Zora's Cry

Tia McCollors

MOODY PUBLISHERS
CHICAGO

© 2006 by
TIA MCCOLLORS

All Scripture quotations are taken from the *New King James Version*. Copyright © 1979, 1980, 1982 by Thomas Nelson, Inc. Used by permission. All rights reserved.

Cover Design: Carlton Bruett Design
Editor: Angela Brown

ISBN: 0-8024-9861-2
ISBN-13: 978-0-8024-9861-8

5 7 9 10 8 6 4

Printed in the United States of America

Library of Congress Cataloging-in-Publication Data

McCollors, Tia.
  Zora's cry / Tia McCollors.
    p. cm.
  ISBN-13: 978-0-8024-9861-8
  1. African American women--Fiction. 2. Female friendship--Fiction. 3. Adoptees--Fiction. I. Title.
  PS3613.C365Z67 2006
  813'.6--dc22
                                    2006009590

*To all of my dear and powerful Women on the Path sisters,
as you live through and walk out the teachings of Titus 2:3–5.
May you forever be yielded vessels unto the Lord.*

. . . the older women likewise, that they be reverent in behavior, not slanderers, not given to much wine, teachers of good things—that they admonish the young women to love their husbands, to love their children, to be discreet, chaste, homemakers, good, obedient to their own husbands, that the word of God may not be blasphemed.

Acknowledgments

To God—For the creative breath You blew into me even before I was born. This gift has been dedicated back to You to use as You choose. My continuous prayer is never to write based on what the current trend dictates, but according to the words and stories that You whisper in my ear.

To my husband, Wayne—You've sacrificed so much to support my vision—our vision. Thank you for jumping on a plane at any given time so I wouldn't have to travel alone. Thank you for being my personal chauffeur, photographer, and publicist. It's amazing how a passerby rarely left my book signing table without a copy of a book in his or her hand. You certainly do your thing!

You never complained about the sandwiches and store-bought meals while I worked on this manuscript. I even appreciate you fussing at me to get in the bed, and helping me get up in the morning when I wanted to cry and stay nestled under the covers. You know you spoil me, right?

To Elder Vanessa Long of New Birth Church in Lithonia, GA—In 2002, I anxiously applied to participate in the nine-month intimate discipleship groups you'd birthed through the Women on the Path program. At the end of the nine months, not only had I been birthed into a new woman, but God begin to birth things through me. Your obedience has changed and strengthened more women than you probably know.

To my family—Who doesn't give a shout out to their parents (LaVerne Carter and Woodrow Webster) and their siblings (Trey and Jamie)? Other than that, you know it's too many of you guys to name. There will be plenty more books for that. In the meantime, know that I honor the lineage and legacies of the Enoch, Carter, Webster, and McCollors families.

To my friends—Being a new author and a new wife within three months of each other definitely changed the amount of time I've had to spend with you guys over the last year or so. But the great thing about it is that you understand me and support me. You know how we do—when one makes it, everybody makes it. We've got so many great things in store. And to my spiritual mothers/sisters/friends Cavell Dudley and Kimberly Thornton. You prayed, pushed, and wouldn't let me let go of God's promises during critical stages in my life. In case you didn't know, I always keep that close to my heart. You are truly women of power.

To the bookstores—(especially B's Books and More), libraries, radio stations, event coordinators, book clubs, and other organizations that invited me to do book signings and sit in on discussions, and/or gave me a platform to tell my story— I can't place a value on how much I appreciate your support. May the seeds you've sown return to you one hundredfold.

To Jamill and Shunda Leigh of *Booking Matters Magazine*—You host and coordinate high-quality events that help spread the word about authors like myself. Thanks for your continuous encouragement and making me look good in those ads! I'm excited about working with you this year and beyond to help take things to another level for both of our visions. Can't you see your full-color glossy magazine around the corner?

To God's psalmists—Your songs and life of worship help keep me in that special place when I write. It's always the perfect song at the perfect time. Your CDs constantly rotate through my CD player—Kirk Franklin, Israel Houghton, Yolanda Adams, Elder Darwin Hobbs, and Elder William Murphy III.

To the literary trailblazers, my mentors and author friends—The list of literary greats and trailblazers keeps growing every year. Like I told my family—there will be plenty of other books for a shout out, but this time I'd like to note some of you who've either touched me by your special words, presence, passion, or diligence in stepping out to deeper waters—Jacquelin Thomas, Victoria Christopher Murray, Kendra Norman-Bellamy, Patricia Haley, Angela Benson, Stephanie Perry Moore, Stacy Hawkins Adams, Dr. Gail Hayes, Valorie Burton, Marilynn Griffith, Karen Kingsbury, Elder Dane Cunningham, Sha-Shana Crichton, Deborha Parham, Caterri Leaks, Vanessa Miller, and Tyler Perry (Tyler—I'm right behind you).

To Cynthia Ballenger and the Moody family—You continue to believe in me, and for that I'm grateful. Working with you during the publication and release of *A Heart of*

Devotion was a pleasant and exciting experience. You've gone out of your way to ensure that I've been represented well and taken care of. Unfortunately, not all authors at other publishing houses can say the same. Thank you for your excellence and professionalism, but most of all your prayers. I know we'll continue to grow together for many years to come.

To my readers—All I can say is "Wow!" It's comforting for authors to know that some of their biggest supporters aren't just our family and friends. The e-mails, guest book signings, and testimonies are evidence that I'm walking the right path.

To our baby boy—At the time of this writing, you're still a busy little boy in my belly. The world will be introduced to Mommy's new book and to you at about the same time. Right now, Daddy and I can't wait to see how you'll look, breathe in your powdery scent after a fresh bath, and figure out whose personality you'll have. We're excited about the great destiny God has given you to walk out. The world will never be the same. XOXOXO, Mommy and Daddy

Dear Reader

God coexists as a Trinity (Father, Son, and Holy Spirit). God is one in essence, but with three distinct and separate functions. The Holy Spirit is the third "person" of the Trinity (1 John 5:7–8).

When a person accepts the Lord Jesus Christ as Savior, he or she is born again by the Holy Spirit. The Holy Spirit dwells within, convicts people of sin, instructs, and empowers (John 14:17, 26; Romans 8:9; 1 Corinthians 12:13). In *Zora's Cry*, the italicized bold print is used to indicate the internal prompting of the Holy Spirit.

Part One

Prologue

Zora Bridgeforth eased open the door of her childhood home. The crisp March morning wind beat against her back as she pulled her key out of the latch. She couldn't believe her parents were dead. How could a drunken New Year's reveler take her parents? How could this happen when they were on the verge of planning one of the biggest days of her life?

Every morning when she awakened, Zora prayed that God would teach her how to breathe again. It had been a struggle to remember even the most natural things. *Inhale. Exhale.*

It was only six thirty in the morning, but Zora wanted to come early before her parents' circle of friends and the volunteer members from her church arrived to help her pack. She needed to remember the house one more time like it had always been—before they would begin to haul her parents' belongings away. It was too much trouble to have a yard sale, and Zora would feel funny if she profited from the situation. She wanted her parents to be a blessing to someone else, even in their deaths, and had opted to have most of the items donated to local shelters and group homes.

Zora sat down in the middle of the blue cotton twill couch. Although the furniture designs changed in the living room over the years, the layout always stayed the same. And whenever they shared a family movie night together, Zora always had the center seat, tucked in between the arms of her parents. Sitting here with nothing but cold space around her, she wished she would've cherished the last time. From this day on, she'd relish every moment in her life.

Zora stood up when she noticed the stack of cardboard boxes leaning against the bookcase. She'd set them aside to pack some of the sentimental items she wanted to keep. There was a particular one she wanted to find before she started sifting through the memories.

It was the other reason she'd arrive early—to find her mother's wedding veil and tiara.

Yesterday, Zora had visited the wedding boutiques with her best friend, Monét, and Mama Jo—her mother's best friend who also happened to be Monét's mother. After one boutique, Zora was convinced she'd found the perfect dress for the perfect day. She was quick to turn down the consultant's offer for a coordinating headpiece and veil. Her parents' wedding photograph had a permanent home on her dresser, and she knew exactly what her mother's veil with the pearl and rhinestone tiara looked like. It was the only choice.

It took most of Zora's strength to push and pull the wooden hope chest from the back of her parents' closet. An ache settled in her heart when she remembered again that her mother wouldn't share her wedding day. Her father wouldn't be there to tighten his heavy hand around her fingers as they rested in the groove of his arm. He would've led her down the aisle, then released her from his care and responsibility, into the hands of the man who would vow to be her covering forever.

Zora eased open the chest that held her mother's precious wedding memorabilia, among other sentimental items like Zora's favorite childhood blanket. She found and opened the sealed bag, then unfolded the delicate veil that would adorn her head on her wedding day.

That blessed night, Zora would unveil her womanhood for the first time. Many a heart-to-heart talk with her mother had been about the importance of preserving her chastity until she became a bride. But above even her parents, Zora had promised God first that she'd present her virginity to her husband. It was a gift she'd vowed to sustain. Virginity in these times may have been hard, but it wasn't impossible. Wearing her mother's veil would be a dedication to her parents.

There's no way I'll be able to move this chest any farther on my own, Zora thought, bending down on her knees in front of it. She lifted out another box that she hadn't seen since her late teens.

On Zora's sixteenth birthday, her mother had walked into her room with the box lovingly tucked under her arm. That night, Sonja Bridgeforth shared the romantic love letters that she and her boyfriend had written to each other when they were dating while he was stationed overseas.

Albert Bridgeforth's love had grown so deep for his beloved, and his heart so anxious, that he hadn't been able to bear waiting until they saw each other again to ask for her hand in marriage. He'd penned the proposal on a piece of wrinkled brown paper that looked as if it had been salvaged from the trash. Her mother had found a special frame for the letter and glued it to the front of a piece of white lace. As another special touch, she surrounded the letter with pink rose appliqués. Zora thought it would be special to incorporate it somehow into her wedding.

Zora set the veil, tiara, and framed letter on her parents' four-poster bed. She remembered that she had to find the rest

17

of her parents' insurance policies, and needed to do it before it slipped her mind again.

She walked to her father's side of the bed and opened the top drawer of the metal file cabinet. Despite her mother's request, he'd refused to move his files to the back room they'd converted to an office and sitting area. He needed to keep his important information at his fingertips in case he needed to get to it in an emergency, he'd rationalized.

Zora laughed at the thought. It was impossible to make Albert Bridgeforth change once his mind was set.

Zora almost felt as if she'd get a scolding once she'd found the insurance papers and continued to look through the files. She'd been reared as a child not to touch an adult's personal belongings without permission. Well, she wasn't a child anymore. It was a possibility that the cabinet held more information that she needed to know.

Zora flipped past the folders tabbed for the household utility bills and car insurance. She came across an unmarked manila folder and pulled out the single sheet of paper inside. Zora panicked as she read the words that followed. She was sure that her eyes had deceived her. She read the paragraph again. And again. And again. She could feel the blood rush to her face and the aching like bile in her stomach already beginning to swirl. Her fingers gripped the letter, and for a moment she considered ripping it to shreds along with any evidence of the secret it held. Tears rolled down her cheek and salted her lips. *How could she be adopted?*

Zora found herself too shaken to stand and, with trembling hands, finally managed to call her fiancé, Preston Fields. She could barely understand her own words through her sobs.

It couldn't be true.

Every imaginable emotion fought to push itself to the surface. She succumbed to her agony and balled herself into a fetal position on the plush tan carpet of her parents' bedroom floor. She didn't move until she heard Preston ringing the doorbell and banging on the front door. She opened the door, handed him the letter, then slipped into the arms of the only truth she'd known.

And Zora cried.

1

Three months later

Rays of the June Maryland sun poured through the glass patio door of Zora's townhouse. Its natural light warmed her face, even in the coolness of the air conditioning. She took a sip of her cranberry juice, then sat the glass flute in the middle of the breakfast table. Her eyes caught the corner of the envelope sticking out of her wedding planner notebook. Zora pulled out the envelope, then the letter.

She read it again. The questions far outweighed the answers. She'd folded and unfolded it so many times over the past three months that the creases had nearly worn the paper thin. She leaned closer to the page and rested her forehead on her palms, fighting to postpone her tears until she was alone.

Preston had seen her break down too many times over the past months. He'd suggested they postpone the wedding. It would give her time to heal and sort things out, he'd said. Zora refused. She knew her parents would want her to press forward. *To be absent from the body was to be present with the Lord.*

Zora brushed away a single tear. Why had they held her adoption a secret. *Why?*

Zora had dealt with the disbelief of the situation a month ago, only to have confusion and anger follow. Now there was just hurt.

But I'm more than able to heal.

Zora tousled her hair and let out a deep sigh. She lost her thoughts amidst the Weed Eater humming outside where Preston was tending to the small yard in the back. She'd bought her home two years ago, right before they'd met. It wasn't long before he'd taken on the responsibility as her official lawn caretaker. The act had won him high marks with her father.

In Zora's quiet neighborhood in Bowie, the brick-front townhouses were clustered in threes, and her two-story home sat nestled between two ranch-style homes. Although the townhouses in the subdivision shared the same architectural design, each owner had taken care to add a bit of his or her own personality to make the home unique. Zora and her mother had planted purple hostas between the bushes and added a gold framed storm door to accent the brick front of the home. This year, her father had planned to fence in the backyard, claiming it would up the resale potential once she and Preston married.

Zora looked out the sliding glass patio doors at Preston. The mere sight of him brought a smile to her face. His countenance was peaceful, though it seemed a man with his angular features would naturally wear a stern expression. The sun heated his dark cocoa complexion, and sweat glistened on his face. She wondered what he was thinking.

As usual, her mind dwelled on the option of looking for her biological family.

Preston looked up to meet Zora's glance and blew a kiss with his free hand.

She stretched across the table and pretended to catch the

fleeting kiss, pressed her hand to her cheek, and then returned one of her own.

In his usual playful manner, Preston held up the Weed Eater in defense and pretended to ward off her affections, before turning it off and making a run for the door. He ducked and dipped with ease, showcasing his athletic prowess. Preston squeezed through the small crack he opened in the door, bringing the smell of fresh-cut grass inside.

"Hey! Watch the shoes," Zora said before he could take another step. "That grass'll be everywhere."

"My bad, baby," Preston said. He pulled off his shoes and went outside to beat the soles on the concrete patio.

Zora slid the letter back into the envelope and into her notebook's pocket. Preston had said she brooded over it too much lately, bringing mental anguish on herself. On one hand, she knew he didn't understand the depth of her pain. But on the other, he was right. Besides, she had work to do. It was six months and counting until the wedding. Time was of the essence.

Her wedding notebook was divided into labeled sections for planning every imaginable aspect of their big day. Zora flipped over the last tab of her notebook just as Preston scooted back inside wearing socks but no shoes. He wiped his sweat-drenched face with his T-shirt and sauntered over to the kitchen table. He stood over her, blocking the warmth of the sunlight.

Zora tilted her head back and closed her eyes. The image of Preston's face still floated behind her lids—his deep-set eyes, the thin goatee he'd started wearing over the last month. Even the small scar between his right brow and bridge of his nose was clear—the result of a lost fistfight with his older brother when they were kids.

"Gimme a kiss," Preston said, pinching her chin.

Zora fluttered her eyes open and said, "I seem to recall a

certain person who was just dodging my kisses a few minutes ago. And now that person wants a taste of these lips?" Zora folded in her lips and gummed, "I don't think so. Plus you're sweaty. That's gross."

"Come on, baby," Preston said, squeezing her nose so she'd have to breathe through her mouth. "I only dodged your kiss because I wanted the real thing."

Zora closed her eyes again. She knew he was studying her. She could feel his breath tickling the side of her cheek as he bent closer. He kissed her eyelids. She opened her eyes to catch a glimpse of him before accepting a soft peck on her lips.

"Whatcha working on?" Preston asked, stretching out on the floor by her feet.

"Wedding stuff," Zora said. "I'm going to dinner with Monét down at the Harbor so we can work on a few things."

"I hope you pay this much attention to *me* after the wedding."

He tried to sound sarcastic, but Zora knew it was all an act. She closed the notebook and joined Preston on the floor. She sat cross-legged on the carpet and leaned back on her hands.

"Baby, I'm only doing this one time, so I want to make sure everything is exactly how I want it," Zora said. "How *we* want it."

She pulled a playful but tight grip at the neck of his T-shirt. "And if you decide to act up down the line, then we'll either elope or go to the courthouse." She mumbled under her breath, "Or I'll be by myself."

"I hate to break it to you, but you're stuck with me. From the time we say 'I do' until forever. You're never getting rid of me."

"That might be the case in six months, but right now I'm ditching you so I can get to the Harbor. I'm going to hang out until you meet me there. You didn't forget, did you?"

Zora knew he hadn't, considering she'd reminded him about the annual waterfront concert series every week for the past two months. He'd finally surrendered to her mission to show him that there was more to experience in Baltimore than sporting events.

"Is that the kind of treatment a brother gets?" He rolled over on his side. "Work a man like a dog and send him on his way?"

"Ruff, ruff." Zora rolled out of Preston's reach, then got up and straightened her khaki shorts and pink tank top. She threw her tote bag over her shoulder and reached down for Preston's hand, attempting to lift his dead weight off the floor. Instead, Preston gave her a slight tug, pulling her down to the floor and cushioning her fall with his own body.

"Ewwww . . . come on baby." Zora slid the spaghetti strap of her tank back onto her shoulder. She looked down at her clothes, making sure he hadn't stained her shirt from grass or his sweat. "That's nasty. Go home and take a shower."

Preston ignored her plea. "Who's got jokes now?" He tickled Zora until she could barely squeak out an apology between gasps for air. "Ruff, ruff? What's all that about?" His fingers showed no mercy.

"I'm sorry, I'm sorry," she pleaded.

"Say I'm the man," Preston said.

"You're the woman," Zora said, setting herself up for another tickling episode that lasted until she finally followed his commands.

The laughter rolled from her belly again long after Preston walked her to the car and she'd hit the BW Parkway on the trip from Bowie to Baltimore's Inner Harbor.

She'd originally settled in Bowie after landing a job as a high school guidance counselor in nearby Glen Burnie. Though it was still close to her job, Bowie was far enough for her to escape from the reminder of her students' problems when she needed a breather. She tended to weigh in on some of their disorderly home lives as much as their academic endeavors. She was grateful for the summer break. Her own issues were enough to handle.

Should she search for the life she would have lived? If two people could forsake their own flesh and blood, then they didn't deserve to know their daughter. And she didn't want to know them. Maybe. Maybe she needed closure.

Zora could picture the church pews filled with an adoring family—parents, maybe siblings, on her wedding day. Cousins, perhaps a few nieces or nephews, doting aunts, and proud uncles. Would they all share her soft shoulder-length hair that frizzed up at the slightest smell of rain? Would anyone else have almond-shaped eyes and one deep dimple in her left cheek?

Zora turned off the AC and rolled down the window of her Toyota Camry. She cruised down the BW Parkway as her thoughts sped through the different scenarios that could play out if she ever had the chance to meet her parents face-to-face. *Her parents*. It was almost strange to refer to them that way. No doubt she would be overtaken by emotions.

"Lord, I know you've heard this from me so many times before, but I'm so confused."

Zora spoke out into the rushing wind, as if the breeze would carry her prayer to heaven quicker.

"I know You're a God of perfect timing, and You'll reveal all things in Your time. So I pray for my patience, and above all else, I accept Your will for my life."

By now Zora was nearing the Inner Harbor. She passed by the Baltimore Convention Center and inched her way through the crowded streets.

"This is ridiculous," Zora said, whipping down Pratt Street and into one of the packed parking lots. She fumbled around in her purse for her cell phone to call Monét and connected her hands-free unit. "Hey. Where are you?" she asked when her best friend answered the phone.

"Down near the waterfront looking at the exhibits. Where are you?"

"Looking for a parking space. Have you been here a while?"

"Girl, please. You know I have."

"I know. I don't know why I even bothered to ask," Zora said. "Meet me in ten minutes near that brick wall where that mime performs sometimes."

Zora circled around the block another five minutes before spotting a couple who looked as if they had reached their quota of crowds and fun for the day. Each held a child, limp with sleep and clearly past the age to be carried with ease.

She crept behind them until they reached their minivan and dumped the ragdoll children in the backseats. Zora swung in as soon as they cleared the parking space, stuffed her purse into her tote bag, and trotted toward the festivities.

Even in her haste, Zora noticed a young boy one row over who was standing too close to the passing traffic. The red cape tied loosely around his neck flapped as he swung his arms wildly in the air. In his young naïveté, he wasn't aware of the danger he was in with cars whizzing by, but instead was engulfed in his own rendition of the fighting tactics of a super-hero.

As Zora got closer, she realized he was not alone, though not under a watchful eye. Barely three steps away, a lady whom Zora assumed was his mother was leaning against a black luxury SUV, her head buried in the crook of her elbow.

Her first intention was to keep walking, but Zora's com-passion got the best of her. She approached the car with cau-tion.

"Excuse me, are you all right?" When the lady didn't respond, Zora took another step closer. She thought about touching the woman's shoulder, but changed her mind. She spoke a little louder. "Is everything okay?"

The woman brushed the layers of her jet black hair out of her face and seemed to take a moment to realize her whereabouts. When she caught sight of the small boy, she snatched him out of harm's way.

"Micah!"

The woman's forehead furrowed in anger, then softened when she noticed Zora. "I didn't even realize—" She seemed to shake the thought from her head. "Thank you," she said, grabbing a small Sesame Street backpack from the rear seat. She clutched the boy's arm, slammed the back door, and rushed away.

❧

The city's annual Waterfront Festival was the event of the year to celebrate Baltimore's waterfront and its maritime history. Modern and traditional Chesapeake Bay boats dotted the waters around the Inner Harbor. There were plenty of maritime exhibits, live bands, children's activities, and contests to keep families entertained for hours.

Even in the bustling crowd, Zora immediately spotted Monét. They had a sixth sense for each other—almost like twins. And why not? As children they'd played in the same sandbox, lost their first tooth during the same week, and spent summers at camp together. Since her parents' death, Monét's parents—Zora's godparents—had naturally stepped in as her surrogate family. Zora considered herself part of the Sullivan clan along with Monét and her older sister Victoria.

Zora waved over the crowd's heads at Monét, not surprised at the Afrocentric look she'd adopted for the day. Her blue tunic top was embroidered in gold around the sleeves and neckline. The pants followed the same pattern, with the trim

28

running down the seam. Her recently auburn-streaked hair was slicked back into a low tight ponytail, and her slender face was framed by gold hoop earrings the size of bracelets. Her outfits and style changed like a chameleon, and Monét was never timid about exploring her fashion options.

With Monét's natural flavor, planning expertise, and insight into the Baltimore area, there was no need to hire a wedding consultant. Monét worked as an event coordinator for one of the city's cultural arts centers. Her job events were usually evening soirees meant for fund-raising purposes, but she loved events of all kinds and took advantage of any and every chance to immerse herself into the city's culture and opportunities. She was Ms. Social and Ms. Cultural Events all wrapped into one. Zora knew Monét could handle being her part-time consultant and full-time maid of honor.

"What's in there?" Zora asked, once she made it to her friend. She peered into a small bag Monét was holding.

"Accessories," Monét said. She pulled out a necklace and matching bracelet made from wooden beads and turquoise and held them out for Zora to admire. "I'm gonna wear it with that jazzy white linen number I have. That is, whenever you give me back the jacket."

"I need to hit the stores myself. You can't be cute by yourself," Zora said, sliding the bracelet onto her arm. "Remind me later about the jacket."

"Oh no, sticky fingers," Monét said. "Bracelet back in the bag."

"Fine." Zora wriggled her wrist out of the bracelet. "Lead me to that shop." She slid her arm through Monét's and pulled her toward a row of stores.

"Oh no," Monét protested. She unwrapped Zora's arm from hers. "I'm starving. Let's get something to eat first. No food, no shopping. Much food, much shopping."

"Well, fill 'er up then," Zora said. She cast a side glance at

Monét when a group of men passed by.

One of them, as chocolate as the night is long, made it no secret that he was eyeing Monét. He slowed his gait and looked at her as if she were the only person at the Harbor. As they passed each other, he and Monét exchanged pleasantries, but continued walking.

Zora looked back and saw the admirer had stopped, as if he hoped Monét would do the same. His eyes beckoned for conversation.

"Monét," Zora said, nudging her friend, "you've got eyes on you."

Monét didn't miss a step as she made long strides in the direction of a line of eateries. "I'm not interested in some random brother gawking at me on the street." She didn't bother to take a second look.

"You know I met Preston when he walked up and just introduced himself to me."

"One-in-a-million blessing. I'd rather be introduced to a man by somebody I know so he can at least vouch for his character."

Too bad for him, Zora thought, leaving the brother behind with his dashed hopes. "Well, Preston can vouch for Jeremiah's character," Zora said, bringing up her fiancé's best friend and best man.

"No long-distance love," Monét said matter-of-factly.

Zora adjusted her tote bag on her shoulder and bumped her hips against Monét. "I'm telling you, I think there could be a love connection between you and Jeremiah. You might be the one to bring him out of his own little world that he lives in."

"If he plans on staying in Houston, count him out. You know for yourself long-distance relationships don't work for me. Been there, done that."

Zora knew she could only be referring to Terrance, the aspiring filmmaker Monét had dated during their senior year in college. After graduation, he'd jetted to California in pursuit of his career. Monét became an afterthought to him even though she had tried everything to make it work, even scheduling regular trips to the West Coast. She had laid out her heart, and Terrance stepped on it. After that, Monét had shut down when it came to love.

She needs to let that go, Zora thought. *Monét has so much to offer, but it had to be for the right man.*

"So if your knight in shining armor wants to rescue you and whisk you off to his castle, you'd rather stay in Baltimore than leave with the man of your dreams?" Zora asked.

"Yes," Monét said without so much as a second thought. "So then if the dream turns out to be a nightmare, Daddy won't have to drive too far to jack him up."

Zora smacked her lips. Monét had written off so many men in her life that Zora could only recall one who made it past six months since the Terrance episode. Bryce. She still couldn't conceive why he'd been around so long. Good looks and a good job could only carry a man so far. Thank God, Monét hadn't seen or mentioned him lately.

Zora and Monét found a restaurant where Zora could order her usual chicken and pasta meal and Monét could have her choice of vegetarian entrées. After placing their orders, they began prioritizing their endless to-do lists for the wedding.

Monét passed an envelope of wedding invitation samples back to Zora. "We can't do anything with these invitations until you make a decision about the reception. I don't see why you're having this last-minute grand idea anyway. Mrs. Fields is a classy lady, but she'll turn this city out if her son's reception isn't at her husband's church. If nothing else, look at the money you're saving by not having to pay for a location. If I were you, I'd save that money and lose my mind while I was honeymooning on Paradise Island."

31

"Okay, okay." Zora dropped her napkin on the table as a sign of surrender. Her future father-in-law was the pastor of Zion Tabernacle. The sanctuary, with its arched ceilings and intricate woodwork, would make for a beautiful ceremony. It had only crossed her mind the other day to move the reception. "I hadn't even talked to Preston about it anyway. It was just a suggestion."

"We're too far in the game for suggestions," Monét said. "We need decisions." She pulled out her list and a highlighter. "Now getting back to business. Have you decided on the wording?"

"Got it," Zora said, flipping to the invitation section and sliding her notebook to Monét. She'd even taken the time to type out the invitation using a calligraphy font so she could envision how the invitation would look.

While Monét studied the invite, Zora noticed the lady from the parking lot walk into the restaurant. She seemed to survey her seating options and pointed to a booth near the back. Her hair shone like silk and swayed with body as she followed the hostess. She didn't remove her shades until she was seated. The boy with her crawled into the booth on his knees, then wrapped his arms around the woman's neck. She laughed and returned the kisses he was planting on her nose.

Zora concluded they had to be mother and son, the more she studied them. They shared the same honey-toned complexion and wide, expressive eyes.

Zora stared at the lady for quite a while before Monét clinked the side of her water glass with a spoon.

"Please, Zora," Monét said. "Not today."

"What are you talking about?" She squeezed a lemon into her ice water before dropping it in the glass.

"You've got that *look* on your face."

"Not true." Zora picked up the laminated dessert menu and fanned her face.

"True."

"Maybe a little."

"A lot."

Zora threw up her hands. If anyone knew her, Monét did. Zora had an almost uncanny gift for getting people to open up. She could coax a professional mime into telling his life story. She'd never been shy about approaching anyone she was drawn to, most of the time to Monét's embarrassment.

Zora volunteered her own analysis. "She's happy, but there's no joy. She's smiling, but look at her eyes. Can't you see that?"

"No," Monét said, looking to the corner of the restaurant where the woman had been seated.

"Well, what do you see?"

Monét sipped her sweet tea before spilling her personal assessment to Zora. "First of all, we're about fifty yards away, and I can see that she practically needs a sling to hold up her arm because of the size of the rock on her hand." Monét scooped a teaspoon of sugar into her glass. "Does she look like she's in need of anything?"

"What's that got to do with it?"

Monét held her fingers up. "Case in point number two. I can spot an original Gucci purse with my eyes closed."

Zora shook her head. "It's more than material things. She needs love. I saw her in the parking lot on the way in, and she looked out of it."

"Maybe she's tired. Little boys will wear you out."

Zora watched the lady pour out a box of crayons onto the table and share a coloring book with the child. Monét was probably right. "Yeah, she's probably just tired."

"Tired of spending money," Monét added.

Zora was caught off guard when the woman looked up at her, then turned away quickly. Even in the parking lot, she'd refused to let their eyes meet. It was as if she wanted to keep

33

the secrets of her soul hidden.

Zora dismissed Monét's assumptions. She knew what she saw. It was more than what was on the surface. That was only half of it. And the familiar knot in the pit of her stomach told her that their paths would cross again. Soon.

Paula Manns stared at her face in the bathroom mirror, wondering if she looked as exhausted as she felt. The sagging under her eyes was more evident, and the dark circles weren't hidden by the concealer she'd applied earlier that morning. No doubt she was physically exhausted, but the emotional drain was taking a toll on her body as well. The way the woman down at the Harbor kept staring at her in the restaurant, Paula wondered if her loneliness was seeping through her pores, making her look older than her thirty-five years.

She hated that she'd given off a perception earlier today that she was an irresponsible mother. She couldn't believe she'd lost her bearings, even for a minute. Tragedies happen in a minute. Lives change in a minute.

Too many days of fatigue and occasional nausea had finally led Paula to the drugstore. She unfolded the brown paper bag and pulled out the pregnancy test. She sat on the closed toilet lid and the chill of the porcelain penetrated her linen shorts. The house was void of the usual sounds of her son, Micah, screaming her name as if every situation were an emergency. There was no crashing of his action figures and toy trucks around the room. He'd worn himself out at the festival and had fallen asleep on the way home. *Thank God.*

Some days Paula craved peace and quiet, but now it was her enemy, forcing her to face the thoughts she'd rather avoid.

The questions rushed at her at one time. How could her husband let another woman lay in his arms? *What's her name? What does she have that I don't?* The thoughts refused to be pushed out of her mind, each one instead battling to be in the forefront. *How long can I pretend? Will Darryl ever walk away and leave me alone?* Alone.

He'd never admitted to infidelity. Denied it like the plague, in fact. Darryl said the only affair he was having was with his hospital pager, but she was no fool. Her womanly instincts told her something was happening, and that was enough.

Things had plummeted downhill since Darryl began to consider leaving his stable and lucrative career as a cardiologist. Of all things, he'd been sucked into the real estate game. It was the most unpredictable industry, Paula thought. They'd already lost several thousand dollars on defunct investment opportunities when Darryl had jumped headfirst into the game with more passion than knowledge. Passion didn't pay the bills.

Paula wasn't willing for their bank accounts to be eaten away while he chased his dream. Since the last episode he'd started to take more time to educate himself, but that didn't matter to her. He'd found a group of investment partners, but Darryl's deep pockets—which were her pockets—were the only ones that could bring money to the table. He'd even said they should consider downsizing their standard of living. What sense did it make to go backward? She didn't need him to be anybody but the great Dr. Manns.

Paula ripped the clear plastic from the package and pulled

the test out of the box. *Just take the test.* She lifted the toilet seat, but had to sit awhile before her body responded. It had to be psychological. Before she returned home, she'd had a sixteen-ounce fruit smoothie and enough water that her bladder should've been ready to burst.

She set the indicator on the back of the toilet and waited for the hour-long minute to pass. Paula willed herself not to look back and watch for the indicator sign to appear.

If she were pregnant, she'd undoubtedly know when it happened. She'd only been with her husband once in the last month. Darryl was rarely home at night anyway. She believed he made an obligatory appearance each morning for his son's sake, but a piece of Paula's self-esteem walked out of the door whenever Darryl did.

There was always the occasional night when they went out to portray a picture-perfect marriage at one of his social events. As a matter of fact, there was one coming up this Friday. This time, it was a silent auction for the foundation for which Darryl served as president. Paula knew the drill. She'd be proudly paraded in public, but placed back on the shelf in private.

Never once had she considered leaving him. Truth be told, she was too unsure of herself to be alone. She'd gotten used to a certain lifestyle and knew she couldn't maintain it on her own. She wanted to pray about it, but didn't feel worthy to ask God for anything. It had been too long since they'd talked.

Hello, God. It's me, Paula.

Paula who? He would probably ask.

Paula had accepted God into her life during a worship service she'd attended with a friend six years ago. From that point, while she and Darryl were dating, she'd tried to learn more about God and teach Darryl what she learned. He wasn't receptive and wouldn't attend church with her. He didn't need to go to church to believe there was a God, he'd said. Before

37

long, he'd smothered the flame of her desire to know more, and she'd continued to grow distant from God since they'd married. Paula learned that the salvation that Darryl claimed to have was more to appease her. God and true friendships were a memory. If only she could have both in her life again.

You can.

Paula was sure God was disappointed and believed this hand she'd been dealt in life was her punishment. Regardless of their problems and disagreements, she missed her husband. She wished he'd see that their lives needed stability.

Some nights, like last night, Paula sprayed her pillow with his cologne so she could inhale his essence; pretend he was there, holding her, sleeping in late on Saturday mornings with only Micah and a bowl of cereal separating them. It was like that a year ago. She missed the security she felt when Micah was a newborn, lying on Darryl's chest with her nestled under Darryl's arm.

But now it was different. Even when they were in the same bed, his heart was far from hers.

Paula longed for a friend to help carry her burden. Darryl's rude attitude toward her girlfriends from church caused her to coil into a shell and eventually push them away. If they were true friends they would've stayed, she told herself. The fact that they'd pulled a disappearing act gave Darryl more evidence for his case. "They were fake anyway," he said.

Paula was too embarrassed to share her marital problems with her mother or sister. They'd warned her before that she was settling and her vision had been cloaked by the dream of being a doctor's wife. Hindsight was twenty-twenty. She married for status over salvation, income instead of integrity. She wasn't born with this silver spoon in her mouth, and now it was choking her.

"Mommmmmyyyyyyyy!" Micah's voice broke her thoughts and she headed for her son's bedroom. He kept her strong because he was a tangible reminder that unconditional love still existed.

"Hi, pumpkin," Paula said, walking in and sitting on the edge of the bed. "Did you have a good nap?"

"Yes." Micah hopped onto her lap. She relished every minute of his boyish ways. He was becoming more independent in some ways, and there were days when he didn't want to be babied. Today was not one of them.

Paula wrapped her arms around Micah's lanky frame and kissed the top of his head. His hair smelled like a mix of shampoo and the tang of a child after playing outside. She'd let him spend extra time playing in the bathtub tonight.

"Dadddyyyy!" Micah jumped from her lap when he heard the entry door from the garage slam. He took off down the stairs, skipping as many steps as his legs would allow.

Paula walked to the end of the hall and looked over the banister into the spacious foyer, covered with mahogany hardwood. Darryl dropped his golf bag at the door by a large Byzantine glass vase. *I wish he'd be more careful.*

Darryl pulled off his cap and plopped it on his son's head, then scooped Micah up and set him on his shoulders. Micah yelped in delight and caught hold of his father's head to balance himself.

"I'm surprised to see you home so early," Paula said, making her way downstairs. She'd left the house earlier than he had that morning, and she had no idea where his obligations, as he called them, had taken him for the day.

"Why? I live here, don't I?" Darryl didn't bother to look at her.

Sometimes, she wanted to say. Her thoughts were always a lot more courageous than her words. If she said the wrong thing, he'd find another reason to leave. But what did it matter? He'd given up fishing for excuses over five months ago.

"Are you hungry?" Paula asked. "I can make something or order Chinese."

"I've got to go to the hospital."

"For what? I thought you were on call last week," she said as calmly as she could.

Micah interrupted the brewing storm. "Chinese, Daddy. Please stay and eat Chinese," he said, drumming his small fingers on top of his father's head.

Paula's heart ached. Maybe Micah could convince him to have a change of heart. She let her son take her usual place and convince her husband to stay.

Darryl lifted his son over his head and set him on the bottom step. "Maybe tomorrow, big man." He squatted down to his son's eye level. "Can you take care of Mommy till I get back tonight?"

"Yes," Micah said, turning his father's cap backward on his head.

Paula was disgusted with Darryl's entire act. Her son had already become her surrogate husband.

"What time will you be back?" Paula knew he hated when she questioned him, but he was her husband. She was entitled to ask as many questions as she wanted.

"I don't know. I'm meeting with some investors later."

Here we go with that again. "You met last week."

Darryl glared at her. He turned his attention back to Micah, who'd been watching the episode from the spot where his father had set him.

"How about setting up your race track and we'll race the cars before I leave? Let me take a shower first."

Micah's eyes brightened, and his countenance quickly shed the disappointment it held just moments before. "Okay, Daddy." He took his father's hand and pulled him up the stairwell. Halfway up Micah bounded up as fast as he'd come down. Darryl pretended to race him, but faked a fall before disappearing into the master bedroom.

Paula's marriage was proving to be a test of her faith. She was failing. She'd vowed to stand by him for better or worse, but back then she didn't know what the worse would be. The burden weighed heavier each day and she needed for someone to help shoulder the load. Why did life keep testing her?

Test! Oh my gosh, the test! If Darryl hadn't gone into the bathroom yet, Paula could slip in and slip out before he noticed anything. Now wasn't the time to deal with the news—whatever the result.

Paula rushed up the steps and saw Darryl's backside just before the bathroom door closed. When she heard the sound of the lid hitting the back of the toilet, she knew it was too late. Seconds later Darryl opened the door holding the pregnancy test in his hand.

"What's this about?" The words hissed from his mouth as he walked over and tossed their future on the bed. It landed face up, the plus sign staring back at her. He didn't wait for an answer.

Darryl walked back into the bathroom, and Paula heard him turn on the shower. Anger and hurt commingled in her heart.

She doubted the streaming water could outcry her eyes.

3

A tickling breeze from the waterfront circled through the festival-goers. It carried with it the music from the performing jazz band and the light scent of buttered popcorn from a nearby street vendor. Satisfied with her shopping excursion, Monét went to bid adieu to her friends before leaving.

She combed the crowd for several minutes before she finally spotted Zora and Preston. Zora was leaning back onto Preston's chest and joining her sway to the melodies with his. Even from afar she could see his arms wrapped securely around her waist. Their relationship was one she adored.

Monét pushed through the crowd until she stood in front of the couple.

"What's up, guys?" she said, dropping her large shopping bag at their feet.

Zora shook her head. "How much damage did you do?"

"Not as much as you think," Monét said. "They ran out of small bags." She massaged the top of her aching left shoulder. "So how are the bands?"

"Loving it," Zora answered without hesitation. She winked at Monét and looked over her shoulder at Preston. "This isn't so bad, is it?" she asked.

Preston kissed her cheek. "Not the Raven's game, but it's all right. I can stand it."

"Good. Get used to it. We're going to do lots of cultural things."

"I do cultural things."

"Eating at the Chinese restaurant down the street from your house is not cultural."

Monét crossed her arms over her chest. The bell sleeves of her tunic fell almost to her waist. "Well, I'm impressed," she said, nodding her head in approval. "Jazz festival this week and my silent auction at the center next week. You'll be well-rounded before you know it," she joshed, patting Preston's shoulder.

Preston unwrapped his arms from around Zora and lifted her left hand to Monét's face. "It was the ring. She's locked me down already."

Monét shifted her weight to her left hip, her arms still crossed. "The ring?" she repeated.

"Uh-huh. You know what they say about a woman when she gets a ring on her finger."

Zora turned around to meet Preston face-to-face, and Monét stepped up beside her, shoulder to shoulder, tight as the front lines of an army.

"They look more beautiful every day," he said. "Yep. That's what they say."

"That's what we thought."

Monét turned to watch the upcoming band set up. Behind the stage, the heavens were painted with stripes of orange and gold against the water's edge. Night began to settle, and the occasional flicker of lightning bugs danced in front of the stage. It was the perfect night to eat a cup of chocolate chip mint ice cream by the moonlight.

"Oh, Monét," Preston said. "You know my boy Jeremiah is coming up here next month. Maybe we can get together and do something."

Here we go again, Monét thought. Lately she felt she'd become the pity case for all of her single dating friends, and she made sure to give Zora a look that showed her disapproval. She wasn't interested in charity dates.

Preston looked backed and forth between the two friends. "Can you let a brotha in on the secret? Did I say something I wasn't supposed to?"

"Seeing that I mentioned Jeremiah earlier today, she probably thinks we're plotting," Zora answered.

"Bingo," Monét said.

"I'm not trying to play matchmaker. I'm just seeing if you wanted to get together and do something." Preston shrugged. "Besides, if a woman can bring Jeremiah out of his own world, more power to her. You may be the woman with the power—who knows?"

"Okay, why does that sound so familiar?"

Zora covered her mouth and lowered her voice. "Actually, I dipped in on one of his phone conversations, so we're not going to make that little phrase a point in this argument right now."

Preston cleared his throat and leaned his six-feet, two-inch frame over between the women's heads. "Speaking of dipping in people's conversations, let me drop my two cents. I've got to vouch for my boy even though he doesn't need my assistance. He can stand on his own."

"And he's a good man," Zora added. "Birds of a feather flock together."

Exactly. Eagles and chickens, Monét concluded. She could take her chance to see who was flying in the flock, but why waste her time?

"I'll think about it," Monét said, knowing she wasn't giving it a second thought. "No promises."

Monét picked up her shopping bag and hugged Zora and Preston with her free arm. "I'm out of here. Zora, I'll catch up with you after service tomorrow. I have to sing, so I'll be at church early."

Monét pressed back through the crowd. In her haste, she sideswiped her bag against the knees of an unsuspecting man.

"I'm so sorry." She apologized for her carelessness and looked up to meet the victim. She found herself a face's length from the familiar eyes she'd briefly locked with earlier during the day.

"No problem. You can just make it up to me." His smile invited her into his world.

"I'm sorry, but I've got to go," Monét said. She turned to walk away, but he reached out and tapped her arm.

"We can't even talk for one minute?" He held up an index finger in front of his lips. They seemed to move in slow motion. "Just one." He stepped in front of her to help clear a path through the crowd.

Monét didn't accept the invitation, though it would have been easy with a smile like his. It was alluring, even with the barely noticeable knick on his front tooth. She was sure he'd flashed it on a number of women throughout the evening. His cell phone was probably full of new numbers.

"If it's meant for us to talk, our paths will cross again—" Monét paused when she realized she didn't know his name.

"Solomon," he said. "But they call me Solo. And you promise you'll give me a minute?"

"Monét," she introduced herself, "and I'll give you ten minutes." She smoothed back one side of her hair. "If you don't mind me asking, why do they call you Solo?"

"Because I live in this world alone until I'm blessed with a beautiful woman like you."

Here come the pick-up lines, Monét thought. "Well, nice to meet you, Solo."

He held out his palms and Monét placed a hand between them. "Nice to meet you too, Monét. And I'm holding you to that ten minutes."

Solomon's grip was secure, yet almost tender. When he didn't immediately let go, she slowly slid her hand from his grasp. He definitely wasn't a blue-collar man. His hands were too soft.

"Until next time," he said, leaving her with a smile like he wanted her to remember him late into the night.

Monét willed herself not to look back, knowing he was watching her walk away.

⁂

Every good man is not God's man. Was the "good man" title supposed to change her expectations about Jeremiah or any other man?

His name flashed again on the caller ID, and Monét ignored it for the third time since she'd returned home that night. Bryce Copeland was ambitious, and he didn't stop until he got what he wanted. He was like that with his ascending quest for a future political office. He was equally persistent with working at the top of his golf game. And he was just as persistent when it came to Monét.

Monét believed it was because she had been the one to walk away. He'd confessed that a woman never left him. If anyone was going to call it quits, it was always him. He had a knack for keeping otherwise intelligent and level-headed women dangling from the end of his string. But not Monét. She'd cut herself off. To a point. Her refusal of him only heated his pursuit.

Monét lit the cinnamon spice candles arranged on the iron

holders inside the fireplace. A blazing fire and smoky embers had never dirtied the fireplace, and Monét doubted that it ever would. To her, it was merely an accessory and the focal point for the expansive loft apartment. Lined across the fireplace mantle were some pieces that she'd been given as gifts from the artists who'd exhibited as the cultural center.

A single beep alerted her to the phone message. At one time in her life she'd wanted to be with Bryce more than anything. That is, until she found out his relationship with God was a facade. She wanted it to be real, for him to have a heart of devotion to God. He wanted a Sunday-only convenience. She'd prayed until she was at a loss for words. It wasn't enough. He had other things that were a priority over his relationship with God. She'd given him two on-and-off years.

Right now she was in the off position. Every once in a while she'd surrender and answer the phone, but a phone call was all he was ever granted. She constantly turned down offers of starlit picnics in the park and tickets to theatrical performances. It was easier to turn him down as long as she didn't see him. The last time had been February.

A streetlight shone through the window of her loft apartment as she looked out past the third-floor balcony. The open square footage was one of the amenities that had drawn Monét to the living quarters. She was also partial to the hardwood floor in the living room and had only added an ivory Persian rug to anchor the area between her sofa and love seat. Her taste for art was reflected in her home's décor, and the furniture—hues of earth tones—was punctuated with subtle hints of bronze and gold using small throws and pillows.

Monét went to her bedroom closet and unzipped the monogrammed garment bag on the door. As she pulled out the purple and gold choir robe, she filled her apartment with the melodic sound of her alto voice. She practiced the selections that the choir rehearsed the past Tuesday.

Since joining Trinity Chapel, she'd been a member of the fifty-plus chorale. To Monét, singing was as natural as breathing—effortless to the point that sometimes she discounted her own gift.

As an adolescent, Monét had carried many a solo part at her family's hometown church nearly forty miles away in Prince George. She was the choir director until she graduated high school and left to attend Coppin State. After college, she settled in the Baltimore area. It wasn't long before she'd found the perfect church to feed her soul, and Zora joined her. There, she was content to blend in with the sea of angelic voices. She sang because of her love for God, not for the attention from people.

The ringing phone interrupted Monét's practice. She picked up her cordless. Bryce was taking it overboard tonight. She was two seconds from turning off the ringer until a glance at the caller ID revealed her parents' name and number. J & J Sullivan.

"Hello, Mother," Monét chirped into the phone.

"I can't believe I caught you," Josephine Sullivan said. "You didn't have one of your little shindigs tonight?"

Monét could imagine her mother gliding around the house in a floor-length satin gown. She couldn't recall a time when she'd seen a cotton or flannel nightgown touch her mother's body.

"Thank the Lord, no." Monét breathed a sigh of relief. "My next event isn't until next week."

"Is that the auction you were so bent out of shape about?"

"Key word *were*. Everything worked itself out after I stopped worrying so much about it. The only thing I did today was go to the festival down at the Harbor and meet Zora for lunch."

"I haven't talked to her this week. How's she doing?"

Monét could hear the clatter of dishes and running water in the background. No doubt her mother had just finished

49

preparing a Sunday feast. "Wrapped up in wedding plans, of course. About as sane as a bride-to-be can be."

"That's why she's got you to keep her calm and be the voice of reason."

"True. She'll survive, but you know Zora. She doesn't stop until she gets what she wants and every little detail is in place." Monét filled her mother in on the latest wedding updates.

To satisfy her mother's need to contribute to the wedding, Monét had assigned her to the bridal shower brunch for Zora. Even though it was supposed to be a small, unpretentious event, the function had escalated to an affair almost as expansive as the wedding. It was Josephine's—or Mama Jo, as Zora called her—gift for a daughter that she'd always treated as her own.

Losing her best friend was heartbreaking, Monét had been told by her mother. And although Zora was almost thirty years old, the Sullivans wanted to take care of her in the same way she knew Albert and Sonja Bridgeforth would've watched over their daughters.

Monét knew her mother's love ran deep for Zora. She also knew her mother was trying to ease Zora's pain. They all wanted to. But this was something Zora would have to endure with the help of God more than anyone else.

Monét remembered the day Zora found out about her adoption. It was nearly unbearable. Monét was just as stunned, and her parents were floored. There was no way someone could've convinced James and Josephine that Zora was adopted. They'd known the Bridgeforths since Monét was four and Zora was three.

"As far as they were concerned, you *were* their real daughter," Mama Jo had told Zora as she lay weeping in her lap. "You always will be." She stroked Zora's back. "God saw to it that you were taken care of. He has a special plan for your life. You're going to be a stronger, wiser woman with a testimony. Just you wait and see."

That chilly March night after Preston had retreated to the couch, Monét stayed in Zora's childhood bedroom and held her through the night as if she were a child. She could never imagine the pain, but only hoped her presence would ease the shock of it. When the endless night finally broke to dawn, Zora had finally fallen asleep, and Monét's restless slumber had been close behind.

"I'll let you know about the final menu for the brunch as soon as your sister calls me back," her mother was saying. "When's the last time you talked to Victoria, anyway?"

"Probably about two weeks ago," Monét answered.

Six years her elder, Victoria was always busy with her eleven-year-old twin boys. Soon after college, she'd married her high school sweetheart, Scott Watkins. Their life was a made-for-television romance and a stark contrast to Monét's. By thirty-one, Victoria had hung up her corporate briefcase to homeschool her then five-year-old sons. But for Monét, now one month away from thirty, marriage—much less children—was the furthest thing from her mind. Her mother thought about it enough for them both.

Ever since Zora had gotten engaged, it seemed everyone thought it was their personal responsibility to hook Monét up. Out of her circle of friends and family members her age, it was obvious that she was the last one standing, so to speak. Well, stand she would. It was possible to be single and satisfied. Evidently, she was the only person left in the world to think so.

By the time Monét caught up on the latest family issues from her mother and chatted briefly with her father, she was in her room and ready to unwind and settle in for the night with a read from the growing stack of books on her nightstand.

No sooner had she hung up the phone, it rang again instantly. Assured it was her mother's usual callback, Monét picked up the phone without a second thought.

"Yes, Mother," she sang in her all-too-knowing tone.

"I'm not your mama, but I'd love to be your daddy."

"Hello, Bryce." Monét didn't bother to feign any enthusiasm. She wouldn't let him sense a hint of anything but irritation in her voice.

"Do you have to sound so mean?" His voice slinked over the phone lines. "You know you want to smile."

"Doubtful," she rattled off, refusing to be wooed by his seduction.

"Why do you give me such a hard time? You know I only live to make you happy."

He'd told Monét that thousands of times. It no longer gave her goosebumps like it used to. Well, maybe one.

"Then why don't you leave me alone?" she said with as much sarcasm as she could manage. Monét's unsuccessful attempts to ruffle his feathers with cruelty had never worked up to this point. It's like deep inside Bryce could sense her last remaining ounce of care for him. She shot back again. "That would make me happy."

"Would it really?"

Silence hung in the air. Monét took it back.

"Look. I'm getting ready for bed. I've got church in the morning."

"Maybe I'll see you there."

Monét didn't believe her ears. Surely they had deceived her. "What? Commissioner Wagner can't be coming through to stand on his political soapbox. It's not election time."

"Can't I come on my own accord?" He had the nerve to sound offended.

"I've never known you to do that," she said. Most of Bryce's appearances at church were attached to the political agenda of his mentor, the commissioner.

"And if I do?"

"And if you do what?" Monét sat down on the floor and

muscled open the overstuffed drawer of her armoire. "You expect some kind of bonus points on your scorecard with me? Go because you want a relationship with God, not a relationship with me."

"That's why I need a woman like you to keep me on track, Monét."

"You're not ready for a woman like me."

"How would you know?"

"Like two years hasn't been long enough to figure it out." She huffed into the phone. "I can't do this tonight. We'll talk tomorrow. At church," she added sarcastically. She hung up before he had a chance to respond, then regretted that she'd been so rude. The hang-up was uncalled for, but she wasn't going to call back. He'd be back at it in a few days.

Monét didn't know why Bryce still had a hold on her. The fact that he didn't have a relationship with God was enough to disqualify him from the running.

Still, he respected her Christian walk. He got used to the fact that she wouldn't budge about giving him her body. It wasn't an option. Sure, he'd tested her commitment, but she stood, even during the incidents when the temptation with Bryce nearly sucked her in.

Monét had committed herself to a life of sexual purity five years prior once she'd had enough of men walking away with a piece of her soul. Three men total; three men too many.

She commended Zora and often prayed God would honor her friend's faithfulness.

Monét tossed a blue nightgown on the bed, then turned out all of the lights except a hall night-light and another in her bedroom. She ran a warm bath, added a cup of Dead Sea salts, and slipped down into the tub of stress relievers. The echo of her silvery voice bounced off of the tile in her bathroom as she sang a song of worship. All thoughts of Bryce and the guy with the gorgeous smile from the Inner Harbor were pushed aside. She should be the one they called Solo. Life was good. Without a man.

4

P.O.W.E.R. During church announcements, First Lady Alana James delivered an enthusiastic introduction about the new women's discipleship group. Pastor Bernard James followed up with a reminder after the benediction. The anxious women were already crowded around the registration table in the vestibule. One of the committee members shoved a form in Zora's hand as she passed.

"Bless you, sister," she said. "You can bring it back next Sunday, and we'll be happy to answer any questions you might have."

Zora smiled, but didn't share the excitement that lit the woman's heart-shaped face. The lady scurried away to another group of women, leaving the citrus fragrance of her perfume behind.

Maybe next session, Zora thought, as she rushed toward the exit without fellowshipping with her church family. It had been her regular timed escape route over the past three months. None of them knew about the recent turn of events in her life. She wasn't ready to disclose it until she had a grip on it herself.

Zora didn't see Monét among the parishioners, so she didn't have time to catch up with her. During worship service, she could never catch her friend's eye from her spot in the pews to Monét's seat in the choir stand. It seemed to her that Monét was preoccupied with watching the door. Even during song selections, she'd noticed her gaze float between the sanctuary entrance and the choir director.

Zora would call her later. She needed to swing by the mall and pick up a birthday gift for Preston's mother. Thoughts related to birthdays only served as a memory that her own hadn't been a day of celebration. Instead of celebrating her birth, she was probably seen as an unwanted burden.

Was she the result of a teenage pregnancy? The remembrance of a night her birth mother wanted to forget? Was her adoption a tearful separation from parents who weren't financially able to raise a child, and chose to afford their daughter a better life? Her mind was jumbled with pressing issues, and birthday presents weren't one of them.

You should keep your mind on Me. I'm the One who can give you perfect peace.

Zora reached the mall in twenty minutes flat. Following a quick ransack through the department store, she was on her way out of the mall and back home. She changed out of her peach two-piece suit, slipped into a baby blue sundress, then went into the living room to await Preston's arrival. She pulled a chair up to the card table she'd placed near the sliding glass door, and opened the new puzzle she'd recently bought. It depicted a serene photo of a teal body of water, dotted with sailboats and set against a setting sun. Just the thing Zora needed to relax.

She turned over the box and dumped part of the five-thousand-piece jigsaw puzzle on the table, running her palm over the clumps until she had a single layer. Zora picked up the remote to her stereo and hit the power button. Her CD player, set on random selection, ran through a set of her jazz collection. Using the box top as her guide, Zora separated the border pieces and then the puzzle pieces according to color and shading. The growling in her stomach intensified as the minutes passed, and she considered eating a small cup of fruit. She abandoned the idea when the doorbell rang.

Zora grabbed her purse and store-wrapped gift and met Preston at the door. She walked out and locked the door before he could consider coming inside.

"I'm starving. Let's roll," she said, playfully punching him in the side.

"Well, hello to you too. Can your future husband get a hug at least?"

"I'm sorry, baby," she said, melting into his arms. She gripped his back and rubbed her hand down the grainy texture of his linen shirt. He looked nice in the tan shirt and slacks. She'd known it would complement his skin tone and physique when she bought it for his birthday last year.

Preston grabbed her hand and led her to the car. "You know, you've been getting a little comfortable lately. I'm telling you, I think the ring has changed things. What's going to happen when we get married?"

"Will you stop saying that? People are going to start taking you serious. I'm the same Zora pre-ring and post-ring, and you know it," she said, waving the ring in front of his face.

"I don't know."

"You know," she said, and slid into the passenger's seat.

Preston wheeled through the complex and pulled out onto the main intersection. He whizzed down the busy streets, only getting caught occasionally by the traffic lights.

Zora stared out the window for most of the ride, waiting for Preston to address the weekly question that hung in the air. He'd been her strongest support since she found out she was adopted, but more so after her parents' death. He'd already formed a bond with them, and viewed them as second parents instead of a dreadful set of in-laws.

Zora knew he wasn't sure how to start the conversation, since it usually brought an outburst of emotions with it. She couldn't predict herself what her reaction would be, seeing that her feelings seemed to change daily.

The biggest thing on Zora's mind during the ride to Preston's parents' house wasn't even the adoption. She couldn't shake the faces of the woman and child she'd seen yesterday at the Harbor. More than that, she couldn't release the feelings for them that had attached themselves to her heart. Almost sorrowful.

Zora's astounding sense of discernment kept her from being unsympathetic. She often carried more than her share of other people's burdens. As she'd grown in her relationship with God, she'd learned that it wasn't always her place to rescue people from their trials. The heat in their lives often served as a molding tool as God tested their faith and perfected their patience. But even this feeling was different, much stronger than what she was used to.

Zora said a silent prayer and pushed them to the back of her mind right at the exact moment that Preston asked *the question*.

"Have you thought yet about looking for your family?"

There it was. Zora was slow to answer. During the first two months after she discovered the letter, her health, sanity, and their relationship suffered. Her sleepless nights left her not only irritable, but physically and mentally drained as well. She'd promised Preston that she wouldn't drive herself into the ground. But he didn't understand. The proof of his lineage was reflected in every sharp, angular feature of his face that was also etched on his father's and two brothers'. His roots

58

were undeniable, and hers were unknown.

No one in Zora's small family, or her parents' circle of friends, knew any details. Either that or they were being tight-lipped in allegiance to her parents' wishes. She didn't have far to dig. She was the only child to two parents who were only children as well. Her only surviving grandmother was living in a nursing home. Dementia was beginning to kidnap her memory, and the news of her only son's death wreaked havoc on an already deteriorating body and spirit. She hadn't been the same since. Zora was convinced she was suffering from a broken heart.

"Zora?"

"Yes, Preston. I'm sorry, baby." She floundered. "Umm. I've been preoccupied with stuff for the wedding." *That's true.* Zora reached over and squeezed Preston's leg. "Not right now, baby. Let's just enjoy the day together. Can we do that?"

Preston coiled his fingers through hers and brought her hand to his lips, warming her skin. "Yes, we can," he answered, and switched his conversation to the chore of narrowing down his invitation list for the wedding. By the time they reached his parents' house, Preston was still just as undecided about the additional forty people that he needed to trim from his list. As far as Zora was concerned, that was a good problem to have.

※

The laughter and loud voices of the Fields family could be heard through the open screen door. Sundays regularly brought at least one of the three sons over to their parents' house for dinner, but today's special occasion was a call-out to the entire Fields clan and a host of close friends.

The couple was welcomed with embraces and kisses from the moment they stepped into the Fields' home. Zora cherished the love she felt there. Before her first visit two years ago, she'd thought it would be stale with a living room that only visitors were allowed to enjoy. Instead, the rooms were cozy, with furniture that beckoned you for an afternoon nap. And in place of what she envisioned would be priceless pieces of art were family pictures of the Fields' pride and joy—their three sons, Andre, Kenneth, and Preston. The kitchen, Mrs. Diane Fields' favorite room of the house, had been remodeled to afford her all of the latest luxuries of a culinary chef. Hidden beneath her designer first-lady hats was a woman who could "burn" with the best of them.

Zora survived a round of introductions and reintroductions of faces that she couldn't pair with names.

"All right now. There's my new daughter."

Zora heard the voice before she saw the towering figure of William Fields enter the den. His voice resonated like thunder even when he wasn't in the pulpit. It had taken Zora some time to get used to the fact that he was a naturally loud man. The only feature of his that his sons didn't share was the wide gap between his two front teeth.

"How are you, Baby Z?"

"Fine, Pop." She leaned forward and accepted the signature kiss he always planted in the middle of her forehead.

"Watch it, Pastor," Preston joked. "Don't get too carried away."

Preston's father pulled Zora into his side with a strong arm. "This *is* my daughter."

"Not yet," the eldest son, Andre, said. He was the stoutest of the sons and carried the same tall and prominent presence as his father. His voice roared when he spoke too. "Zora still has six months to come to her senses and make a run for it."

Preston clasped hands with his brother. "And she'll run right back into my arms, won't you, baby?"

"You know I will," Zora said, stroking her man's ego.

Andre's wife, Lynnette, came over to hug Zora. After two miscarriages the year before, she was hesitant to mention her pregnancy this third time around. But now at the end of the first trimester, she and Andre had recently announced the upcoming addition to the entire family.

"How's the baby?" Zora asked.

"Fine." Lynnette rubbed the area that was on its way to being the size of a beach ball, but was currently a pudgy lump. "This child is zapping my energy, but of course I'm already used to that," she said, referring to her four-year-old, Andre Jr.

Preston approached them with a sly look on his face. "Hey, Sis, how are you going to manage that thing when it's time for the wedding?"

"This *thing*," Lynnette pointed to her stomach, "is your niece or nephew, and we'll do just fine. I'll be there even if you have to roll me down the aisle." She held her hand up to silence the remark that was surely poised on the end of Preston's lips. "Don't go there," she warned.

Andre sneaked up from behind and unleashed an unexpected tackle on his youngest brother, nearly making Preston lose his balance. The elder Fields secured Preston in a headlock.

"Don't make me come in there," Mother Diane said. Preston's mother walked far enough into the den to warn all of her sons. "It's my party, and I can be my own bouncer."

Mother Diane's hair was a deep brown, although Zora knew it was with the help of a coloring kit and not by genetics. The cheeks of her round face sat nearly as high as her eyes when she smiled. She couldn't hide it, even when she was scolding her sons.

Preston muscled his way out of the headlock that loosened after his mother's warning.

"Your playing around is what got me this—" he pointed

to the scar above his nose—"in the first place."

Kenneth, the middle son, butted in from his seat on the couch. His eyes never left the television, and he looked determined to claim dibs on the TV remote for the rest of the day. "Not this story again. Please, Bro, spare everybody here since we've all heard it at least a hundred and seventy-two times."

"Both boxers to their separate corners," Mother Diane said. She walked into the den wearing a blue and white windbreaker set with matching tennis shoes. No matter the outfit, she always wore gold hoop earrings and an armful of gold bangles that clanked to announce her arrival. Today, her tinkling jewelry joined the chorus of the swish of her pant legs rubbing together when she walked.

Zora adored Mother Diane. The first lady of Zion Tabernacle was equally as cherished by the congregation as she was by her own family.

All eyes, especially the first lady's, were on Zora during her first visit with Preston to his father's church. As the pastor's youngest son and the last to be married, Preston had the attention of most of the single women in the congregation. But his focus was on the things of God and not after the women who tried relentlessly to pursue him. Fortunately, Zora's future mother-in-law took to her soon after she realized the sincerity and purity of their love.

"This is what you have to look forward to, especially if you have a house full of boys," Mother Diane told Zora when she walked over to greet her and Preston with a kiss. She took a seat in her favorite recliner. "The Fields men are famous for making boys, so I hope your side of the family brings some strong female chromosomes to add to the mix."

Zora didn't know what she was bringing to the family. She didn't know anything about her family's traits and tendencies. *Do I have siblings who know nothing about me too? Are my parents even alive?*

She made Preston promise he wouldn't disclose her situation to his family. Not now. She wasn't ready for the questions she couldn't answer. She couldn't imagine what they'd think of her parents. What they'd think of her.

Pop held up his massive hands to quiet the rumblings around the house. His gestures had the same effect as they did when he was in the pulpit. A hush eventually fell, even from the rowdy children who'd been ushered in from the backyard. Zora felt like the call to salvation was coming next.

"It's time to serve the queen," Pop announced.

"Amen to that," Mother Diane said.

Pop went over to help his wife out of her chair. "Let's bless the food."

They grabbed hands until everyone in the room was connected. Connection, that's what Zora wanted in her life again. To know her life was tied to someone else.

Mother Diane wrapped her arm around Pop's waist. For the first time, Zora noticed their identical outfits, only Pop wasn't wearing his jacket. That was something her mother and father would've done. Zora would've had to talk her way out of her mother making them triplets. She missed the closeness she shared with her family.

Mother Diane winked at Zora before she bowed her head. And like any bride-to-be without her parents, Zora missed her mother.

5

M*others don't live forever.*

It was a fact that Belinda Stokes had never thought of before. But now, hoisting her portable files and laptop case into the backseat of her car, she realized again for the countless time that week how true it was. You never knew what the next day would bring. It wasn't that she thought her mother was going to die. Her eyes were just opened to the reality that every moment in life should be cherished.

Belinda wiped the sweat beaded on her nose. She was thankful for the occasional breeze sprinkling dandelion seeds across her front lawn. It was an almost perfect Sunday. It would've been perfect had it not been for the trip she was taking to Baltimore this evening.

When she'd received the call about her mother's breast cancer diagnosis a month earlier, she'd dropped everything and frantically driven the over three-hour ride from Danville, Virginia, to Baltimore to spend time at her mother's side. The oncologist had ordered immediate rounds of radiation and chemotherapy for her mother, Bernice. Nausea, vomiting, profound fatigue, and hair loss followed.

Then the second blow followed a week ago. Mastectomy. The chemo and radiation weren't effective.

Since arriving back home, Belinda had spent the last three days in shock. The only thing she could think about was getting back to her mother's side as soon as possible.

To aid in her recovery, Belinda's husband, Thomas, had agreed that it would be beneficial for Belinda to stay with her mother periodically. Fortunately, her duties as a magazine editor could travel with her, and it would do both Belinda and her mother good to be with each other. With her older sister in California and her brother stationed in Japan, Belinda would be one of her primary caretakers.

The ordeal made Belinda think about her father.

He had died eight years earlier after a long battle with heart disease. Walter Allen had been the only man who'd held her mother's heart. The same love that blossomed when they were nineteen had carried them through forty-seven years of marriage.

Belinda moved the diaper bag from the backseat to within easy reach on the front passenger seat. She wouldn't accept the doctor's diagnosis as the final report, no matter what his medical expertise predicted. God held all power in His hands.

God, please don't take my mother, she prayed.

"I wanna stay, Mommy. Please let me stay with Daddy."

Belinda turned around at the sound of the faked childlike voice. Too much bass. Her husband of ten years, Thomas, stood on the porch of her home, his face hidden by the pudgy body of their six-month-old daughter, Hannah. The baby was dressed in a yellow and white checkerboard sundress with a bib shaped like a daisy. Thomas, who had been inside feeding and dressing Hannah, had taken his best stab at slicking the baby's short ringlets into two pigtails on either side of her head.

Belinda pushed the button on her car remote to lock the doors. "You'd never survive more than eight hours at a time by yourself with her. If I leave her here, I guarantee you'll call me to come back tomorrow and pick her up," Belinda said.

"Yeah," Thomas said, "because I'd be tired of *your* crying, not hers."

"Ain't that the truth."

As Belinda walked toward the patio, Hannah flung her arms and legs about wildly. She'd recently found a new use for her mouth and found great joy in blowing spit bubbles until they dribbled over her chin.

"Hey, sweetie." Belinda took her daughter and lifted her above her head, rocking her body back and forth until a string of spit threatened to land on Belinda's forehead. "Yuck," Belinda said, wiping the bib across Hannah's mouth. She propped her daughter on her hip and followed Thomas inside.

Belinda walked upstairs to the nursery. She had taken special thought in choosing the soft yellow color of the room. The accenting teddy bear decor could grow with Hannah at least into her elementary years. A musical mobile danced over the crib that was designed to convert first to a toddler bed, and eventually a twin-sized bed fit for an adolescent. The plush stuffed animals that currently lined the bookcase shelves could easily be replaced by books or whatever would become Hannah's collectible fascination. Maybe dolls. Or tea sets.

Hannah grabbed the necklace around Belinda's neck, then dug her head into Belinda's neck so she could stuff the pendant into her mouth. Belinda pried the necklace from Hannah's tight grip and dropped the chain inside her shirt. Hannah's quick hands reminded her that they'd have more baby-proofing to do to the house soon. Before she knew it, Hannah would be crawling and walking.

Both Thomas and Belinda were still adjusting to being parents. Although they'd tried endless times over the first eight years of their ten-year marriage, they'd never been able to conceive. Afraid that her biological clock would soon stop ticking, Belinda began to consider adoption after turning thirty-eight. With so much love to give between her and Thomas, they couldn't see denying it to any child. Now at forty, Hannah's adoption had made her a first-time mother.

In a way, Thomas' son, Thomas Jr., had been a staple in their lives years ago. His mother, Juanita, was tolerant, though not thrilled when Thomas asked her to introduce Belinda to T. J. when they were dating. But once Belinda and Thomas had announced their engagement, Juanita's acceptance of Belinda was out the door. Things only worsened with Thomas's intention to file for custody of his son. He wanted to rear his son in a God-fearing home instead of Juanita's home where there were no rules.

Juanita was furious. She limited, then eventually cut off Thomas's contact with his son. She and T. J. relocated without a trace.

That was part of the reason why Belinda prayed so hard to give her husband a child. Their marriage had withstood a test that they never thought would happen. She'd questioned her womanhood with her inability to conceive, but Thomas reassured her by his unyielding devotion to his queen. For better or for worse. And he meant it.

Belinda looked around the nursery one last time. Thomas stood outside the door in the hallway. He'd changed out of his pajama bottoms and into a T-shirt, jeans, and his house slippers.

"Can you think of anything else I need?"

"Really, Belinda. What are you going to do? Strap the furniture to the top of the car and haul it to Baltimore? You're only going to be gone for a week this round."

"The one thing I don't take is the one thing I'll need."

Thomas shook his head.

"Woman thing," she said. She pressed Hannah's hand to her lips. "One day you'll understand." Belinda rubbed her nose against Hannah's chin. "We've got to get ready to go."

Thomas held out his hands for Hannah. "We're going downstairs to wait for you."

"I'll be down in a minute," she said, kissing Hannah, then Thomas, on their cheeks.

Belinda sat down in the gliding rocking chair by Hannah's crib. She covered her eyes with her clasped hands. Despite the circumstances, she knew something good would have to come out of this ordeal. God's Word said that *all* things work together for the good of them who love the Lord, not *some* things. She didn't immediately wipe away the tears that trickled down her face until she was ready to leave the room.

Belinda lazily pushed herself off the comfort of the plump cushions, walked over to pull the blinds together, then went downstairs.

"Okay," Belinda said, rapping her knuckles on the wooden banister. She picked up her purse hanging from the end of the banister and threw it across her shoulder. "I'm ready to roll."

Thomas walked out of the kitchen with a frozen treat in his hand and Hannah cuddled in the other arm. He ran the strawberry-flavored fruit bar across Hannah's lips. Hannah smacked her lips, obviously thrilled at the sweet taste, and followed Thomas's hand with an open, drooling mouth.

"Give me my baby before you give her a sugar overload," Belinda said. "I've got to ride three hours with this child."

"At least it has fruit in it," Thomas said, hoisting Hannah up to her mother with one hand so he could catch the ringing kitchen phone. "Hello? Yes, ma'am. She's walking out the door right now." He nodded his head and mouthed the words "your mother" as Belinda walked toward the door. "Okay, Mama. I'm always praying for you. I'll try to see you the next trip," he said, and hung up the phone.

Thomas opened the front door for his wife and led her down the steps with his hand in the curve of her back. Belinda felt a spring of emotions well up inside of her. The seriousness of her mother's condition was frightening. Thomas seemed to sense his wife's thoughts and hugged Belinda into his chest. Her eyes watered. She took a deep breath then slowly tried to exhale the pain from her chest.

"I didn't think I had any tears left."

Thomas lifted her chin with his finger, then cupped her face between his hands. "You don't have to be strong right now," he said. "I can carry you."

Words weren't necessary. They always discerned each other's thoughts. They stood on the porch wrapped in each other's embrace.

"Let's pray before you get on the road," Thomas suggested when they finally withdrew from each other's arms. Hannah squealed in agreement and went back to blowing bubbles.

They strolled down to the middle of the driveway. Belinda gave Thomas a smile that reflected her sincere adoration of him, then bowed her head in prayer. After Thomas prayed, they hugged each other again until Hannah, lodged in the middle of their embrace, started to squirm for air.

"All right, little mama. Let's go," Belinda said, and opened the back passenger door to buckle in Hannah.

Hannah latched her chubby fingers onto the collar of her mother's shirt while Belinda adjusted the car seat straps. Belinda wiggled the chair for security and double-checked the position of the Winnie the Pooh window shade before walking to the driver's side, where Thomas was waiting with the door open. She couldn't resist falling into his arms once more and accepting the kiss that told her that she would be missed.

He'd given her the same message last night. They made love, not once, but three times. She slept in and skipped church this morning. As far as Belinda was concerned, she'd received the ministry she needed.

"What are you smiling about?" Thomas asked. He closed the door after Belinda was situated and leaned down to the window.

"Ministry." Belinda cranked the car and rolled down the window, smiling seductively. She'd been using her shades as a makeshift headband for her growing natural twists; now she slid them down on her nose.

"I'm glad I left you with something to think about while you're gone," Thomas said, returning a sensual gaze to his wife.

"Don't make me come back in that house," she said, backing out into the empty street. She bid her final good-bye with the toot of her horn. "Love you." Belinda blew a kiss and headed toward the entrance to their subdivision.

♋

Fortunately, Hannah easily entertained herself during the ride from Danville to Baltimore. Distracted by the colorful interactive toys attached to her car seat and her other new fascination of playing with her toes, Hannah wasn't a problem.

It seemed like no time before Belinda was pulling into the neighborhood where she'd grown up as a child. When she was younger, she and her friends either walked or biked the short distance to her elementary school. The streets were lined with cookie-cutter houses, only made distinguishable by the cars in the driveway or the occasional personalized name marker attached to a house.

Belinda crept down the street. She beeped her horn and waved at Marcus Cain, who still lived three doors down from her mother's house. His dreams of owning an auto repair shop had never ventured further than the old Chevy Impala propped on bricks parked in his parents' driveway.

Belinda eased into her mother's short driveway and looked back at Hannah through the rearview mirror. Her baby had finally cooed herself into a deep slumber. Belinda shifted the car into park and grabbed her purse and baby bag. She went around to the back and opened the passenger door.

Belinda lifted her daughter's head and ran her hand down the side of Hannah's black ringlets. The hair on the back of her head and around the side of her hairline was soggy with sweat from being pressed against the fabric of the car seat.

Belinda leaned in to put her cheek close to Hannah's lips, much like she sometimes did at night to make sure Hannah was breathing. She smelled the faint smell of apple juice from her mouth mixed with the soft scent of baby powder from her body. Belinda often thanked God for such a mild-natured child. A gift from God, as she was so appropriately named.

She unsnapped the belt and lifted out her daughter. Hannah's body, limp as a rag doll, hung over Belinda's shoulder. Belinda's feet felt as heavy as lead. She was walking into an emotional time in the household. "God, help me," she prayed.

Don't I always?

Belinda blew out a quick breath before she turned the key in the door.

Zora had slept soundly through most of the night, awaking only once from the dream that Tuesday morning. It had been at least three weeks since the recurring dream had pushed itself into her slumber. Since childhood she'd dreamt of chasing a figment of her own image down a white hallway. It never caused her alarm, only perplexity. Lying under the crumpled sheets, she finally understood the symbolic meaning behind it. She was chasing her own identity.

Zora's vision blurred the red digital numbers of her alarm clock until she rubbed the sleep from her eyes: 5:09 a.m. She'd made a decision. She'd search for her biological family or at least some type of closure so she could move on with the rest of her life. It was the only way to keep her nights and soul at rest.

"Good morning, Lord," Zora said, pulling the sheets up to her neck.

The sunrise wouldn't awaken the horizon for at least another two hours, but Zora still basked in the dawning of the new day. It was time to exchange her sorrow for joy. The world was saturated with opportunities and, somewhere, an answer.

"I've been a mess, haven't I, God? I've been walking around like my life is over, and You give me new mercies every day. I'm sorry for taking Your grace for granted. Every answer can be found in You."

Zora rolled over to the left side of the bed and opened the top drawer of the nightstand, feeling around for her book lamp. As always, she'd fallen asleep after reading a chapter of Psalms, and her Bible an arm's length away on the pillow beside her.

Zora couldn't remember a time that she hadn't slept with her Bible on the bed. Like most children, she experienced a stage of being afraid of the dark, but she'd found comfort in the Scripture her father highlighted in her Bible. Proverbs 3:24 was forever etched in her memory. *When you lie down, you will not be afraid; yes, you will lie down and your sleep will be sweet.*

Every night she and her father had read the verse together until the supposed monsters under the bed were the least of her worries. By twelve, she was more concerned with trying to sneak lipstick to school instead.

Zora flipped on the book lamp and a sliver of light seeped on the page. Her parents had raised her to seek God's Word faithfully and she still held their teachings close to her heart. She'd gleaned the pearls of wisdom from the book of Proverbs for years and had committed a lot of Scriptures to memory.

The clock blared out at her. 5:14. She thumbed the pages of her Bible to find another passage to read. She stopped in 1 John chapter 15 verse 14 and read a passage highlighted in pink. Verse five, chapter fourteen.

The time and the verse? May be a sign, huh, God?

She pushed herself up against the bed's headboard and clicked on the bedside lamp for more light.

Now this is the confidence that we have in Him, that if we ask anything according to His will, He hears us.

Zora meditated on the Scripture until she was drowsy again. She slid down and pulled the sheets over her head, drifting into a place of peace. It was ten o'clock before she awakened to a blaring car alarm down the street.

"Thank God for summer break," she said to herself and stretched her body across the length of the bed. Before she even opened her eyes, her mind ticked through the day's obligations. *Pack picnic basket. Make hair appointment. Pick up clothes from cleaners. Meet Monét at florist.* But none of them at the moment was as important as one of the steps she was going to take this morning. Fear of the truth had paralyzed her before.

Not anymore. The "what ifs" hung over her head. She needed to be free. Knowing something was better than knowing nothing.

Zora stretched her limbs from her toes to her fingertips, then rolled out of bed. She pulled and straightened the flat sheet until it was tight enough to bounce a quarter on—her bed-making skill complimentary of her military-groomed father. She jerked her arms up and whipped her new lavender comforter into the air, landing it almost perfectly across the bed. She smoothed the wrinkles before finishing up with the coordinating pillows. She'd read recently that the color lavender was not only a calming shade, but the flower emitted a relaxing fragrance—floral, yet slightly fruity.

Zora carried the color theme into her master bath, accenting with lavender towels and plush rugs. She enjoyed expressing her femininity and was eager to incorporate a lady's touch into Preston's decor. Once she moved in, his place would come alive with bursts of color, instead of the drab shades of brown and black that were currently prominent in every room of his house.

"All right." Zora walked into the spare room she used as an office. "Now down to business."

She planted herself in front of the computer, then opened the high-speed Internet browser.

Maryland, adoption. The words she typed in the search engine opened an endless list of Web sites.

"The power of the Internet," Zora said, and pulled a notepad out of a nearby drawer. "Might as well start at the top."

Zora scrolled down the site for the Maryland Department of Human Resources. She had no idea whether her adoption was finalized through a public government department, private agency, or if it was an independent adoption. But according to the information, all legal documents related to the adoption were held by the court where the adoption was finalized, whether it was public or private.

"That narrows it down," Zora said. Her parents had only lived in two counties since they were married. When God gives you an unction, it's worth following it, she thought. If things were going to be this easy, Preston's guest list may not be the only one that needed to be trimmed.

Zora's plans for the day wouldn't give her enough time to visit the courthouses in both Anne Arundel and Howard Counties. She opened another window browser and found their addresses. She had a clear calendar for tomorrow and could spend as much time as she needed. But now, she needed to get dressed.

Midmorning sunlight spilled into the bedroom when Zora opened the blinds, and she prayed incessantly within the thirty minutes that she showered and changed.

God, I'm going to have to believe that You have my best interests at heart. I'm tired of crying myself to sleep, so now

I'm crying out to You. I don't know why I was put up for adoption, but I do know that You placed my life in the hands of two people You trusted. Still, my heart needs healing. I believe You spoke to me through Your Word this morning, and I need to be able to stand on faith. Amen.

Zora had planned a picnic for the love of her life. Last night, she'd driven to Preston's place and used his spare car key to leave an invitation to lunch on his dashboard. The note instructed him to meet her two blocks down from his office building at one o'clock. His duties as an accountant often left him crunching numbers at his desk during lunch, instead of escaping for a breath of fresh air.

Two years ago Zora had been hesitant to fall in love for fear her heart would be crushed. Like Monét, she'd had her share of heartache. But with his godly compassion, Preston had shown her how to live and love again.

Zora found the picnic basket that she'd vowed to put to good use when she splurged on it last summer. She flipped open the brown wicker lid and stocked it with the items she'd bagged the night before—everything they needed for chicken pita sandwiches, including Preston's favorite ranch dressing. The only thing left to do was brown the chicken cubes. In the meantime, she tossed in a couple of bags of baked chips, a container of fruit and two bottles of juice, then cushioned the food with a traditional red and white checkerboard tablecloth. Twenty minutes later with her summer cuisine in hand, Zora headed out the door to meet the finest man on this side of heaven.

❧

"I'm looking for them," Zora said. She smoothed out her jean skirt and spread a cloth napkin over her lap. She and Preston had found a picnic table outside and slid in beside each other on the bench.

Preston took a hefty bite out of his chicken pita, then wiped the ranch dressing off the corner of his mouth. He'd come out of his jacket and tie for lunch. The crew neck of his white T-shirt peeked through the unbuttoned top of his blue dress shirt.

Zora jumped in as Preston seemed to search her face for an explanation.

"My parents. My real parents," she said, as if it needed to be clarified. It didn't.

Preston unbuttoned another button on his shirt. His eyebrows raised with what at first Zora thought was skepticism, but then realized was concern. "Are you sure you're ready?"

Zora nodded. She was surer now than she'd been this morning. She pulled the pita bread from one side of her wrap and added a scoop of diced tomatoes. "Definitely."

"What made you come to this decision?"

"A feeling I had this morning. At 5:14," she recalled. "It was right after I woke up from my dream." Another comment she didn't need to explain. Preston was well aware of it—they'd prayed many times together that the mystery of the dream would be revealed.

"I finally figured out why I've had that dream all my life," she said, and explained her deduction to Preston.

He twisted the bottle tops off their fruit juices and handed one to Zora. He tilted his head back and downed nearly half of the beverage before coming up for air.

"Drove you to drink, huh?" Zora laughed.

"Nearly." He slid closer to Zora and picked up her hand. He pressed his lips to her knuckles, then squeezed her hand reassuringly. "If this is what you want, I'll support you. But you have to be prepared for what you do or don't find."

That was just like Preston, always wanting to protect her.

"I know. I have faith that I'll find some sort of closure. Even if I never see them, it would make me feel better if I knew why. When I woke up this morning I read the Scripture in 1 John 5:14. The time, the Scripture. I can't pass that off as coincidence."

Preston stared at her. His skin was smooth and the creamy color of dark chocolate. His eyebrows were as wide as they were thick, nearly connecting in the center. They were expressive and told his thoughts when he didn't.

"We can never have the answer to every question we have in life," Preston finally said. "That's where faith steps in. And that's where I come in to help hold you up. And remind you."

"That's why I love you." Zora wrapped her arms around Preston's neck. He was wearing her favorite cologne. She held on to him as if her life depended on it. In some ways it did, she felt.

Preston hugged her and rubbed his hand down the center of Zora's back. "How much do you love me?" He pulled away slightly so he could see her face, then covered her lips with his.

After a few seconds Zora leaned away from him. "That's not fair," she said. "You're trying to influence the jury." She pulled out of his arms and crossed her hands on top of her heart. "There's no measure to the depth of my love for you," she said, batting her eyes.

"And the Oscar goes to—" Preston held an imaginary microphone to his lips.

"Preston Fields for lead actor in the movie *Only God Loves You More Than Zora.*"

"So that means you love me enough to ask Monét for another ticket to the auction?"

Zora opened a bag of chips and dumped them out on her plate. "For who?"

"Jeremiah," he said, stealing one of her chips.

"So you must want to meet me at the altar at my funeral instead of at the wedding. Monét is going to kill me."

"All she can do is say no. At least ask her."

"I will," Zora said, popping a grape into her mouth. "So why is Jeremiah coming up?"

"His firm is sending him up for a meeting. Something about a possible buy-out or merger. He's on the fast track to becoming one of their junior partners, so they wanted him involved."

"Already?" Zora was impressed. "His ex-fiancée, what's her name? Ingrid? She missed out, didn't she?"

Zora had only had the chance to spend time with Jeremiah a few times since she and Preston met, and only one of those included Jeremiah's former intended wife. She wasn't cruel, but Zora thought she lacked personality. She had an unsociable disposition, totally opposite from Jeremiah. Ingrid and Jeremiah used to work together. That seemed to Zora to be their only common ground. Both were engrossed in their jobs and spent more time at the office than at home. Zora had always thought the relationship had started out of convenience.

"That man is focused," Preston said. "Always has been. It's either his blueprints or his music. Anything or anybody besides God who can tear him away from his loves has got to be heaven-sent, especially after Ingrid. She didn't believe in his vision beyond the workplace. That's a surefire way to run a man off."

"I bet Monét can take his thoughts off his blueprints and his music. She's so eccentric and different. Confident in her unique style, you know?" Zora brushed a crumb off Preston's goatee.

"If she can, then more power to her. I kid around with Monét a lot, but the two of them are too caught up in their own worlds to notice each other. Jeremiah is in love with his keyboard all the way in Texas, and props to the man who can pencil himself into Monét's schedule."

Preston definitely had a point, Zora thought. She spun the top of her juice bottle on the wooden table, catching it each time a split second before it toppled over. Regardless, she had a feeling about those two.

Preston opened the picnic basket and began packing their leftovers. "If he can't go, then I'll probably skip the auction and hang out with him. I can't abandon my boy. I hardly see him as it is."

"You'll come up with any excuse, won't you? Don't worry —we'll get him a ticket."

Zora sipped the rest of her juice and tied the empty bottle up in the plastic bag they were using for trash. She shook the crumbs from the napkin on her lap, then wiped her hands, paying special attention to the ranch dressing smeared on the side of her engagement ring. She was still in awe at the pear-shaped solitaire sitting on a platinum band. It was more than she'd expected.

When the table was clear she opened her wedding organizer.

"I already know what you're going to say," Zora said, and flipped to the sheets she'd torn from a magazine. "But let's look at these one more time."

"Baby, I give you a hard time about some of this wedding planning stuff, but it's really not that bad. I've heard some of my brothers' horror stories, so I know I've got it good."

"Remember that three months from now when it's crunch time. Writing out checks, stuffing envelopes, assembling favors."

"Hold up. I don't have a problem writing the checks, but can't you have your bridesmaids or somebody help you do that other stuff?"

Zora laughed. "Don't worry, sweetheart. Everything will be taken care of well in advance. Monét and I will have everything under control."

"That's what I need to hear. Whatever you ladies need that day, food, whatever. It's on me."

"That's all *I* need to hear."

"I don't know what I just got myself into." Preston pulled the notebook closer to his view. "Now show me some carnations. You know we can get those ten for a dollar at the convenience store on the morning of the wedding."

Zora pressed her palm against Preston's forehead. "I think this heat is scorching your brain."

"I'm hot, but it's not from the sun," he said, grabbing her side and pretending to bite her neck. Preston growled.

"Preston!" Zora playfully slapped his arm. She looked over her shoulder to see if the couple behind them or the elderly gentleman reading the paper was privy to Preston's teasing. She lowered her voice. "Five more months and I'll unleash the tiger on *you*."

They shared a laugh loud enough to turn heads.

Shame on me, Zora thought. *It's not five months. It's ninety-nine days.*

Zora and Preston scanned the magazine pages of some of their preferred flower choices and designs before she left. She zipped to meet Monét at the florist to discuss options for bouquets, ceremony decorations, and reception centerpieces. After all, tomorrow she'd only have ninety-eight more days to go.

Zora considered several approaches to ask Monét about the extra ticket for the auction. By the time she pulled into an empty space in front of Bailee's Blossoms, she'd decided to wait and see if an ideal opportunity presented itself.

The name of the flower shop was painted in red and yellow across the front of the window. Green ivy had been stenciled around its edge, and a bright yellow awning hung over the door. It beckoned passersby to visit. Based on Monét's recommendation, Bailee's reputation for excellence preceded her.

Zora reached for her tote bag in the backseat and turned back around to see Monét standing on the sidewalk tapping her watch. Her conservative navy blue suit was jazzed up with a set of bold accessories. Monét's shapely calves and legs, shown off by her knee-length skirt, testified that she wasn't a stranger to the gym. It prompted Zora to promise herself to hit the weights and treadmill soon. She didn't want Preston to have any unpleasant surprises.

"It's about time," Monét said when Zora swung open the car door. "Need I remind you that I'm working double duty here? I had to finalize the centerpieces for the auction too. At least you have some time. I've got two days."

Definitely not time to ask about the ticket, Zora thought as Monét switched into wedding coordinator mode.

"I talked to Bailee about some of the styles you and Preston like, and she knows about the budget you're working with. We started to play around with a couple of ideas for the bouquets while we waited for you to get here."

"Great. I trust your judgment as much as my own. Nobody knows me better."

"Except Preston."

"Well, right now he's running a close second. But after we truly become one—"

"I get the point," Monét said, opening the door and leading Zora into a room full of God's handiwork. The scents of the flowers mingled together, bringing their fragrant dance of nature inside the store.

Zora had become quite the flower expert, recognizing many of the petals from her endless hours poring over wedding magazines and Web sites for the past six months. Groupings of red roses burst color out of the mouths of glass vases. Long-stemmed Oriental lilies exploded in shades of pink, white, and yellow. Dutch tulips, orchids, and her favorite purple hydrangeas were bunched in separate vases.

A pecan-tan woman with a heart-shaped face appeared from a door behind the counter. Her auburn sister locs were bustled into a bundle on top of her head, and her floor-length tunic flowed behind her like ocean waves when she walked. She looked like the kind of woman, Zora thought, who would sell her possessions and live as a missionary in Africa.

"You must be Zora," she said. Her deep alto voice belonged on a late-night jazz station. "I'm Bailee Thompson. Nice to meet you."

"You too," Zora said, shaking Bailee's outstretched hand. Even at arm's length, Bailee's perfume wafted to Zora's nose. It was a soft floral scent. *How appropriate.* "Monét raves about your work."

"It's God's work. He just uses my hands." Bailee pointed toward a nearby countertop where several portfolios lay open. "Shall we get started?" she asked.

Zora walked over and flipped through the books to compare Bailee's work with her examples.

"I can do some quick mock-ups for you, and we can arrange them until it suits your liking," Bailee suggested.

"Sounds good."

"How much time do you have?" Bailee checked the watch hugging her thick wrist.

"I'm open for however long you need me, but Monét has to get back to work."

"I have about forty-five minutes," she told Bailee, then turned to Zora. "But ultimately the decision is yours. I don't have to be here."

"I know, but you're my second set of eyes. I don't want to make a bad decision."

"Trust me. With Bailee's work, you won't even have any bad choices. We haven't priced another florist for events at the center since I don't know when."

"How much money do I owe you for that plug?" Bailee asked.

"Just remember it for when it's her turn," Zora said.

"I had no idea," Bailee said, looking between the girls for a sign of confirmation. She put her hands on her hips, and her balled fists disappeared in the roundness of her waist. "Monét, I didn't know you had a romance brewing."

"Neither did I." Monét fingered her chunky necklace.

Bailee went to a shelf on the wall and brought back two vases. "Zora's fiancé doesn't have any single friends?"

"He certainly does. He has a very single best man," Zora emphasized, "but he lives in Houston."

"Maybe he'll find his way to Baltimore before the wedding," Bailee said to Zora.

Monét posted herself between Bailee and Zora. "Are you two going to continue this conversation like I'm not here? We're supposed to be talking about flowers, not my love life or lack thereof."

Zora talked around Monét. "As a matter of fact, he will be in Baltimore. This Saturday." She chose a blooming red rose from a nearby arrangement and handed it to Monét. "And I know he'd appreciate a seat at the auction." *There. I kept my promise to Preston. At least I asked.*

A smirk lined Monét's face. "So I'm visible again?" She ran the flower under her nose, broke off the blossom, and put it behind her ear. "We'll talk about it later."

Zora watched as Bailee worked effortlessly, her hands creating her mind's picture. "Elegant. Simple, yet classy."

"I picked that up," Bailee said, her eyes never leaving the work in progress. "You can tell a lot about a person's taste in flowers by the way they dress." She finally looked up at Zora and seemed to assess her client. Bailee crossed her arms around her ample bosom. "Your jewelry—the small diamond studs and cross pendant—are timeless." She pulled out one of the pictures of Zora's choices. "Just like these hydrangeas are age-less. Then you have your cute V-neck sleeveless sweater and jean skirt. Those are classic pieces too, no matter the decade."

Zora snickered and looked at Monét who nodded her head. "I don't know whether to take that as a compliment or not," she said.

Bailee continued even though her eyes were back on her work. "Monét, on the other hand, will probably go a little bolder. I wouldn't be surprised if she took a step on the wild side." She cupped her chin in her hand, then shook an assured finger at Monét. "I wouldn't be surprised if you got married on an island somewhere. Barefoot in the sand with an endless ocean behind you."

Monét gave her a high five. "You couldn't have said it better. I spend so much time planning other people's events that I'll want to escape the drama of it all."

Forty minutes later, with Zora and Monét's input, Bailee had transformed three of her working tables into reception centerpieces, and used another to showcase her ideas for the bouquets and church decorations.

"These are absolutely amazing," Zora said. "You were able to interpret what I was trying to explain, but still add a splash of individuality. And it's not overdone. Thank you so much. Preston is going to love these."

Bailee beamed. "Don't thank me; thank God. He's the awe-some Creator of these flowers, and He gave me the gift for me to give back to Him. I'll be right back." Bailee slipped between the two sheer panels hanging over the opening to the back room.

Bailee's presence could no longer save Zora. The conversation was bound to come up sooner or later. Deal with it now and get it over with, she thought.

"I promise you I didn't set this up," Zora said.

"You sound guilty already."

"Preston just told me at lunch today. Jeremiah has to come up for some meeting for work."

"Zora. I'm not in the mood to try and mooch a seat out of Dr. Manns. He's already done so much. He gave me three of his twenty seats."

"Preston doesn't want to abandon Jeremiah, and if he can't come, then Preston is going to ditch the event."

"I'll see what I can do." Monét said. "If Preston backs out, at least let me know so I can fill the seat. I don't want to seem ungrateful."

"I will. Hopefully the only seat you'll have to fill is an extra empty one and I already have a taker."

"I'm sure you do," Monét rummaged through her purse and pulled out a small tube of lip gloss. She glided the wand across her lips. "For this to be a coincidence, you're a little too happy."

Zora held out her hand for a tube. "Seriously. This isn't a setup," she said between puckers. "You can ask Preston."

"Like I can really expect a straight answer from him. He's your accomplice." Monét picked up a corsage and held it to her chest. "Any other surprise news I should know about?"

"I'm looking for my biological parents."

Monét put down the corsage. She pulled out two of the chairs around the table and sat down in one. Zora joined her.

"I know what you're thinking, but I can handle it. The denial and then the initial shock was too much for me to handle at first. God spoke to me this morning. I'm sure of it."

"That's all I need to know," Monét said.

Zora knew Monét meant it.

Bailee returned with her digital camera. "I'll take pictures and e-mail them to you so you can show your fiancé."

"Good idea," Zora and Monét both chimed.

"You act out together, and now you're talking in unison. You sure you're not sisters?"

"Practically," Monét said.

"Possibly," Zora said, making light of her own situation.

"I think I better sit down and talk to my folks," Monét said. "I'm not up for any more surprises like that."

Zora noticed the puzzled look on Bailee's face. "Don't mind us." She picked up a bouquet and pretended to march down an aisle.

Bailee snapped a picture. "What's the countdown, Zora? Every bride knows how many days she has left."

"Who, me?"

Monét picked up a bouquet and started down the imaginary aisle behind Zora. "Don't even try it. You know it."

Zora looked over her shoulder. "You're a natural. All you need is a wedding dress." She turned back around, and Bailee caught her with a candid shot. "And a man." *All I need is another auction seat.*

7

The flowers for the auction were one less thing Monét had to worry about. Bailee's centerpieces were being delivered and set up on Friday morning. She'd turned in Bailee's invoice to the accounting department, so the check would be ready for Monét to pay on delivery.

Now to the seating chart.

Monét added paper to her laser printer, then swiveled around in her high-back chair to face the window. She stared at two squirrels chasing each other up and around the tree until the computerized voice alerted her that the printing job was complete. She pulled a florescent pink highlighter from her rotating desk caddy and set her mind to the task at hand.

Only an act of God would open up an empty seat at the sponsorship table, or any other table, for that matter. She lined the five pages of the spreadsheet with the invitees and confirmed RSVPs across her desk. Every seat was accounted for.

Jasmine, the summer intern, tapped on Monét's open door. She struck a pose like a game show hostess and ran her hand around the silhouette of a single red rose in a crystal vase.

"Well, well." Monét got up from her desk. "Must be from Maurice," she said, matching the excited look on the zealous college junior's face. Maurice was Jasmine's boyfriend and the topic of ninety-eight percent of her conversations.

"I wish." Jasmine held the vase out to Monét. "This is for you." She crossed her arms and leaned against the door frame. "So you're keeping secrets?" She pursed her overly glossed lips together in a pout.

Monét fanned away Jasmine's comment with a flick of her hand. Probably a client or artist appreciation gift, she thought to herself. "Thank you," she said, and set the vase on the coffee table in the middle of her office.

"What?" Monét asked when she realized Jasmine hadn't left her post.

"Mmmmm . . . Uh-huh." Jasmine didn't sound convinced, and her tone showed she was far from believing her supervisor. She spun around on her chunky heels for a dramatic exit.

Monét thought nothing of it. She received flowers and other tokens of appreciation from her clients on a regular basis. It was probably from Jacqués, she thought. After the hassle she'd endured trying to pull off his debut exhibit, a show of gratitude was the least he could do. The rose was nice, but a bottle of aspirin would've been just as appropriate to fight the headaches he caused her every time his voice was on the other end of the phone line.

No matter how worrisome, Monét always handled even the worst clients with finesse. The cultural arts center had created the events coordinator position for her after a three-year stint as their summer college intern. Before her, the events were contracted out to a freelance event planner. Fortunately for Monét, the woman gave birth to twins and dropped the cultural center from her client list.

Monét opened the small white envelope attached to the

side of the vase. The card was sprayed with cologne. Smells familiar, she thought.

Missed church. Missing you. A single rose, but wishing there were two . . . of us. B-

Bryce. He was a client all right. One with a terminated contract. He never stopped, and his game rarely changed. She tossed the sad excuse for an apology in the wastebasket beside her desk and refocused on the spreadsheets, frustrated that she actually expected him to walk through the door on Sunday.

Monét gathered together the papers across the desk and stapled them. Unfortunately for Zora, it looked as if Preston would be having a night out on the town with his boy. But fortunately for Monét, she wouldn't have to endure an awkward matchmaking session.

Monét checked the room's layout plan to make sure the tables were arranged according to sponsorship levels and that individually ticketed guests were seated at tables suited to their character—and pocketbooks.

As tedious as the logistics of events like these could be, Monét thrived on the details and rush of pulling off another successful affair. She had the winning record to prove it.

Zora's wedding was no different. She deserved a grand affair, an occasion to experience how much she was loved and honored. Planning a wedding and preparing to be a wife were stressful enough. She was glad Zora was moving forward, despite the recent events in her life.

Jasmine buzzed through on Monét's phone's intercom speaker. She'd forwarded all her calls to Jasmine so she could concentrate.

"Dr. Manns is on the line. Should I put him through?"

"Please," Monét said. What could it be? So far the event was progressing without a flaw. A call from the head honcho this far into the game usually meant a monkey wrench was about to be thrown into the system. Dr. Manns was the board chairman for a foundation initiated bya group of black cardiologists.

"Monét Sullivan," she answered.

"Are you counting down the days yet?"

"Of course I am," Monét said. "But not in the way you probably think. I can't wait for the auction. It's going to be a successful event."

"If I could work with someone like you every day, my life would be much easier."

"Thank you, Dr. Manns."

"You've worked with me long enough to call me Darryl," he said. He proceeded to ramble about two presenters he wanted to add to the program.

Calling him Dr. Manns worked fine for her, Monét thought, as she scribbled down his notes. She didn't want to give him any inkling that their professional relationship had the possibility of crossing into the personal realm. A few of his comments in the past had made her uncomfortable, and she knew she wasn't overreacting. Both times she'd ignored his come-ons. He was a married man with a loose tongue. He probably put out bait to see who would bite. She felt sorry for his wife.

"I truly appreciate the work you've done," Dr. Manns said. "Which is why when a seat opened at the association's table, I thought of you first. My assistant won't be able to make it. Her niece went into labor early, so she went to New Jersey to help her for a few weeks. You're more than welcome to invite another friend."

"That's nice of you," Monét said. *I can't believe it.* "I'm sure I'll find someone who would be delighted with the offer." She didn't have to look far.

"Great," Dr. Manns said. "The love of my life just walked in, so I better go. I'll touch base at the end of the week."

"Sure thing." Monét released Dr. Mann's call from her line, then picked up a clear extension on the phone to call Zora.

"God has surely worked in your favor," she said, dialing Zora's number. When Zora didn't answer her home phone, she left a message on her cell. "You've already been praying hard today, haven't you? Call me."

The hands on Monét's crystal desk clock rounded closer to six thirty, and Monét finally decided to pack up her work. She typed a priority list for the following day, then picked up the vase she'd placed on the coffee table. On the way out she left it on Jasmine's deserted desk. Somebody might as well get some joy out of it.

8

The love of his life? At one time she would have believed his words. But now, watching him walk by and barely take note of her, they couldn't seem further from the truth. Paula's husband had transformed into a man she barely knew.

Darryl had been home for two hours and had only spoken to her three times. Four if you count the grunt when she warned him about pulling his car too close to the garage wall.

"By the way. I can't find a babysitter," Paula said, smoothing lotion around the cuticles of her perfectly manicured nails. She couldn't resist purchasing the spa's latest body butter earlier that the day after her monthly deep tissue massage. It smelled exactly like honeydew melon.

Darryl had just come down from upstairs and had made it his business to hound her about the upcoming auction. Now he paced around the living room like a lion stalking its prey. She watched his movement through her peripheral vision. Even though her heart thudded against her chest at the anticipation of an argument, she ignored him.

Paula wasn't up for playing the part of the socialite on Friday. She could plaster on a cookie-cutter smile and make it through the evening like she'd done at three other events over the past few months. Tonight she was sick and tired of being sick and tired. Why should she try anymore if he wouldn't?

Darryl stopped at the foot of the ottoman of the love seat where Paula was sitting, his hand posted on his fit waist. She caught the glimmer of the pinkie ring on his left hand. It had recently replaced his platinum wedding band. Supposedly the metal of his wedding band irritated his finger, but Paula couldn't see why it had taken five years for that to happen.

"What do you mean you can't find a babysitter? You've known about this silent auction for months. How is it going to look if the wife of the association chairman isn't there?"

She repeated the same sentence that a moment before had nearly caused steam to blow from his ears. "I can't find a babysitter."

The fury built on Darryl's face. He gritted his teeth together and shoved his hands in his pockets.

"Please don't yell," she forewarned. "My son is sleeping."

"*Your* son?" His voice dropped almost in a whisper. He shook the phrase off as if he refused to be distracted by her. He began pacing again.

Paula swallowed the lump in her throat. Her boldness was at its climax today. She'd cried enough. How long did he expect her to be pitiful? If he wanted to leave, she'd help him pack. *Maybe.*

Darryl burst into her thoughts.

"Take him to his grandmother's."

"She's out of town at her sister's house. It's Aunt Kelda's birthday."

"What about Kelly?"

"Away in college."

"School is out."

96

"She's in summer session." It was an assumption. Paula had known she'd attended the summer session at Norfolk State for the last two years. Why would this year be an exception? Paula actually hadn't bothered to call.

"Did you try the girl down the street? What's her name? Uh . . ." He snapped his fingers as he tried to recall her name. "Regina," he finally said.

Now you want to be helpful? Paula took her time putting on her jewelry—a two-carat diamond ring for her left hand and a stylish bracelet from Tiffany's on the right. It was a gift to herself for being an expectant mom. If Darryl wouldn't acknowledge her pregnancy, his American Express Platinum card would.

Paula let Darryl hang on her silence before she said, "Oh, Regina? She's at cheerleading camp." That she knew for a fact. She'd run into her mother last week at the grocery store.

Darryl's voice rose. "I can't believe you. You're just doing this to spite me."

Evidently he didn't care about his sleeping son at the moment. Obviously he didn't care that it had taken her two hours to settle the cranky child for a nap because of the sugar-loaded punch they'd given the children at his playgroup.

Any other day, Paula would've broken down in tears if his voice escalated the slightest decibel. But not today.

He'd seen the pregnancy test three days ago and still hadn't said anything else about it. If their child was nonexistent in his eyes, then the same went for his wife. She was worried about herself, Micah, and the baby. She wouldn't react. Stress and pregnancy were like oil and water.

"*Me* doing something to spite *you*. Now that's a change." Paula brushed past Darryl. "I need to change clothes."

She left Darryl standing in the living room. She gloated as she climbed the stairwell to the master bedroom. *Paula one point, Darryl zero.* Time had slipped away from her. She had

97

less than thirty minutes to change clothes and get Micah ready to leave the house.

Paula walked into the closet and chose a sundress from her rack of spring apparel. She tore the price tags from the label in the neck and paired it with a matching cardigan to tie around her shoulders.

"Where are you going?" Darryl appeared at the bedroom door.

She wasn't used to having him around questioning her moves. "Tuesday night Bible study," she answered curtly. Paula ran a comb through her tresses and was thankful for her standing hair appointment on Thursday mornings, even though it looked as if she'd just left the stylist's chair.

"Why are you running to church all of a sudden?"

"I haven't been in a while. I need it right now." Paula had decided to focus on growing her relationship with God and trusting Him to take care of the rest. What other option did she have?

Darryl disappeared, but not before he grunted a remark under his breath that Paula was glad she couldn't make out. She didn't want to carry his bad attitude with her to church.

In fifteen minutes, she was in Micah's room. Though he was heavy and wobbly as a sack of potatoes, she did her best to dress him while he half slept. In another ten minutes, she was out the door on the way to Berean Christian Cathedral. Her life seemed better already.

※

Paula peeked past the usher through the sanctuary door's window. The pews weren't nearly as full as they would've been during a Sunday morning worship service, but it was still more than Paula had remembered. After signing Micah in to children's church, she hurried back to the main sanctuary with the other adults. It was a welcome change after spending the majority of her waking hours without adult conversation.

She greeted everyone within speaking distance as she walked down the blue-carpeted aisle. Familiar faces welcomed her return and sometimes questioned her whereabouts. "I'm just happy to be back," she graciously answered with a smile, then accepted a hug. Her spirits lifted. Each embrace brought her closer to home. Paula slid into the sixth row and sat down beside a woman who smelled like an entire bottle of baby powder. As she settled into the pews, Paula sent a silent prayer to heaven that the Lord would touch her soul.

Before praise and worship began, First Lady Claudia Griffin approached the pulpit to read the church announcements.

"Ladies, I'm excited to bring you information about a program that I know everyone will want to be a part of. We have the opportunity to join other daughters of Christ. We, Berean, can be a part of a women's discipleship group with our sisters at four other churches in the community.

"P.O.W.E.R." she said. "Purpose-Oriented Women Equipped and Righteous." Sister Griffin went on to explain the purpose, mission, and expectations of the program, along with the date for the upcoming orientation.

That's two weeks away, Paula thought. She jotted all the information about the program that she could remember across the top of a blank page in her journal. A new page—a new beginning.

As First Lady Griffin instructed, Paula would be certain to pick up the information packet after church from the ushers. She made a note to herself to make early arrangements for child care for Micah for two Saturdays a month over the next nine months. Saturday mornings were always hard to secure sitters, but she'd make the hourly rate more than worth it.

Paula expected a dynamic word from Pastor Jesse Griffin and was prepared to hear from the Lord. What she didn't plan for was the conviction she felt from the sermon. While she'd pointed her finger and blamed Darryl for all her problems and misery, the Holy Spirit gently chastised her for her actions.

You've contributed your part.

Pastor Griffin walked to the edge of the pulpit steps and looked out into the crowd of parishioners in each pew. "How can you pray to God about somebody else's attitude when you haven't checked your own? If you want to change the heated environment of your home, then check your own temperature."

He held the microphone so close that it grazed his lips. He dropped his voice to a bass tone. "Are you always hot, blowing up at everything, or on constant simmer? Are you waiting for someone to say that one word that will make you—" He held his hands up and clinched them together like he was choking someone's neck.

The congregation roared in laughter. Paula knew the feeling.

"Turn with me to Proverbs 15:1."

Pastor Griffin waited until the rustle of the turning pages silenced.

"We all need to read this aloud together."

The congregation read in unison. Some people stood in reverence of the Word being read from their Bibles, but it seemed to Paula that every person in the place had their heads buried in their Bible.

She turned her pages quickly to find the verse.

"A soft answer turns away wrath, but a harsh word stirs up anger."

Pastor Griffin seemed to let the words seep in.

The words rammed against Paula's heart. If God changed Darryl, then it would be easier for her to act right. Her fleshly mind fought with the Word going out from the pulpit, but the part of her that knew God's Word seemed to awaken inside of her.

"Oh, but Pastor, I don't let people get to me like that," Pastor Griffin squeaked. "You let somebody hit the wrong button at the wrong time and then come back and tell me that."

Chuckles and "amens" rolled over the sanctuary.

The lady sitting beside Paula jabbed a chubby elbow into Paula's side. A puff of white powder escaped through the thin fabric under her armpit.

"People think just because you have money you don't have problems," Pastor Griffin said. "There are more problems in this world than financial hardship. Where's the prosperity in having money in your bank accounts, but a negative balance in your relationships?"

Amen to that, Paula thought.

"We've got to start in our own homes. How can you be pleasant to your coworkers, but come home and be nasty to your spouse? There used to be a time when all you wanted to do was sit close and snuggle on the couch."

The pastor scrunched up beside one of his associate ministers in the pulpit and batted his eyes. He couldn't keep a straight face and had to laugh at himself.

"Now you can hardly stand to be in the same room with them. In the same house, for that matter."

Paula nodded in agreement, but didn't make eye contact with her powdery neighbor.

Pastor Griffin walked to the podium and closed his Bible. "Lean forward. I've got a secret for you. You know how to get a person to change?" A beat passed. "*You* change."

Humph. Paula still warred in her mind. *He doesn't know my husband.*

Paula hit the remote to the three-car garage as she rounded the corner to her cul-de-sac.

Their four-sided brick home was one of only four in the circle. The gated community wasn't enough privacy for Paula. She'd wanted to be in the back of the development. The lake behind their house assured her that the builder wouldn't renege later on his plans and decide to build another house close enough to see through her kitchen window.

Paula was surprised to see both Darryl's Jaguar and Mercedes Benz in the garage. She parked her Range Rover between his two pride and joys. Darryl kept on the cusp of the latest Jag body styles and upgraded to suit his fancy. On rare occasions, a speck of dirt found a home on his chrome rims for more than a week.

She swung open the driver's side door and was still three feet from his Benz. She grabbed her belongings and juggled them in her arms while she lifted Micah out of his booster seat. Her sleeping son clutched his Noah's ark project and instinctively wrapped his legs around her waist. It was a struggle now to carry him. And to think, she would be starting this experience over in nine months.

The chirp from the door chime announced her arrival, but there was no sound or sight of Darryl. The click of her heels echoed in the foyer, and she wondered if her husband was home after all. He had a tendency to play the prodigal husband. She trudged up the steps with Micah. At the top of the stairs, a light seeped from under their closed bedroom door. As she walked closer, she heard a low murmur. Her heartbeat quickened. She put her ear to the door to distinguish the voices.

She exhaled.

Realizing it was the television, Paula continued on to Micah's room and took her time getting him ready for bed. *Why am I stalling?* She pulled his arm through the sleeve of his pajamas, then tucked him in bed.

When she opened the door to the master bedroom, she immediately noticed papers strewn on the bed.

"Hi," Paula said, leaving a crack in the door to listen for Micah. Upon a closer look, she realized Darryl was looking through a real-estate professional's newspaper. *He must be working on that business plan as usual. That's going to be our financial downfall.*

Darryl looked up from his laptop. "Hey."

Paula tossed her Bible bag on the bed and disappeared into the walk-in closet to find a pair of pajamas. Folded on the bottom closet shelf were three sets saved especially for her bloated weeks. She pulled out the most unattractive pair she could find, even though she wouldn't have her monthly visitor for a while.

"How was church?"

His question caught her by surprise. They rarely spoke unless they were arguing.

"Fine," Paula answered, her voice muffled by the sundress she was pulling over her head.

She tossed it into the dry cleaning hamper and then stepped into the frumpy cotton pants.

Darryl was a stranger. They had no common ground to tread upon for conversation.

Maybe he'd mention the pregnancy test tonight.

"What's this about?" Those were the first and last words he'd said about it.

Paula scoffed at the thought. *And it's my attitude that I'm supposed to change?*

She went into the bathroom. It was almost half the size of the bedroom, with his and her marble sinks with gold fixtures. She'd insisted on those fixtures and the Jacuzzi tub suitable for two people, but it had been a while since she'd shared it with Darryl.

Paula smoothed a cleansing mask on her face and brushed her professionally whitened teeth. She tried to ignore the words of Pastor Griffin's sermon playing in her head, but it was no use. The Word has already begun to change her temperament. She finished her bedtime regimen and walked back into the master bedroom.

"I can check with Jeanette's daughter to see if she can babysit next week." It took a lot out of her. Paula didn't want Darryl to think she'd cowered down. When he didn't respond, she swallowed her smart aleck remark and sat on the edge of the bed.

She opened her Bible bag and thumbed the pages to the text from Bible study. Paula reviewed it before turning to the first chapter of Psalms.

Tap. Tap. Tap. Pause. *Tap. Tap.* Darryl's fingers ran across his laptop's keyboard. She closed her eyes. The sound was annoying. Even the whish of the shuffling papers at his side made her hairs stand on her forearms. She knew the small things working her nerves were just that—working her nerves. He was only doing what he was doing before she came, not anything purposefully to annoy her.

Paula drowned out the tapping with other thoughts—the opportunity to participate in the women's discipleship group. God knew what she needed. It was an answered prayer, and it would be foolish for her not to jump at the chance.

Paula pulled the folded registration form from the pages of her Bible. The tapping had stopped. She looked back at Darryl, who had engulfed himself in a magazine. She found a blue ballpoint pen in the side pocket of her Bible bag and completed the P.O.W.E.R. form. Taking the first step increased her faith. It also gave her a reason to attend church the upcoming Sunday to turn it in. She'd find God again yet.

Paula pulled back the covers.

"Good night," she said.

"Night," Darryl said.

The tapping resumed.

Paula turned out the lamp on her side of the bed. She didn't remember falling asleep, and now she was being stirred out of her slumber by Darryl's cell phone. She didn't budge, only opened her eyes to see the clock on her nightstand: 12:36. The bed shifted as Darryl reached for the phone, then took it into the bathroom.

Paula strained to make out his words, but the fan he turned on in the bathroom hummed over his whispered conversation. When Darryl put on his clothes and left, she knew the answer.

9

Mastectomy. Belinda could still hear the doctor's voice. The words released fear into her body. She knew it was the best thing, the only option at this point. She combated her fear with prayer and immersed herself in the Bible, looking for peace.

After staying at her mother's for three days, Belinda decided to stay for two weeks instead, and had made a trip to the grocery store to stock up on extra formula for Hannah and the foods she preferred for herself. What she thought would be a thirty-minute trip ended up being an hour-long ordeal because of the rain showers moving through.

Belinda could barely stand leaving Thomas for two weeks at a time. Even after ten years, their love was as fresh as newlyweds. Unfortunately, Thomas's hectic work schedule would most likely prevent them from seeing each other. Still, Thomas promised he'd come visit if the opportunity presented itself.

With her last bag in hand, Belinda walked into her mother's home, and the familiar faces of the angel figurines inside the glass curio in the front family room stared back at her. As always, the house smelled like potpourri.

"This is the last bag, Aunt Wanda," Belinda said, looking to where she'd laid her napping daughter against the back of one of the sofas. She had buffered her body with pillows. From where she was standing, Belinda could see Wanda Jakes, affectionately known as everybody's aunt, busy chopping carrots on the cutting board.

"Hey, baby," Aunt Wanda answered. Her entire face, shaped almost in a perfect circle, smiled, and her gap-toothed grin took up over half her face. Her gray tresses were pulled back into a clip, making her face look even rounder.

"I'm juicing some carrots and celery for your mama so she can have something for later," Aunt Wanda said. "She's been reading every health magazine on the shelves in the grocery store. I think I buy a new one for her every day."

"Hmm." Belinda walked into the kitchenette and picked up a celery stick. "Where is she?" she asked, biting into the crisp stalk. Before Belinda left for the store, her mother had been watching a game show in the living room.

"Taking a nap. She said she didn't sleep well last night." Aunt Wanda stuffed the last carrot into the top of the juicer and shoved the top onto the opening until the juicer started automatically. Within seconds, the natural juice dripped into the container underneath the spout.

Belinda waited until the juicer stopped so she wouldn't have to talk over the groan of the machine. The doctor had forewarned them about the side effects of the chemotherapy and radiation. It was the main reason her mother was opting for a natural and organic diet with as little processed food as possible. Now she hoped the new lifestyle would aid in her speedy recovery after the surgery.

"How is she?"

"You know as much about the doctor's report as I do," Aunt Wanda said. She washed a carrot under the kitchen faucet. "Once they remove—"

Belinda put her hand on top of her Aunt Wanda's and stopped the annoying clack of the knife tapping against the wooden chopping board. "But how is *she*?"

Aunt Wanda laid the knife on a napkin and wiped her hands on a dish towel. "About as good as can be expected, I guess. She's adjusting. We're all adjusting. None of us have ever been through anything like this before. And what's amazing is that she's never complained out loud, but I know she's trying to carry the burden alone."

Aunt Wanda paused, as if listening for the creak of the back bedroom door. She picked up the knife and went back to her task. *Chop, chop.* "She's not the same when you're not around. And I know I don't expect her to be. Bernice has always taken care of everybody else in her life," Aunt Wanda said about her childhood best friend. "And now this." Aunt Wanda's voice cracked. *Chop, chop, chop.*

Belinda could tell Aunt Wanda was forcing the threat of sobs back down her throat.

Belinda wouldn't allow herself to break down today either. She had to be the strong one. She grabbed another celery stick, then walked down the hall to peek in on her dozing mother. Her mother's face carried the Morris family's strong traits of high cheekbones and petite figures that were only slightly interrupted by their plump hips. Belinda watched to make sure she saw the rise and fall of the single sheet that covered her mother's body, before going back to ball up in the corner of the sofa in the family room. Hannah slept at her feet.

Aunt Wanda juiced enough vegetables and fresh fruits to fill two small pitchers. When she was finally finished, she joined Belinda in the family room. She tenderly scooped up Hannah and laid her across her ample lap. Hannah's small body jumped from the unexpected movement, but then she found a comfortable spot on her new napping place. Aunt Wanda bounced her leg and patted Hannah's pampered rump until she settled back to sleep.

"Now my question is, how are *you* doing?" Aunt Wanda asked Belinda.

Belinda sat up and leaned over Hannah. "Six months ago was one of the happiest times in my life," Belinda said, referring to their final adoption of Hannah. She rubbed her pinkie across the smooth skin on the top of Hannah's hand. Her daughter instinctively grabbed for the finger. "I'm making it. I believe God has the final say, but that doesn't mean my emotions don't sometimes try to override my faith."

"While you're going back and forth up here, it might be a good idea to have some shoulders to lean on."

Belinda nodded. "I know you all are here for me."

"Always will be," Aunt Wanda said. "And I'm also on a committee at the church that helps put together a discipleship for women from St. Paul and two other churches. There's nothing like having God-fearing women around you. Pass me my bag beside the coffee table."

Belinda reached for the overstuffed canvas bag and hoisted it to Aunt Wanda's side.

Aunt Wanda moved slowly so as not to arouse Hannah.

"The deadline is in a couple of weeks, but I can turn in your registration packet if you're interested. You grew up in St. Paul all your life. Come home for a while."

Belinda read the top of the paper. P.O.W.E.R. She could use some of God's strength. Trying to operate in her own had proved to be useless. *"Not by might nor by power, but by My Spirit," says the Lord.* Zechariah 4:6 was one of her favorite Scriptures.

"If I was at home, I wouldn't give this a second thought." Belinda kicked her shoes off. She refolded the crocheted afghan slung over the sofa arm. "But I'm here to take care of Mama, and I don't have anywhere to leave Hannah."

"It's only for two hours twice a month on Saturdays, so I

can sit with your mama just like I do when you're not here,"
Aunt Wanda said. "And as far as Hannah, I've raised three
children of my own, lest you forget. She won't be any trouble
at all."

"You know she's spoiled. She's not used to many people."

"Well, it's no better time to get her used to her family."

In Belinda's mind, she grappled whether it would be selfish to tend to her own emotional needs when her mother was
suffering. Looking up into Aunt Wanda's eyes, she was assured
that it was okay.

They heard the creak of the bedroom door down the hall
and knew that Bernice was making her way toward them. The
soft shuffle of her bedroom shoes scooting across the carpet
was a sure sign. Belinda wanted to rush to her side, but her
mother was stubborn about being fussed over.

"Hey, baby," she whispered to Belinda when she was in
sight. The words stumbled from her mouth.

Belinda jumped up to meet her mother anyway. "Hey,
Mama. I was wondering when you were going to wake up."

Belinda couldn't help but notice how her mother's jaun-
diced face robbed the cheerfulness and the light from her eyes.
Genetics had dealt a good hand to her mother, and she'd
always looked younger than her age. The rounds of radiation
and chemotherapy seemed to have added more than the sixty-
six years of age to her body. Even her silver hair had lost its
luster and begun to thin around her temples and in the middle
of her crown.

Belinda took her mother's hand and helped her into the
brown recliner, which over the years had molded to the shape
of Bernice's body. Belinda tried to adjust a pillow behind her
back to make her comfortable, but just then, Hannah aroused
from her sleep and let out a low whine. She began to cry for
Belinda's attention.

"Bring her to me," Bernice summoned.

Immediately when propped on her grandmother's lap, Hannah's crocodile tears dried up. She pulled at the bracelet on her grandmother's wrist and tried to shove the accessory into her mouth.

"She tries to put everything in her mouth now," Belinda said. She squatted down at the foot of the recliner and pulled down slightly on Hannah's jaw. "I think she's teething."

"Babies grow up so fast," her mother said. "Look at my baby," she said, pinching Belinda's cheek. "I used to take care of her; now she has to take care of me."

Those words almost caused Belinda to tear up.

"Not for long," she assured her mother. "I know you. You'll be on your feet before you know it. You've got a lot of fight."

Bernice pulled Hannah closer to her stomach and straightened her twisted pink footie. "It'll take more than my fight. I've got to have God's strength and power."

Belinda eyed the P.O.W.E.R. form on the coffee table. "I do too, Ma. I do too."

10

The rain pounded the windshield as Zora drove to the courthouse in Anne Arundel on Wednesday morning. The wipers tried to brush away the downpour in the same way that she was trying to push the thoughts out of her head. Both the rain and her thoughts kept coming.

Most often her thoughts floated to what she may have missed. She'd never doubted that her parents afforded her the best opportunities or showered her with love. It was the unknown that constantly played with her mind. As a teenager, she'd wished for an older sibling—especially a brother. It was her dream to have a star athlete sibling who overshadowed his younger sister with love and protection.

The rain beat harder to the point that Zora could barely see in front of her. She maneuvered off the road into a gas station parking lot and pulled under a covering. The pelting on her car temporarily stopped.

Her thoughts didn't.

She tried each day to go about life as if her world hadn't

shifted, but the world still revolved. People walked past her every day, never knowing her pain. She wished the world would stop and listen to her cry.

Hopefully, today they would.

Keep your mind on Me, not your circumstances.

Her meditation Scripture from yesterday morning came back to mind. *Now this is the confidence that we have in Him, that if we ask anything according to His will, He hears us.*

⁂

Zora took the elevator down to the ground floor of the courthouse and walked through the muggy, empty hallway. It smelled like old, wet paper. She wouldn't be surprised if her adoption file was covered with mold.

"Good morning," Zora said to the attendant sitting behind the front counter. Her desk plate read *Angel Harrisburg.* "I'm coming to get information about an adoption that occurred in 1976."

"Okay. What information do you have?"

"Not much. I have my information, of course, and the information of my adoptive parents."

Angel reknotted the silk scarf hanging from her neck. All of her accessories were a perfect match to her bright outfit and facial expressions. It was a nice change for such a dreary day. She smiled until she realized Zora had finished. "That's all?"

"That's absolutely it," Zora said.

"Do you know if the adoption was handled by a public or private industry?"

"No."

"Your search may be like looking for a needle in a haystack," Angel said.

Zora laid her dripping umbrella by her feet. Her clothes and hair were already dampened, but she refused to let her spirit be. *It's already rained enough on me this morning, and now you have to put a damper on my day. Some angel you turned out to be.*

"But it's always possible that someone will find the needle," Zora said.

Angel shook her head. "Can't argue with that," she said, her fingers running across her keyboard. "If your adoption was facilitated at a local department of social services or at a licensed child placement agency, I'm 99 percent sure the records have been stored in the state archives by now."

Zora propped her elbows on the counter and leaned forward to see if she could get a peek of Angel's computer screen. "What if it was private?"

"If the attorney who performed it retired or left the practice, then the records might be destroyed. Or if a private agency handled it and they closed, then again, the records may be either at the state archives or destroyed."

"They don't mind destroying vital information, do they?"

"Client confidentiality," Angel said. "Space limitations." She hit a return key on her keyboard and a sheet of paper rolled out of the printer on her desk."

"I guess I jumped ahead of myself by not doing my research."

"Don't worry about it. That's what I'm here for."

Angel laid the piece of paper on the counter and stood so she could review it with Zora.

"Here's information that will make your life a lot easier, because the system can be so confusing."

"I see." *More confusion is the last thing I need in my life.*

"The state provides an Adoption Search, Contact, and Reunion Service that you can use to authorize the Department of Human Resources to initiate a search for your birth parents. In short, once you complete the consent and the other required documents and pay the required fees, a confidential intermediary will work on your behalf."

"That's all I need to know," Zora said, taking the sheet outlining the information and process. She folded it in half and stuck it in her purse. "You just saved me time from going on a wild goose chase."

"Well, if I think like you do, I'd say at least one goose could be caught."

"Can't argue with that," Zora said, mimicking Angel's earlier comment.

"I would also suggest adding your name to an adoption registry. You never know."

"I'll definitely do that," Zora said.

And she did. As soon as she walked back in the door at home. The rain had finally tapered off, but the thick humidity still hung in the air. Zora pinned her hair back with a clip. It was a lost frizzy cause.

Adoption registry, she typed once she settled at her desk.

The chances of discovering a long-lost family member this way were probably slim, but anything was possible. God could reunite her family in a way she least expected. Even via the Internet. These days the world was a keystroke away.

Zora had seen the daytime talk shows about the miracles of how families were reunited—accidental wrong numbers, repairman casually talking with homeowners only to unearth a long lost brother. Why not?

She scrolled down the page, then clicked the first link on the list, and the computer screen opened to a vast array of resources on the web site's colorful home page. There were listings of agencies and true stories of reunion. This one Web site alone was enough to keep her occupied for a week, if not longer. She saw links for photo galleries of searching adoptees, birth families seeking adopted children, and children seeking adoption.

Zora immediately delved in.

The true stories, testimonials, and online journals were what Zora found to be the most touching. There were adoptees who shared their lives with both their biological and adoptive parents. There were parents who shared stories about why they adopted. Others told accounts of adoptees who, after years, had never found anyone in their biological family.

Those were the ones that tugged at Zora's heart. *I can do this.*

Zora pulled a tissue from the box on her desk and pressed it around her eyes. The area behind her eyes throbbed, and the pressure moved to her temples. Her nose was so congested that she couldn't sniff or blow. She wasn't sure how long her crying lasted before the phone rang. She let it ring three more times.

"Hello?"

"Hey, baby."

It was Preston. "Hey."

"How did it go today?"

"Fine." Her answers were brief. She didn't trust her voice not to quiver.

"Okay." Preston paused for a moment as if waiting for Zora to jump in with her usual rambling of details. When she didn't, he asked, "Did you find out anything?"

"Can we talk about it later tonight?" The first crack trailed from the end of her last word.

"Zora, what is it? What happened?"

Zora heard the concern in Preston's voice, and his tone almost demanded an answer.

"I'm sorry." Her voice squeezed through her nasal passage. "I know you're tired of me crying all the time."

"Listen to me, Zora. I'm here for you. For better or for worse doesn't begin for me at the altar."

Zora pushed away from the desk and turned her back to the

computer screen. His words were a balm to her aching soul. "I didn't find out anything at the courthouse other than the fact that I ran down there too soon without doing any research." She cleared her throat. "I was on this adoption Web site reading some of the personal stories, and I was touched. That's all."

"Do you need me to leave work now? I was going to leave in about thirty minutes, but it's no problem."

"No, don't do that. I'm fine. Honestly, I don't feel like talking right now. Nothing personal. I'll see you in a little while, okay, baby?"

"Are you sure?"

"I'm sure."

"Call me if you need me."

"I will. I promise."

Zora put the cordless phone on the cradle and pulled out a fresh tissue. She patted her face and let out a deep sigh. Closing her eyes, she concentrated on the rise and fall of her chest. She filled her lungs to capacity and exhaled until the tightness pressing down on her chest lifted.

If she was going to make it through this search, then her faith needed to be strengthened.

"Blessed is the woman who believes," Zora said aloud, searching her memory for the Scripture she'd come across many times before. She went to her bedroom to get her Bible. By the time she returned to her home office, she'd located Luke 1:45.

Blessed is she who believed, for there will be a fulfillment of those things which were told her from Lord.

Zora typed the Scripture, then cut and pasted it down the page. She cut out the individual verses and attached them to the areas in her home where she'd always see them—the bathroom mirror, bedroom closet door, refrigerator, the front clear sleeve of her wedding organizer, and one at eye level on the front door.

"Believe," she said.

I can do this. Back on the initial Web site, Zora followed the directions for creating a log-in name and password so she could access the members-only pages. Curiosity led her to the chat room, but finding no one there, Zora went back to combing through the plentiful resources until the evening crept upon her.

Preston was coming over before he went to Bible study. Their imminent wedding put a halt to their frequent dinner outings, and they had agreed to alternate turns cooking dinner when they could.

Zora went into the kitchen and combined the leftover chicken and the rest of the ingredients for chicken and broccoli casserole. She had to do something to spruce up the two-day-old poultry. By the time Preston arrived, the table would be set with the main entrée and a garden salad. She was setting the table when she heard a chime similar to the instant message alert for her e-mail. That was funny. She wasn't even logged on, she thought.

The screen saver disappeared when she wiggled the mouse. There was a message on the chat-room screen.

Solo: Hello, Baby Z.

This person was talking to her. That was the log-in name she'd given herself. Zora was hesitant at first to answer, but remembering that she was hidden behind anonymity, her fingers flew across the keys. *Hello.*

The response popped up on the screen in seconds.

Solo: Are you new to the family?

It must be a tight group to call themselves family, Zora thought, as she typed *"yes."*

Solo: Welcome. What's your story?

These people don't waste time, she thought. She thought a second, then typed. *Looking for anybody. Found out about adoption three months ago.* It was amazing how she'd summed up such a complicated situation in ten words.

Solo: Wow. I've known all my life. Closed adoption, so no information. I'm one of three adopted sons. I chime in for support. But maybe someone will find me. Like on the talk shows.

Zora laughed at the same thought she'd had. She didn't know what else to say to this person. She wasn't ready to give up any other information. At least she'd found out Solo was a guy. Maybe she should have chosen a gender neutral log-in name. Baby Z was far from masculine.

Solo: You'll like this family. I live in Randallstown, MD. You?

Too close for comfort, Zora thought. What were the odds of that? She waited for a minute, then decided that his chances of knowing someone on the West Coast may be slim. *California.*

Solo: Really? What part? I'm originally from San Francisco.

The world was smaller than Zora thought. She knew that Sun Valley was at least five hours away, because she'd visited the area once with a college roommate and was disappointed because she thought she'd get to experience the cable cars San Francisco was known for. *Sun Valley,* she typed.

Solo: Not my side of Cali.

Zora was quick to change the subject.

Baby Z: Why the name Solo?

Solo: Because I feel like I'm in the world alone sometimes.

Baby Z: Know what you mean.

Other screen names started to pop into the chat room. She declined when Solo invited her into a private room. It was time for Preston to arrive any minute.

The doorbell confirmed her thoughts.

Preston greeted her with a kiss before Zora had time to close the door behind her. "What did I do to deserve that?"

"For being you," he said.

120

"And that's for me being me too?" She pointed at the present he was holding.

Preston opened the silver gift bag and held it up by the satin ribbon handles. Zora pulled out the object, wrapped in pink tissue paper, and felt the cool hardness through the paper. She unwrapped the paper gently, figuring the gift was fragile.

Zora looked up at Preston for an explanation of the jar she held in her hands. It was empty except for a pink piece of paper rolled up on the inside. She turned the jar around until she could see the words hand-painted on the outside: Psalm 56:8.

Preston nodded his head, signaling for Zora to open the top.

She twisted it off, took out the paper, and gave Preston the jar to hold. She unrolled the paper and read the message he'd written.

*You number my wanderings; put my tears into
Your bottle; are they not in Your book? (Psalms 56:8)*

*He's counted your tears, and I'm always
here to wipe them away.*

Forever and always, Preston

Zora took the jar from Preston's grip, set it on the kitchen counter, then slid into his arms. She accepted the comfort from the strength in his fingers as they kneaded her back. She squeezed her arms around his waist, pressing herself into his chest. She felt the side of his jaw moving against her cheek and heard his whisper. Even though she couldn't make out his words, she knew her fiancé was covering her in prayer.

"Amen," he said a couple of minutes later.

"Amen," Zora said, knowing that his prayer for her was

according to God's will. Having a man who had a true relationship with God was a benefit she would've waited for all of her life if she'd had to.

Zora leaned into Preston, desiring the warmth of his lips, and truthfully much more. Each day the flame within her blazed stronger for him. It was only a matter of time before her passion could be quenched.

"Mmmm . . . ," Preston said, squeezing her tightly. He chuckled and Zora looked up, resting her chin on his chest. A smirk spread across his face. "I know what you're thinking." He cupped her face between his hands and ran a thumb across the outline of her lips. "It's only a matter of time."

"Whew." She laughed. "I'm glad one of us is strong today. I better get away from you." She wiggled out of his arms and went back to the open pantry. She pulled two place settings from her stash, and Preston followed behind her with the utensils from the drawer.

"We've both had our days. Thank God we haven't been weak at the same time."

Zora stacked their plates with food, and Preston carried them to the table.

"One last finishing touch," Zora said, and went down the hallway into her bedroom.

When Bailee heard of Zora's new affinity for the lavender herb yesterday, she made a small arrangement combining it with three purple-hued flowers that Zora had chosen during her florist visit.

Zora returned to the dining area and set the arrangement in the middle of the table. She pointed to the flowers and explained which ones would be incorporated into the wedding bouquets, church decorations, and reception centerpieces. She'd sent him the pictures, but they didn't do justice.

Just as she thought, Preston was pleased with the final choices, but was more interested in eating dinner.

They bowed heads, and Preston blessed the food.

"I've found so much on the Internet today, baby," she said, poking her fork through her salad. "I haven't even scraped the surface of one site, and there's tons more like it."

"Don't get overwhelmed. Take it one day at a time."

"I will." Zora noticed they didn't have anything to drink. She went to the refrigerator to get the raspberry tea she'd made earlier that day. "One neat thing is that I joined a chat room," she said, cracking the ice tray. She expected to meet an excited look on Preston's face when she turned around.

"A chat room?" Preston's brows furrowed. He held his fork suspended midway to his mouth.

"It's for people who are going through some of the same experiences. Like a network."

Preston's fork clinked against the plate when he put it down. "I don't know if I agree with this whole chat room thing. People are too crazy these days."

"You don't even have to use your real names. I could be anybody as far as that's concerned."

"Exactly my point. You never know who you're dealing with. I'd feel better if you didn't do the chat room thing." He went back to eating, signifying the conversation was over.

Zora set the glasses on the table. She didn't say a word. She couldn't promise him that she wouldn't go back into the chat room. She wouldn't lie. She just wouldn't tell him.

❧

Zora wasn't in the mood to do anything but surf the net; not even talk to whoever was calling. Preston was off to Bible study, and she planned to go back on to the adoption registry sites.

"Tell me you love me," Monét said when Zora answered the phone.

"Love ya. Now why am I making this confession?"

"Did you get my message I left on your cell phone yesterday *and* today?"

"Nope. I didn't check them yesterday, and I was out most of the morning. Remember, before we left Bailee's I told you I was going to the courthouses today." Zora didn't feel like talking about the courthouse ordeal again and hoped to God Monét didn't ask. She probably shouldn't have reminded her.

"Sorry," Zora said. "Was it important?"

"Not unless you consider an extra ticket for Jeremiah to the auction important."

"Stop lying."

"I'm serious. I didn't even have to ask Dr. Manns. He called and offered."

At least I know my prayers are getting through. Evidently some just take longer than others, Zora thought. "Thank you for even considering asking."

"You're welcome," Monét said. "And you can thank me again by bringing me that linen blazer that goes with my pant suit to Bible study."

"I'll bring it to your job tomorrow. I'm not coming to church tonight."

"Is everything all right? What happened at the courthouse?"

"Nothing worth mentioning right now. I'm tired—that's all. A woman's entitled to a break every now and then."

"I feel you," Monét said.

Zora heard Monét's car horn blast in the background.

"People act like they can't drive when it's raining," Monét fussed.

"It's raining? Girl, get off the phone and drive. I'll see you tomorrow."

Zora didn't have time to entertain her friend and distract her from driving. Monét needed to concentrate, and so did she. She went back on to the Department of Human Resources Web site to review all the information she'd overlooked in her haste. After that, she'd log back on to the chat room. Solo was sure to have some advice.

11

Zora sat in Monét's desk chair and rolled closer to the window. Her promise to drop off Monét's linen blazer on Thursday had gotten her drafted to stuff gift bags for the auction attendees.

It was a drive and a visit she didn't mind making. She enjoyed seeing the latest exhibits, mostly to admire the work of the center's local artist of the month. She didn't think most people realized the talent and culture birthed in Baltimore. Zora was ignorant herself until Monét opened her eyes.

After strolling through the halls, she'd finally go upstairs to Monét's office and steal the comfort of her friend's office chair, just like she'd done today. Being able to stare into the trees outside of the office window helped her think.

"I don't have time to participate in that P.O.W.E.R. thing," Zora said. She'd considered it, but decided her time wouldn't allow. Still, no matter where she stuffed the registration form, she seemed to keep running across it.

Monét was walking down the assembly line of gold gift

bags that were spread across her office floor. The two hundred bags were already wide open and stuffed with royal blue tissue paper. She walked over to them, dropping one of the sponsor's key chains in each.

"We should do it," Monét said. "What other chance will we get to fellowship with women from four other churches?"

"I have too much on my plate already." Zora picked up a bin of ballpoint pens. She started at the beginning of the line and followed Monét. "I can't commit."

"It only meets twice a month, once when all the churches come together and then one time in the smaller groups they're going to divide us into. At least that's the way I understood it."

"I'm too busy."

"This is an opportunity for us to walk with women in different stages of life and in their walk with Christ." Monét wasn't one to give up easily.

"I'll pass this time. Maybe I'll do it next year. Right now I don't believe God is leading me to do it." *Maybe.*

"How do you know what God is leading you to do? You haven't even asked Him. Tell the truth. You're going off of your predetermined schedule."

"Uh-huh," Zora muttered. Point-blank, she was busy. Evidently Monét failed to remember she was not only planning a wedding, but she was searching for her biological family. This wasn't about scheduled social events.

Knock. Knock.

"I see this is your week for special deliveries." Jasmine walked in holding a hot pink box balanced out on the palm of her hand, steady like a skilled waitress. She stepped over the bags on the floor and set the box on Monét's desk. "Now I *know* you're holding some secrets. Another client gift?"

"Thank you," Monét said, setting down her empty bin and picking up one with lapel pins. "I'll get to it." She started her trek from the first gift bag again, ignoring Jasmine.

"I'd be glad to help you ladies," Jasmine offered. She picked up a handful of wrapped mints and let them fall between her fingers and back into the plastic tub.

"Nice, try, and no thank you." Monét perched the bin against her shapely hip and waited for Jasmine to leave.

"I guess I'll go back to my desk and finish licking and sealing envelopes."

"Yum." Monét smacked her lips together. "Sounds good."

Zora's curiosity ate at her patience as soon as Jasmine walked out, but Monét didn't seem to notice. "Are you going to open it or pretend like it's not there?"

"The latter." She picked up a lapel pin that had missed its toss inside a gift bag.

"Well, pretend like you don't see me when I open it." Zora didn't move. Neither did Monét.

"Go ahead," Monét said. "I know it's from Bryce. He's on bended knee for saying he was coming to church Sunday and not showing up."

"Not surprising," Zora said, ignoring the fact that she thought Bryce had been officially cut off since Valentine's Day. "Let's see what beg mode has gotten you this time."

Zora headed for the desk. When she turned around, Monét was two steps behind her. Monét couldn't play nonchalant for long. Zora held the box while Monét pulled the white satin ribbon, then lifted off the box top.

Monét opened the white note card that lay on a bed of pink tissue paper. "We can make beautiful music together. My heart sings for you," she read.

"Please." Zora was not, and never had been, impressed by anything Bryce did. She knew that deep inside Monét wanted Bryce to measure up. But with his record of inconsistency, Zora knew he wasn't the one—the two, three, or four, for that matter.

Monét pushed away the crumples of tissue paper until she saw the CD of Yolanda Adams's latest release. "I was going to pick this up after work today." She pulled open the tab and tore the plastic from the case. She slid the CD into the disk drive of her computer and snapped her fingers at the first bar of music. "I like this already."

Music was the way to Monét's heart. Bryce knew how to play his game. "He'll probably run after you until your wedding day," Zora said. *Because he sure won't be the one you marry.*

"It's just a shame he won't be the one up there standing beside you." Zora chuckled when her thoughts made it through her lips. She picked up one of the chocolate heart-shaped candies that was in the box and peeled off the silver foil paper. She plopped back down into Monét's chair and crossed her legs, thumping her slip-on sandal on the bottom of her heel.

Silence came between the friends for the first time since Zora had arrived. It was as if each were engulfed in her own thoughts. Yolanda's voice serenaded them with her love ballad to God.

"Can I be honest with you?" Zora asked Monét.

"I've never known a time when you weren't."

"I'm scared," Zora said. She noticed the confused look on Monét's face. "Not about the Bryce thing, though that's frightening too." Zora had to take one last shot. "I've prayed about searching for my biological parents. I thought I heard from God, and I told myself I could handle it, whatever did or didn't come out of it. But I'm still scared." She gathered her hair at the nape of her neck. "What if I do find my biological family? What then? It may not be the best thing. It might make my life more confusing than it already is."

"God knows what's best," Monét said. "If it's meant for you to find them, then you will. If He wants to protect you from even more heartache, He'll do that too." She sat down on the edge of her desk. "Just the other day you were so sure. I think you should stand on that and not let all of these scenarios play back and forth in your mind. Sometimes we can think *too* much."

"Tell me about it."

"When I think about you, I think about the Scripture in the book of Luke when Mary went to visit Elizabeth and Elizabeth's baby jumped at the sound of Mary's voice. Mary told her that because she believed, God was going to fulfill His promises to her."

"God just used you to confirm something He'd told me," Zora said. "That's amazing. That's just like something God would do."

"He loves you that much, Zora."

"This calls for a celebration," Zora said, and picked up two more chocolate candies. "Might as well add a few more miles to my workout," she said, and tossed the empty silver foil among the other balled-up remnants. "It'll give me something to blame Bryce for."

Zora swiped her hand across the desk and pushed the trash into a wastebasket. "I know the commissioner is coming to the auction. Is he bringing his shadow with him?"

"Fortunately not," Monét said. "He's bringing his administrative assistant instead."

"Good." Zora licked a smudge of chocolate off the side of her finger. "And I'm not going to say anything about Jeremiah."

"Your break is over," Monét said, pulling off her Anne Klein pumps. She wiggled her stocking feet and, standing up, thumped Zora on the shoulder. "These bags aren't going to stuff themselves, and the auction is tomorrow."

Zora moaned. "Am I going to get paid for this?"

Her best friend showed no mercy.

"I'll deduct it from your wedding coordinator expenses. In the meantime, get moving."

"I'm coming," Zora said. She pushed herself from the chair and dodged a piece of candy that Monét threw. "Whatever happens at this auction better be worth my free seat."

12

Zora reared back in Monét's office chair and flipped through the pages of the *Black Enterprise* that she'd confiscated from the in-box on her desk. She knew enough not to bother Monét with idle chatter once she'd slipped into her zone. Monét circled the room, reciting the speech she'd prepared. Not wanting to be handicapped by a stack of note cards, Monét had memorized her remarks for tonight's event.

Zora tossed the magazine on the desk when she realized she had the same issue at home. None of the other magazines in Monét's in-box caught her interest. A yellow Post-it note stuck to Monét's P.O.W.E.R. registration form was lodged in the stack. *Finish. Add meeting dates to Palm Pilot.*

P.O.W.E.R. dropped in her spirit whenever she had her personal devotion time in the morning and at night. Like every time, she picked it up and threw it out with an excuse about her schedule. There was still tons to do before the wedding.

Somewhere her wedding to-do list was tabbed into Monét's

Palm Pilot too. *I'll knock some things out on Monday,* she thought.

When Monét glanced at her watch, Zora looked at the time on the small crystal desk clock. It was twenty minutes until six o'clock. Guests would be arriving soon for the six-thirty event.

Admiration swelled in Zora as she watched her friend. She wouldn't be surprised if her face graced the cover of *Black Enterprise* one day.

Monét stared in the full-length mirror on the back of her office door. She adjusted the twisted bodice of her chiffon dress. Her toes barely peeked out of the hem of her floor-length dress. Zora was glad they'd chosen the shimmery peach polish for Monét's pedicure. It matched perfectly with her dress. After one last examination of her pinned-up coif, she turned toward Zora.

"What are you staring at?" Monét walked over to the desk and picked up her portfolio.

"Just watching you do your thing."

"Instead of watching me, how about grabbing the rest of those programs?" She pinched Zora's arm as she walked by. "Make yourself useful."

Zora pulled the makeup compact from her handbag. "You sure have been bossy lately. I'm here for moral support, not manual labor. I've already put in my time yesterday," she said, dabbing the cosmetic puff under her eyes.

"You copped a seat at the bigwigs table tonight," Monét reminded her. "It's the least you can do."

"Well, since you put it like that." Zora snapped the compact closed. The evidence of her late nights and eyes strain had started to surface on her complexion. She'd stayed up late last night again registering on adoption sites and talking to Solo in the chat room until midnight. Preston had kept himself preoccupied with Jeremiah after his friend's flight, but she was still on the computer when he called at close to one in the morning. They never went to bed without saying good night.

"Didn't get much rest, I see?"

Zora crossed her arms. The fact that they were as close as sisters authorized them to speak their minds. Zora had done her fair share lately, and Monét was taking her turn. All in love.

Monét rescinded. "Okay, granted, I could have said it with a little more tact. But you know your face can't hide anything."

"Is it that obvious?"

"Probably just to me," Monét said, seemingly trying to soften the blow. "Don't worry about it."

"It's a little too late for that now."

"It's not like you're after prospects. You've hooked yours."

"The way you're stepping out tonight, you might reel in a few of your own. Or at least one great catch I know of."

"So much for dropping subtle hints about Jeremiah."

"I didn't say a word about Jeremiah." Zora pulled at the spiral curls she'd set in her hair for the night. It was a different look, but it went well with her dress. She hoped Preston liked it. He could be particular when it came to new hairstyles.

"Not directly just then," Monét said. "But you've talked about him so much since—"

Zora stood up and picked up the programs. "We better get downstairs. I need to wait for Dr. Manns."

Monét grabbed her office keys. "Guilty as charged."

Zora walked out behind Monét and waited for her to lock her office door. Their heels clicked on the spotless tile floor as they made their way down the hall to the elevator.

Monét hummed to the sync of their footsteps, and her melody birthed into a song. Zora snapped her fingers to the tune, and they maintained their orchestrated sound until the elevator bell dinged and carried them downstairs.

"The concert is over," Zora said as the doors opened to the plaza level hall.

As always, the expansive area was sectioned off for visitors to take self-guided tours of the visiting exhibits. Tonight, however, white lights streamed from the ceilings, then draped down the walls.

Zora greeted the other center employees and volunteers. She'd become closely acquainted with the staff during her frequent visits. Monét thanked the volunteer committee as she passed the registration table, nodding her head and commenting that everything was in order.

Jasmine, dressed in a simple but sophisticated black dress, whistled when she noticed the ladies. Zora knew Monét had prepared her mental checklist, but Jasmine updated her on all that had been done before she could rattle it off.

"You're trying to take my job, aren't you?" Monét said, showing her appreciation of Jasmine's capabilities.

Jasmine's faced glowed while she soaked in Monét's compliments. Before long Jasmine's excitement about her boyfriend's visit the upcoming week usurped the conversation about the auction. Anything about Maurice usually did, Zora had noticed during her two visits to the center since school let out.

"Puppy love," Monét said when they finally escaped. "She's never been hurt before."

Not a word. She wasn't going to say a word about Monét's tendency to hold on to her past issues.

Zora and Monét went to the front entrance of the building.

"Looks like the man of the hour is here," Monét announced after five minutes. "That's Dr. Manns," she told Zora.

"He's handsome," Zora said. The tuxedo was cut for his body, and he donned a soft gold tie and vest.

"And he knows it," Monét muttered.

136

Dr. Manns trudged up the sidewalk with a look of irritation etched on his face. A woman—who Zora assumed was his wife—lagged two steps behind him with an equally annoyed look. Monét couldn't make out the words from his pinched mouth, but his lips seem to spit fire. As they neared the door, he paused briefly and held out his arm.

The woman hooked a hand in the crook of his arm, and they left their argumentative countenances outside. Dr. Manns opened the door, and the couple entered with distinction, their heads held high like a cross word hadn't passed through their lips.

The dashing physician beamed when he saw Monét. His facial hair and the tapering of his hairline were cut with flawless precision. A person could surf on his hair's natural waves.

"Nice to see you, Monét," he said. He planted a kiss on her cheek.

Zora noticed the quick cut of the woman's eyes at him. *If looks could kill,* Zora thought, *he'd be a dead man.* The woman, shapely and tall with impeccable makeup, looked familiar. Zora couldn't place her face.

"I'd like you to meet my wife, Paula."

"Nice to meet you, Mrs. Manns," Monét said.

"Likewise. And please, call me Paula." She swooped her bang behind her ear, and the massive rock on her finger gleamed. Her ears were home to a set of dazzling diamonds.

Zora was sure they were real. She and Preston could pay for her wedding and honeymoon with her accessories alone.

"This is my best friend and drafted assistant, Zora," Monét added.

Zora shook the couple's hands and thanked Dr. Manns for the tickets. She noticed how Paula was quick to avert her attention to other parts of the gallery. While Dr. Manns rambled about his excitement for the night, his wife wandered over to an exhibit of abstract paintings. She held up the hem of her strapless bronze floor-length gown as she moved to each piece of artwork.

Where do I know her from? Zora thought. She looked too young to be the mother of one of the students at her high school. Then again, these days you could never assume.

Laughter from Dr. Manns and Monét brought Zora back to their conversation.

"Jasmine wants to go over the program one last time with you," Monét told Dr. Manns. "If you'll give me a few minutes, I'll be happy to answer any questions you have."

"That's fine. I'll see you shortly." Dr. Manns looked at his reflection in a nearby glass door and adjusted his tie. "Are you ready, dear?" he called to his wife.

Paula looked up with a forced smile and walked over to her husband.

Finally out of earshot, Zora asked, "Have we met Paula somewhere before?"

"First time I've met her." Monét started rehearsing her remarks. She'd done it so much that Zora could recite the introduction.

"Monét, there is such a thing as over-rehearsing. You know the speech," Zora said. "Besides, you're working my nerves."

"Practicing helps me relax," Monét explained. "Be an attentive audience." She went back to her remarks.

Zora went back to her thoughts about Paula Manns. It hadn't been that long ago since she'd seen Paula. That much she knew.

A few minutes later, other guests began to arrive. Their attire ranged from elaborate traditional garb and head wraps, to black-tux corporate executives and artists just as expressive with their clothes as they were with their work. They strolled around, networking and commenting on the ornate decorations that had been chosen for the event. Everything was a soft orange and ivory, highlighted with white lights.

It wasn't long before Preston and Jeremiah were among the attendees traipsing up the sidewalk with twenty minutes before the auction's start. Monét was busy greeting guests and wasn't aware of their arrival.

Zora hawked her fiancé. She wouldn't deny she was biased, but Preston was the finest man who had entered the doors all evening. He wasn't suited in a tux, but his black suit measured up to the best. Clean shaven and handsome, it wasn't hard to see why he'd had to run from the women at his father's church. Good thing he'd run in her direction.

"Hi, handsome," Zora said, accepting Preston's kiss on her cheek when he walked in the door.

"I have to keep my eye on you tonight," Preston said. He held Zora's hand in the air and twirled her around.

Zora put her hand on her hip and let Preston admire her dress, a jazzy red number with a forties flair. It was covered in sequins, and the hem flared open when she switched her hips. "Hey, Jeremiah," she said in the middle of her spin.

"I haven't seen you since last year," Jeremiah said. "Can I get a little love?"

"I think I can spare a dose," Zora said, and gave Jeremiah a squeeze.

Zora was anxious to make introductions. She spotted Monét, who was still talking with one of the attendees. The woman was dressed in a kente cloth smock and wore long wooden earrings shaped like giraffes. She didn't look like she planned on letting Monét get away. Once Monét got a peek of Jeremiah, Zora was sure she'd divert the talker somehow.

Jeremiah ran a close second to Preston in the looks department. His skin was the color of a walnut, and baby smooth. He stood a few inches over Preston—at least six feet, three—but they shared the same athletic build. During the times he visited, he and Preston hit the racquetball court for their mandatory challenge. Either that or they showcased their strength and eye coordination at the batting cage. "Friendly competition never hurt anybody," Preston would say.

Zora finally caught Monét's attention and motioned her over. She had a feeling when it came to this matchmaking assignment. She'd let God do His thing, but had volunteered her services as a vessel to help get the job done.

"Hi, Preston," Monét said as she joined the three. "And you must be the famous Jeremiah." She offered a hand, but Jeremiah bent over to give her an innocent embrace.

"And you must be the even more famous Monét." He pulled away, but kept a hand on her shoulder. "It's a pleasure to finally meet you. I've heard good things."

That was Preston's doing, Zora thought. She hadn't had a chance to drop any words on Jeremiah. Relationships went far beyond looks, of course, but they even made a cute couple. And until now, she hadn't considered their similar interest in music. With Jeremiah's gifting on the keys and Monét's angelic voice, they could make more than beautiful music together. Bryce was a sour note in comparison.

Jasmine appeared from around the corner and summoned Monét's help.

"Come on," Monét said. "I'll show you guys your seats."

Zora matched her gait with Monét's swift steps. "Cute, isn't he?" she whispered.

"Uh-huh," Monét hummed. "He's a looker."

"A saved, intelligent, and driven looker."

"Uh-huh," Monét hummed again. "A looker about a twenty-four-hour drive away."

"Just over three hours by plane and distance doesn't matter when your souls are connected."

"Love has made you so sappy," Monét said. She led them around the perimeter of the room to their assigned head table in the front. Like the others, it was adorned with off-white tablecloths, chair covers, and Bailee's exquisite centerpieces. For the night, Monét had chosen gold vases overflowing with orange Asiatic lilies and white lilies.

Zora looked at her watch. Attendees were still huddling in small groups outside the foyer and inside the ballroom.

"It's almost time to start," she said, scoping the room. Zora was about to comment on the crowd when she noticed the expression on Monét's face. She tried to decipher it. It ranged somewhere between surprise and disgust.

Zora followed the gaze of Monét's somewhat panicked look.

Bryce. Standing at the double oak doors that opened into the ballroom. He looked in their direction. He was like a radar when it came to Monét.

Preston and Jeremiah had taken their seats at the table and were talking about who knows what. They were oblivious to the unfolding scene, and Zora was thankful. Monét looked as if she'd seen a ghost.

"Fix your face," Zora told Monét, turning her back to the doorway. "I'm sure he'll be coming in our direction," she reported.

"No, in your direction. I'm disappearing to take care of some business."

Monét walked away before Zora had time to convince her otherwise. She nearly crashed into a tuxedoed waiter balancing a tray of Caesar salads. Her exit was perfectly timed.

Moments later Bryce's voice followed the touch of a hand on Zora's shoulder. "Ms. Zora. How's the soon-to-be blushing bride?"

"I'm doing great. And you?" Not that Zora really cared, but it was the polite response. Zora pulled out a chair and scooted up to the table, hoping her actions would send Bryce away. They didn't. Bryce proceeded to list his recent accomplishments and too many of the happenings in the commissioner's office.

Zora sipped her water. "Life is definitely keeping you busy," she said, cutting him short when he stopped for air.

"Things couldn't be better. Unless, of course, Monét was part of my life."

Surely he didn't consider Monét as an accomplishment, Zora thought. *It figures.* But despite his arrogance, it was easy to see why Monét had been smitten. Most women were—that was part of the problem. He had too many choices. Unfortunately, he hadn't made the distinction between quality and quantity.

Zora didn't have to tolerate him much longer, as he soon went off to find his seat when Monét approached the podium. When dinner started, he'd undoubtedly start to showcase his knowledge of current events and politics to the people at his table.

Don't count on my vote, Zora thought as she watched him shaking hands. I'm supporting a more qualified candidate.

Jeremiah leaned up and whispered past Preston.

"Your girl knows her stuff. Smart. And fine too. She should be scooped up by now."

Zora nodded and spread her napkin across her lamp. *Oh, she will be.*

After Monét's introduction, Paula tiptoed in and sat at the only empty seat beside Jeremiah. She'd left soon after Zora came to the table, and had just returned. During dinner, she rarely joined in conversation with her neighbors or anyone else at the table. She finally opened up when Jeremiah pried a conversation out of her. Monét kept an ear to their conversation.

"So are you a member of the association hosting the event?"

Paula dabbed her mouth with a napkin. "No. My husband, Dr. Manns, is the chairman." She pointed him out among the other officers seated on the stage.

"So you must go to events like these all the time."

"I'm afraid so," Zora heard her tell Jeremiah. "I'm sorry. I don't think that came out right." She spread the napkin back on her lap. "Don't mind me. I'm thinking about my son. He wasn't feeling too well before I left home."

"You think it's separation anxiety?"

"No. He loves his babysitter. He was talking about her all day. I think he caught a bug from his playgroup."

"How many children do you have?"

"One son. Micah."

It was amazing how her countenance had changed from earlier that day to now when she spoke about her son, Zora thought.

The light went off in Zora's head. Micah. The boy with the red cape down at the Harbor. The frantic way his mother called his name.

Zora's instinct hadn't lied. Their paths had crossed again. Tonight she'd find out why.

As soon as their feet hit the hardwood floors in Monét's loft, Preston and Jeremiah peeled out of their suit jackets. They headed straight for the couch to surf the sports channels for the Orioles score updates. The volume was turned so high that Zora and Monét could barely hear themselves in the kitchen area.

Monét filled a red teakettle with water, while Zora turned on the stove. After a successful affair, the four had retreated to her abode for a nightcap. That was fine with her. When heavy sleep crept up on everyone else, she'd have the luxury of the trip from her sofa to her king-sized bed in less than twenty steps.

"You know Paula isn't going to like you very much if you try to dig around in her business again."

"That might be the last time our paths ever cross," Zora reasoned. "I had to make sure she wasn't my long-lost cousin our something. I'm on a mission right now."

"And?"

"And she pretty much thinks I'm crazy, but at least I won't

be left to wonder." Zora slipped out of her high heels.

"You must have been asking more than about her bloodline," Monét said. "By the time I walked up, she already looked irritated. People don't act that way just because you ask about their family."

"The only thing I did was try to see where she was in life. Get a feel for her."

"She's seen you twice in her entire life." Monét finally pulled off her pumps too. High fashion wasn't always worth the price of sore feet, she thought. "The woman's not interested in baring her soul to a stranger."

"Anyway. Enough about Paula," Zora said. "You pulled it off again. I think that's the best function of yours I've been to so far."

Monét thought so too. "Except for Bryce's appearance, it was near perfect."

Zora opened the pantry and pushed two wheat cracker boxes aside to find a tea box. "I thought he wasn't coming," Zora said. She pulled four Earl Grey tea bags from the box and put them in the deep clay mugs Monét set on the counter.

"Supposedly the commissioner's assistant had a family emergency, so they called Bryce. The commissioner never makes an appearance alone."

"I saw him hawking over you every time he caught you alone."

"Tell me about it," Monét said, playing with the tag hanging on one of the tea bags. "He's a chameleon, Zora. You know that I have to stay away from him or else I find myself being sucked into his trap."

Monét had felt the pull of his allure from the time he walked in. He turned heads and hearts without even trying. He was the classic pretty boy, and Monét thought if she could erase his face from her memory, he'd be easier to flush from her system. Their pictures and other memories were finally trashed from the photo box at the top of her closet.

Then he came tonight, and his face etched in her subconscious again.

"Charm *is* his middle name," Zora was saying. She leaned forward and rested her elbows on the counter and propped her chin between her hands. She directed her gaze toward the men on the couch.

Monét knew what was coming. She opened the cabinet and pulled out a variety box of Pepperidge Farm cookies. "He's sweet," she said, running her finger under the unopened box tab.

"And?" Zora prodded.

"Polite."

"And?"

"Definitely eye candy," she surmised. "Who lives in Texas."

Monét couldn't deny that Jeremiah was eye candy. He had a tasty smile set between two dimples. And on top of his looks, he conducted himself with suavity and was as much a gentleman as his best friend. It was a sweet encounter. But that's all it would ever be. She didn't do long-distance relationships. They either lost their flavor or went sour before they had time to ripen.

Zora searched through Monét's cabinets, looking for a serving tray. "You never know where life will lead you," Zora said.

She never gives up. "What's the probability that I'll move to Texas or he'll move to Maryland?"

"I wouldn't say that if I were you. God specializes in answering my prayers, you know."

"You're right. There was no way I thought we'd have an extra seat tonight." Monét walked to her small pantry and found a serving tray. "Why can't you accept the fact that I'm single and happy? The two can coexist, you know."

The doorbell chimed over the ruckus blasting out of the television.

"Who in the world is that?" Zora asked. She held the serving tray while Monét poured out the cookies.

"Probably Casey. I've never known a neighbor to make so many grand appearances when she thinks I have company. Can you handle her for me?"

"Gladly," Zora said. "Who needs building security when you have neighborhood watch?"

Zora kissed the top of Preston's head on the way to the door. She looked through the peephole, but didn't say anything or open the door.

"Who is it?" Monét asked from the kitchen.

Zora turned around and shrugged. The uninvited guest rang the doorbell again. "Their back is turned."

"Open the door, Zora," Monét said. She practically had to yell. "We've got two strong men to come to our rescue."

"Who can't hear or see anything but the TV right now." Zora turned the latch, but still blocked her body in the crack of the door when she opened it.

Oh, that's really going to help, Monét mused to herself.

Zora opened the door wider, and the next shock for the night hit Monét in the face. She couldn't believe it. Surprise and anger thudded her heart.

Bryce. Again. He stood confident in the doorway, his hands stuffed in his pockets as if he were posing for a *GQ* spread. He said something to Zora, a smile punctuating his face, then brushed past her and strode into the apartment as if he paid the mortgage. He took in the scene and, noticing Monét, headed directly to her. Zora followed behind him.

"What's up, fellas?" Bryce patted Preston and Jeremiah on their shoulders as he passed.

Monét walked from around the counter. The feelings from when she first saw him that evening returned. Love and hate lived simultaneously.

Bryce wrapped his arms around her waist, though her arms

148

dangled at her side. She couldn't move them. His embrace nearly lifted her off the ground, and Monét instinctively had to grab his arms to keep her balance.

The blasting volume of the TV had diminished. Preston had abandoned the sports channel and posted himself in the kitchen, standing behind Zora. He held her against him, their faces pressed cheek to cheek.

Monét knew his presence was meant to intimidate. Preston had tolerated Bryce over the years, even though he never cared much for him.

"Nice event tonight, wasn't it, man?" Preston said.

"Definitely. I came to congratulate Monét, but it looks like she's already having a victory party."

Monét finally found her voice. "Thank you. And now that you've done that, I'll let you out."

Bryce wasn't shaken by her coldness. She didn't expect him to be. He was used to it.

"Am I missing the party in here?" Unaware of the room's tension, Jeremiah joined them in the kitchen. He extended a hand to Bryce.

"Bryce. Mr. Bryce Coleman."

Mister?

"Jeremiah Hartgrove."

"You're the lucky man who's stealing Monét's heart from me?"

Monét sensed that Jeremiah had picked up on the tension. It was probably by the way everyone froze as if they were about to watch a ringside event.

Jeremiah laughed.

Monét caught the look he threw at Preston.

"We just met today, so I haven't had the chance to try. Yet." Jeremiah pulled out a seat at the kitchen table and sat down, propping one ankle across the other knee. "And I don't believe in luck."

The teakettle whistled. It was a high-pitched shrill that matched Monét's scream inside. She turned to cut off the stove eye. It must have also been an alarm to Bryce.

"I'll give you a call tomorrow," Bryce said to Monét.

She walked behind him to the door and let him out. "Now that our station break is over, we'll return to our regularly scheduled program."

"Gladly," Zora said. Accustomed to Monét's mode of operation, Zora turned off the television and hit the power button on the stereo.

It calmed Monét's nerves and immediately changed the atmosphere. "Zora, can you light the candles in the fireplace?"

"I'll take care of it," Jeremiah said, taking the lighter from Monét. He walked over to the fireplace and knelt down to open the glass door. "You've only burned candles in here, huh? No smut at all."

"Of course." Monét sat on the brick edge of the fireplace. "It's more of an accessory than anything else."

"You don't know what you're missing. I'm from Chicago. I know fireplaces."

"Should I be ashamed to say that I don't even know how to light it?"

"If it wasn't June, I'd show you how we did it in Chi-Town."

Monét looked at Zora, who sure enough was eyeing their interaction, but trying to pretend she was preoccupied with putting the tea and cookies on the table. She left Jeremiah to light the candles and decided to pull back the curtain sheers. If she stayed around him any longer, Zora would have them married off by the end of the night.

❧

It wasn't long before Monét's disturbed mood caused by Bryce's visit had disappeared. Her body and emotions had simmered down, and she was able to enjoy the conversations with her company. They talked about the upcoming wedding, family values, their careers, and world issues. When stories of sibling rivalry and differences in childhood upbringings dominated the conversation, Zora chimed in every once in a while. Her thoughts, Monét sensed, seemed far off.

"Zora! Back to earth over there," Preston said. "What's the biggest fight Monét ever had with Victoria?"

Zora didn't hesitate to respond. "Without a doubt the time she thought Victoria stole a shoebox of her cassette tapes. It was ridiculous," Zora recalled. "If her mom hadn't come home, I was two minutes from calling the police. The aftermath was not a pretty sight."

"So you went to blows over a shoebox of cassette tapes? You must be a music woman."

"In a sense," Monét said. "I lose myself in the lyrics. You can feel the ones that are written from the heart. It's their heart's song. And for the record, Zora is exaggerating about the fight."

It seemed Jeremiah had found a common thread that he wasn't letting go of.

"I think it's the music that evokes the emotions of the song," he said. "The lyrics and the music dance together."

He had sparked her curiosity. "So you play an instrument?"

"The keyboard. And if you're the lyrical lady, you must sing."

"I can do a little something."

Zora butted in. "She's being modest. My girl can blow."

Jeremiah pushed away from the table so he could stretch out his legs. He clasped his hands on top of his chest. "Can we have some entertainment tonight, then?"

151

Monét felt her face blush. "How did I know you were going to ask that?" She leaned back in her own chair and crossed her arms, her mind made up that there would be no serenades tonight.

"If I had a keyboard here, I'd play for you guys."

"And I'd enjoy every minute of it."

"At least tell me who your favorite singers are. I mean real singers, not voices that have been manipulated in the studio."

Preston pushed his chair back and went to the refrigerator. "Needless to say, Zora and I have nothing to contribute to this conversation," he said, and helped himself to a bottle of water.

Monét and Jeremiah dove together into the world of music. She thought she was a walking musical archive, but her knowledge seemed nominal compared to Jeremiah's endless bank of facts and trivia. Monét held on to their common thread too. At least for tonight.

Monét looked around after a while and realized they were the only two at the kitchen table. Zora had evidently found better entertainment with Preston. They'd changed the area near the stereo into an impromptu dance floor to enjoy a slow drag to the radio station's quiet storm.

"What do you have planned for the Fourth?" Jeremiah asked.

"There's usually a celebration with fireworks down at the Inner Harbor. I'll probably check that out after I have dinner at my parents'. They threw a guilt trip on me so I'd come over for my birthday."

"Your birthday is on the Fourth?"

"Yes. You haven't noticed? The nation celebrates every year."

"You must be some kind of woman." Jeremiah pulled his chair closer to Monét. "But I should've known. You have men following you home."

152

"Bryce? He's an old friend."

"An old friend can mean lots of things."

Monét didn't respond. She didn't want to think about Bryce. She'd done enough of that for the night. She wasn't naive to Jeremiah's tactics. He was trying to find out if she and Bryce had anything going.

"I bet you're taking your girlfriend to a romantic picnic under the fireworks for the Fourth. I can see you doing something like that."

"With who? Because I don't have a girlfriend," Jeremiah said. "I'll be here that weekend again for work. Maybe I'll come to the Harbor."

"That would be nice."

Real nice. If only the owner of those dimples didn't live so far away.

14

Zora slipped into the sanctuary at the exact moment that the three pastors' wives of the participating churches of P.O.W.E.R. approached the podium. She spotted a seat near the back of the full room. She slipped past two ladies sitting at the end of the row, being careful not to crush their toes.

She mouthed "excuse me" to the women as she passed, then scrunched between them on the empty seat.

Zora was well aware that her plate of responsibility was already overflowing. She'd reasoned with herself and God all night about why she didn't have time for this. Another activity was the last thing she needed on her list.

God won. Obedience was better than sacrifice. On the third Saturday in October, she'd be crossing the burning sands from singleness to marriage. There was still a lot for her to learn about womanhood based on God's terms and not what the world's current trends dictated.

Zora slid her purse under the seat in front of her and finally relaxed. Time had slipped away that morning from her once she got engulfed with filling out the required forms to start the adoptee registration and search through the state system. Then, it was imperative that she take the package to the post office since she'd missed her neighborhood mailman's prompt pickup and delivery. She was surprised her car hadn't become airborne as she sped from the post office to the church. She'd have Monét fill her in on the fifteen minutes she'd missed.

"One thing this is not, ladies, is a gossip circle," Sister James, the first lady of Zora's church, Trinity Chapel, was saying. "If you have problems with loose lips, then we need to get that issue settled before we get in too deep. So the power of the tongue is the first issue we'll address."

Sister James's hand gestures accompanied the excitement in her words. "Over the next nine months we're hoping that your new level of intimacy with God and your fellow sisters will bring forth something great.

"There are dreams and visions that will finally be birthed. Amen!"

"Amen," the women echoed.

Sister James passed the microphone to a petite woman who introduced herself as the first lady of Berean. Sister Griffin stood barely over five feet, and her high-heel sandals cheated her at least three more inches.

"Purposed-Oriented Women Equipped and Righteous. The name says P.O.W.E.R. in more ways than one, doesn't it, ladies?"

The women clapped in agreement. Some threw up their hands and shouts came in the form of "Amen," "Hallelujah," and "Praise the Lord."

"Not only should we honor God by living a righteous life, but we have a duty and responsibility to raise righteous and godly seed. Like it or not, everybody is leaving this earth one day. Am I right? Do you want to leave with regret, or do you want to leave a legacy?"

"Legacy," the women chimed together.

Sister Griffin pranced across the front of the room. She held out her hand and admired the ring on her finger. "I love it when my husband comes home with one of those little blue boxes. They say diamonds are a girl's best friend, but I believe wisdom is our best friend. The Word of God says in Proverbs 8:11, 'For wisdom is better than rubies, and all the things one may desire cannot be compared with her.' And there is power in being a wise woman."

Zora looked at the women sitting on either side of her.

"Amen to that," one woman said.

"She's preachin', ain't she?" The lady to Zora's right waved a hand with ruby red nails in the air and in front of Zora's face. She slapped the lady in front of her on the back.

The woman nearly jumped out of her seat. She grabbed her shoulder and looked behind her with alarm.

"She's preachin' ain't she?" Zora's neighbor repeated.

The woman nodded, though a frown covered her face. She turned back around, rubbing the whacked spot on her shoulder blade.

"It's time we do something. We need to be equipped so we can take back our generation, raise godly children, and be effective in our communities." Sister Griffin pointed a finger in the air. "No, in this world. The earth is the Lord's and the fullness thereof. Enough is enough."

Zora applauded along with the roomful of women. When a few of them stood, others followed, until the entire room exploded in praise.

"Take a look around," Sister Griffin said. "You should be honored to be in the company of a group of powerful sistas!"

It was the first opportunity Zora had to absorb her surroundings. The cheerful and excited faces belonged to college-aged youth to ladies with hair streaked silver by age and, most assuredly, wisdom. Exhilaration blanketed the room.

Zora's joy increased as her spirit fed off of the other women's enthusiasm. The praise was contagious, and she'd been infected.

It was nearly five minutes before the room settled enough to proceed. Following the program's overview by St. Paul's first lady, Sister Desiree Kilpatrick, the women were instructed to pick up their manual and study guide based on their last names. Those who were turning in their registration forms that day were told to wait in the room and find a seat in the first two rows.

Zora gathered her belongings and waited until the rest of the crowd bustled out of the room. She'd hoped to catch Monét during the women's stampede exit, but the crowd prohibited her from seeing little more than the women passing directly in front of her. When the room was nearly empty, she joined the twenty or so women up front.

She sat down beside a woman with natural twists, pinned back by a small clip in front. The woman pulled off her reading glasses and hung them on the neck of her shirt.

"Good morning," Zora said.

"Good morning. How are you?"

"Great now that I'm here," Zora said. "I can't believe I was about to pass up this opportunity. Even after the welcome and introduction I know I'm supposed to be here."

"I know what you mean. I considered not coming myself."

"Really. Why?" Immediately Zora was embarrassed for being so forward. She placed a gentle hand on the woman's shoulder. "I'm sorry. That was so rude."

"That's okay," the woman said gently. "From the sound of things, we need to get used to being transparent." The woman crossed her legs and adjusted the straw purse on her lap. "My mother was recently diagnosed with breast cancer and is recovering from a mastectomy."

"I'm sorry to hear that," Zora empathized.

"It's definitely turned my world upside down. I have more respect for caregivers, and I honor my mother more than ever. I could go on and on about how it makes you examine your life," she said, rubbing a silver necklace between her fingers. "So I'll be traveling back and forth between here and my home in Danville for the time being while she's recovering. A family friend who's helping care for my mother told me about P.O.W.E.R., and St. Paul is the church I grew up in, so it's just like home. She thought I could benefit from it. At first I felt selfish for wanting to do something for myself."

The woman's easy demeanor reminded Zora of her mother. Even though she was walking through a trying time, she could tell her relationship with God was seasoned.

"Zora Bridgeforth," a voice from the front of the room called.

Zora excused herself from the conversation and checked in at the registration table. She was handed her materials along with a postcard with the number six printed on the back.

"Group number six is meeting in classroom three. Down the hall and to the left," the woman at the table directed.

Zora watched every movement of the woman's lips. They were covered with so much deep rum-colored lipstick that Zora was sure they'd get up and walk off the woman's face.

"You can go out this door," she said, pointing to the exit behind her.

"Thanks," Zora said. She started toward the exit, then turned around to go back and speak to the lady who was still waiting to be called.

"It was nice meeting you—"

"Belinda. Belinda Stokes."

"Zora Bridgeforth. And who is this?" Zora asked, noticing the small picture pendant on the end of Belinda's delicate silver chain.

"My daughter, Hannah. She's six months."

"She's adorable," Zora said, leaning in to get a closer look.

"Thank you. She's a blessing." She lifted the silver pendant to her lips.

"Trust that your mother is in God's hands," Zora said, feeling the need to leave behind an encouraging word. She embraced the woman she'd known for a brief time, but felt a connection to. "I'll pray for you and your family, Belinda."

"Thank you, Zora. I appreciate it more than you know."

Zora hurried down the back hallways of St. Paul and followed the P.O.W.E.R. signs to her assigned classroom. The entrance to the corridor was pasted with bulletin boards of children's Sunday school projects. She looked through the tiny window of classroom three before easing open the door. The faces on first sight were all unfamiliar, until her eyes landed on Monét, and then on the doctor's wife seated beside her—Paula Manns.

15

Zora left the house at exactly nine o'clock, allotting extra time to pick up Monét and factor in traffic for their ride out to Sister Oda Barnes's house. Monét held the directions to the house and was responsible for navigating them through the community once they exited the highway. Until then, she'd buried herself in wedding magazines.

The weeks leading to Zora's first group session of P.O.W.E.R. flew by before she knew it. For every one task she crossed off of her wedding to-do list, she added three more. Moreover, she'd been chatting online with Solo about his adoption experiences, and he'd given her more advice on how to proceed with her search.

Zora still hadn't heard a word from her appointed intermediary. She was aware that he had ninety days to report the outcome of the search, but she had expected to hear something before that. God had made her a promise. In the meantime, she did her part by registering with other adoption sites.

Preston had joked that she was having a love affair with her computer. She spent more time with it than anything or anyone else lately. But being the understanding man that he was, he'd given her the space that she needed.

Still, guilt rode Zora's conscience. She hadn't told Preston about her online buddy, Solo. Solo's advice had been helpful, and even though it hadn't uncovered any answers for her yet, she was sure it would eventually. Preston would be grateful if he only understood how much support Solo had been.

"This is my favorite one," Monét said, leafing through a bridesmaid catalog. Zora had dog-eared the pages to her top three choices for her ladies of honor. She wavered between the spaghetti strap dress or the two-piece ensemble with a halter top and A-line skirt. Both would fit all of her bridesmaids' figures.

Zora wanted them to complement her gown perfectly. Her own dress was an exquisite strapless satin A-line gown with embroidery along the train. It was as pure white as the first overnight winter's snow.

The decision about the dresses was long overdue, which was why Zora and Monét were meeting Victoria at the bridal salon after the midmorning P.O.W.E.R. meeting. Monét had been riding her back to get them ordered. She'd reminded her that Stacy, her bridesmaid who lived in Louisiana, needed ample time for her dress to be shipped and altered.

Enough about the dresses, Zora thought. She wanted to pick Monét's mind about Paula.

She hadn't been able to find out anything on her own the night of the auction, but with Monét's help, things could change. Paula always gravitated to Monét.

Zora eased into a conversation.

"So when's the last time you talked to Paula?"

Monét looked up from the bridesmaid catalog. "Not since orientation. We exchanged numbers, but neither of us got around to calling." She pointed to the upcoming street. "Turn here."

Zora merged into the right turning lane. "I'm still wondering what her deal is."

"Don't start this again."

"Seriously, though. Remember how I told you how she looked like she'd been put through the ringer the first time I saw her? And you saw how she and Dr. Manns were arguing before the auction."

"All married couples get into it every once in a while," Monét rationalized. "They were just having one of those days when the angels weren't flying over their heads playing harps. Aren't we all entitled to having a bad day?"

"You're talking to someone who has had her share of them lately, so yes, we're all entitled. But I'm telling you, she's dealing with something more."

"If she is, then she's in the right place. Promise me you won't hawk the woman down again. Like I told you the first time, if she's going through something like you think she is, then she doesn't need to feel uncomfortable. The best thing you can do is pray, pray, and pray some more."

Zora slowed for a group of young boys ahead pushing their bikes across the street. "She avoids me anyway. You see how she left after orientation as soon as I walked over to you."

"Here it is on the right," Monét said. "Come on, Zora. You hounded her like the FBI the last time you saw her. What do you expect?"

"Okay, I'm dropping the subject," Zora said, pulling against the curb behind the line of vehicles already in front of the house. "I love this neighborhood," Zora said, pulling up the gear shift and turning off the car. "I can see me and Preston settling in a neighborhood like this."

Sister Barnes, their group's facilitator, volunteered to host the first meeting. Her home, a brick ranch, was tucked between coves of towering evergreens. The front of the house was lined with thick bushes that sat on beds of pine needles.

"We better get inside." Zora grabbed her purse, study guide, and Bible from the backseat.

"What's Preston up to today?" Monét touched up her lipstick.

"He has to pick up Jeremiah later today from the airport."

"That's right. I forgot he was coming up this weekend. I can't believe they'd make him travel on a holiday weekend. You should tell him to come over for dinner tomorrow with you and Preston. My parents won't mind one extra person."

"I'll ask him. All I know is that I've been officially kicked to the curb today."

"I don't believe it. You two can't stand to be apart from each other for too many days."

"I haven't seen him since Thursday."

Monét smacked her lips. "It's Saturday morning." Monét shook her head and laughed at her best friend.

"No comment," Zora said, closing the driver's side door and walking around the car to catch up with Monét. "Just wait," she said, putting an arm around her shoulder. "One of these days your nose is going to be wide open too."

"Not like yours. I need a man who's like me and needs his space."

"Whatever. You're going to be head over heels, and I can't wait to say I told you so."

Zora rang the doorbell, and she and Monét were greeted a few moments later by a man with a thick mustache that hid most of his top lip. And despite his overgrown facial hair, not a strand of hair was found on his head. After introducing himself as Sister Barnes' husband, Howard, he led them to the back den. As they walked through the house, Zora admired the couple's taste in furniture and African-American art. Every area put the best two-page spreads in the top home décor magazines to shame. The home that looked so modest from the outside was decked out.

"Hello, ladies." Sister Barnes swept over to them wearing an ankle-length cotton skirt and short-sleeved denim shirt. She greeted them with a kiss on the cheek and a hug.

Zora knew it was coming. She'd done the same thing to the group on orientation day, and she'd witnessed her reaction with other women when they fellowshipped afterwards in the vestibule. She'd lay her anointed lips on just about anybody's cheek.

"We're going to wear name tags until we remember everyone's name," Sister Barnes said, pointing to the four tags remaining on the coffee table. "Grab yours, and then you can sit wherever you want. We're waiting for two more ladies."

"Hi, everyone," Zora said as she picked up her name tag and noticed that both Paula's and Belinda's tags were still on the table. They were the only two people besides Monét whose name she could match with a face. There wasn't anyone else from her church in the group.

Zora apologized as she passed over two of the women to claim the corner end of the long leather sectional. She was usually good with remembering faces, but was astonished that she didn't recognize either of the women. She looked at their name tags. Jewel's lips moved a mile a minute as she constantly interrupted the sentences of Celeste, the woman she was talking to. Celeste's face seemed to beg for relief from the incessant conversation, but the chatty Jewel was oblivious to it all.

"Hi." Zora leaned forward slightly so she could see the name tag of the rail-thin younger woman seated to her right— "Peggy."

Unlike the chatty Jewel, Peggy seemed aloof, almost timid. She croaked a response barely above a whisper, then opened her Bible. Evidently she didn't want to be bothered, Zora concluded.

165

Sister Barnes returned to the room with a bamboo serving tray of lemonade and coasters. Jewel jumped to her assistance and passed the glasses around. Just as Zora put her glass to her lips, both Paula and Belinda walked into the room. Zora didn't look in Monét's direction a few seats away; she would undoubtedly have a look of warning on her face.

After the twelve women were settled, Sister Barnes opened the session with prayer. Her mighty petitions struck a chord in every one of the lady's hearts, evident because not a dry eye was in the room when she finished. One of the women dug around in her purse and pulled out a small travel-sized package of tissues. She passed them around the room, and when they reached Zora, she pulled out two. If the rest of the session dug as deep into her soul as the prayer, then she'd need them.

"As you all know, ladies, our first study is on the power of the tongue," Sister Barnes began. She paused when murmurs and comments rose around the room. She peered over her red-rimmed reading glasses. "I struck a nerve with about half of you all, and we haven't even got started yet. Lord, help us." She chuckled.

"I don't know a woman who doesn't have a problem with this one," Jewel said.

"A man either," another lady said. She blushed when she realized her voice wasn't as low as she'd thought.

"Well, honey, I like to speak my mind," Jewel said. Her cowry-shell earrings jingled as she shook her head.

Zora could tell that Sister Barnes had a patient way about her. She slid back into the leather love seat.

"Regardless, you still have to speak the truth in love," their group facilitator explained. "And then you have to determine whether you're correcting a person based on what the Word of God says, or based on your opinions. People's opinions are usually what get us in trouble."

"That's right," Celeste said.

Sister Barnes opened her Bible across her lap.

"Let's review our Scriptures, and then we'll talk about some practical applications. The Word won't work in your life unless you put some action behind it. Would anybody like to read Matthew 12:36–37?"

"I will," Jewel said, standing up with her Bible already turned to the passage. She waited while the other women found the Scripture.

"'But I say to you that for every idle word men may speak, they will give account of it in the day of judgment,'" she read. "'For by your words you will be justified, and by your words you will be condemned.'"

Zora was aware of every syllable and letter in each word as Jewel read the Scripture. She wasn't the only one who noticed.

"All right sister. You read that Scripture like you meant it," Sister Barnes said.

"I'm a drama teacher," Jewel announced. "We project and enunciate. My mother poured that into me, God rest her soul."

That explains it.

"Would anyone like to comment on the verse?" Sister Barnes peered around the room.

"I think it speaks for itself. Basically you're held accountable for the careless words you say."

Zora couldn't see the woman's name tag, but she reminded her a lot of her seventh-grade teacher.

"That's right. And what about the Scripture that says the tongue is like fire? Why is that?" Sister Barnes looked around the room.

Zora looked down at her Bible, avoiding eye contact. She'd read her lesson, but the women looked so mature in the Word, and she didn't want to make a fool of herself. Personal devotion time didn't compare to this.

"I see you all are playing shy, but that's okay, because we're going to break down the walls by the end of these nine months. And age has nothing to do with it. Everyone has something to contribute, and we're here to help each other grow."

Go ahead, Zora.

"I'll take a stab at it," Zora said. "What I got from the Scripture was that the tongue is like fire because it can spark altercations and evil that can spread. It only takes a few words to destroy a situation."

"And you know most fire damage is irreparable," Sister Barnes added.

The group's study on the tongue continued for the next hour, reviewing issues of gossip, lying, and words that bring destruction. Then they reviewed ways to use the tongue as a powerful tool to uplift, exalt God and one another, and activate their faith.

Zora made up her mind to make a declaration every day. She started penning them across the top of her study guide.

I believe that my true identity and roots will be revealed. My mind rests in the peace of God. I will not falter, but be like a tree planted by the water, and whatever I do prospers.

After closing their lesson in prayer, Sister Barnes invited the women into the kitchen, then out onto the deck for brunch. A selection of pastries, fruit, yogurts, and juices covered the kitchen island.

Zora chose an apple cinnamon croissant and a cup of yogurt, and then congregated on the deck with the other women. She noticed Monét and Paula standing near the deck steps and debated about whether to join them. She had a good idea what the result of that would be. She didn't get a chance to consider it much further.

Belinda walked up, giving Zora a gentle hug from the side.

"How are you doing?" Zora asked.

Belinda nodded her head slowly. "I'm doing," she searched for the word, "better. It's been a rough week."

"Is it your mother? How is she?"

Belinda dunked a tea bag in the steaming Styrofoam cup of water she was holding. "The recovery medications are taking a toll on her body and her energy. Her spirit is strong. It's just tough to see her body go through the changes. She's teaching me a few things about perseverance."

"I think God gave women an extra dose of tolerance for pain," Zora said. "You probably thought you were going to pull your husband's head off when you were in the delivery room. But the pain didn't compare to the first time you held your daughter and looked into her eyes for the first time."

Belinda blew the steam off the top of her tea. "It's a bittersweet situation that I received the blessing without the physical pain. Hannah is adopted," she explained. "Thomas and I have had her since she was two days old."

The words had rolled off her lips without a care or thought. Belinda's unexpected comment stunned Zora. She felt Belinda's hand on her forearm.

"Are you all right?"

Zora managed a weak smile. "I'm fine. I got a little lightheaded. Probably because I haven't eaten this morning." She peeled back the pink foil top of her yogurt and realized she didn't have a spoon.

"Here you go." Belinda passed Zora the basket of plastic utensils.

"Thanks." Zora stirred the fruit in the bottom of the cup until it mixed throughout the cream.

"I'm going to grab a plate," Belinda said after Zora spooned yogurt in her mouth. "Maybe you should sit down awhile until you get your bearings."

"That's a good idea," Zora said, walking off to a chaise lounge in the corner of the deck.

P.O.W.E.R. was supposed to be an outlet away from her issue. Instead, it was confronting her. What she was ashamed of most had reared its head.

Perhaps it was the circumstances. It may have been different if she'd known from the beginning. But her parents' deceit was accompanied by her shame. *No. I'm not going there.*

Zora saw the faces of her group members, but the world around her was on mute. Their mouths were open with laughter, but all she heard were her own thoughts. The questions and insecurities rushed in. She began mentally reciting her declaration Scriptures. Again. And again.

"Hey." Monét walked over with a plate of fruit in one hand and a cup in the other. "Why are you over here being unsociable?"

"Sit down," Zora said, moving her purse so Monét could sit at the foot of the chaise lounge. She could sense her friend's immediate concern. "Belinda just told me her daughter is adopted," she said, not holding back. "I hope she explains it to her daughter when she's old enough to understand."

"If she was so readily open with you about it, then it's probably no secret. You never know the circumstances behind it, but I'm sure she'll make the best decision for her child."

"The best decision is to be honest. Nobody—" Zora lowered her voice—"should have to go through what I'm experiencing right now. It's not fair."

"Did you tell her about your situation?"

"Of course not. And it's going to stay that way." Zora leaned closer to Monét. "I'm not telling these people—who are practically strangers—that I lived in a lie for practically most of my life."

"Like I've told you a thousand times, I can't begin to imagine what this has done for you. But you can't stay locked up forever. Maybe it's time for you to be open."

She's right.

Monét swirled a pieced of watermelon around on her plate like her statement was a simple revelation.

Zora tensed with frustration. Monét was right—she couldn't imagine what this had done to her. Instead of getting upset, Zora thought it best to change the subject.

"Where's Paula?"

"She had to pick up her son."

"I'm sure Paula's a decent lady. Reviewing our lesson with other women really made me see how judgmental I am. I should be lifting her up."

Monét shook her head because her mouth was stuffed with an assortment of fruit. The look on her face was like she'd eaten a slice of heaven.

"Me too," she finally said. "I might not always make a comment, but I think about it. We're supposed to esteem others higher than ourselves, and I for one have to do better about that."

Belinda walked up and handed a bookmark to each of the ladies and said, "Compliments of the hostess."

"For I know the plans I have for you, says the Lord," Zora said, reading the Scripture on the front of the laminated bookmark. *At least you know, Lord.*

Belinda knelt over and tried to shove her Bible and bookmark in her oversized purse. It wasn't working. She repositioned a diaper cloth and clunky rattle to make room.

"I better get going. Hannah is probably wearing Aunt Wanda out. She's so spoiled. I had to wait until she was getting her bath so I could sneak out."

"That sounds like Monét," Zora teased. "We've been best friends for all of our lives, and when she slept over at my house when we were little, most of the time she'd wake up in the middle of the night and cry for her mom."

Monét set her empty plate at the foot of the chaise.

"Don't make me pull out my arsenal of stories," she said.

171

"Belinda, I have some I could tell you, but I'm going to be nice like a best friend and maid of honor is supposed to be."

"You're getting married?" Belinda tried to snap her purse, but it was about to bust at the seams. "Congratulations. For some reason I thought you already were. When's the big day?"

"October. And it's coming faster than I expected."

Belinda held out her hand so Zora could help her get up. "These knees can buckle sometimes. You'll see one day," she chuckled, dusting off her pants. "I know you've been given enough advice to write a book about marriage, but I'm still going to add my page to it. Don't listen to people who have let their marriages grow stale. I've been married for ten years, and it's only gotten better with time. Much time." She winked. "In *every* area."

"All right now."

They gave each other a round of high fives.

Zora picked up her purse. "We better get going too. I've got to choose bridesmaid dresses today."

After bidding their good-byes and "Happy Fourth" to Sister Barnes and the lingering group members, the women escorted themselves through the house and to their cars. Belinda was just as excited to share her insight into the joy of marriage as she was to disclose her experiences of being a first-time mother at forty.

"I'm an open book," Belinda told Zora and Monét. She popped the trunk of her Volvo station wagon and slid her manual into a plastic crate in the back. "You can ask me anything."

Zora looked at Monét, then back to Belinda.

"Well, there is one thing I want to know."

16

Aunt Wanda was right, Belinda thought on the ride home. The sisterhood of women would help her cope with her mother's illness. She drew strength from being in their presence.

It was a blessing to see women at different places in their walk with God. No doubt they'd all witness miraculous changes in one another by the end of nine months. *I could stand to birth some perseverance,* she thought.

Riding helped Belinda think. She especially needed to clear her mind to write the magazine's feature. Her initial idea about chronicling her own experience from her mother's diagnosis until now was harder than she expected. When she sat to put pen to paper, the words didn't flow; only tears did.

On the other hand, a stoic, fact-filled medical article wouldn't be true to her creed. She always pressed the other writers to dig deeper and find the story behind the story. This time, her life was the story. She'd try again tonight. She had to press through the pain so someone else could find hope in her testimony.

Belinda slid on her hands-free earpiece and called Thomas. When he didn't answer at home, she called his cell. It rolled into his voice mail, but she didn't bother to leave a message. He'd see her missed call and return it when he could. One of his calls to his wife and daughter always came around one o'clock. It was only eleven thirty, so he was probably with the men at church working on the new handicap ramp.

It turned out Belinda didn't have to wait for her one o'clock call from her husband.

"That's my baby," Belinda said, pulling into her mother's driveway beside Thomas' black Jeep Cherokee. She spotted his garment bag hanging in the rear window and knew his visit was for more than that day.

When Belinda walked into the house, her husband's cologne welcomed her at the foyer. She followed his voice down the hall to her mother's room. Thomas was adjusting body pillows behind Bernice's back. Hannah was sprawled out on her play mat at the side of the bed, kicking the dangling octopus toys.

"Your wife," Bernice managed to say. She tried to lift her body to find a more comfortable position.

"Take it easy, Ma," Thomas said, then looked over his shoulder. "Hi, queen. I was wondering when you'd get back."

Belinda smiled as wide as the Jordan River. "I just called you not too long ago." She sat down on the floor beside Hannah.

"See, all you have to do is think about me and I show up," he said. He squatted down beside his wife.

"Mmmm," Belinda said, as Thomas's lips grazed hers. His kiss still warmed her insides.

"Ma, you didn't know I had such a romantic, did you?"

Her mother laughed and patted the side of her hair. It reminded Belinda that she was supposed to shampoo and roll it up for her later in the evening. Though still thin in some areas, it was starting to grow back and regain its shine.

"Of course I did," Bernice said. "He's been taking such good care of me. He wouldn't do any less for his wife." She shook a finger at him. "Or else."

Belinda was glad to see her mother was regaining some of her spunky personality.

"Now, Ma," Thomas said. "In ten years has she ever called you about me?"

"That's your house," Bernice said. "I stay out of it."

Thomas slid down on his stomach beside Hannah. "You don't have to worry about me," he said. "I'm prepared to handle anything thrown our way."

Thrilled to have a face at her eye level, Hannah bobbed her head up and down and tried to pull her body forward like a seal. She scooted a few inches and moved her head faster, as if the act would propel her chubby body. Hannah squealed in delight.

"That's remarkable," Thomas said and patted his daughter's pampered bottom. "T. J. used to do the same thing. He'd get that head going, and it was like he couldn't stop."

Belinda saw the joy of the distant memory in Thomas's eyes. She pictured his seven-year-old son from their last outing together at the state fair. He probably looked like a man by now compared to what she remembered. Then he was lanky with a mouth mixed with both baby and adult teeth.

She couldn't picture him at seventeen. Like most boys at that age, his voice had probably dropped a few octaves. She wouldn't be surprised if he'd be obsessed about the two strands of hair growing from his chin that he considered a beard. That probably made him think he was a man. Seventeen hadn't reached the point of manhood in Belinda's book. At seven months, Hannah already showed signs of independence. She couldn't imagine dealing with a teenager.

"Daaaa," Hannah sang. "Daaaaa, daaaa."

"Did you hear that? She said Daddy." Thomas scooped Hannah up and lifted her over his head. "I haven't heard that in a long time."

Joy and pain struck Belinda's heart at the same time. She lifted up Hannah's yellow unbuttoned onesie and kissed her pudgy belly. Her husband had waited over ten years to hear someone call him Daddy.

Why me, Lord? Belinda's heart screamed inside. *I wanted to give that to my husband years ago.*

I know the plans I have for you.

17

Reading *it was a lot easier than doing it,* Paula thought. How was she supposed to bridle her tongue for a man who had the audacity to ask her if she was sure the baby was his?

Dr. Darryl Manns, Ivy League scholar and renowned cardiologist, suddenly seemed to have lost every lick of sense he was born with. She'd always heard that beating people over the head with the Word was not the way to win their souls. She thought differently. The Bible she'd been holding last night could've worked wonders in knocking some godly sense straight into his head. She fumed now just thinking about it.

"God, this is one I'm going to need help with. He talks to me like I'm his child instead of his wife. Don't you think I've held my tongue long enough?" Paula said out loud.

She drummed her finger on the steering wheel, anxiously waiting for the traffic light to turn. Paula looked over to the car next to her, and an elderly woman in the passenger's seat waved frantically. She said something to the driver, who looked over and also acknowledged his recognition of Paula.

Paula waved even though she had no idea who they were.

Not today, she thought, when she saw the lady roll down her car window.

The woman proudly announced to Paula that she'd attended the auction a few weeks ago to show her appreciation to Dr. Manns because he'd saved her life. "Anything to help Dr. Manns," she said. "He does so much for his patients."

Yes. He mends hearts at the hospital and breaks them at home.

The green light gave Paula the great escape.

❧

During her first year as a stay-at-home mother, Paula looked for anything to keep her connected with the outside world and had found an area playgroup. Today's morning playgroup at the home of one of the mothers was perfect. She trusted Micah's care in the hands of Patricia, and her son, Trey, was Micah's best friend.

Patricia was the creative stay-at-home mother. Micah would come home with an insect made of clothespins or car-shaped cookies sealed in a sandwich bag. She was a good person. Paula just didn't consider her, or any of the mothers in the playgroup, as a friend. Associate was more appropriate.

Paula couldn't share her marriage woes with them. Mrs. Darryl Manns was envied. She had the home they all dreamt about, the cars they envied, and a bank account to keep her expansive walk-in closet stocked with clothes that still had tags.

But Paula the individual needed a touch. She needed to know her life wouldn't always feel like a boulder teetering on the edge of a cliff.

Paula prayed the P.O.W.E.R. group would grow into something more than a typical church function. Today's session was all right, but she could tell the women weren't as open as they could be. Everyone, except Jewel, seemed kind of stiff, herself included. She didn't blame them. People shouldn't be privy to all of her business. As far as Paula was concerned, she and God could work out her marital issues in private.

Paula looked at the console clock. She still had time to see if Neiman Marcus had updated their inventory. The department store was around the corner and not too far off her route to Patricia's house. She needed a few pairs of casual slacks and tops anyway. She could also stand one more pair of sandals, she decided, pulling into an empty parking space.

"Paula Gilmer?"

Paula turned in the direction of the voice as she closed the car door.

"The years have treated you well," a man said. "You don't remember me, do you?"

No doubt he was a man she'd seen before. His features were the same, but his look had evolved; a maturity reflected in his dress slacks and crisp shirt as opposed to his oversized athletic gear. He smiled, and his inch-deep dimples jogged her memory.

"Victor Humphries," Paula said.

How could she forget? As the star wide receiver, he'd owned the front page of the campus newspaper's sports section in his junior and senior years. "The Victor," as he'd been called, was known on campus just as much for his academic genius as he'd been for his athletic skills.

"How have you been?" Victor asked.

They shared a friendly hug, keeping that unspoken amount of expected personal space between their bodies.

"I can't complain," Paula said. *I really could.* "Did you end up in Detroit? Last time I saw you, the scouts were beating down your door."

"No, I'm actually back here now. I'm working on a new development project in Prince George's and Montgomery Counties. You know real estate is the name of the game around here." Victor reached in his back pocket and handed her a business card.

Oh brother. "I never would've put you in real estate. I thought you would retire from the NFL."

"Everybody did, but that wasn't my passion. My father has had a contracting business for years, so the way I see it, I might as well take the legacy to the next level. It's in my blood." He laughed. "Not to mention I got a bum knee. But enough about me." He leaned against Paula's SUV and out of the way of oncoming traffic in the parking lot. "So what road did life take you down?"

A bumpy one. "I'm married. I'm actually Paula Manns now." She felt embarrassed that it was her only claim to fame. "Keeping busy with a four-year-old," she added.

"That's definitely a full-time job. So what kind of work does your husband do?"

"He's an interventional cardiologist," she said, wondering why men always asked that question. They seemed to measure success by careers. "Are you married?" Paula asked.

"Separated."

Paula wondered why. Maybe he had the same problem her husband did.

"So do you have time to grab a cup of coffee?" Victor asked.

Victor looked good. Point-blank, the brother was fine. *What's the harm with a cup of coffee?* Paula looked at her watch.

"No coffee, but I could use some tea and a muffin."

Neiman Marcus could wait. If there were anything outstanding on the racks, Susan, her personal shopper, would set some items aside, call her, and have her wardrobe room waiting for the next time she came. Then there was the fact that she'd only had a small cup of cranberry juice at Sister Barnes's house. She'd felt queasy earlier, but the feeling had passed.

Don't do it.

Why am I trying to justify a cup of tea? It's no big deal. I'm not doing anything wrong.

It's the appearance of it.

Paula and Victor walked to the coffee shop inside of the mall. When she'd been pregnant with Micah, the smell would have sent her running for the nearest bathroom. Compared to her first, this pregnancy was a breeze.

Victor offered to pay for their order, and then they found a table for two.

"Paula, Paula, Paula."

"What?" Paula ran the stirrer around the edge of the cup and put the beverage to her lips. She batted her eyes. Was she flirting? It felt good in a way. Besides, it was harmless.

"I can't believe how much you've changed. You were quite the conservative one in college. Now look at you."

"What?" she asked again, fishing around for compliments. It had been a while since she'd had one.

"No need to be modest. You could walk out of here and put supermodels to shame, and you know it."

Paula looked sharp. She had to admit it. She was glad she hadn't chosen to put on her yoga pants and grey T-shirt this morning. Instead, she'd matched a pair of black capris with a raw silk, red, wrap-style blouse. It accentuated her waist and toned hips. She felt good. The extra money for the personal trainer was worth it.

"I see you haven't lost your charm," Paula said.

"Seems my wife is right."

For a minute she'd forgotten he was married too.

"Who's the lucky lady anyway?" She wondered if it was Sheila. They'd been inseparable during college, but mostly because Sheila didn't let him far out of her sight. She'd staked her claim on him and showed no intentions of loosening her grip.

"Her name is Maria, and I can bet she doesn't consider herself lucky. What I call being friendly, she calls flirtatious. If I say up, she says down. If I go right, she'll fight to go left."

Paula nodded, but didn't comment. She wasn't interested in getting involved in anyone's marital woes, and she definitely wasn't qualified to give any advice.

Paula and Victor became so occupied reminiscing about the old college days that she hadn't noticed anyone walk up until the person cleared his throat.

Paula looked up.

Her heart dropped from her chest to her toes. She pushed a napkin aside and set her cup down slow and steady, easing as if a sudden movement would spring Darryl into attack.

"Darryl Manns," her husband said, offering his hand to Victor.

Victor stood, seeming pleased to meet her husband's acquaintance.

Darryl began again before Victor could speak. "So you must be the father of my wife's baby?"

Paula's heart found its way back from her toes and up into her throat. Her shock matched the look on Victor's face. Her hands trembled.

"Evidently you're mistaken," Victor said, shaking his head and shoving his hand into his pocket. He was calm and unmoved by the confrontation, unlike Paula. "We ran into each other in the parking lot. We went to college together. I'm Vic—"

"Is that the story you two concocted?" Darryl's words were slow and steady, easing out of the subtle smirk on his face. "Really, Paula," he said. "I thought you were more intelligent than that. And to think you said you were going to meet with a women's church group? Is that what this group does? Teaches women to cheat on their husbands. Can I get an amen, Paula?"

182

It's not what you think.

Darryl hovered over her, waiting for a response. Her body betrayed her. She couldn't get her lips to move or her legs to stand. She almost wished he'd cause a scene. At least then she'd be sure of where his head really was. His impassive reaction was more threatening. He was calm. Too calm.

"Her things will be packed tonight so you can pick her up," Darryl said, landing a heavy-handed slap on Victor's back. "I'll see you then." He walked out and took Paula's courage and ego with him.

Paula exhaled. She literally felt the blood rush through her body. Frantic, she pushed away from the table, the force knocking over her cup of tea. Now the heads turned.

"I'm sorry," she said to Victor. He was still standing, dumbfounded by the accusation thrown at him.

Paula sopped up the spill on the table, but the brown liquid still dripped to the floor. "This is so embarrassing. I didn't mean for this to—I'm sorry." She picked up her purse and ran out of the coffee shop.

Paula looked for a sign of Darryl. Nothing. She literally wanted to run for the exit, but instead hit a stride like a New York businesswoman battling the brisk downtown winds. She clutched her handbag against her chest. She couldn't get to her car fast enough, the threat of tears rushing her more than her feet. Paula clicked the car remote to unlock the door as soon as her vehicle was in sight.

She pulled the handle, but the door didn't open. What else could go wrong? She shoved the key into the lock. It wouldn't turn. Paula shielded her eyes from the glare of the sun and looked into the driver's side window. She didn't remember having a magazine on the front seat. The earpiece hanging on the rearview mirror wasn't hers either. *This isn't my car.*

Paula walked back out into the middle rows of the cars and pushed the panic button on her remote. Her car horn blared from two rows over, and she cut through the parked vehicles. Three steps away from safety another car horn blasted.

Darryl?

Paula swung around, prepared for a verbal attack.

"Hey, Paula." Zora and Monét cruised to a stop behind her vehicle.

Paula smoothed her bangs behind her ear, then pulled her damp shirt away from her stomach. She felt a drop of sweat trickle down between her breasts.

"I'm late picking up my son. I'll see you guys next time." With that the conversation was over. She opened the car door and slid inside on the blazing hot leather seat. She reached for her shades over the visor. She had to get Micah and get home before Darryl made good on his threat. Imagine her packed bags on the doorstep. That was like a scene from a movie.

Paula gunned the gas to make it through the yellow light. What if Darryl really did put her stuff out?

"God help me," she said. "Something told me not to do it."

I told you.

Paula barely made it through the second yellow light. She thought being at home was bad before. Paula knew she probably hadn't experienced the worse of it.

W hat's up with her?" Zora wheeled into the parking space left empty by Paula's frantic departure. "She nearly left skid marks."

"She was supposed to pick up her son. She was probably late." Monét brushed her hair back into a hair clip. "I can't believe how hot it is."

Zora opened the driver's door. The heat rushed into the car, and she slammed the car door behind it. She shook her head. "Can't you see it?"

"See what?"

"Forget it. I'm still working to apply our lesson to my life. I'm going to keep my mouth shut." Zora checked her watch. "We've got thirty minutes before we have to meet Victoria."

"Enough time for me to grab a cup of coffee."

"You just ate."

"But I need my sixteen-ounce hazelnut. It's my once-a-week treat. And you don't want a cranky maid of honor."

"To be so health conscious, how can you down a week's worth of caffeine?"

"You have your chocolate. I have my coffee," Monét said.

That wasn't a lie. The evidence of Zora's chocolate affinity still sat on her hips. She'd only run twice in the last two weeks, and neither time was enough to break a decent sweat.

"You know my heart dropped to my feet when you told Belinda you had to ask her a question. How do you keep your trunk so organized? Girl, I thought you were about to drill her about whether she was going to tell Hannah she's adopted. You know I can never be sure what's going to come out of your mouth."

"Have a little faith in me," Zora said. "I'll ask her that next time," she joked.

Zora followed Monét to the coffee shop, and she grabbed a table in the corner while her friend placed an order. She pulled out the list Monét had e-mailed to her on Friday afternoon. The proposed errands for the day were bulleted down the page. *How in the world are we going to do all this?* She dare not ask Monét. When it came to finishing lists, she was a machine.

Zora flipped open her cell phone and pushed the number preset to dial Preston. She hung up when she remembered he and Jeremiah were doing their male bonding thing. Unlike her, he seldom had the chance to spend any quality time with his best friend.

She turned her attention to Monét, who was at the counter talking to a handsome gentleman. He held what looked to be coffee-drenched napkins in one hand, but still managed to slip into his back pocket and retrieve a business card. Monét took the card and said something to him before walking away. He bent down to wipe up the mess left by his dripping napkins. A teenager with an irritated look on his face mopped the man and his mess out the door.

"Were you being picked up at the cash register?" Zora asked.

"Only as a potential client. He's in real estate—an agent

and a developer," Monét said.

"Victor Humphries." Monét read his card and dropped it on the table beside the sugar jar. The wooden legs of the chair scraped the hardwood floor as she took her seat.

Zora turned up her nose. "How can you drink something steaming hot when it's like three hundred degrees outside? I've never understood how people can do that."

"Only a coffee drinker would understand." Monét took another quick sip of the coffee before she switched her hat from girlfriend to wedding planner.

Zora only had herself to blame for falling behind schedule. She still had three months to go and the novelty of planning the wedding had worn off. Monét rattled off their priorities, and Zora was content to let her take charge. Eloping looked more tempting.

Zora was tired just thinking about their errands. Thirty minutes later she packed her notebook and Monét trashed her empty coffee cup.

"Isn't that Dr. Manns?" Zora noticed the man sitting on a bench near the elevator as they left the coffee shop.

"It sure is," Monét said, looking in his direction. She walked within his sight range so she wouldn't disturb his phone call.

"One minute," he mouthed, then ended his call shortly after.

Paula must have stopped by to meet her husband, Zora thought, looking at Dr. Manns. She wondered why he opted to wear that gold pinkie ring instead of a wedding band.

"I hope he doesn't try and turn this into a meeting for his association's next function," Monét said. "His mind is always thinking about business. Act hurried."

"It's not an act," Zora said, as Dr. Manns stood and slid his cell phone into the clip attached to his belt. "Make it quick."

Dr. Manns' conversation with Monét was less than inter-esting and proved Monét's theory that weekends weren't reason enough for him to rest from discussing business.

Zora noticed the man from the coffee shop coming up the nearby elevator. Evidently, Dr. Manns did too.

"See you tonight, Victor," Dr. Manns said.

Victor didn't break his stoic expression. He walked past Dr. Manns as if he were invisible.

"You know that guy? I just met him a while ago," Monét said. "He was talking about one of his real estate projects. Some land he's developing out in Prince George, I think."

Dr. Manns shoved his hands in his pockets and watched Victor walk out of the mall. "I don't know him, but evidently my wife does."

Awkward, Zora thought. Even Monét didn't know how to respond. They bailed out as soon as they scooped their chins off the shiny mall floor.

Zora didn't say what she wanted to, and she knew Monét wouldn't mumble a word of what she was thinking. Silence ushered them to the bridal boutique, and Zora's assumption never left her mind the entire time Monét and Victoria were trying on dresses.

Paula was cheating on her husband.

19

I *must've awakened yesterday morning with one less brain cell,* Monét reasoned to herself. Had thirty crept up on her and planted a seed of desperation? No. She wasn't desperate. Thirty was a reason to celebrate, and she intended to accept every offer to celebrate her entrance into her third decade of life.

Even Bryce's.

His walk had been smooth, almost a glide, as he entered the sanctuary on Sunday morning. Bryce had followed the uni-formed, white-gloved usher to the end seat on the fourth row. After sitting on the blue cushiony pew, he had propped his right leg over his left, showing his two-toned loafers.

Stacy Adams for sure, Monét had thought. Her seat from the choir stand had been the perfect angle to see him, yet pre-tend that she hadn't.

The agitation she felt from his unexpected visit to her home after the auction dissipated to a certain degree. He wasn't a bad person. His heart was in the right place. His character just needed to catch up.

Bryce's presence had made her anxious, though she wished it wouldn't. Nervousness had kept her eyes glued to the director during their song selections. Her eyes closed during her solo, then focused on the back of Pastor James's head during the sermon.

After the benediction, Bryce had waited at the bottom of the steps where she had to exit the choir stand. *Zora must not be around,* she thought at the time, knowing her friend would have intercepted him. It wasn't until later that evening that she realized Zora's disappearance was because of her surprise birthday party. The low-key family Fourth of July and birthday cele-bration on Sunday evening turned out to be an all-out bash.

Bryce had stood with his hands clasped in front of him. The lines of his suit were cut specifically for his body. The neck of his blue dress shirt stood open, free from the constriction of the tight-knotted tie he wore to work every day.

Monét had accepted his waiting hand and tripped down the steps. Bryce had placed her hand in the crook of his arm and escorted her to the side set of pews, away from inquisitive ears. He had turned to face her.

"Three minutes. That's all I need."

Monét nodded. That's all she could do.

Bryce had led them to the back pew in the corner section of the sanctuary and let her sit down first. Monét unzipped her robe and wiggled her arms out of the sleeves. It was getting hot.

Sister Maybelle had crept by, scooting her aging legs along and steadying herself every few steps at each pew. "I was blessed to hear you sing today," she told Monét. "You sing like an angel."

"Thank you, ma'am."

"And you're a handsome young man, too," she said to Bryce. "Real handsome," she said, and patted him on the cheek. She had caught her slipping dentures with her tongue and pushed them back in place.

Oh, my Lord.

Monét and Bryce had held their snickering until Sister Maybelle shuffled along.

"I need three more minutes," Bryce had said. His face turned serious. "First of all, let me apologize for my actions that Friday after the auction. In person. I know you got my messages, even though you never returned my calls."

Monét had stretched her arm across the back of the pew and turned her body toward Bryce. Two of her fellow choir mates caught her eye over his shoulder. She didn't react to their looks of wonder and attempts to talk to her through hand signals. She knew what their next conversation with her at choir rehearsal would be about.

"When I realized other people were there and you may have been seeing Preston's friend—"

"Jeremiah told you. We met that day."

"I know now. And I shouldn't have shown up unannounced. But when I saw you that night . . ." His words had trailed away.

Monét had almost felt bad. He seemed as if his feelings were truly hurt.

"You don't have to," he had continued, "but can you give me the chance to redeem myself? Let me take you out for lunch tomorrow. Consider it a birthday gift."

Before Monét knew it, she'd said yes.

Now she was waiting for him, sorting through the mail in her in-box to pass the time.

She unlocked her bottom desk drawer to get her purse. She wished she'd had time to change out the brown chunky bag for her everyday black tote. She unzipped the side pocket after noticing the bulge on the outside. The purse was barely used. It smelled like fresh leather.

It was her gift from Jeremiah causing the bulge. She'd

forgotten about it. He'd run back inside the house last night to give it to her after he and Preston said good-bye. She squeezed the square package. It felt like a padded envelope underneath the wrapping.

Jeremiah's presence had been a nice addition to the night. He'd mingled easily with her family and friends. Her mother, of course, had nothing but good things to say about him. Monét had kept an eye on her throughout the evening to make sure they were never alone for extended periods of time. It wasn't safe—for her or Jeremiah.

Monét had been pulled in every direction after the party. She didn't feel as if she'd spent the amount of time she wanted to with each guest. There were at least seventy or eighty people there. She couldn't believe they'd pulled it off without her finding out.

Nice wrapping job, she thought, taking off the red envelope with a miniature silver bow attached to it. The paper had red, white, and blue balloons. *Cute.*

Monét pulled out a clear CD case and could see the words "Lyrical Lady" written in black ink on the front of the CD. She opened the card first.

You said the whole nation celebrates, and I didn't want to miss out. I composed this piece, but words don't flow for me like music. This song is especially for you. Let's see what the "Lyrical Lady" can do. Happy Birthday. Love, Jeremiah.

Monét pushed the open button on her disk drive and slid the CD in. *An original song. This is a first.*

The computer hummed as it read the CD and automatically opened the music software. The first five seconds boasted Jeremiah's natural ability on the keys. She closed her eyes and enjoyed his jazzy style.

Knock, knock.

Monét opened her eyes to the light tap on the door and Bryce's voice.

"Looks like I need to learn to play the keyboard." Bryce walked over to her desk. "You ready?"

"Hi. Give me a sec," she said. *If only he knew.*

Monét hit the stop button, ejected the CD, and slid the case and envelope into her desk drawer.

"You look nice," Bryce said, commenting on her linen pantsuit.

I wish he wouldn't look at me like that. "Thanks," she said, following him out of the office and closing the door.

Thankfully, Jasmine had deserted her desk for her usual lunchtime stroll.

"Where are we going?" Monét asked when they reached his midnight blue convertible BMW. He opened the door for her, and she sank into the beige leather seat.

"Your gift, your choice," he said, shutting the door.

"Just ride and see what the stomach says," she said, and laughed when he said the phrase with her. It was the answer she usually gave when they were faced with choosing dining options. Before.

I'm fine with this, she convinced herself. Bryce filled her in on the latest news and developments brewing in the commissioner's office. His passion for his career was one of the things that had impressed Monét when she first met him. He wasn't shy about approaching her at the Young Professionals Mix & Mingle event. She'd been tired that night, but went anyway because she'd paid the fee for the network dinner. Bryce invited himself to sit beside her, and it turned out his presence made the night worthwhile.

Halfway to the strip of restaurants, Monét decided she wanted to eat sushi. She wouldn't mind a platter of California rolls and shrimp tempura. The lunchtime crowd was already bustling in and out of the restaurant. Patrons were packed shoulder to shoulder on stools at the bar. Those at the table barely had room to scoot back their chairs without bumping into the person behind them.

Good. Monét didn't have to worry about lunch being romantic. It was too bright and too noisy.

By the time they placed their orders and were served, Monét felt even more comfortable. She couldn't remember why she'd been so cold toward Bryce. Sure, he had a long way to go in his spiritual walk, but did it mean they couldn't be friends? Maybe she'd been too hard on him.

Monét felt the vibration on her leg from the cell phone set on silent in her purse. "Excuse me," Monét said. "This may be work calling."

It was Zora. Monét could imagine Zora's reaction when she found out about her lunch date—if she found out. She wouldn't be answering that call.

Bryce dropped a lemon in his water. "I'm glad you let me treat you today," he said, once she tucked her cell phone back in her purse. "How does it feel to hit the big three-oh?"

"I feel great." Monét pushed her glass back for the waiter to put down her platter of food. "I don't see why women get so bent out of shape. Thirty is great. I feel liberated in who I am."

"You do look settled," Bryce observed. "Life must be good."

"I'm blessed. Work keeps me busy, the city is alive, and my best friend is getting married."

Bryce dumped a bowl of rice on his plate and covered it with soy sauce.

"What are you going to do when Zora is a married woman?"

"Keep living," she told him, just like she'd told the countless people who approached her with the subject.

"Zora won't be able to roll out when and where she wants to. Your running partner can't live the single life anymore." He reached across the table and squeezed her hand. "If you get lonely, call me."

"I'll keep that in mind."

The waitress brought the rest of Bryce's order, and he held out his hand for hers. She bowed her head and let him bless the food. That was a change. She was usually the one who prayed.

Several times during lunch her thoughts traveled back to Jeremiah's gift. She needed to get his number so she could call and thank him. An original song had to be one of the most thoughtful gifts she'd ever received. The music had already burrowed its way into her mind. She couldn't wait until she could steal a free, relaxed moment with a pen and her journal of God-inspired poetry and psalms. Lyrics for Jeremiah's musical composition were sure to spill from her soul.

It turned out to be a day full of surprises, especially when Bryce started a conversation about Sunday's sermon. There was a time when getting him to remember, much less discuss, sermons was like pulling permanent teeth. Pastor James's topic on water-walking faith had left an indelible impression. It was a start.

"I know this gift is a day late," Bryce said, reaching into the pocket of his suit jacket that hung on the back of the chair. "But I couldn't come without getting you something."

"Lunch is more than enough," Monét said, though she still picked up and opened the envelope he slid across the table.

"A gift certificate for a couples' massage," she said.

"One for you and the person of your choice. Maybe you can take Zora."

Nice try, Monét thought. She knew he wanted her to take him, but she'd let him flounder and wonder. Maybe it *would* be him. If he acted right.

I don't think so.

Then again, Jeremiah was bound to be back to Maryland soon. Maybe I'll invite him. The corner of Monét's lip turned up at the thought.

"What are you smiling about?" Bryce asked. "I hope about me."

Monét's mouth was too full of shrimp and rice to answer. *If he only knew.*

And God, she thought to herself, *You know me better than that.*

20

Paula shuffled through the wad of bills and stack of mis-
cellaneous receipts stuffed in her red leather wallet. She knew
it was here somewhere. After the embarrassing episode at the
coffee shop a month ago, she at least owed Victor an apology.
She'd run off and left him with a pant leg soggy and stained
from her tea spill.

That day of her personal disaster, the nation had been preparing for fireworks for the next night. But none compared to the
explosion that erupted in her house when she returned home.
Both of Darryl's cars were in the garage when she pulled in.
To her relief, there was no sign of her luggage or any tossed
clothing along the front lawn.

Paula took a deep breath before she turned the doorknob.
She didn't know what awaited her behind closed doors. She
hurried Micah to his room and went into her bedroom.

"I hope you don't think you're staying here tonight,"
Darryl said, once she walked into the bedroom and closed the
door behind her.

"I'm not going anywhere." Paula tried to keep her voice

and legs steady. They'd already betrayed her once today. She put her purse on the edge of the bed. "It wasn't what you think. It was on old friend I happened to run into."

"How long ago was that?" Darryl walked out of the master bedroom closet with a piece of Paula's Louis Vuitton luggage in each of his hands. He unzipped them and opened them up on the bed.

"Today." Paula zipped them back up when he walked into the closet.

Darryl's face was covered by the stack of clothes in his arms when he returned. He dumped half a row of her slacks on the bed. The reaction she was waiting for finally came.

"Don't play me, Paula!" he yelled. "You think I'm stupid. Is that what you think? I'm a *doctor*, Paula. There's not a stupid bone in my body."

"You're the one who thinks I'm stupid. You walk in and out of here at your own free will. Staying some nights, going to sleep with your little side gig on the next. You think I don't know?" Her throat felt raw from screaming.

"What do you know, Paula? What have you seen? Huh? Tell me that." He walked into the closet and grabbed another armful of clothes. This time when he walked out, he slung them on the floor.

She had to jump back so they'd miss hitting her legs. "I've seen you walk away emotionally from me and Micah. I've seen you not give a flying flip about the baby I'm carrying. Your baby, Darryl." Tears stung her eyes. She could tell without seeing them that they were bloodshot red.

Their argument lasted until the entire room was blurry. He accused, she denied. She accused, he denied. They were both worn out by the time they noticed Micah standing in the door-way with tears in his own eyes. They retreated to their separate corners.

Paula sat down in the chaise on her side of the bed and let

Micah crawl into her lap. She comforted him until his sobbing stopped and his conversation turned to the latest action figure toy he wanted her to buy. Darryl grudgingly picked up her clothes and hung them back in the closet.

It was the end of what could've turned into a night of terror, had it not been for their innocent son.

Paula finally found Victor's business card stuffed between two Neiman Marcus receipts. She leaned the card against the base of the phone in her office. She'd call from her business line, or rather what she called her business line. She'd insisted that Darryl have it set up to help her field calls coming in for them regarding his latest association function. Paula wasn't for having their personal information floating amongst any event committee members.

The number on Victor's card was listed as a cell. She called, half hoping she'd have to leave a message and spare herself the shame. Still, part of her wouldn't mind a couple of minutes of conversation. He made good company.

"Victor Humphries."

"Victor. Hi, this is Paula Gilmer. Well, Manns. I hope I didn't catch you at a bad time." She heard the noise of machinery in the background.

"Paula." His voice sounded surprised. "Hold on for a second. Let me go where I can hear you."

Paula heard the faint crunch of gravel under his feet. The sound soon quieted along with the other machinery grumblings.

"Hello?"

"I'm sorry to disturb you," she said. *Maybe I shouldn't have called.* "I don't want to pull you away from business."

"I was just walking through one of the development sites, taking it all in."

Paula felt bad about disturbing him at work. "Don't worry about it. I can give you a call another time."

"Paula," Victor said, "it's okay. I was leaving anyway to go pick up my boys from summer camp. I'm glad you called. I've been worried about you."

"You were worried, and I was embarrassed," she admitted. "That's why I was calling. To apologize."

"No need to apologize. When you step back and look at things, the scene could've easily been twisted into something that it wasn't."

Paula settled back into her high-back leather chair. "I think Darryl did a little more than twist it." She swiveled her chair around, looking up and down the ceiling-high bookcases.

"Paula, if you remember anything about me, you know I shoot straight from the hip," Victor said.

"That I do know."

"So tell me. What's really going on between you and your husband?"

"I'm not tipping out on him, if that's what you're thinking." Paula stood up and walked over to one of the shelves that covered an entire wall. She pulled out a book about avoiding marital conflicts. It looked like the pages had never been turned.

"Never thought or said that, but I can tell when something's going on." Victor laughed. "That exhibition at the mall made it pretty obvious."

Paula had to join his musing for a minute. It was easy to laugh things off in hindsight. At the time she didn't see the least thing funny. Paula thought she heard a car door slam. She walked to the hallway where she could hear better.

"Plus I'm going through my own situation, so I can feel things," Victor said.

"You can feel things, huh?" Paula peeked in on Micah sleeping. He'd curled himself into such a tight ball that she could barely see his face. She opened his door all the way, then went downstairs.

200

Paula felt safe putting a small piece of her personal business in his hands. After all, he'd seen the drama with his own eyes. "Our marriage is going through some challenges right now."

"As all marriages do," Victor said.

"Insecurities on my part and his, I assume." She didn't assume anything, but the reason sounded good.

Was she supposed to admit to the possible infidelity in her household? She still hadn't proved it, and Darryl wouldn't admit it, but she wasn't convinced the real estate ventures were the only thing keeping him away from home.

"We're working it out." She opened the door leading out to the garage. The car door must have been her imagination.

"As long as you feel safe." Victor paused a minute. "There aren't any other issues, are there?"

"No." She knew where he was taking the conversation. "He's not putting his hands on me."

"Verbal words can hurt just as bad. We're all guilty."

Who was he telling?

The only reason she hadn't had to go off lately was because she and Darryl had rarely been home at the same time.

"I don't want to keep you." Paula didn't want to be drawn into a conversation about her marital woes. "I just wanted to call and say I'm sorry for the way I ran out and offer to pay for the dry cleaning for your pants."

"The pants were brown. You couldn't see the stain anyway."

"I'll take your word for it."

"Or I can send your husband the bill."

"Funny. Real funny." Paula watched a butterfly land on her kitchen windowsill. Its wing fluttered, inviting her outside to enjoy the remainder of the day. Maybe she'd take Micah to the park. He'd need to release some of his boyish energy after being cooped up inside.

"You call me anytime, Paula. I mean that. Sometimes you just need somebody to listen."

"I know what you mean." At least she knew someone had his ear out. Evidently God was ignoring her pleas. She'd wasted so many words praying for Darryl already.

21

August had to be the hottest month of the year, and this would probably be the hottest day, Zora thought. She rang the doorbell at Celeste's apartment. The temperature had hit eighty before Zora returned from her jog at nine o'clock. If it wasn't for this P.O.W.E.R. meeting and having to meet Preston to pick out tuxes, she would've hibernated in the comfort of her air-conditioned home.

Then on the other hand, she needed to get out of the house so she wouldn't spend the day strapped to the endless Internet sites or stacks of resource books from the library. A month had passed, and Zora still had no solid leads in her search. *Faith without works is dead.* It wasn't always enough to believe if she didn't put action to it. God couldn't say she hadn't.

Zora had to do something. Her intermediary hadn't returned any information, though he'd assured her that he was following every basic search protocol, and then some. He was committed to searching for her family as if it were his own, and would work until all reasonable leads had been exhausted, or so he claimed.

Her online comrade, Solo, shared the information he'd collected for himself, with hopes that it would help her, though it had brought disappointment for him. Her results were no different. She'd done almost everything she knew to do.

God, don't You see my effort?

"Hi." Celeste startled Zora when she swung open the door. "Zora, right? I still need to work on putting names with faces."

"You're probably doing better than me," Zora said, stepping inside. She walked directly into the living room and, looking around, realized she was the last to arrive.

"Hi, ladies. Sorry I'm late." She sat down beside Belinda, who patted her knee.

"Hey, girl."

"Hey."

Zora looked around Celeste's living room. Her green thumb showcased an array of pothos ivy houseplants, hanging fern baskets, and other greenery. Even the air fresheners made the room smell as if she were sitting in the woods, instead of in an apartment building in the city.

Monét sat on the other side of Belinda, engulfed in a conversation with Paula for most of the time before Sister Barnes quieted the group and opened the session in prayer. Afterwards, the women explored the Scriptures during their study of serving others. Although women shared their experiences and battles with the issue, Zora still sensed a barrier. Their conversations and confessions were safe.

It was, after all, their second monthly meeting together. She didn't necessarily expect them to divulge all of their personal matters. She held her own secrets. Who didn't? Maybe that was part of the problem. Her own were getting heavier to carry alone.

You don't have to.

Casting this care on God wasn't as easy as other problems she'd endured in life. At the time those seemed insurmountable. But looking back, all of them together weren't as taxing as this one. Zora fought to pay attention during the session, but her thoughts kept floating off.

Following the lesson, the women were divided into smaller groups according to their seating arrangements, leaving Zora in a group with Belinda, Monét, and Paula. Sister Barnes assigned each subgroup to a presentation based on one of the upcoming precepts.

Zora considered it a blessing to work with at least two people she connected with. Her bond with Monét went without saying, and Belinda was warm—a mother figure of sorts, even though there was only eleven years' difference in their age. Then there was Paula.

Zora figured she'd only have to endure her coldness for as long as it took for them to finish their project on hospitality. But known by now for her fabulous ideas, Jewel suggested they keep the same groups for a prayer circle.

It was actually a great idea to have prayer partners. Zora wasn't against praying. But to have to pray with and for someone who had made a career of giving her the cold shoulder whenever she came around . . . that was unfair. But then again, with all the things God had shown her mercy and grace toward, she didn't want Him to be fair. His way was fine with her. She'd deal with it. She'd said to herself before that she would pray for Paula, but never did.

She'd been drawn to Paula since the first time she'd seen her. Maybe this was the reason—to pray for and with each other. Zora was doubtful she and Paula would ever be friends, but at least they wouldn't be enemies.

You have to pray for your enemies too.

Zora made plans with Monét, Belinda, and Paula to meet

next Saturday. Today was one of those days when she preferred to be alone, so she headed out.

Confess your trespasses to one another, and pray for one another, that you may be healed. The effective, fervent prayer of a righteous man avails much.

The Scripture in James 5:16 stuck in her mind. It was the one nugget from the session she remembered hearing. It was the only word God needed to speak to her heart at this moment.

Yes, God was with her. But her sisters in Christ were too.

God, is it time? Do I really have to share the secret I'm ashamed of?

Zora didn't hear an answer.

❧

Preston could tell Zora's mind was elsewhere. He said he was going home to let her spend some quality time with God, and then he'd meet her later at the house for a quiet evening and a stack of rented movies.

Zora had been dealing with an undeniable push to obey the voice of God. It had grown stronger from the time they chose Preston's tuxedo cut, and heavier on her heart through their decision on the coordinating vest for his groomsmen. She had to get home to find her father's proposal letter to her mother.

The other half of the time, she'd brooded over her unwillingness to share about her adoption with her group members or anyone else. She'd convinced herself that it was a situation that couldn't be helped by the ladies, unless there was the far-fetched possibility that one of them held a piece to her puzzle. But this feeling wasn't about finding someone who could lead her to her biological family. It was about being set free.

It's time. There's no shame in My plan for your life.

Yes, Lord. Zora pushed the remote and backed her car into the garage. *I hear You.*

৯২

Zora pulled out the hope chest, tucked away in the far corner of her bedroom closet. She opened the chest lid and lifted out a quilt her mother had made when Zora was first born.

Her mother loved to tell the story of how Zora always wanted to drag the quilt around from the time she could walk. Everywhere she went, no matter the season, Zora wanted to bring it with her. Her mother finally had to break her of the habit the summer before she started kindergarten. From what her mother said, it was worse than the horrors of teething, ear infections, and potty training combined.

Zora propped the quilt on top of her dry cleaning pile, then lifted out the box that held her father's proposal letter to her mother. She'd been so bitter at one time that she'd decided not to use the framed memoir. Zora sat on the edge of the bed, then slid back to the middle of the plush comforter. Zora moved slowly as if a sudden movement would cause the box to explode.

The memory that led to the morning when she first discovered about her adoption opened fresh in her mind as she lifted off the box top.

Zora, Monét, and Mama Jo had met for an early breakfast before arriving at the first bridal boutique when the doors opened. She'd scheduled three appointments for that day and wanted to get an early start.

Monét and Mama Jo's reactions to the first three dresses had been nominal. Then Zora slipped back into the dressing room to try on the fourth gown, with the boutique consultant close behind her.

Even she hadn't realized the splendor of her fourth option

207

until she walked out of the unmirrored dressing room and onto the stage of the showroom floor. Mama Jo teared up, and Monét just looked and covered her mouth. Other future brides and their entourages stared at the sight before their eyes. She felt and looked like an angel.

Then the next morning she went to her parents' house to find her mother's veil, and she ended up feeling like an angel who'd crashed from heaven. Her life changed. Then . . .

Then I stepped in to carry you.

An overwhelming peace that Zora couldn't describe swept over her as she looked at the proposal letter. She would find a special place for it in her wedding ceremony, after all. Her parents were part of God's plan for her life. She wept and released the weight of harboring her secret.

"You're right, God. There's no reason to be ashamed of the life and family You chose for me. Your will and Your ways are perfect."

As always, God's Word that Zora held hidden in her heart was unearthed. *He heals the brokenhearted and binds up their wounds.*

It was time for the true healing to begin.

Part Two

One secret." Zora folded her arms then propped her elbows on the table. She, Belinda, Paula, and Monét were cramped close enough around the small table for their knees to touch. They were supposed to be discussing the presentation for their P.O.W.E.R. project, but after praying for God's direction over the past week, she knew there was a matter to be taken care of before they could move forward.

Belinda took off her reading glasses and set them on the crease of her open notebook. Zora sensed that Belinda thought this little secret confession was child's play. Monét's pursed lips were turned up slightly on the side—a smile hovering at the corner of her mouth. Paula snapped her compact closed and slid it in a leather makeup case. She'd popped a piece of gum in her mouth before she finally realized she was being stared down.

"This façade is getting old," Zora continued. She shook her head. "All of this . . . this . . . this pretending we have it together when we don't." Zora felt more relaxed. To know she was delivering a message from God eased her stress. All she could do was be obedient. The rest was in God's hands.

"If we're going to walk together, then we've got to be real," Zora said. "How can we bear one another's burdens if we don't even know what the burdens are?"

Belinda nodded, picked up her glasses, and used them to push back her hair. She closed her notebook. "You're right. It's a trust issue. Sisters have to trust each other."

Zora repented in her mind for being skeptical at first. Belinda had connected with her, and she knew the other ladies would follow suit.

"I'm glad somebody agrees with me." She held her index finger and thumb less than an inch apart. "Because I was this close to quitting. I keep thinking about other things I could be doing."

"Me too," Belinda said. "My mother isn't progressing as quickly as we'd hoped."

"Considered it myself," Paula said, with no reason attached.

"I need as much Jesus as I can get, so I'm in it to the end," Monét said. "Dare I admit I do have a confession, or secret, as you say, to own up to?"

Zora cocked her head to the side and lifted her eyebrows in wonder. "As does everyone at this table." She shook a packet of sugar, then ripped it open. "No time to sugarcoat anything," she said, dumping the contents from the package.

"Let's pray first," Belinda said, holding her hands out. "I know we've been placed in each other's lives for a reason."

"God doesn't operate by coincidence," Zora said.

"How did I know you were going to say that?" Monét hooked her hand in Belinda's and held open her palm for Paula's commitment. "Let's commit to holding each other accountable."

Zora took a deep breath and felt the veil covering their

lives lift as Belinda began to pray.

"God, I thank You for the women's hands that I hold. I thank You that You've called us to walk together for such a time as this. Use us to be a blessing and speak into each other's lives. We lay down our perceptions and reservations. Do what needs to be done. Move how You want to move. In the matchless name of Jesus we pray. Amen."

Zora clasped her hands together and put them in her lap, then set them on the table. "I guess I'll go first," she said, bringing her hands up to her lips. She closed her eyes. When she opened them she looked at Monét first. Monét's eyes held reassurance. She already knew.

Belinda was rubbing her silver locket between her fingers, and even Paula sat motionless.

"Five months ago I found out I was adopted. My parents never told me." She added to Paula and Belinda, "They were killed in a car accident on New Year's Day."

"Oh Lord," Belinda said, and closed her eyes. She shook her head like the news had come about someone in her own family.

"It's okay, Belinda," Zora said. "I take it one day at a time. God is keeping me."

"Bless the Lord," Belinda said.

Five months ago I found out I was adopted . . . The confession set Zora free. She'd been trapped by her perception of what others would think. Of her. Of her parents. She didn't cry. It was amazing how much of a relief she felt.

"I may never know why they didn't tell me, or if they planned to tell me later. Right now, believe it or not, I know about as much as you do."

"I never expected you to say that," Paula said in disbelief. "Any of it."

Zora saw compassion in Paula's face for the first time. "And I never expected any of it to happen," she said, then took them back to the day of how and why she found the letter. "I've been too ashamed until now."

"Of course this makes me think about my own daughter," Belinda said. "How and when we're going to tell her."

"Your daughter is adopted?" Paula asked. She didn't seem disinterested like she had earlier. "Why did you decide to adopt?"

"I guess that means I'm next," Belinda said. "I don't really consider this a secret, but it is an *issue*," she said, choosing the word as if she'd be judged by them.

But Zora knew their critical eyes of judgment had been discarded.

"My husband, Thomas, and I wanted to start a family as soon as we got married. I was thirty, and he was thirty-three, so we felt we were established and ready to handle the responsibility of having a child."

Hannah, who until then had been sleeping peacefully at Belinda's side, began to whine.

"Right on cue," Belinda said, and unsuccessfully tried to give her a bottle. She cried even after Belinda checked her diaper and found it dry. Hannah made it clear that neither hunger nor a soggy diaper was the problem. She simply wanted out.

"After eight years and no pregnancy we considered adoption, because we knew we wanted to be parents. We have so much love to give. Not to mention that the way the world is today, somebody had to raise a godly seed."

"Amen to that," Monét said.

"To make a long story short, Hannah came into our lives on December third. She was two days old. We went through a Christian adoption agency and had countless interviews with the counselor and biological mother. She was a teenage mother who wanted a closed adoption. No contact at all."

Belinda counted the steps on her fingers. "The interviews,

background checks, the whole gamut. And I would do it all over again."

"What about your husband?" Paula asked.

"Thomas was more than supportive when I went through times of questioning my womanhood because I wasn't able to have children. I've had problems with polycystic ovarian cysts since I was in my twenties. I was pretty resigned to the fact that I probably wouldn't carry children. Then I met Thomas, and our relationship grew to thoughts of marriage, and it became a reality. I thought I'd experience motherhood from the start, because Thomas had a son, and we planned to file for full custody when we married."

Zora pushed her seat away from the table and crossed her legs. "I didn't know you had a son too. I've always looked at you like you'd be a compassionate mom. The kind everybody wished they had."

"Evidently, Thomas Jr.'s mother didn't think so," Belinda said. "She didn't like it one bit. And let me tell you, it was not pretty. She fought tooth and nail and eventually disappeared. It was literally like she dropped off the face of the earth."

"And you've *never* seen him again?"

"Never."

Paula shook her head. "If my husband ever disappeared with my son—" She took a sip of her cranberry juice. "I don't want to think about it."

Belinda put her hand over her heart. Tears began to fall. "At the time I felt that us having a child together would help heal his pain. It's not that I felt like I could replace his son. It's so hard to explain your reactions when you let your emotions rule your life."

The atmosphere at the table was thick, but the ladies continued to press through. Thoughts about their presentation had been shoved aside, along with their study manuals and café menus. While Belinda had poured out her heart, a cautious waitress approached their group. After the waitress saw Zora pass Belinda a tissue, she quietly turned aside.

Monét spoke up after the women had a chance to digest Belinda's testimony.

"Even after what you shared, Belinda, I can tell you're happily married," Monét said. "I can see it all over you. You too, Paula."

Zora hoped so. They might all find out differently before their confessions were over.

Monét patted Zora's shoulder. "My best friend is about to join the ranks with you ladies, and most people think I'm about to go through some sort of depression. But I can honestly say that I'm fine with it. It blesses me to see her with a man that I know God chose."

"Thank God," Zora said. " 'Cause you should've seen the ones *I* chose." She looked at Monét. "Don't say a word."

Monét ran her fingers across her mouth like she was zipping her lips. "Anyway. Like I was saying. I've tried to walk upright. I've kept myself celibate for seven years and literally had to flee from some situations."

Zora could vouch for that. Most of her running was from Bryce.

"I can't look at Zora's reaction on this one," Monét said.

What in the world is it?

"This guy Bryce—"

Not Bryce!

"—has all the pieces, but he has the one missing key element. His relationship with God is not like it should be. I admit that, but he's grown. A lot. Especially over the last month or so. He took me out to lunch for my birthday, and even the changes since then have been more than over the past two years. He even prayed for me last week when I was having a bad day. He's never done that before. He's still got things to work on, and I admit that. But don't we all?"

216

Zora crossed her arms. She wasn't saying a word.

"We do," Belinda said. She lifted Hannah to her shoulder. Her daughter had grown tired of the stuffed bunny rabbit keeping her entertained, and wanted to see what was going on around her.

Monét glanced at Zora, then turned her conversation to Paula.

"Why should I totally cut him off because of that? At one time my relationship with God wasn't where it is now, but somebody took the time to lead me back on the right path when I strayed."

Paula was sliding her wedding ring on and off her finger. She must've thought Monét's question was rhetorical, because she didn't say anything.

"Zora can tell you. My parents were strict when it came to living according to God's Word, but I still had to go through my process of coming to God on my own, with my own heart. Bryce didn't have the benefit of being taught as a child. As sweet as his parents are, they don't have a relationship with God. Bryce isn't at fault for that. Is it fair for me to turn my back on him because he doesn't meet a certain standard? How effective would I be in the body of Christ if I only ministered to other Christians?"

Zora slid her chair up to the table. She had to add her two cents even though Monét had heard it from her a hundred times before.

"It's not entirely about Bryce meeting a certain standard. It's about keeping yourself emotionally distant and not becoming involved with him when you know you're not equally yoked. It would be different if there were never any interest, but you were mutually attracted to each other, so there's a fine line there."

Belinda cradled a now calm Hannah in her arms and rocked her back and forth. She stuffed a handful of Belinda's shirt into her mouth, soaking it with dribble. Belinda didn't try to pry her shirt out of her daughter's grip. Anything to keep her calm.

"So there's always that chance of slipping back into a non-platonic relationship," Belinda added. "Before you know it, your friendship will be more about the two of you and not about leading him to Christ."

Exactly, Zora wanted to exclaim. It was so clear, but for some reason Bryce always clouded Monét's vision. Monét was fine as long as she didn't see him. His auction appearance must have opened the door again, she assumed. *Monét was rambling*, Zora thought. Who was she trying to convince, the ladies or herself?

"Maybe you can refer him to one of the young men at your church to disciple him," Belinda suggested. "Or what about your fiancé, Zora?"

Both Zora and Monét knew that wouldn't fly. "They're cordial to each other, but they've never hit it off like that," Zora said.

"Oh, I see."

Paula finally spoke up. "I wouldn't suggest getting involved with a man who's not on your spiritual level or doesn't want to be. Like one of my girlfriends says about her husband, you might as well marry the devil."

"I wouldn't go that far," Belinda said, even though she laughed. "Marriages can be restored, but it does take a lot of work. Thomas and I have counseled couples at our home church. We've worked with couples working together to save their marriage and those where only one spouse was willing to fight. Sometimes that's all it takes. That one person. Everything in marriage is not always fifty-fifty."

Paula leaned forward. "Why should you fight for something if your spouse doesn't want it?" she asked, tapping her index finger on the table to emphasize her point. "The way I see it, a woman should have a little dignity."

Belinda passed Hannah to Monét, then was quick to share her knowledge. "To you, Monét, when it's all said and done, you have to make your own decisions. God isn't going to force you to do something, but He will give you all of the signs to warn you ahead of time if the choice is wrong."

She then turned toward Paula. "It's not about dignity. It's about honoring the covenant that you took before God. Even if the marriage fails, you can stand before God and say that you gave it everything you had."

"Hmph," Paula huffed.

She muttered something under her breath that Zora couldn't quite hear. "What?"

"Nothing," Paula said. She looked at her watch as if the conversation about marriage had ruffled her feathers and it was time to change the topic. "I guess it's my turn." She called the waitress over and insisted to the ladies that they order food first because she was starving.

"I have two secrets," she said, once the waitress scampered away. "Well, not really secrets. More like a confession and an announcement."

Paula turned to Zora.

Why is she looking at me?

"Zora, the first thing I want to do is apologize for being so cold toward you. This day has helped me see that you're a nice person and not the nut I thought you were."

Zora had to laugh at that one. She didn't take offense to Paula's words. When she thought about it, her approach had been rather aggressive.

"I'm woman enough to take that," Zora said. "I should be the one apologizing to you not only for *my* actions, but for my perceptions of you. As far as I was concerned, you had rich snob written all over your face."

This time it was Paula's turn to laugh. "Well, half of that is true," she said. "But I'm not snooty. At least not all the time."

Belinda stepped up to her usual role as counselor and mother figure. "It seems to me it was just the Enemy's plot to bring unnecessary friction between two godly women. So since we know he's not capable of telling the truth, we're going to dump these preconceived notions and start from scratch. Fair?"

"That's more than fair to me," Zora said. "We're too old for this nonsense anyway." She stood up and walked to Paula's side of the table and opened her arms for a hug. They'd finally accepted each other. "Besides," she said, "you wear some cute clothes, and we look like we're about the same size."

"Pretty soon I won't be able to squeeze into them anyway." Paula patted the bottom of her abdomen. "Which leads to my other announcement. Surprise. I'm pregnant." She bit her lip and cast an apologetic glance at Belinda. "I didn't know if it was appropriate considering the conversation we just had."

Belinda stood and hugged Paula. "Of course it's appropriate; don't be silly. It's a blessing from God." She reached to the table, picked up her glass of cranberry juice, and lifted it in the air. "To new life," she said.

Monét bounced Hannah in one arm and passed each of the ladies their drinks. They circled together, shoulder to shoulder, signifying their new bond together.

This was what Zora had envisioned. From this point on they would bear one another's burdens.

Paula sipped off the top of her juice before raising her glass. "And new expectations."

"And new trust," Monét said, holding her glass beyond Hannah's busy hands.

"And new friendships," Zora added last.

They clinked their glasses together, then had to break up their circle to let the waitress by. This time, they sat down as sisters instead of group members.

220

Finishing their project was a breeze, and they held their table hostage long after the waitress cleared away their empty plates. They babysat their drink refills and shared a slice of banana cream pie. The meeting was supposed to last an hour, but three passed with no thought to the time.

"Uh-oh," Belinda said when Zora's cell phone rang. "Somebody forgot to check in."

Zora looked at her watch. "We're supposed to do our wedding registries today."

"Hi, baby," she sang into the phone. She winked at the ladies and stuck out her tongue. "Yes. I'm almost finished. Uh-huh." She crossed her eyes when Preston reminded her of their obligations. "All right. I'll see you in a bit."

"Party is over, ladies," Monét said, turning up the last sip of tea in her glass. "I need to get out of here myself."

Paula slung her Louis Vuitton purse over her shoulder. She pulled her shirt down over her pants' waistband. It was the first time Zora noticed the stomach pooch.

"Big plans, Monét?" Paula asked.

"If you call a pedicure and manicure big plans, then yes."

Belinda buckled Hannah into her stroller and squeaked one of the toys attached to it when Hannah started to whine. "We should get together more often. P.O.W.E.R. doesn't have to be the only thing that brings us together."

"You ladies are more than welcome to come to my make-a-wedding-favor party in a couple of Sundays."

"That's a new one," Monét said. "How many other people are invited?"

"Just you guys so far."

Belinda pulled the shade over Hannah's stroller and unlatched the brake. "I have the feeling we'll be the only ones. Just call me. I'll be there if I'm in town. I'm looking forward to some time at home with Thomas soon."

That wasn't the only thing that was going to happen soon,

Zora thought. Everyone's life had entered another dimension. When Paula prayed, and they'd stood in agreement, the Lord saw their desires. He was even going to deal with the secret things of their hearts that only He knew.

Zora just wondered whose breakthrough would be first.

23

Paula couldn't bring herself to tell the truth. Besides, the situations of Zora and Belinda were something they had no control over. Monét still had time to make an intelligent decision. Paula prayed she did. No one, not even her worst enemy, deserved the walk she'd made for herself. She wasn't a saint, but at least she was making an effort to do right.

As she drove to pick up Micah from her mother's house, she questioned her actions, or lack thereof, over the years of her marriage. Though she didn't think she'd done anything deliberately to tear her marriage apart, she certainly hadn't contributed to making it more successful.

Paula hadn't planned to announce her pregnancy yet. It wasn't her first child, so she was starting to show much earlier than she had with Micah. Her clothes still hid her growing frame enough to go another few weeks without anyone noticing, but she'd had to say something convincing. A woman saying that her marriage was failing was like a woman admitting that she was a failure.

Speak life over your marriage.

Paula's eyes began to burn. She reached into her purse for a handkerchief and dabbed it under her perfectly lined eyes. The more she dabbed, the heavier her tears flowed, pouring out her frustration, anger, and self-pity. The handkerchief was smudged with black mascara. She could imagine how her face looked. She was desperate for a touch from God. Anything to change her life and set it and her marriage on the road to restoration.

Paula knew she had a tough exterior with a soft interior. The stress she carried couldn't be healthy for her baby. Their baby.

At least he'd acknowledged the baby last night.

"How are you feeling?" He'd tossed his briefcase onto the bed and loosened the tie around his neck. He slid the loop over his neck and walked into the closet.

Paula knew he was hanging the tie on the rack with the others in the same color family. They all looked the same to her, but he was particular about their grouping.

"Fine, for the most part," she had answered. "A little nausea here and there. Tired. But that's about it."

"Didn't you say you had a doctor's appointment?" He had unbuttoned the white dress shirt and slipped his arms out of the sleeves.

"That was last week," she had said, watching him tinker around the closet in his cotton T-shirt and work slacks. She'd told him with hopes that he would want to come to the appointment to hear the baby's heartbeat for the first time. He'd been on clinic rotation and couldn't get away.

"Everything was routine, and the doctor gave me a prescription for prenatal vitamins."

Darryl had put on a lightweight polo shirt and changed his belt. "I'm going to meet with some of my partners. I'll take Micah with me."

How does he expect Micah to entertain himself while he conducts his so-called business?

"He's not going to be able to sit still. You might as well leave him here."

"I was trying to get him off your hands for a while so you could rest."

"Fine, take him. But don't call me to come pick him up later."

Darryl had walked out of the room shaking his head. She could've handled it differently. She hadn't accounted for the fact that he had tried to make an effort. The damage for that night was already done.

At today's meeting Paula thought Belinda had made a good point about keeping her covenant with God. *"Even if the marriage fails, you can stand before God and say that you gave it everything you had,"* she'd said.

But giving all she had was so hard. Paula was truthful with herself. Her last attempt to live her marriage according to the Bible and not her emotions had lasted all of two days, if that.

You're operating in your own strength.

Now Paula was prepared to fight. She deserved it; her children deserved it. As far as she was concerned, Darryl deserved it, even if he didn't realize it. What man in his right mind wouldn't want a woman like her? The thought boosted her ego.

God, I'm going to fight for my marriage. I promise.

Paula pulled over into a gas station and wheeled her Range Rover into an empty parking space blocking a pay phone. She wasn't worried about someone having to use it. Every person walking around these days seemed to have a cell phone strapped to his or her ear.

She folded the tear-soaked handkerchief inside out. She opened up a bottle of water in her cup holder and put the handkerchief over it, tipping it just enough to dampen the cloth. Pulling down the sun visor, Paula did her best to clean her tear-streaked face and raccoon eyes, then remembered her mother's home remedy for makeup removal. She dug around in her purse for the tube of petroleum jelly lip balm. *Perfect,* she thought, squeezing a smidgen on her index finger and rubbing it under her eyes. The makeup was easily removed with the handkerchief. It was a little greasy under her eyes, but she'd wipe off the excess before she arrived at her mother's.

Since Paula had dropped Micah off at her mother's house on Thursday night, her mother, Rosanna Gilmer, had added a new hanging plant to the rows that already lined both sides of the screened-in porch. After pressing through the miniature jungle, Paula rapped on the screen door and pulled the handle, knowing it was unlocked. Despite Paula's urgings, her mother walked around as if her community and the world were as safe as they were forty-three years ago when she first moved into the house.

Paula jumped when the door with the loose hinges slammed behind her. She grabbed her chest. The security of her gated community made her tense up at every unsuspecting noise.

"We're back here," Rosanna called from the backyard.

Paula found her mother rocking on the only glider chair that would fit on the small back porch. Unlike the small front yard and cluttered screened-in porch, the backyard was fairly spacious, with only a small garden patch that her mother used experimentally to grow vegetables. Other than that, there was a colorful plastic jungle gym she'd purchased for the grandchildren.

Rosanna was wearing her favorite outfit—an ankle-length jean skirt with a yellow cotton T-shirt. She had a closet full of identical skirts, but changed the shirt color to suit her mood. A black headband pushed back the hair she refused to cut above her shoulders.

Rosanna waved at her daughter. "I didn't expect you to —"

"Hey, Aunt Paula," her seven-year-old nephew, Javon, yelled as he bolted past her. A red cape flapped wildly behind him. It had to be Micah's. It had the same rip in the corner.

Javon's ten-year-old sister, Yvette, followed closely behind him, but she stopped for a breather when she saw her aunt.

"Hi, Aunt Paula," she said, brushing her frizzy bangs aside. "Watcha doing here?"

"I'm coming to pick up my son, if that's okay with you," Paula said. She lifted Yvette's ponytail tied on top by a yellow ribbon with pink polka dots. Never mind that she wasn't wearing either color.

"He's not here," Yvette announced just as Javon swept by and slapped her shoulder.

"Tag," he hollered.

"Ow, boy," Yvette screamed and took off behind him. "I told you I wasn't playing anymore."

"What does Yvette mean, Micah's not here? Where is he?"

"Darryl came to get him. I thought you knew. I figured you were coming back to get his cape. I can imagine he's screaming to high heaven for it."

Of course she didn't know. The cape was the last of her worries. "Probably miscommunication."

"Right. I thought he'd be here until at least this evening."

"What time did Darryl pick him up?"

Rosanna looked in the air like the answer floated above her head. "Around eleven." She looked at her plain white-faced watch with a fake leather strap. "So just a few hours ago," she said, staring at her daughter's face. "Why does your face look so greasy?"

"Oh." Paula ran her pinkie under the rim of her eyes. "A new eye cream I was trying."

"Another fancy treatment to break your purse. All you need is a little Vaseline."

It does work wonders, Paula thought. "I better get home before Micah wears Darryl out."

"Let his daddy take care of him for a change." Rosanna cocked her neck up toward Paula.

You got that right. Paula kissed her mother's waiting cheek. "Don't start, Mother." She felt the need to protect her husband. Or was it her marriage's image? "Darryl spends time with Micah."

"Whatever. And don't call me Mother. I'm Mama. Like I always have been."

Paula saw her mother's eyes travel down to her belly. She pulled her shirt down, straightened her posture and tried to suck in her stomach. Not today. Her mother could be, as sweet as she wanted to be, or as bitter as she wanted to be on any given day. She'd be thrilled about the prospect of another grandchild, but would find something negative to say regardless.

"Bye, guys," Paula yelled to her niece and nephew. She picked up her step and ran out of the house for two reasons. One—she didn't want to chance running into her sister, who was sure to join her mother in any insults they could conjure up about Darryl. And second—she wanted to know what possessed Darryl to pick Micah up out of the blue.

Paula repeatedly called home and to Darryl's cell phone, but both phones kept transferring to voice mail. Even paging him didn't work.

He wasn't making her promise to God easy.

You promised Me, not your husband.

At least Darryl was at home. Paula pulled between Darryl's vehicles. The convertible top on his Jaguar was folded into the compartment on the back of the car. Surely he hadn't ridden home with Micah with that top down. It wasn't safe for a child, even if Micah was in the backseat.

"Hello, guys," she sang, putting as much sweetness in her voice as she could muster.

Paula wanted to set the right temperature in her house. She thought back to Pastor Griffin's sermon from when she first returned to church. There had been many of his messages that she'd enjoyed in-between, but that one struck close to home. She reminded herself to go back and review her notes and Scriptures.

Paula didn't see or hear Darryl or Micah, though the evidence of their arrival was spread across the marble countertop on the kitchen island. A half-eaten order of French fries smothered in ketchup lay beside a kid-sized soda cup. She shook it. Empty. It was going to be a long, hyperactive night. She lifted the corners of a hamburger wrapper and dumped it and the rest of the meal in the stainless steel trash can by the refrigerator.

That's when Paula noticed them. The scene unfolding outside was the picture she wished she could see more often—Darryl pushing Micah on the swing. It was swinging too high for her taste and motherly protection, but Micah was oblivious to any possible danger. Fear of broken bones or knocked-out teeth evidently didn't live in the mind of her husband. Still, it was a sentimental thing to see, and it chipped away at the fury that had encased her from the time Yvette had made her innocent announcement.

Suddenly, it didn't matter that Darryl had picked up Micah. Why should it? He should've called to let her know. True. It would've been the considerate thing to do. True. He could've at least answered her pages. What if it had been an emergency? It was all true and valid. But in the large scheme of life, did it matter?

One thing Paula's mother had told her before she got married was to pick her battles. This one she'd lay aside. She had a larger battle to fight—the one to save her marriage.

Paula opened the patio door and stepped out into the eighty-nine-degree summer. She squinted from the high afternoon sun as she walked down the deck steps and into the expansive backyard. The landscaper nurtured the golf-course-green grass until it felt like carpet under their feet.

"Mommy, watch this!" Micah yelled. He pumped his legs back and forth furiously, as if doing it hard enough would make him fly. And fly he did. He let go of the swinging chain when he reached the peak of his ascent. It was so sudden that Paula didn't have time to react. He landed on all fours.

She looked at Darryl, who seemed more amused than concerned about his son's circus act. When he looked at Paula, his jaws tightened. It was amazing how they'd both mastered jumping between emotions.

Set the temperature.

"Wow. Make sure you're careful when you do that." She'd be sure to tell Micah about the danger when Darryl wasn't around.

Micah ran up to her, his chest swollen with accomplishment. "I've been practicing," he announced. "Daddy taught me how."

Paula kept the look of disdain from her face. She looked at Darryl as she kissed the top of Micah's head. When Micah took off for the slide, she walked over to her husband. "Thanks for getting him something to eat. Have you had anything yet? I was thinking about broiling salmon and making a field green salad for lunch."

"That's fine."

What? "All right. I'll go in and get started." His responses

230

never ceased to amaze her. Of course, he was probably wondering why she hadn't questioned him. She wasn't going to give him the drama he expected.

"I don't think it's a good idea for you to dump our son off just because you want to go hang out with some of your girlfriends."

"It was actually a meeting with a women's discipleship group from church."

He grunted. "Oh, that again. We know what it led to last time. A secret rendezvous."

She overlooked his comment.

"Mama has been wanting Micah to come spend the weekend with her for a while, so I don't consider it dumping for him to go to his *grandmother's* house." She turned around before he had a chance to respond. "I can't believe how hot it is today. I'm going inside where it's cool. I'll call you when your salmon is done."

ᘓᘐ

After taking Darryl his lunch outside, Paula pulled out a dining room chair and ate her lunch inside alone—with her thoughts. It had been a long time since Darryl had spent quality time with Micah, and she could tell that her son was soaking up every minute of it. Since his flying trapeze stunt, he hadn't run inside the house once to plead for a snack or explain his latest imaginary invention. He hadn't even asked for the cape she forgot to reclaim from Javon.

Micah had found a yellow oversized plastic bat under a bush and was swinging at the air, so far missing every pitch Darryl threw. It took several chances before he finally connected a hit, running around the bases but forgetting to drop the bat. Paula was the missing piece to the happy picture outside.

After she ate, Paula retreated upstairs to her bedroom. She pulled out her Bible, ready to arm herself with ammunition for her battle. She wasn't sure where to start, so she leafed through the pages, praying God would send her a sign—like blink a light, slam the bedroom door, anything. She laughed at the absurdity of it all. If God did deliver a sign like that, the last thing she'd be doing was sitting there reading her Bible.

Not knowing what else to do, Paula stopped to read a Scripture whenever she saw a highlighted passage in her Bible. There was a time years ago during her thirst and hunger for God that she read her Word more frequently. Then she quenched her desire for God with a desire for Darryl, but that was about to change.

One particular Scripture stood out to her as powerful. She digested the words from Isaiah 55:11. *So shall My word be that goes forth from My mouth; it shall not return to Me void, but it shall accomplish what I please, and it shall prosper in the thing for which I sent it.*

Paula prayed. She didn't try to use eloquent words to make her sound spiritual, but words of sincerity. Her spirit was broken and her heart contrite.

Lord, show me. If I have to sit here all night, I will.

She didn't have to sit all night. God's direction was clear.

Speak life to your marriage. Speak My Word.

If His Word always did what it said it would do, there was no reason why she couldn't pray God's Word for Darryl's life. It only made sense to pray God's Word back to Him so it could touch their lives. Duh? Hadn't they talked about that in their first P.O.W.E.R. meeting? She had the power in her tongue.

Paula remembered that her P.O.W.E.R. manual had a section on marriage. She pulled out the notebook she'd tucked under the bed, away from Darryl. She'd written some personal notes along the margins and the self-assessment exercises that were reserved for her and God's eyes only. The lesson on mar-

232

riage wasn't for another two sessions, but she needed it now.

Paula carried her materials into the office. She shuffled through the caddy on her mahogany desk and found a pink highlighter. She crawled into the love seat by the bay window and propped her feet on the round ottoman. She read the study Scriptures from the P.O.W.E.R. manual and highlighted them in her Bible, until the business phone rang.

That was rare for a Saturday unless an event was close on the horizon. Paula had the annual events memorized. She was in the clear, at least until the holidays.

"Manns residence." Silence. "Hello?"

"Paula?"

"Victor?" *Victor!*

Paula ran over to the window. Darryl and Micah were still outside, though Darryl was taking a break and eating his lunch at the patio table. Micah, however, was still in high gear.

"Victor. I don't think it's a good idea for you to call me. What if Darryl had answered the phone?"

"I would've said I had the wrong number." Victor exhaled into the phone. "I'm sorry. I just wanted to talk to you. It's been one of those days, you know?"

Paula went back to the love seat. She held her page with the highlighter and steadied her Bible on the arm of the chair.

"Okay. But next time, let me call you."

24

Even without ten years of marital counseling experience, Belinda would've been able to see that Paula's marriage was in trouble. Because of her ministry, God had sensitized Belinda to the heart of women, especially hurting ones like Paula. Whether it was clothed behind a secondhand store dress or a designer boutique dress, the hurt was the same.

In due time Belinda would speak a word into Paula's soul. It had to be when Paula was open to receive it and when she could believe that restoration was possible. Right now, she was acting as if her situation didn't exist. She'd attributed her own troubles to that of a friend. That was about the oldest trick in the book, Belinda thought.

She opened the front door and was surprised to see that the house was as lively as it would've been before her mother's illness. Her mother was still weak, which kept her from moving about as much as she wanted, but Bernice sat in her favorite recliner with her feet propped up on an ottoman. The television was on full blast.

She's definitely getting back to her normal self, Belinda

thought, turning the volume down as she passed the television.

"Here she comes, trying to run stuff in my house," Bernice said. "Leave my television alone."

Belinda set Hannah on the floor and propped up her body with pillows from the couch. "Hello to you too, Ma."

"I already told her that thing was too loud," Aunt Wanda said. As usual, she was in the kitchen, preparing enough meals to last Bernice for a few days. "She acts like she's deaf, but she can hear somebody whispering from the next room."

"Only if they're talking about me or something I need to know about," Bernice said. "God gave me extra radar after I had those kids."

"Belinda should know that. She jumps up at every grunt and whimper Hannah makes no matter where she is." Aunt Wanda set the timer on the oven and settled at the kitchen table with the daily newspaper.

Belinda poured herself a cup of orange juice and sat down on the arm of her mother's chair. The color was trickling back into her mother's face as the days passed. She could tell her mother was getting better because she was growing vainer with each passing day. Last week she asked for Belinda to paint her toenails. Belinda acquiesced, even though she didn't do feet. And her mother knew it.

"Just to make you feel better," Belinda had told her mother. "But this is the first and last time this will ever happen." She'd spread a towel out on the floor in front of Bernice. "Ever."

Bernice had tried to hide the smirk spreading across her face, but it was as if her expression were taunting Belinda for a comment. Belinda bent over and rubbed the cotton ball soaked with polish remover across her mother's toes. She wasn't going to humor her that day, even though she was tickled on the inside.

Belinda's mouth spread open with a yawn.

"Good gracious," Bernice said, patting Belinda on the back. "I could see your stomach when you did that. Why don't you go take a nap?"

Aunt Wanda butted in the conversation from the kitchen. "Don't worry about Hannah," she said, looking over the top of her reading glasses. "It's not like she can go anywhere."

Hannah was finding pleasure in beating on the pillows around her and stopping every now and then to clap her hands together.

"I think I will," Belinda said. "I'm pooped."

She got up and headed back toward the bedrooms. "Just bring Hannah to me if she starts acting out."

"Go," Bernice shooed. "She's not even paying attention to you right now. Scat out of here before you give her a reason to cry."

"I'm going," Belinda said.

As soon as she changed into more comfortable clothes and stretched across the bed, she was glad she'd stolen some moments away by herself. The times were rare. She was thinking about going home on Monday. Her mother was fairing well and was able to do more things on her own now. She just had to take it easy and not push herself. God was working things out in His timing.

That's the same thing she was going to tell Zora. God's plan would never fail as long as she stayed obedient to His voice, like she'd done today by challenging them to be honest.

As for Monét, she'd just have to see. Monét admitted that she knew better than to connect herself with someone who— she wasn't equally yoked with. When people can't warn a person, God has a way of opening her eyes.

25

Bryce had left a voice message on both Monét's home and cell phone while she was meeting with her P.O.W.E.R. prayer partners. He'd offered to cook dinner tonight.

While most men would throw together a pot of spaghetti and heated a pan of frozen garlic bread, Bryce boasted the skills of a master culinary chef. Lemon-crusted salmon, sautéed asparagus, brown rice, and squash casserole were set for his dinner menu. Monét could taste it already.

Monét had called him back and accepted the invitation for an eight o'clock dinner, despite the discussion and advice she'd received earlier that day. It was about what she wanted right now. *What's wrong with that? I'm a grown woman. If things get too deep, I'll pull back like I always do.*

If she wanted to be honest with herself, she'd tell herself that things were getting deep. The more time she spent with Bryce, the more Monét felt her grasp slipping from the strings holding her heart.

But she was still in control. On two occasions Bryce had

escorted her home after they met for a late evening movie. There had been no sexual innuendoes or aggression. He kissed both cheeks and left like a gentleman. Was it wrong for her to wish he'd at least tried? Whoever held the rejection held the power. She needed to reject him. She needed to know she held at least an ounce of power over him.

Monét hit the prompt on the phone to play the next message.

"Hi, Monét. This is Jeremiah. I'm sorry it's taken so long for me to call you back."

Oh, now you want to call back after over a month.

"I know," the message continued as if he'd anticipated her thoughts. "A month is pretty ridiculous. I've been working a lot of overtime, and I didn't want to call you too late at night. But enough of the excuses. Whenever you get a free moment, give me a buzz back. Hope you're somewhere writing lyrics for your song. Talk to you later, Lyrical Lady."

Jeremiah was a sweetie. His voice was as relaxing as his music. Now was as good a time as ever to return his call. She didn't want another month to pass. Besides, she wasn't expected at Bryce's for another three hours.

Jeremiah answered the phone with Fred Hammond's latest CD playing in the background.

"Hey, you. It's Monét." She pulled off her flat embroidered slip-in shoes and plopped down on the beige microsuede sofa. "Did I interrupt the maestro while he was composing a masterpiece?"

"The maestro is too tired right now to be creative."

"I can call you later," she offered, though in her mind she was disappointed. She enjoyed their conversations.

"You're harder to catch up with than me," Jeremiah said. "I'm not letting you go anywhere."

"Well, I guess that settles it," she said.

"As a matter of fact, I will call you back. Hang up and I'll call you so you won't be charged for the call."

"You don't have to do that."

"I want to," he said. Jeremiah hung up.

Monét did the same, and her phone rang a few seconds later.

"I never thought you'd be the kind of guy to hang up in my face," she teased.

"How can I make it up to you?"

Was he flirting? "Let me think about that one."

Like the two times before, their conversation flowed with no effort. Even after two hours on the phone, a lull never settled on their conversations. Jeremiah was easy to talk to. They related to each other in more ways than their musical talents. He was an African-American history buff as well, and read about the history of other cultures. Monét's love of the same is what sparked her interest in working for the cultural arts center in the first place.

Jeremiah didn't try to impress her with a list of achievements. He was comfortable being himself. More so, he was confident in his faith and didn't try to downplay his love for God. She could sense it in his character and his conversation.

Monét knew she wouldn't mind getting to know more about Jeremiah on a personal level, but the miles between them prevented that. It wasn't worth the trouble or the possible heartache. She'd thought she would've been able to sustain a relationship with Terrance, an old flame, but she soon learned that their levels of commitment weren't mutual after he moved to California. It wouldn't have taken her as long to come to her senses if he'd lived close enough for them to spend quality time together. Quality time was one of the glues that helped hold a budding relationship together. Glue wouldn't stick from Maryland to Texas.

So far, she and Jeremiah had never mentioned their past relationships, although Monét was curious about his. She guessed that was a little too personal. How much should she expect him to divulge after only three conversations?

Zora had already told her that he had previously been engaged. It seemed to her that his ex-fiancée had missed out on a good thing. But then again, there were two sides to every story.

"So what are your plans for tonight?" Jeremiah asked.

Monét looked at her watch. Another hour had slipped away. She was supposed to be on her way to Bryce's by now. She walked into her room to decide if she should change out of her clothes.

"I'm having dinner with a friend," she said, noticing a tiny nick in her fresh manicure. "I should be headed out the door," she said, though she was disappointed to have to end the conversation.

"If you don't mind, I'd like to give you a call every now and then," Jeremiah said.

Of course. "I'd like that," she said.

"And next time I'm in town, you'll have to show me the culture of the city. I may have to come back up in a few weeks."

Monét was amazed that her heart fluttered. No one since Bryce had been able to do that. "You've been up here a lot lately." She joked, "Are you sure it's for your job, or does Preston need a little moral support before he takes the plunge?"

"Preston would get married tomorrow if he could," Jeremiah said. "Zora doesn't have to worry about him getting cold feet. She has him—hook, line, and sinker. That's what a good woman will do to a man."

"So I've heard," Monét said. "Speaking of being hooked, seems like your job has you pretty reeled in."

"My company is doing a lot of reorganization and is going to merge with one of the Baltimore firms. I'm on the team to help ease the transition and help the project manager divvy up the new and existing projects."

"Sounds exciting."

"Sometimes. But I'm ready to have my life settle down. Have the Lord bless me with a wife, start a family. Settled."

At least he's not running away from commitment and responsibility, Monét thought.

"The Bible does say that he who finds a wife finds a good thing. You might want to start looking," Monét said.

"Who said I wasn't?"

All righty then. Monét stretched across the foot of the bed. She decided not to change out of her Asian flair kimono and wide-legged drawstring pants. That would buy her some conversation time.

"What kind of woman are you looking for?" Monét asked. *This should be interesting.*

"God-fearing, focused, supportive of God's vision for our family. Beautiful—inside and out," Jeremiah added. "I'm not going to act like I don't care about waking up every morning beside a fine woman."

Here it comes. "Halle Berry fine, huh?"

"No. A woman who carries her unique beauty like she knows she's a queen. Like she knows she's fearfully and wonderfully made."

Now he's trying to drop a little Scripture on me.

"I need a woman who can roll with me," Jeremiah added. "There's so much to offer in Houston. I can't imagine myself living anyplace else."

The dream bubble in Monét's head popped. God's man for her was in Baltimore. She was sure of it.

"Hello?"

"I'm here," Monét said.

"Well, you probably shouldn't be," Jeremiah said. "I don't want to be the reason you're late for dinner. I'll catch up with you soon. I still want to try and hook up next time I come up there."

"Call me," Monét said. "We'll work it out. Better yet, drop me a quick e-mail if you're busy with work. I know how that is," she said, and gave him her work e-mail.

"Will do."

"I think I'll work on my song when I get back," Monét said. "Did I tell you how much I play it? It was the perfect gift."

"Good. That means you owe me a personal serenade. Talk to you later."

"Bye," she said. Singing in front of a crowd was one thing. One-on-one was another. Besides her family and Zora, she'd never been that bold, not even with Bryce.

Monét freshened up a bit, grabbed a bottle of sparkling grape juice, and headed out the door. Bryce lived in Pikesville, a short ride, but long enough for her to think about Jeremiah the entire time. Long enough for her heart to do that thing again that she was going to ignore.

≈

Bryce's cooking skills were more than fabulous. By the time Monét finished dinner, she was starting to think that Bryce had missed his calling.

"Are you sure your heart is set on politics?" Monét tipped back the last sip of sparkling juice that Bryce had poured in wine glasses. She'd thwarted his attempts to be romantic and requested they eat by the fluorescent kitchen light instead of by the candlelight he'd planned. She'd also nixed the radio's quiet storm and turned on the television.

Bryce had jazzed up his apartment quite a bit since the last time she'd been there. He'd thrown splashes of color around the room with red accent pillows on the couch and an area rug. There were also two impressive pieces of Black art added to the wall decor in his entryway. Monét could tell they were prints by Romare Bearden.

No doubt, the changes came from a woman's touch. She knew. Besides, Bryce wasn't the type to have scented candles in his bathroom either.

Throughout dinner, Monét saw the line that Belinda and Zora had talked about. She was trying to stay on the friendship side, but she could tell he was crossing it, despite his assurances before that a friendship was all he wanted.

"I know the way to a man's heart is through his stomach," Bryce said. He rinsed off their plates and put them in the sink. "I hope it's true for a woman."

"Bryce." Monét stood to help him clear the table. She knew what was coming.

"I'm just kidding," he said, and winked at her.

That wink. He used to always get her with that wink.

"Just admit that we've been having a good time together lately," he said.

Monét handed him the two glasses. "I'll admit that."

"So I hope you'll consider helping me entertain my parents in a few weeks. They'll be here for nine days, and that's eight days more than I can bear."

Monét knew where he was coming from. Bryce's father, Floyd Coleman, was laid back, but his mother was more than a handful. Because he was an only child, Sylvia Coleman had a tendency to hover over her son. She was as involved in his life as much as she could be at five hundred miles away in Pennsylvania. If it weren't for her husband's stubborn insistence that he'd never abandon his home of thirty years, she would've made a move to Maryland by now.

"I'll consider it," Monét said. "It depends on how my schedule is looking. I've got so much on my plate planning Zora's wedding and all."

"My mother would love it."

Monét smirked. She didn't bother to respond. She knew Bryce was being sarcastic, because they'd had numerous discussions about Sylvia's overbearing ways when they were dating. She leaned against the kitchen counter and adjusted a stack of coasters. *He's come a long way since the round disposable ones he used to have, she thought.*

"Speaking of your mother, did she add this flavor to your apartment?"

Bryce laughed, but didn't respond.

She knew what that meant. A twinge of jealousy arose in Monét. She dried their glasses and put them back in the cupboard. *That's new too,* she thought, spotting a crystal punch bowl. Not that a man couldn't have a punch bowl, but Bryce didn't roll like that.

"I hate to eat and run," Monét said.

"We didn't finish watching the rest of the movie," Bryce said. "That's the least you can do to please the chef."

"You're not being fair. That's manipulation."

"I can't help that I like spending time with you. I'm not being manipulative. I'm being real."

The phone rang, but Bryce ignored it. He ignored it the first time and the next five consecutive times that it rang, even after looking at the caller ID.

"Maybe you should get that. Evidently it's an emergency if a person is calling back-to-back like that," Monét said. It was starting to work her nerves.

"Don't worry about it."

The phone rang again, and Bryce finally turned off the ringer. He took Monét's hand and led her around to the couch.

Monét sat down, but she had no intention of staying.

Bryce's cell phone began to ring and vibrate across the coffee table. He turned it off immediately.

"I'm sorry, Bryce. I can't. Dinner was wonderful, but I have to go. My choir is singing in the morning, and I don't stay up late on the night before the mornings I have to minister." Monét put her purse on her shoulder and went to the door.

"I'll see you in the morning then," Bryce said.

Tonight, he knew not to push it.

"Pastor James said that this week he is going to start part two of his sermon on living the abundant life," Bryce recalled. "He really said some things that stuck with me a few Sundays ago." He slipped his hands around Monét's waist and pulled her to him.

Bryce leaned forward to kiss her, but Monét turned her face. His lips landed on her cheek. Soft and warm. Then they went to her neck. "If I could just experience love with you for one night," he breathed. "Just one."

Monét let his lips find hers. It had been a long time. She dug her fingers into his biceps and pushed him away, though it wasn't immediately.

"I'm sorry," he said. "You're just—" he ran his palm down the side of her face "—so beautiful."

He was trying to take her there, but she wasn't going to let him. It would be so easy to slip in, close her eyes, and. . . . She felt it from the touch of his lips. It was a familiar place that she would visit one more time. *Just this once.*

I shouldn't be doing this, she thought as Bryce covered her lips again. She pulled away.

"See you later," Monét said. She bit the corner of her lip and shied away from him.

"Tomorrow," he reminded her, turning her face back to his before he let her go.

Bryce walked her to the car and pulled her into a tight embrace before he opened the car door. He didn't have to say much. His body spoke for him. Monét jumped into the car and sped away. She couldn't handle it tonight. She tried to keep her mind off him, but their kiss and embrace kept trying to replay in her mind.

Her attention was soon diverted to the driver trailing close behind her with his lights on high beam. The one-lane road to the highway didn't allow for the car to pass or for Monét to pull over.

A mile down the road, Monét pulled into a gas station, and the car followed. She pulled up to the gas pump, and the car crept by. A girl with tousled hair pulled into a ponytail on top of her head peered into the car. Monét watched the car circle around the gas station, then leave in the direction they'd just come from. *Evidently a case of mistaken identity,* Monét thought. A woman scorned on the hunt for her man. Well, he wasn't in her car.

The gas station was in a well-lit and fairly busy area, so Monét decided to fill her tank. She'd noticed on the way to Bryce's that it was creeping down to just above a quarter of a tank. Her dad wouldn't be pleased. He didn't believe in letting a gas gauge drop to under half-full.

She slid her debit card in the automated machine and unhooked the gas pump handle.

Before she knew what was happening, a car screeched to a halt in front of hers. Within seconds, the deranged-looking woman who'd left the scene earlier was in her face, spitting out a string of curse words.

"I don't know who you think you are, trying to sneak around with somebody's man, but don't try to play me."

"I think you've got the wrong woman." Monét shoved the gas pump into her tank and tried to stay calm. "I don't know anything about your man."

"Oh, so now I'm stupid," the girl yelled. Her eyes nearly bugged from her head.

Monét saw a woman peek her head from around a gas tank from two stations over. The patrons going in and out of the store didn't seem to be paying them much attention.

"I just saw you hugged up with Bryce outside of his apartment. I just told you, don't try to play me."

Monét's defensive instincts kicked in, and she raised her

voice to match her attacker's volume. "It seems to me you should be taking this up with Bryce, not me. Trust me, I'm not so desperate that I need to be with somebody else's man."

Calm down.

Monét had to stop herself from going off. Better to err on the side of caution. She didn't know what this chick was capable of. Her heart pounded in her chest.

"Is everything all right out there?" A voice from an overhead speaker disrupted their altercation. "I'll call the police."

"Please do," Monét said. She glared at the girl, but remained calm.

"Watch yourself," the girl said. She went back to her car and disappeared as fast as she'd come.

"Thank you, sir," Monét said. She waved at the cashier attendant who was looking out of the bullet-proof window. "I think everything is fine now."

Monét finished pumping her gas, the whole time watching to see if the woman would make another appearance. When things looked safe, she hit the route back to her house. She was still shaken up and decided to call to chat with Zora on the way home. It would help calm her nerves, but there was no way she'd tell Zora about what had just happened. She couldn't believe it herself.

☙

Monét entered the dark loft, lit only by the angel nightlights her mother bought for the hallway and the small light she'd left on over the stove range. She immediately noticed the blinking red message light on the phone cradle and figured it was Bryce calling to wiggle his foot further into the open door. If it was, she'd call him back with a few words of her own. Of course, if she did that, his fatal attraction was bound to be at his house and retrieve her number from his phone. She looked like the kind of woman who'd do that. She'd wait.

Monét pushed the code to retrieve the message, then cradled the phone between her shoulder and chin.

"Hi, Monét. This is Jeremiah. I know you're somewhere enjoying your dinner. My turkey sandwich was off the chain too, just in case you wanted to know."

She laughed with him.

"I wanted to call back and tell you how much I always enjoy talking to you. I can tell you're one of those good women who can make a man want to be hooked. Whoever finds you will definitely find a good thing."

So sweet.

"And for the record," he said before he hung up, "you've got Halle beat."

Zora was going to flip over that.

Monét found her journal and got under the covers, fully clothed. She turned to the empty page after the last poem she'd written. She couldn't let these feelings pass without putting them to words.

Bryce. Despite the craziness she'd just experienced, there was a part of her heart that wanted him.

Then there was Jeremiah. He wasn't like anyone she'd met before.

Was it possible for a woman's heart to want to be in two places?

26

Three hours passed before Belinda opened her home office door. Thomas had graciously offered to tend to Hannah while she caught up on the magazine's production schedule. Her eyes had grown weary from proofreading the article copies. It seemed like the font size shrunk with every issue. She straightened the papers and slid the manila folder into her desk stack file.

Belinda pulled off her reading glasses and let them dangle from the chain around her neck. She walked out into the hallway and lifted her arms, stretching the tension from her back, then sank her toes into the plush almond-colored carpet. When they first moved into the house after getting married, she'd insisted they install new carpet instead of keeping the light ivory color the previous owner had throughout the house. Her choice was in anticipation of the small tribe of children they'd have that were sure to leave smudges, spill juice, and walk around with their feet dirtied from outside play.

It was nice to have slept in her own bed for the past two

days. Belinda missed the familiarity of home—the smell of Thomas after a fresh shower, the warmth of falling asleep snuggled close to him while he prepared for his Sunday school lesson. Then there was her morning routine. At seven o'clock she was awakened by the strong aroma of the dark coffee dripping from her automatic coffeemaker that she'd preset the night before. Getting a good night's sleep and sleeping in to well past mid-morning was like heaven.

As Belinda walked toward the wonderful aroma coming from the kitchen, she thought about how nice it was that Thomas could take care of Hannah, cook, and not even have to wake her once. She pushed aside two boxes of clothes that the UPS man had delivered earlier that morning. They were addressed to Thomas, but didn't have a return address. They'd been collecting items for a church clothing drive and had sent out a mass e-mail to their e-mail address books. No doubt someone had cleaned out their teenage son's closet and donated them to charity. The young fellow's closets were probably so packed with the latest fashions that he wouldn't miss them, she and Thomas had mused.

Belinda heard the faint sound of music. She rounded the corner and saw Thomas standing by the stove. With his back turned she could clearly see his birthmark—a small patch of grey hair—about the size of a silver dollar—on the left side near the crown of his head. When they'd first started dating and she'd met his parents, his mother shared the story she used to tell Thomas as a child about his patch. God, she said, had dropped an extra dose of wisdom on his head as a child. His mother's theory proved to be true. He'd always been wise beyond his age. Most importantly he was wise in the Word of God. The fruit he bore in his life proved it.

Belinda walked over and kissed his shoulder blade. She rubbed her hands down the slope of his shoulders.

"Mmm . . . smells good in here."

"Thank you." Thomas picked up a bottle of marinade sauce and shook it over the chicken cubes browning in the skillet. "Hannah is down for a nap. Not sure how long it's going to last though."

Belinda leaned against the kitchen island and watched Thomas prepare the chicken. He slid it on the skewer along with slices of red and yellow peppers and grape tomatoes. Her stomach rumbled. She didn't realize how hungry she'd been.

"You've got a whole island thing going on here," she said, just noticing the Caribbean flavor to the music.

"I'm taking you on a mental vacation," Thomas said. He lined the skewers on a platter and covered them with foil. "Stay here," he instructed. He opened the patio door and squeezed outside without opening the wooden vertical blinds.

Belinda was thankful for her husband. She needed a break from her caregiver role. A teething seven-month-old and recovering mother had exhausted her. For the next week, her mother was in the able hands of Aunt Wanda.

During the time she was at home, two of the college students from Thomas's Sunday school class had volunteered to take turns babysitting Hannah. Thomas had arranged it himself. God knew what she needed. He always did.

She also knew that God knew her heart. How it still ached to conceive a child. To experience the miracle of life inside her belly. She'd felt jealousy creep in over her joy for Paula. She didn't like that feeling, and it was one she didn't want to repeat.

Then there was Zora's confession. Two years ago, Belinda experienced peace and joy in accepting God's call to adopt. Now she began to wonder how their choice to adopt would affect Hannah when she was old enough to understand.

"Honey, can you pour two glasses of pineapple tea?"

Belinda looked toward the patio door. Only Thomas's head was visible, stuck between two slats of the blinds.

"Sure," she said.

Then there was Thomas. He'd nurtured her through the shame she felt and the unending questions of when she'd give her husband a child.

Thomas said their lives were one. She hadn't failed to give him a child. God was the giver of life, and He never fails at anything. Belinda didn't want to burden him with her insecurities again. These feelings were selfish. Her thoughts should be on her mother and the blessing God had given them with Hannah.

The tea, Belinda reminded herself. She got two glasses from the cupboard and filled them with chipped ice from the automatic dispenser.

Thomas is my husband. There shouldn't be any feelings I can't share with him.

"Ready to eat?" Thomas walked inside and pulled the cord to open the blinds.

The tiny sip of tea made Belinda's taste buds dance. She tipped back the glass and took another swallow of the sweet, tangy beverage before handing a glass to Thomas. She followed him to the deck, grabbing the baby monitor along the way.

"What's that?" Belinda peered out into the back of her manicured lawn. A huge red ribbon flapped against one of the oak trees.

Thomas headed out toward the area and she followed, setting their tea and the baby monitor on the patio table. Getting closer, she noticed a rope hammock fastened between the trees. It was the exact one she'd had her eye on at the lawn and garden center for some time.

"Now you can steal away anytime," Thomas said. He held down the side of the hammock so Belinda could ease on. "It's not on a deserted island, but it's as far away as Hannah and I can stand you being away right now."

"You're pitiful," she said, and caught her balance before

swinging the rest of her body into the hammock.

When Thomas released the hammock, Belinda and the hammock flipped over.

Belinda yelped. She caught on to one of the knots above her head and barely caught herself from falling out. Her laughter and her nearly upside-down state prevented her from regaining her balance.

Thomas jogged to the opposite side of the tree and steadied the hammock again. "And I'm the pitiful one?" He jerked the side, threatening to dump Belinda on the carpet of grass beneath her.

"Don't you dare, boy," she said, grabbing to the leg of his jeans.

"Oh, so now I'm a boy?" He rocked the hammock again, and Belinda squeezed his leg tighter.

They'd always been a playful couple. It was one of the characteristics that kept their marriage fresh.

"I give," he said, rubbing his leg after she loosened her grip.

Belinda looked up at Thomas, standing over her like a guardian angel. She needed to talk to him. She wanted to dump some of her feelings so somehow he and God could help her put the pieces together.

"Lie down with me for a minute," Belinda said. "Very slowly," she cautioned, in case Thomas still had a trick up his sleeve. She let him adjust himself on the hammock, then positioned her body so she could lie on his chest.

His heart's rhythm spoke in her ear. The breath streaming from his nostrils tickled her forehead. She matched her breathing with his. He was calm and peaceful.

She was, too, after sharing her thoughts.

"There's no reason to be ashamed of our feelings," Thomas said. "And the worse thing to do is bottle them up and not talk about it. Whatever, whenever, you come to me.

We'll work through this no matter how long it takes."

"I just don't think it's fair for me to think this way when we've been so blessed with such a beautiful child," Belinda said. "I want to be the kind of parent to Hannah that God is to me as His child."

"You are." Thomas kissed her cheek. "And you will be. To Hannah and any other children God brings to our lives."

Belinda was nervous at that thought. She'd barely gotten used to one child, and here Thomas was talking about another one.

"One at a time. We're not spring chickens."

"Speak for yourself," he said, covering her face with kisses. He lifted her arm and ran his lips from her forearm to her fingertips. "Tonight might be our blessed night."

"What about our food? We need to eat."

"We will. Later. I've got something tastier in mind."

Thomas swung himself off the hammock, then scooped up Belinda. He moved as if he had the bedroom or the closest room he could get to on his mind.

She didn't care what this man said. She was hungry, and she was eating first. From the looks of things, she was going to need her energy all night.

※

Belinda had just pulled the bed comforter up past her waist and turned on the light on her nightstand. Aunt Wanda called right when it crossed Belinda's mind to call and check on her mother before she went to sleep. It was a luxury to make it to bed before midnight these days.

"I'm fine, Aunt Wanda. I was just about to call you."

"Belinda, is Thomas there with you?"

Belinda's heart quickened. Aunt Wanda would only ask that if something was wrong. "Aunt Wanda, what is it? Please.

Just tell me." Belinda's demand held more than she might have been able to handle.

"We're at the hospital. Your mother fainted while we were at home so I called the ambulance. They rushed her back to ICU, but we're still waiting to hear from the doctor."

"I'll be there as soon as I can." Belinda had already kicked the covers back and was shedding her pajamas.

She turned on the bedroom light and looked around the room for the jeans she'd worn earlier. After their romantic dinner and time alone, the last thing they'd been concerned about was putting their clothes in the hamper.

"Thomas," she called out. She made her way to the den where he watching the late-night news. "Thomas."

He stood when he saw her, obviously alarmed by the frantic look on her face.

"It's Ma. They had to rush her back to the emergency room. I need to go."

Thomas threw out questions, digging for more information. It only irritated her. The only thing she knew was that she needed to get to her mother. She turned around and ran up the steps, with Thomas's footsteps pounding behind her.

"Sweetheart, I know you're scared, but you've got to calm down and get yourself together. It's not helping anything for you to be frantic."

Belinda paused for the first time since she'd hung up the phone. Thomas walked to her and wrapped his arms around her waist. Her head fell against his chest, and the tears took over her frenzy.

"God please touch my mother," she cried. Belinda didn't think she had the strength or mind-set to pray, but the words flowed. "You can do what the doctors can't, and we know You have the final say. I pray for the doctors who are with her. Anoint their hands. Use their minds to think, and give them clear and precise direction. In Jesus' name, amen."

Thomas kissed her eyes and ran his thumbs under the wetness gathered around her eyes.

Belinda rubbed the muscles in Thomas's back. "I already know what you're thinking, but I'd rather you stay here with Hannah. Diane is still coming over to babysit for the rest of the week, and God willing, I'll be able to come back and pick her up."

Thomas agreed. They threw together enough belongings to last Belinda a few days. She tiptoed into Hannah's room and leaned over the crib rail.

"Be good for Daddy," she whispered, and kissed her forehead.

Thomas followed her out to the car and put her bag on the backseat. "Don't worry about anything here. We'll be okay. Things will be just like they were when you left."

Belinda nodded her head, though Thomas's comment left her wondering. If his words were true, why did she feel the uneasiness in the pit of her stomach?

27

Four voice messages, four hang-ups. Monét was fed up. Whoever was pulling this childish prank accomplished what he or she had set out to do. Annoy her.

She'd drilled Bryce about the incident the other night, and about whether the girl that had accosted her had any way of getting her information. There was no way, he'd said.

"Baby, that girl is crazy. You saw for yourself. Why do you think I let her go?" He had sounded convincing. "That's been a while ago, and she's still trying to recuperate. She's got serious problems."

"Well, her serious problem became my serious problem when she followed me to the gas station."

"It won't happen again," Bryce had said. "I'll check her on that. I have some things I can hold over her head if I need to, and I know she'd want me to keep my mouth shut."

"Do whatever," Monét had replied. "Just make sure she's never in my face again. I don't need the drama, Bryce."

That had been the end of that conversation.

Monét recalled that conversation as she walked out of her office and to the assistant's area where Jasmine sat. The intern was neck high in mailings, as usual.

"Jasmine, have you transferred any calls to me today?"

Jasmine swept a loose braid behind her ear, then decided to add it to the stack of braids piled in a ponytail on top of her head.

"Just two," she said, flipping the pages of the message pad. "Both were from the same man calling about displaying his collection of historical quilts."

"Right. I got those. I'm asking because somebody keeps hanging up without leaving a message. Whoever it is must have my direct line. You'd think they'd realize they have the wrong number."

Monét picked up the day's stack of mail on the corner of Jasmine's desk. "It's annoying."

"You don't seem like the type to have any enemies, so I say it sounds like a fatal attraction case to me." Jasmine swiveled her chair around and crossed her legs.

It better not be. Monét thought back to her talk with Bryce again. She wasn't going to let Jasmine take her there. *This girl can make drama out of any situation,* Monét thought. "None of the men I've ever dated have been that crazy. Plus I'm not seeing anybody right now."

Jasmine's eyes widened and her head shot back against the chair's headrest. "Please, Monét. You must think I'm blind." She sat up straight in her chair. Her tone changed. "I mean, if you don't mind me being frank."

"What? And go ahead and be frank."

"Bryce," she stated matter-of-factly. "He's through here more times than the mailman. And if it's not him, then it's something he's having delivered."

Jasmine was right. Bryce had upped his gifts and his appearances lately. They'd been out to eat four times in the

260

past two weeks. He always picked her up—whether from home or from work—with a single rose in hand.

Monét tossed the mail that wasn't addressed to her back in Jasmine's in-box. "We're friends."

"I don't know a man who would put out that much money for someone who's just—" she mimicked quotation marks with her fingers "—a friend."

Jasmine looked set to grill her, district–attorney style. Monét didn't feel as if she needed to be put on trial by a twenty-one-year-old who knew nothing about the complexities of relationships. She pulled over an extra chair from an empty desk anyway. She needed the break. It had been a long day, and it was just two o'clock. She might as well entertain Jasmine.

"If you must know, we've been friends for about three years," Monét said.

"So you're telling me you've never crossed the line from friendship to relationship?" She cut the air with her hands. "I can't believe that."

There goes that line again. "I never said that. But that's not the case now."

"So why do you spend so much time with him?"

"I wouldn't call it a lot of time. It's something to do. We enjoy each other's company."

"And you honestly think he doesn't want anything more?"

Monét shrugged. "He may. But we've tried before, and it's never worked."

"People change."

"True." *Bryce has.*

"All I'm saying is that you don't want to walk around with your eyes closed and miss a good thing that's right in front of you. You never know. He might be the one."

Hmph. That's the first time she'd heard that one. Monét looked at the row of pictures of Jasmine and her boyfriend hanging by pushpins around her cubicle wall. She decided to let Jasmine take her turn in the hot seat. "What about your good thing? Maurice."

"He's around."

"Around? That's a total change from the way you used to talk about him."

"We're going through some changes, I guess you could say." Jasmine didn't seem so comfortable in the exchanged roles. She pulled on the bottom of her shirt, then bent over and adjusted the strap around her shoe.

"Don't get shy now," Monét said. "You were the one who asked if you could be frank."

Jasmine looked directly into Monét's eyes. It was the first time Monét had seen her look that serious.

"Maurice wants to be intimate, and I'm not ready for that yet. I love him, but I want to make sure it's right. I want to make the decision on my own, not be pressured."

"What kind of pressure is Maurice putting on you?"

"Mostly just in things he says," Jasmine said. "He questions my love for him, especially when I put the brakes on him after we go a little too far. Do you know what I mean?"

"Jasmine, I'm thirty years old." Monét wondered if she should've said that. She didn't want Jasmine to feel she was making light of her situation because of her age. *I should fix that.*

"Trust me, I know what you mean. It can be hard to keep your physical desires under control, especially if you love a person. But then that voice pops into your head and says that you know you're not doing the right thing."

"Exactly." Jasmine's eyes lit up at the connection she'd just made with her supervisor. "I can't even believe I'm having this conversation with my boss."

"We're two women," Monét said. "And you can bet if you're going through it, then I've already been through it."

"So you're telling me that you and Bryce aren't—you know?"

"Having sex?" Monét finished. "Don't be afraid to say it. That's how you got here, you know?"

"I know, but at my church, it's like a dirty word. Nobody wants to be real about it. People act like it's not happening until somebody shows up pregnant, and then they talk trash about them."

"Well, God designed sex, so it's not a dirty word. But it's a beautiful thing if it's enjoyed between two married people. Anything besides that just brings too much drama that you don't want to have to deal with. And no, to answer your questions, Bryce and I aren't having sex."

"Are you a virgin?"

"In most people's eyes I wouldn't be, because I've had sex before. But I've rededicated my life back to God, and I know He's made me pure and whole again. So to me, yes."

"I never knew you thought that way."

That was an eye-opener to Monét. People should be able to distinguish her walk with God, as far as she was concerned. Evidently, her light didn't shine as bright as she thought it did.

When was the last time she'd shared her convictions with a coworker or another associate? *I can't remember.* She crossed paths and talked to people every day who probably didn't know the beauty and restoration of God's love.

God, I'll do better. I want everyone to know You.

"I'm glad we had this talk," Monét said, getting up and pushing her chair back to the empty desk. "There's nothing like a heart-to-heart with another woman. My whole attitude has changed from earlier."

Jasmine stood too. "I'm glad we talked too. I feel better. If you can save yourself, then I can too."

"Yes, we can." Monét turned to go to her office, then turned back around to Jasmine. "Maybe we can catch dinner or something after work one day. That is, if you don't mind going out with an old woman."

"As long as we can get a senior citizen's discount, I'm down for it."

"Very funny," Monét said. She reached out to hug Jasmine. "Don't forget that I sign your paycheck," she said while she embraced her intern.

"Yes, boss."

Monét went back to her desk and opened her e-mail account. She'd ignored the e-mails all morning so she could focus on the copy she was writing for their upcoming exhibits brochure. If somebody needed anything important, he'd call.

The first e-mail in her in-box that morning was from Jeremiah. It had been that way since their phone conversation last week. It was their only form of communication lately because of both of their schedules.

Jeremiah always ended his e-mail with a Scripture for the day. It was astounding how it always spoke to where she was in her life that day.

My Word is always in season.

Today the Scripture was from James 1:5–8.

If any of you lacks wisdom, let him ask of God, who gives to all liberally and without reproach, and it will be given to him. But let him ask in faith, with no doubting, for he who doubts is like a wave of the sea driven and tossed by the wind. For let not that man suppose that he will receive anything from the Lord; he is a double-minded man, unstable in all his ways.

Monét responded to his e-mail. *Hi, Jeremiah. Hope all is going well with you. I don't think I've ever known a person who works as much as I do. Thanks for the Scripture. As always, it was right on time.*

Monét scrolled through her in-box past the spam and the reminders about the quarterly event planners' meeting. She spotted another message from Jeremiah. The time tag showed that he'd sent it twenty minutes prior.

Just found out I'll be in town this weekend, he wrote. *Maybe you can take me to some of those historical sites you told me about.*

Talk about bad timing. This weekend she was supposed to meet Bryce for the outing with his parents. *Tied up on Saturday*, she typed. *Let's do dinner on Sunday though. Call me Sunday afternoon.*

"This better not be my prank caller," she said, picking up her ringing line.

"Monét Sullivan."

"I think Monét Coleman would sound a lot better. See how that just rolls off the tongue."

"Hi, Bryce."

"Hey, love."

Monét paused. That's what he had always called her when they were dating. She overlooked it. She knew Bryce was looking for a reaction.

"What's up?"

"I don't know," he said. "I was calling to ask you the same thing."

"It depends on how I feel after work. I may just want to crash."

"I can do that too. At your house," he added.

"So I guess you've invited yourself over."

"Me and whatever I decide to pick up for dinner. You do the dessert."

That was easy enough. She could swing by the grocery store on her way home. "What do you want?"

"You."

"You know that's not going to happen."

"Pastor James has been preaching about water-walking faith. Don't forget that."

"I'll pray for you," Monét said, and hung up the phone. She

meant it. And she'd drop a word in for herself, too. Another kiss like the last time and she'd have to put on her running shoes.

28

Paula's prayers hadn't brought a tremendous change in Darryl's treatment toward her. Yet. The only things that had changed were his smart-aleck remarks whenever she left the house for church. He'd seen that they hadn't deterred her, so he'd retreated to his side of the ring.

Once he'd lodged a complaint that his son didn't need to be dragged to church on Tuesdays and Sundays. She obliged his request and left their kicking and screaming son in his hands twice while she went to worship. Micah hadn't missed children's church since.

Victor's voice was a welcome change from her disagreements with Darryl. Their marital problems had brought them closer. He understood her pain. He gave her insight from a man's point of view to understand the things her logical female mind couldn't conceive.

"Moooommmmmmmmmmyyyyyyy?"

Micah was intent on getting her attention. She could tell by his voice that it wasn't an emergency. It was his usual act that occurred whenever she was on the phone.

"Mooommyyyy," Micah bellowed again.

"Duty calls," Paula told Victor. "This boy is going to drive me crazy."

"He's a kid. That's what he's supposed to do. Give him about six years and he might not want anything to do with you."

"Remind me about that later," Paula said when Micah yelled again.

"Call me later," Victor said.

"If I get a chance. Darryl's been home more lately."

"See. Things are getting better."

"Depends on how you look at it. Being here physically isn't the same as emotionally."

"In time," Victor said. "Until then, you've got me."

Micah came into the room, dragging his yellow toy construction truck behind him. Nearly his weight, he was having trouble transporting it and bumped it against the eggshell-white wall. He looked up at Paula as if he were prepared for a scolding for the black mark left on the wall.

When Paula laughed and patted the bed beside her, Micah dropped the truck and jumped on the bed.

"Mommy, I can make you laugh more." He peered into her eyes. "Watch this," he said. He started an acrobatic act on the bed, flipping and spinning on his head. His grand finale was impersonations of zoo animals.

Micah was taking his freedom of expression as far as he could when he saw it brought no rebuke.

"Watch this." He jumped on the bed, his bent knees nearly touching his ears he sprung so high. "I'm a frog." Micah finally stopped when he tired, then fell back on the bed laughing hysterically. His high-pitched squeal stirred a laugh in Paula's own belly.

Paula stood up on the bed too.

Micah found his second wind and started again. The high ceilings gave Paula the range to see if her toning and flexibility classes at the gym were worth the extra time. The stability of the bed was no worry either. The king-size sleigh bed was no comparison to her childhood rickety iron bed. Its frame used to buckle under the slightest pressure.

Remembering her condition, she decided it best to leave the gymnastics to Micah. Paula was having so much fun with him that she didn't want to answer the phone when it rang.

Micah dropped down rear first on the bed. "Mommy, can I answer?"

"This time," Paula said. She fell to her knees and stretched out between the king-size bed pillows. That was more workout than any aerobics class she had attended at the gym. "But you only answer the phone when Mommy lets you, okay?"

"Okay," he said, picking up the cordless phone.

Paula pointed to the button for him to push.

"Hello?" Micah gripped the phone with both hands. "Yes."

Paula could tell it wasn't anybody he knew.

"Yes, ma'am."

At least he remembers his manners.

Micah handed the phone to Paula and commenced to perform aerial stunts on the bed. She let him. She realized how fun it must be to be a child with no worries.

"Hello?"

"Paula? How are you, darling? It's Sister Barnes."

"Hi, Sister Barnes. I'm doing fine. How are you?"

"Blessed and highly favored of the Lord," she answered in her usual jovial tone. "I'm calling around for Belinda to get some righteous women praying for her mother. She suffered a setback last night, and she's back in the hospital. The doctors didn't know if she'd make it through the night, but I know the God we serve," Sister Barnes said, her voice exuding confidence.

She could ignite a fire for the Lord in anyone's belly.

"Yes, I'll pray for her. And I'm free to go to the hospital too, so I think I'll do that."

"That's sweet of you. You know the Word says in James 5:15 that 'the prayer of faith will save the sick, and the Lord will raise him up.' And you know what else I know for myself? While you take care of God's business, He'll take care of yours. He'll give you a blessing that'll knock your socks off."

"Thank you' Sister Barnes." *Lord knows I need a blessing over here.*

Paula hung up the phone and looked at the clock. The cleaning service was scheduled to come in at three o'clock, but they could let themselves in. Margaret was their regular housekeeper; Paula trusted her.

"Mommy, can we go to the playground?"

"Not right now, sweetheart. We need to go to the hospital."

"To Daddy's job?"

"Yes, Daddy works at the hospital, but he's seeing sick people right now." It was a shame that she could go to the same hospital Darryl worked at and not want to at least swing by and see him.

"Do you remember what I said about hospitals?"

"They help sick people, and you can't run around and be loud."

"That's right. A lady I know has a mommy who is sick, so we're going to go see her."

A look of fear swept across Micah's face, erasing the glee that had been there before. His wide eyes turned down at the corners and his bottom lip trembled. "I don't want you to get sick, Mommy. Will we get sick if we go?"

"Neither one of us will get sick. Now get your shoes on so we can leave. And bring one toy and one book," she hollered after him as he galloped to his room. "Nothing that makes noise," she added.

Paula tried to call Monét at work and on her cell, but didn't get an answer. She left messages and started to reach for the tennis shoes on the side of the bed. She stopped. Then Paula picked up the phone again and did something that up until a week ago, she never thought she'd do voluntarily. She called Zora.

29

Zora had thought her new running short set and other athletic gear she'd splurged on would be enough to spur her into excitement about her workout. It hadn't worked, but at least she looked cute. Half of her bounty would be going back to the store tonight if she had a chance.

Her tennis shoes were tossed in the corner where they'd been since she'd walked in the door at Preston's house.

Preston's exercise equipment was as advanced as any gym, even though he had the majority of it stuffed in the same room as his office. He liked to be able to switch between the bench press and his computer when he pulled late nights. He said it helped him think and work off stress.

Zora knocked her shoulder against the weight bench. She thought the room was too cramped. There was no way she could get any serious work done in this office. It was another project she'd have to put on her list when she became Mrs. Fields.

Five more minutes and I'll start my workout.

Zora turned on Preston's computer. She was going to check

the adoption registry before swinging through the chat room again. Zora was supposed to meet Solo there. Her slip of the tongue was still the butt of some of his jokes toward her. She'd become so comfortable with him that she'd let her guard down and let it slip that she lived in Baltimore. He'd let her ramble on awhile before he called her out on it. In exchange, he'd told her his real name. Solomon. It turns out Solo wasn't just a fitting screen name.

Solomon still knew her as Baby Z, and always would. Even if they met.

The thought had crossed her mind, and Solomon brought it up almost every day. *A public place with people would be safe,* Zora thought. He'd said the Harbor was one of his favorite places to hang out.

Zora would think about it and make a decision by tomorrow. She could take Monét with her this weekend, but tell Solo she was coming alone. That way if anything looked shady, she could bail out, and he'd never know she'd been footsteps away. But then again, if Monét knew, she'd talk her out of it. No. Monét couldn't know.

It was funny how Zora had pushed the ladies in her prayer circle to be honest, but she'd found herself hiding behind lies.

Just for a little while, Lord. Just until I can find some answers.

Solo wasn't logged in to the chat room yet, but then again it was only two thirty by her watch. She stayed logged in. He'd be there around three o'clock. He always was.

Procrastination had been Zora's best friend for most of the morning. There were still final contracts and deposits to be made to the photographer, videographer, and cake designer. She was still behind on assembling her favors, and Monét had just about come to her wit's end bugging her to choose the paper for her programs. Summer break was supposed to be her time to get ahead of the game, but she'd whittled it away.

She was supposed to report for the upcoming school year in three weeks.

That night, sleep evaded Zora. It was nearly four-thirty that morning before she'd been able to get settled. She could only remember one time when the unction to pray had fallen so heavily upon her through the night. Last night she'd prayed over and about everything her mind conceived, but her prayers grew most fervent when she'd interceded for her prayer partners. It was as if God called her to His throne and she entered into one of the most intimate dimensions she'd ever experienced.

Beyond the veil.

She'd lain in complete silence and let the peace envelope her soul. It was a place where no words would suffice. She'd drifted to sleep soon after and slept until the alarm clock reminded her of the busy day ahead. She'd intentionally pushed her workout to the late afternoon.

Zora double-knotted her shoes and stepped on the treadmill for a warm-up. Twenty minutes would suffice before she hit the full-body equipment.

I should've had Preston write me out a plan, Zora thought as she started the treadmill.

Her strides grew progressively shorter and faster as the treadmill adjusted speeds through the programmed workout. Zora's stamina wasn't as strong as it used to be. She settled into a rhythm, her feet thudding on the treadmill's rubber belt.

This actually feels good, she thought. *No pain, no gain.* Zora pushed a button to increase the speed. Three, maybe four days a week until the wedding, and the extra ten pounds would be history.

She ignored the ring tone of her cell and decided to burn out her leg muscles for the last five minutes. Finally, her legs heavy like steel, Zora walked around to Preston's exercise equipment. He'd shown her before which contraption worked specific muscles. Now they all looked the same.

Her phone rang again. Maybe it was Preston. He'd be able to make sense out of the hanging metal bars and leg lifts. Zora let go of the hand bar without thought and the weights banged together. Good thing he wasn't here. He'd have a fit.

Zora picked up her cell phone, but didn't recognize the number. She'd answer it anyway in case it was one of the wedding vendors returning her call.

"Hello?"

"Is this Zora?"

"Yes, it is."

"Hi, Zora, it's Paula."

"Paula?" It took her a second to make the connection.

"Did I catch you at a bad time?"

"Just working out to fit into your wardrobe." She dabbed a hand towel on her nose. "What's going on?"

"Belinda's mother was rushed to the hospital last night." Paula filled Zora in on the scant information she knew.

"I'm going to head out to the hospital for a while. Do you have time to meet me there?"

"Of course. I'll leave here in about ten minutes."

"See you shortly."

Zora tossed her phone into her purse and went into the master bath in Preston's bedroom. She worked around his electric razor and the rest of the junk on the crowded countertop to freshen up. She ran out the door without bothering to pack up the rest of her things. She and Preston planned on cooking spaghetti for dinner, so she'd be back to his house, probably by the time he made it home.

❧

The odor of stale antiseptic cleanser circulated in the corridor. The off-white walls and bland beige tile did nothing to lift the spirits of the visitors or the patients. It reminded Zora of the hallway in her dream, only there wasn't a bright light.

Zora's visits to hospitals were rare. She could count on one hand the number of times she'd been in the last ten years, and three of them were to visit the newborns of some of her church members. After her parents' accident, she'd rushed to the hospital. The first place she'd seen their bodies was in the morgue.

Hospitals were an intriguing place. One floor experienced the miracle of birth, another was full of people saved by the miracle of medical technology, and yet another held patients clinging to life.

After asking the concierge for directions to the ICU waiting room, Zora found the closest elevator and worked through the maze of hallways. There was no warmth there either. The chairs looked more suited for a 1970s doctor's office, as did the unpolished coffee table in the middle of the room. Paula and her son sat in the corner of the waiting room. He had a line of colorful oversized cards lined on the floor between his legs. Paula flipped through a fashion magazine. It must've been her personal copy, because it wasn't tattered with a torn cover like the others on a nearby table.

Zora eased into a chair beside Paula. "Hey."

"Hi." Paula leaned over and hugged Zora.

It was the first time their hug meant more than just being cordial. Zora felt relieved that the unspoken animosity between them was broken, especially since it had no justifiable reason to exist in the first place.

"Belinda just left to go back to her mother's room a minute ago. She'll be back in a few minutes after she talks to the doctor."

"Mommy, can you play Go Fish with me?" Micah practically screamed.

Paula held her finger up to her closed lips and shook her

head. She beckoned him with a finger, and he got up and flopped over his mother's lap. He acted limp as a wet noodle when she tried to stand him up.

Kids. Acting out for company, Zora mused.

She looked at the other visitors in the room. A woman with bloodshot eyes stared at a muted television. Seated next to her, a napping man kept jerking up his bobbling head every few seconds, only to have it fall back down on the lady's shoulder.

Paula's voice went stern. "Stand up, Micah," she said between clenched teeth.

Micah got the point. Evidently he was familiar with the threat behind her tone.

"Do you remember what I said before we got out of the car?"

He nodded.

"Okay. So use your inside voice if you need to ask me something." Paula straightened his twisted jeans and turned him around toward Zora. "Can you say hi to Miss Zora?"

"Hi, Miss Zora," he said. His *z*'s sounded more like an *s*.

"Hi, Micah."

He hid his face and flopped down on the floor, content to play with his cards by himself.

"He's cute."

"A cute handful," Paula said.

"You know, I didn't even think to call Monét," Zora said. "Can we use our cell phones in here?"

"Oh, I finally got in touch with her a few minutes ago. If she can walk out of work at five o'clock, she'll be here a little later. I wanted Belinda to know she had a support group here."

Preconceived notions weren't worth a dime. Paula was even more compassionate than Zora had figured her to be. Behind the brand-name attire and expensive jewelry there was a person. A woman whose feelings were much like her own.

Zora and Paula kept their conversations at a respectable

level for the other three visitors who'd joined them in the ICU waiting room. When Belinda entered the room, she looked worn, but relieved that they were there. Her mother's condition was grave, but her faith didn't let the family settle for anything but the best.

"Her doctor explained that blood clots were common following a mastectomy," Belinda said, "but I know they didn't warn us about them. I would've remembered. I would've had her walking around and being more mobile instead of just resting around the house." Belinda wrung her hands. "One of them traveled into her lung."

Zora didn't know what to say. She let Belinda get the concerns off of her chest.

"My sister should be flying in from California tonight," Belinda said. "The ministers and members from my home church have been in and out most of the day, but only two people are allowed in the room at a time."

"I'll stay as long as you need me," Zora said.

"Just showing your face was enough," Belinda said. "But I could use something to eat. Let's go downstairs to the cafeteria."

Zora, Belinda, Paula, and Micah ventured to the ground floor to the overcrowded café.

"It must be dinnertime for the employees," Belinda said. "Let's come back later. I'll go outside and get some fresh air."

The women headed for the main hospital entrance, saving their conversation until they could get outside. Belinda noticed a sign on the outside of a closed door.

"I was wondering where the chapel was." She opened the door and peeked inside. "Last time I'm changing my mind," she said, and walked in, holding the door for her two comforters.

Zora eased the door closed behind them. The small room was dimly lit with only a small row of overhead lights above the altar. A gold cross hung on the wall. The ladies sat together on one of the six pews, their shoulders touching.

Classical hymns seeped into the room from an unseen source. Zora felt the weight of Belinda's concern. They stared straight ahead, as if drawn to the holiness of the cross.

Zora began to pray silently and assumed Belinda and Paula were doing the same. Even Micah settled into a hush.

"I can't wait to see Thomas and Hannah," Belinda said finally after a few minutes of silence. "They're supposed to be up in a couple of days, if not sooner. Depends on Mama's condition."

"How's Thomas managing with the baby?"

"It's only been one day, and he's had help from one of the college students from our church."

"That's a blessing."

"Definitely. But I'm worried about him. I talked to him three times today and he sounded disturbed."

"He's probably worried about you."

Belinda shook her head. "He says nothing is wrong, but I know my husband. You'll see soon, Zora. You think you know Preston now. Just wait until you become his wife. Am I right, Paula?"

"That's true."

Zora leaned forward and looked around Belinda so she could see Paula. "How is Dr. Manns, by the way?"

"He's fine."

The sound of his father's name brought Micah up from his reclined position across the pew. "Is Daddy coming home tonight?" he asked Paula.

"You know Daddy has to work late sometimes." Paula patted Micah's shoulder, and he laid his head back on his mother's lap.

Zora sat back in the seat. "Tell him I said hello."

Belinda propped her hands under her chin. "We should all

get together," she suggested, "once everybody's lives get back to normal."

"Whatever normal is," Zora said. She soaked in her words until Belinda spoke again.

"Are you ladies ready? I haven't seen the light of day since yesterday. I want to go outside for a minute."

They filed outside again in the same order they'd entered the chapel. As soon as Zora closed the door, she bumped into Bryce. He was carrying a vase of flowers, and all of a sudden his face looked flushed.

"Hi, Zora. I was just bringing some flowers to a friend. A patient. Third floor, I think."

It wasn't like Bryce to stumble over his words. Not Mr. Politician. "Okay," Zora said. "Good to see you again."

"You too," he said, and disappeared around the corner without his usual exchange about his rising political career.

That was strange, Zora thought. Very strange.

30

Zora left the hospital at around six o'clock. After they'd left the chapel, they grabbed a bite to eat and chatted a little while longer before Belinda went back to be by her mother's side. Since they couldn't go into the ICU room, Zora and Paula joined Belinda in prayer and then decided to leave. Instead, they ended up sitting in the parking lot and talking for another hour. Zora knew their friendship would continue to grow past the season of the P.O.W.E.R. group. And finally, Paula thought she wasn't insane.

Life had taken them so many places. Paula was beginning to open up more. Belinda was right; their petty tension between each other was only a device to keep two potential lifelong sisters from connecting.

They'd even continued their conversations from their cell phones on their rides home until Zora pulled up in Preston's driveway. Preston was already home, as she'd guessed. He'd promised not to pull a late evening at the office. Unfortunately, she didn't have any room left in her stomach for the dinner she was sure he'd already prepared.

"Hey, sweetie," Zora said, giving Preston a kiss on the cheek as she whizzed through the door. She pulled off her windbreaker and tossed it on the back of the love seat in the den.

"I'm starving," she said. "Is dinner ready?"

"Almost," Preston said dryly.

"Good." She pulled off her sneakers and set them in the foyer near the door. She didn't see his infuriated countenance until she realized he hadn't left the open door where she'd first greeted him.

With a swift push of Preston's hand, the door closed. Almost slammed.

"Are you okay?"

He didn't answer, only stared down at her. His eyes seemed dark. Preston walked past Zora and disappeared down the hall.

What in the world? Zora followed after him. "What's going on?"

Preston sat down in his office chair and hit the space bar on his computer. "You tell me," he said, nodding toward the screen.

His rotating screensaver of classic cars disappeared, and the monitor opened to the chat room. In her haste to get to the hospital, Zora had neglected to log off, leaving her actions open to Preston's perusal. *Not good.*

She tried to sit on the end of Preston's knee, but his raised hand prevented her backside from connecting with his lap. He meant it.

"Seems like this Solo person is interested in more than sharing adoption resources. The instant message alert is chirping every few minutes. That's why I looked to see what was going on."

"Preston—"

"And what did I see?" He leaned closer to the computer and rattled off the messages from Solo. "Baby Z, where did you go? You missed our virtual date. Got great news. We should meet soon. What day is good for you?" Preston stopped.

Zora didn't want him to read more anyway.

She put her hands on his shoulders, softly kneading them, hoping she could rub away the tension that showed through to his tight jawline.

Preston reached back and lifted her hands. Raising them above his head, he held on to them while he steered her until he could see her face. Zora leaned on the edge of the desk. It wasn't as comfortable as his lap would have been.

"I thought we agreed you wouldn't be in chat rooms."

"Actually, we never agreed to that. That's what *you* wanted," Zora said. "You should be able to trust me. Solo has been able to give me pointers about what he's learned through his own search."

"Like what?"

"You wouldn't even know, Preston. It's so much. You can't relate. You have no idea how I feel."

"We've been through this before, Zora. No, I can't know. I never will. But does that mean you have to run to another man because he can supposedly relate?"

"That wasn't my intention. I'm not trying to run to another man. Trust me."

Preston pushed the chair back and left her sitting on the desk, staring at an empty chair.

"Trust? And then *you* have the nerve to say something about trust," Preston said from behind her. "How am I supposed to feel if my future wife can't be honest with me?"

Preston walked out and left her to deal with the small rift she'd torn in the trust between them. Zora knew she never should have withheld the secret from Preston. Her feelings would've been the same if she were in his shoes.

She logged out of the chat room and packed the rest of her belongings in her duffle bag. When she walked to the living room, she was surprised to see Preston in the kitchen preparing two plates for dinner. She watched silently as he set the table. She wasn't even hungry. Feeling the need to do something, she poured two glasses of lemonade.

Zora wanted to squeeze him until he was assured that he could trust her, but she wasn't sure Preston would accept her touch. He needed to cool off, and she intended to give him time. They had never eaten dinner with the television on, choosing instead to enjoy the time together and not to be distracted by the world around them. Tonight, however, the evening news seemed more important.

31

Belinda flicked on a single lamp in her mother's house and sat down at the end of the sofa. Her mother's prognosis wasn't the best, but she'd held on this far. Even the doctors said it was a miracle she was still alive. Their professional expertise couldn't explain her mother's survival, but her living wasn't for them to decide. Belinda knew that even though her mother couldn't respond, she was holding on to the same faith.

The nurses on the late shift were kind enough to let Belinda stay past normal visiting hours. She didn't leave the hospital until ten o'clock. She'd wanted to stay by her mother's side and pray.

With all that was going on, Belinda knew that it wasn't time for her mother to leave them. At first she thought she was in denial about her mother's possible death. But no, she'd heard God clearly. This situation was perfecting the entire family's faith.

Even her brother Rodney, who'd barely stepped foot in a church or cracked open a Bible since he left his mother's house at nineteen, was seeking the Lord. Whenever he'd been able to call them, Rodney wanted Belinda to end their phone call with a prayer. It helped calm his nerves, he said.

Belinda picked up the living room phone. She was sure Thomas was up waiting on her call. He was probably stretched out on the couch in the den watching the nightly news, and had let Hannah fall asleep on his chest.

"Hello?"

Belinda was surprised that his voice didn't sound groggy at all. "Hi, sweetheart. I thought you'd be barely hanging on trying to stay awake. Hannah must still be up."

"Yes, she's still awake. She can't seem to get settled tonight."

"Make sure her milk is warm enough," Belinda said. "That usually works."

"Okay."

Thomas still seemed distracted. He wasn't his usual talkative self. Belinda would get it out of him by the time they hung up the phone. If something was wearing on his mind, she needed to know, even if he thought she had a lot to be concerned about. If she couldn't be there physically, the least she could do was pray.

"How's Mama?"

"She's in the same condition, but the good thing is that she hasn't gotten any worse."

"That's good to hear. Everybody from the church keeps calling to check on her."

"I appreciate that."

Thomas didn't say anything. It was an awkward silence. Belinda didn't like it.

Thomas breathed heavily into the phone. "Honey, I'm not sure how to tell you this."

"Is it something with Hannah?"

Thomas said nothing.

Belinda gripped the phone. "Thomas, you're scaring me." Tears were beginning to form in her eyes, and she wasn't sure of their cause. *Mama.* "I just left the hospital," she said. "The nurses have my cell phone and they . . ." No. *That couldn't be it. He'd just asked about her.*

"Belinda." Thomas was calm—too calm for the words he'd just spoken. "We didn't lose a life in our family."

Belinda exhaled.

"We've gained a life."

"Who's pregnant?" A surprise, but still a relief considering her last thought. "It's not Carmen, is it?" She'd recently talked to her sister-in-law, Deena, about her niece sneaking out of the house to see her boyfriend. Deena was probably devastated.

"Belinda."

Thomas's voice rescued her from her imagination.

"Belinda."

He called her by her name. Not honey, not sweetie.

"Thomas Jr. is here," he said.

"Thomas Jr. is where?" Belinda's grip on the phone loosened, and she had to steady it with two hands. "What do you mean?"

"He's here. At our house. Dropped off on the doorstep."

"The doorstep?" That was reserved for orphaned puppies and abandoned postal packages, not for a teenage son who hadn't seen his father in ten years. "Make sense of this," she begged.

"I wish I could. His mother drove him from Pittsburgh and left him. Remember the boxes of clothes we thought were for the clothing drive? They're his."

Belinda stood up. The shadows played against the wall in the living room. She walked around, turning on the lights. It didn't feel comfortable sitting in the dark anymore. She heard Hannah wail in the background, and Belinda wanted to join

289

her. Then she heard Thomas scamper around in the back-ground, and soon Hannah's sobs faded to whimpers.

If only it was that easy to calm me down.

Thomas explained how Juanita shipped T. J.'s clothes to them after one of his son's runaway stints. His repeated behavior problems had apparently nearly driven her to a nervous breakdown, from what his son explained. When T. J, returned two weeks later, he'd found his room empty and his belongings missing. She made him get in the car, and they didn't stop until they pulled into the Stokes's driveway.

"This is—" She searched for the word.

"Crazy," he said. "But he's my son. Our son."

"What did Juanita say to you?"

"Nothing. She waited until I opened the door and then hightailed it out."

"Well, what if you weren't home? What was she going to do then?" Belinda went from shock to fury. "I can't believe she would just drop off her son like a box of Salvation Army clothes."

"Don't go there now, Belinda."

She could sense the frustration in his voice. Belinda relaxed as much as she could. She didn't want to add to his stress.

"Where is T. J. now?"

"Upstairs. I tried to talk to him earlier, but he's not saying much," Thomas said. "You should see him. He's practically a grown man. Almost taller than me."

Belinda could imagine Thomas pacing around on the deck like he did when he was trying to clear his thoughts. Then he'd lean on the wooden rail and stare out into the woods behind the house.

"Where are you?"

"On the deck."

"I could hear something wrong in your voice all day." She walked over to the angel figurines her mother kept in a curio.

I'm watching over you.

"I never expected this," Belinda said.

"That makes two of us. But God wouldn't have dealt us this hand if we weren't prepared to play it."

He's right.

That was just like Thomas, Belinda thought. He found God in every situation. She was going to have to dig a little deeper for this one. She hadn't even had time for this to sink in and Thomas was sounding like he was ready to make them into a new happy home.

Things weren't always that easy.

32

Bryce had pleaded with Monét to use a vacation day for Friday and join him with his parents. At his mother's persistent request he was accompanying them on a two-day tour to highlight the sites of African-American heritage. They were starting on Friday in Cambridge and would end the second leg on Saturday in the Baltimore area. That's where Monét would join them. The step back in history was at times an emotional journey, but one that Monét cherished. None of her friends shared the intensity of the emotions she held for history, although Zora was starting to appreciate it more.

Monét arrived in Towson at nine o'clock and met Bryce and his parents at the Hampton National Historic Site. From there they planned to travel back to Baltimore for an afternoon packed with seeing the attractions like the Great Blacks in Wax Museum, the Baltimore Civil War Museum, and a few of the religious structures used by the Underground Railroad.

"Oh, Monét, I'm so thrilled to see you." Sylvia Coleman met Monét at her car as soon as she pulled into a parking space. When she hugged her, Monét breathed in the light floral and citrus scent of her lotion. "I'm so glad you and Bryce are seeing each other again."

Is that what we're doing?

Mrs. Coleman held on to her hand. *Here we go.* It was a sign that she'd latched on again. Monét greeted Bryce and his father, Floyd, with a one-armed hug. Mrs. Coleman held on to the hope that Monét would become her daughter-in-law. It was no secret. She went through a phase where she was too attached and wanted to sit on the phone and talk to Monét all night.

I wish she'd let my hand go.

"Bryce just told me a few minutes ago that you were coming. I guess he knew I'd worry him silly."

Monét looked over her shoulder, and both Bryce and his father nodded. Mrs. Coleman swung her hand like they were two six-year-olds frolicking in a country field of daffodils. All the way during their walk from the parking lot to inside the building, she retold her emotional personal account of their first day's tour along the Underground Railroad Trail. She was overwhelmed by the visits to the Harriet Tubman Museum and the Stanley Institute.

Bryce finally rescued Monét from his mother when Mrs. Coleman slipped away to the ladies' room.

"I see your mother hasn't changed," Monét said.

"She still loves you. Like me. I never stopped."

"Bryce, please don't force it. Let's just—"

"Flow," he said, finishing her sentence.

Bryce picked up her hand and pressed it to his lips. He moved to her cheek, and then to her lips. Monét's face grew flush. If his mother walked in on this scene, their next stop would be the bridal boutique. She looked over at Mr. Coleman, who was preoccupied with tying his shoe. The only person who seemed to notice them was Jeremiah.

Jeremiah?

If it wasn't him, Monét had discovered the identical twin that everyone in the world is thought to have. Jeremiah moved in her direction, confirming her suspicions. He looked better than she remembered.

"I thought that was you," he said.

Bryce stepped up like the question had been directed to him. "Preston's friend, right? Justin?"

"Jeremiah."

"That's right. My bad," Bryce said.

Why is this awkward?

Your heart knows why.

Monét swallowed the lump in her throat and took an inconspicuous step to her right. Bryce's arm didn't budge. *I'm not committed to either of them. I'm a free woman,* she thought. *There's no reason for me to feel this way.*

She had to say something. It was rude for her to just stand there.

"Who did you come with?" She looked around for Preston. As far as she knew, he was the only person Jeremiah really knew in this area besides a handful of business associates.

"I'm here by myself. I didn't have anybody who wanted to roll with me."

Did he have to say that?

Jeremiah's eyes didn't leave hers. She didn't want them to. What she wanted was to walk out of the door with Jeremiah and leave Bryce there to deal with his mother and her shattered dreams.

"Have fun, bro," Bryce said, massaging Monét's shoulder. His hand traveled to the small of her back and rested on her waist.

"Maybe I'll talk to you later, Monét."

Why did he have to say maybe?

Jeremiah's intense gaze stayed with Monét from the

moment he walked away. She couldn't enjoy the wax depictions on the tour. With no thought, she walked past the figure of Henry Brown, the Virginia slave who mailed himself in a crate to freedom. The scene of Rosa Parks being escorted from the bus after refusing to give up her seat didn't evoke her regular emotion.

By the time they reached the Lewis Museum of Art at Morgan State University, Monét was ready to abandon the Coleman clan. Neither Bryce's nor Mrs. Coleman's petitions could change her mind.

Monét couldn't get home fast enough. The red light blinked on her phone. She pressed the code, hoping to hear Jeremiah on the other end. All five calls were hang-ups.

The calls and her reaction today to Jeremiah were enough to open Monét's eyes. She wasn't a fool. Belinda's words came back to her. God had surely given her the signs to warn her that she was making the wrong choice . . . and Bryce . . . was the wrong choice.

33

Love is brewing," Paula said, reading the tag on the end of the tea bag. "That's so creative." She'd just walked back from checking on Micah in Zora's room. She'd packed a bag of his favorite Disney cartoons to keep him occupied so they could work in peace.

Zora snapped in the CD of her and Preston's favorite love songs and closed the plastic cover. Her stack of unfinished favors seemed to be multiplying. She wouldn't have been able to accomplish much without help.

"What did you and Dr. Manns have as wedding favors?"

"We had cute personalized wine glasses and miniature bottles of sparkling cider with the wedding date and our picture on the label." Paula camped out at her spot on the floor and went back to attaching the tea bags to small bundles of Hershey's kisses covered in tulle.

"My folks better be happy with what they get," Zora said. "It's nowhere near that extravagant."

Monét sat at the table stuffing envelopes. With both an

inner and outer envelope, she had even more to finish than Zora. She'd already complained about two paper cuts. "It's the thought that counts," she said.

"Most of it's just for show anyway," Paula said. "The sparkling cider is long gone by now, and the dusty glass is at the back of people's cupboards. As long as the love lasts, that's all that matters."

"It will." Zora slapped another label on the front of the CD case. It was a nice touch that Monét had designed. "You know our next session is about marriage and how to love your husband."

"Actually, I have no idea what's coming up next," Paula said. She pulled off her socks and sprawled her legs open in front of her so she could work closer to her project. "It seems like we just had a session. Time is flying."

"Tell me about it," Monét said. "Ouch!" She shook her hand in the air, then stuck her fingertip in her mouth.

"Fifteen more minutes and we'll rotate stations," Zora said. "I promise."

"Don't worry about me." Monét ran a sponge across the seal of one of the envelopes. "These are your bloody invitations we're sending out."

"That's nasty, Monét," Paula said, scrunching up her nose. "Anyway, I volunteered to host the next meeting, not even paying attention to when it was going to be."

"Remember, the group voted to push two sessions into one month since Sister Barnes is going out of town. The next one is in two weeks," Monét reminded them.

Zora marked the dates on her wall calendar while it was fresh on her mind. "September is always such a busy month. School will be back in full swing then too. I've reported a few days last week already, and parents are already coming in with issues about their kid's summer school grades."

"I don't envy you at all," Paula said. "Micah starts pre-K

this year and I'm already set to stay on his behind for the next thirteen years. He needs a full-ride scholarship to college."

"What does he say he wants to be when he grows up?" Monét asked. "A doctor like his daddy?"

"I wish," Paula said. "Darryl has been taking him out when he goes to look at these old houses with his buddies. Or investment partners, as he calls them." She rolled her eyes. "Even though they don't have a dime to invest."

"He might have the finances and they the wisdom. At least you guys are putting up most of the money so you'll profit the biggest return," Zora said.

"I've seen the accounts, and trust me, money is going out but nothing is coming in. Real estate investing is too much of a risk."

"Most things in life are. It took faith for Peter to walk out on the water. Maybe you should have a little faith in your husband."

"You'll see, Zora. Preston is bound to have a pursuit sooner or later and you'll question his sanity too. Faith checks don't pay the bills."

Zora decided to drop the subject. She and Paula didn't need an unnecessary issue to drive a wedge between them. Preston always said a woman who doesn't believe in her man's vision will push the man away.

"You know, I ran into a man not too long ago at the mall that was a developer or something like that," Monét said. "His name was Vincent, I think. I should've kept that card. I don't even know where it is now. Darryl could've hooked up with him. He came off like he was very successful."

Zora wished she could send a CD across the room that would boomerang against Monét's head. Surely she remembered Dr. Manns's comment that day.

"In fact, I think it was the same day we saw you after we left our first P.O.W.E.R. meeting. We saw Darryl too, and . . . "

Bingo. Zora could tell the light went off in Monét's head.

Monét stretched the crook in her neck. "Forget it. The number is long gone now, so it doesn't matter."

"Was the man's name Victor?" Paula asked.

Zora tried not to show her surprise that Paula had continued with the conversation. She straightened the crooked stack of CD cases in front of her and pretended like she was more interested in slapping on labels.

"That sounds familiar. Zora, do you remember that man's name?"

No, she didn't. "Not at all." Zora got up and put the completed CDs in a box in the corner of the room. "I don't know about you guys, but I'm ready to eat."

After confirming that Chinese food was an acceptable dinner option, Zora went to call Preston. As promised, he was taking care of their food in exchange for being exempt from wedding-favor duty.

Zora peeked in on Micah and, after finding him mesmerized by cartoons, made a detour to check her e-mail. She was so tempted to see if Solo was in the chat room. She logged off and left the room before her curiosity got the best of her. It wasn't worth it.

After leaving Preston's house the night after he'd discovered her online chatting with Solo, Zora had called Monét and told her she was dropping by. She'd needed an outlet to vent and to confess.

They had stretched across Monét's bed staring at the ceiling.

"That's got to be the same guy I met at the Harbor that night when we finalized your invitations," Monét had said. "Remember? You wanted me to stop and talk to him then, but I ended up talking to him later."

"The cutie?" Zora had rolled a pillow in a ball and propped it under her neck.

"The cutie. He had the same name and the same nickname. He told me his name was Solomon, but they called him Solo for short."

"Just think what could've happened if I'd asked you to go down to the Harbor with me," she had said, turning her head so she could see Monét. Her friend's eyes were closed, and she was massaging her temples. "No doubt he would've recognized you."

Monét's eyelids had shot open at Zora's last comment. "There's no way I would've gone with you to meet some random man you'd met on the Internet. I'd have talked you out of it, or ended up telling Preston myself."

"You would've sold me out like that?"

"Girl, yes. There's no loyalty from me when a person's safety is involved. You woulda gotten over it. Anyway, I told that guy our paths would cross again if it were meant to be. Evidently, it wasn't."

"Yeah," Zora had said. She reached over and pulled the side of the comforter over her legs. "He was probably crazy."

"Uh-huh," Monét had said, her eyes closed again. "And who needs crazy in their lives?"

※

By the time Preston arrived, the women had finished assembling the favors and stuffing the envelopes. After eating, they planned to address and stamp the invitations.

Preston greeted Zora with a lingering kiss.

"That was definitely an extra show for the audience," Zora whispered in his ear.

"Always," he said, kissing her forehead.

Preston unloaded the brown paper bag and opened the white containers of Chinese lo mein, rice, and chicken and broccoli. Of course, he had to harass the ladies about their work and throw in a few jokes about his supposedly true reasons for marrying Zora. Despite his jesting, he dutifully set the women's places at the table and served their food and drinks. He even made a pallet with blankets on the floor where Micah could eat.

"I thought you could stay awhile, baby," Zora said. "We're taking a break."

"And be privileged to sit with the ladies of P.O.W.E.R.? I don't know if it's a good idea or not."

Monét twisted her fork through a heap of noodles. "If you've been on your best behavior you have nothing to worry about. It's been a while since we talked anyway."

Paula laughed. "I can tell she lives to give you a hard time."

"It's my duty."

Preston sat in the extra seat at the table. "Monét is salty because I'm moving her out of first place, even though we've offered her a highly available man that I just dropped off at the airport." He spooned a lump of rice on his plate and topped it with chicken and broccoli. "I heard she still wants to play in the little leagues, though."

"So he told you?" Monét asked Preston.

"Told who what?" Zora said. "No secrets in my house."

"I was out with Bryce yesterday and saw Jeremiah."

Zora shook her head. She could save her breath. She knew Monét had beaten herself up enough. Zora had promised to stay out of it. Monét and Jeremiah had quickly bonded, that she knew. They had stayed on the phone for hours the last time they spoke. Monét had told her that the daily e-mails he sent always ministered to her. No telling what the next e-mail would say. If there would be one.

Preston was taking advantage of his time, listing all the reasons Jeremiah surpassed Bryce.

"Why would Bryce ever be an option compared to a man like Jeremiah?" Paula asked.

"Can we talk about something else, please?" Monét said. "Like Belinda. Has anyone heard from her?"

Monét had reached for anything to get off the hook. It worked. The mood in the room shifted. They'd all been connected on the phone line when Belinda told them the news about T. J. She was leaving that morning to address the situation at her home.

"Unless something changes for the worse with her mother, which I pray it doesn't, she doesn't plan on coming back for a couple of weeks," Zora said. "In the meantime, we need to keep her family lifted up in prayer."

The crash made all of them jump. They knew exactly where to look.

Guilt, along with fear of his mother's scolding, had already begun to send tears down Micah's cheeks. Zora's nearly completed puzzle was scattered on the floor with Micah's unfinished dinner. One of the legs to Zora's card table had obviously collapsed from the boy's hyperactive behavior.

"Didn't I tell you to sit still?" Paula said, walking over to pick up the puzzle pieces. "Now look what you did to Ms. Zora's puzzle."

Micah pushed his Chinese food to the side and tried to alleviate his punishment by helping his mother pick up the pieces.

"That's okay," Zora said to Micah. She rubbed his back. His body quivered from his weeping.

"All of the pieces didn't come apart, Micah. I can put it back together in no time." *Even though I was almost finished.*

Zora carefully lifted the pieces that still clung together and waited for Preston to fix the table. She hoped this wasn't an indication of what was going on at Belinda's. She prayed things weren't falling apart.

34

The past four days had been the longest days in Belinda's life. After her sister settled in and her mother was stabilized, Belinda went home.

Now, here she stood, staring at the adolescent version of her husband. His squared, low-cut hairline, the slight hint of a cleft in his chin. Their features were the same. From the times she'd spent with him when he was in second grade, she'd noticed their resemblance. Now ten years of maturity had etched a nearly identical man. He stood before her, his hands shoved in his pockets. From the round bulges, she could tell they were balled into tight fists. Closed. Like his heart.

She couldn't blame him. He'd been thrust into a situation with a father he thought had abandoned him and a mother who'd deceived him. He was uprooted from the place and the friends he knew.

I'd be closed too. God, help him.

Could it be that the answer to ten years of their prayers stood before her? Their desire was to raise godly children who wouldn't be ashamed to change the world and live for God.

Belinda had assumed Hannah was the answer, and perhaps another child in a couple of years. A son. Now what she hadn't been able to give Thomas stood before her. A reminder of her barren womb. *God, help me.* She pushed those thoughts out of her mind. They weren't from God, and she wouldn't accept them.

Thomas walked closer to his son, with Hannah balanced in the cradle of his forearm. He cuddled her closer to his chest and, after a slight hesitation, put a hand on T. J.'s shoulder.

God, help us. Belinda couldn't stop saying it. Her words were few, but her plea was sincere.

"Have you eaten yet?" Once the words left her lips, she realized how ludicrous they sounded at a time like this.

"No, ma'am," he answered.

His voice was deep. Belinda wasn't sure why she expected it to sound like the seven-year-old she used to bake chocolate-chip cookies for. *At least he came delivered with manners,* she thought.

Belinda didn't realize how tightly she'd been gripping the blue handles of her canvas tote bag. She set the bag down and let it lean against the table in the foyer.

Now that her hands were free, she felt obligated to wrap them around T. J. Her reach for him was awkward. He leaned one shoulder into her embrace. He managed to pull his hands out of his pocket and pat Belinda's back. Not with affection, but in the way she burped Hannah.

Belinda squeezed him harder before he could sink deeper into his emotional shed, and before she did too.

"You're so handsome," she said. "I can't believe you're practically a man." *Just practically, she wanted to reiterate.* "It's good to see you again."

"Thank you."

Now that their short embrace was over, T. J.'s hands hung loosely at his side as if he didn't know what to do with them.

Belinda held her hands out, and Hannah dove into her arms. But instead of settling there, Hannah stretched out her hand and leaned toward T. J.

T. J. looked at Belinda before he held up his index finger, probably meant to appease Hannah. Hannah latched on to it and used it to pull herself closer until T. J. finally took her in his arms.

Thomas and Belinda looked at each other. The dynamics of their family had changed in one day. Maybe it wouldn't be too bad after all.

⁂

Belinda had gotten ahead of herself thinking that their lives would continue the way they always had. It had only been three days, but already she and Thomas were bumping heads about T. J. Last night they went to bed with unresolved anger. They never did that. The Stokes family didn't operate like that. Their picture-perfect family scenario had been misconstrued.

Belinda had her expectations for men around the house, and sleeping in until one and two o'clock in the afternoon wasn't one of them. Staying locked up in a room all day with a television and radio wasn't one of them either. Their guestroom had been transformed into a teenage hideaway.

Thomas, the usual disciplinarian when it came to teenage boys at the church, was being soft. Belinda had expected him to lay down the law. He hadn't lain down anything but his soft side.

"He needs transition time," Thomas had said.

"I understand that. But he's not the only person transitioning in this house." Belinda was growing more irritated with each word. "If you're at work all day and I'm home trying to finish this issue of the magazine, keep tabs on my mother, and keep Hannah entertained, then he can do *something* around this house."

"Give him time," Thomas had said, and started to head out of the bedroom. He stopped at the door, a look of disbelief on his face. "I never thought you'd act like this, Belinda. After ten years I never would have thought my wife would be jealous of my son."

With that he turned and took his newspaper downstairs to the den.

Jealous? The heat from Belinda's fury rose to her face. The thoughts of the dinner she was going to prepare evaporated. *Let him make a sandwich.*

When Thomas crept into the bed at almost eleven o'clock that night, Belinda was still awake, but said nothing. A mound of crumpled sheets and her pride were the only things left of her conversation with him.

When the alarm sounded at six thirty and Thomas got ready for work, she still didn't say a word, even though sleep had evaded her most of the night. He went about his morning as usual as it could be without her waking to drink their morning cup of coffee together.

Hannah was her usual perky self and woke up like clockwork at seven. Belinda could hear her babbling from the baby monitor, and Thomas's voice joined her soon after.

"Good morning, sunshine," he cooed. "How's Daddy's girl?"

Hannah gurgled.

"You can lie with Mommy, 'cause Daddy's got to go to work."

Belinda assumed Thomas was changing her diaper like they always did first thing in the morning. "Have fun with your big brother today."

Hannah's big brother rarely cracked the door unless it was to surface for food or a bathroom break, Belinda thought. What fun.

The next thing she knew, Hannah was being nestled in

beside her. Hannah flung her arms, slapping the top of the sheets and kicking her pudgy legs as if she could punch a hole through the sheets that constricted her.

Thomas kissed both of their foreheads. "Love you," he said.

Belinda propped Hannah up on the pillow so she could feed her with the fresh, warm bottle Thomas had brought. "Love you too."

"God, I know my attitude is not right," Belinda whispered when Thomas closed the door. "Help our marriage stay strong, and help me to support my husband in his decisions. He's doing the best he can with what he knows. If either of us is at fault, show us the error in our ways. Show me what I can do. That's something only You can do."

⁂

Around noon Belinda walked past the closed door of T. J.'s room. She paused when a familiar, yet unpleasant scent hit her nose. Her college days in the coed dorm weren't so far behind her that she couldn't recognize the stench. It didn't matter that it was trying to be hidden by a can of cheap air freshener.

"God bless my soul and my temper if this is what I think it is," she said, banging on the door.

This is my house. I don't need permission to enter a room I pay for.

Belinda turned the knob, but the door was locked. "T. J. Open the door."

There was no answer, so she knocked and turned the knob again. Belinda knew he could hear her despite the music that thumped from behind the closed door. "T. J.," she said again.

Her rapping and her words were louder. Another episode like this and she'd take the door off the hinges and store it in the garage. He was only seventeen. There was no such thing as privacy.

Belinda heard scuffling behind the door before T. J. opened it. She glared at him. She was sure he was wearing the same jeans he'd had on for the past three days. His boxes of clothes were untouched, stacked in the corner where Thomas had put them. She walked in and scanned the room.

The television was set to music videos, but it didn't match the music or lyrics coming from the nearby radio.

"Ma'am?"

"What are you doing in here?"

"Chillin'."

That was the problem. That's all he did. Belinda walked over to the window.

"What's that smell, and why do you have this window open?"

T. J. suddenly retaliated as if he were used to a barrage of questions being swung at him.

"I was hot, so I opened it." He nearly spat his words.

It was true, Belinda thought. Teenagers thought adults were dummies. They thought that adults were dropped down in the middle of life and had never experienced or heard of absolutely anything.

Belinda propped her hands on her hips. "The air is on, so if you're hot you can come downstairs and cool off. You're probably getting stuffy in this room." It was more a command than it was a suggestion.

T. J. leaned over to cuff the bottom of his extralong jeans, then pulled down on his white T-shirt, already two sizes too large.

"Can I use the phone? I need to call Ma. She's probably through trippin' by now."

"You can use any of the phones downstairs." That would get him out of this room, and then she'd find something for him to do downstairs to keep him busy.

T. J. slunk out of the door holding up the side of his pants. Belinda followed him. The window could stay open for now. Whatever was in there needed to be out. Thomas had to open his eyes now. If things continued this way without discipline, T. J. may go too far.

T. J. went to the phone in the den, and Belinda appeared to look busy in the kitchen where she could still be in hearing range. Hannah would be waking from her nap shortly, so she made enough bottles to last for the rest of the night. She still had some work she needed to concentrate on before Hannah demanded her undivided attention. The first order of business, though, was to dip in on T. J.'s conversation.

T. J. must've tried every number his mother had, and he left the same message all three times. "Ma, it's me. I promise I'll do better now; just come get me. Call me. Please."

He was still a child, Belinda thought. A wounded one. She felt bad about the negative thoughts she'd had against him for the past three days. Inside there was still the seven-year-old she'd wanted to fight for.

Once after one of his Little League baseball games, T. J. had asked if he could call her Ma 'Linda instead of Miss Belinda. She'd agreed to it as long as it was okay with his mother. Of course, it wasn't. Still, a few times he'd called her that when they were alone. It had been their secret. She wondered if he still remembered.

Belinda heard the television click on in the den. He was still being lazy, but at least he was out of his room for a while. She'd let him be for now. His father was right. He needed to transition.

She owed Thomas an apology. There was still no excuse for what she assumed had been going on in her house upstairs, but she'd let Thomas handle it.

Belinda retreated to her office to catch up on her work and

311

to wait for the call from her sister about her mother's progress. At last word, the clot buster they'd used did the job. They'd been warned that it could possibly cause a mild stroke or a massive heart attack, but at that point, it seemed to be the only option.

It was stressful to make decisions for an incapacitated loved one. It reminded her that when they found the time, she and Thomas needed to sit down and write directives for their family. It was tough to think about, but it was life.

Belinda pushed her office door closed slightly, but she could still hear the television downstairs. *The life we are dealt isn't always what we expect,* she thought.

You may be caught off guard, but I never am.

35

That morning Paula had eased out of her bed and grabbed her silk robe from the bench at the foot of the bed. She didn't want a reason to doze off while reading her Bible, so she had taken it to one of the guest rooms the night before. Her journal and Bible lay exactly where she'd left them. Darryl and Micah never came in this room. It had become her secret place.

Meeting God in the morning proved to be refreshing. *I rise before the dawning of the morning, and cry for help; I hope in Your word*, read Psalm 119:147. Before the bustle of the day set in, she'd sink into a place of peace. It was a joy to welcome the new day by sunrise. It was a sign that she was another day closer to seeing Darryl as the man she married. Or at least she'd been trying to convince herself that was the case.

Darryl's response to her wasn't always cordial, but at least he had gotten better. Last week when nausea got the best of Paula's evening, he bathed Micah and put him to bed early so she could rest. He'd left soon afterward. That's what hurt. So she kept praying, like she had this morning.

Paula had called Margaret to come in yesterday, even though she wasn't scheduled for a cleaning until next week. She wanted the house spotless for the P.O.W.E.R. meeting at her house this morning. The earlier part of the week, she'd been busy finding and scheduling the caterer. She had had her share of hosting parties while working on different committees with the other doctors' wives over the years. Today she'd put her knowledge to work.

Darryl made plans to desert the house all day after finding out about the P.O.W.E.R. meeting. She'd tried to convince him to take Micah with him, but he refused. It hadn't been as easy as Darryl thought to keep Micah preoccupied at his business meetings. He wasn't going to take the chance this time.

"He needs to learn to sit still," he'd said last night.

"He's four. There's only so much sitting still he can do."

Paula was prepared to drop Micah at his grandmother's house. They hadn't visited her since the time Darryl picked up Micah without her knowledge. It would be a good time to share her pregnancy news. So far, it had only reached the ears of her prayer partners. She'd also asked them to pray for her relationship with her mother. It had never been what a nourishing mother-daughter relationship should be. They went about their separate lives and called each other only when they had to. That needed to change.

Paula had so many personal issues on her prayer list, it was a wonder God could get to them all, she thought.

I already know the end to every situation.

Last night she'd wondered how she was going to squeeze in an extra errand to her mother's house, seeing that Rosanna refused to drive on the highway. A call from Patricia spared her the trip. She was taking Trey to the zoo today and wanted to invite Micah along for the day and to sleep over tonight.

Micah didn't even bother to kiss her good-bye when he heard the doorbell ring this morning. He bounded down the

314

front steps and flew past Patricia, dragging his overnight suit-
case behind him. It held more toys than it did clothes. She'd
let him stuff his bag with whatever he wanted. At least he'd
be out of the way for a while.

Paula's food spread and the immaculate layout and decor
of her house had the P.O.W.E.R. women in awe. She graciously
took them on tours through the living room, great room, office,
dining area, five bedrooms, four baths, and sun room.

Afterward, the women got comfortable in the living room,
where Paula had marked each of their spaces with a personalized pillow with their first initial. It was a special touch that
she'd put in a rush order for through her favorite catalog.

"Paula, would you like to lead our discussion today on
marriage and husbands?" Sister Barnes asked.

Paula was intent on playing the part of hostess. She was
holding a tray of spinach quiche, the final round of hors
d'oeuvres.

God, this isn't funny. This week had been busy. Not only
had she not read or studied the lesson, but she was probably
the person least qualified to touch the subject. Her marriage
was still in shambles as far as she was concerned.

When Paula came to herself, she realized the group was
staring at her—waiting for an answer.

She confessed. "Actually, I didn't study the lesson. I apologize, but I want you to know that this is serious to me. I don't
take it lightly." *Please go to someone else.*

Sister Barnes walked over and stood behind Paula. When
she patted Paula's shoulders, she knew her decision stood.

"I really feel like you're supposed to lead this lesson. So let's
move forward and go with the flow. We'll all learn together. Is
that fair?"

Everyone answered yes except Paula. She offered the
quiche one last time before she went to set the tray on the
kitchen counter.

"I guess we should proceed then," Paula said, opening her manual for the first time that week. She sat down beside Zora in the only empty chaise left in the room.

Paula began by reading the lesson's foundation Scriptures in 1 Corinthians 13:4–8. It was the essence of love as God defined it. "Love suffers long and is kind; love does not envy; love does not parade itself, is not puffed up," Paula read. Her heart sank as she continued through the Scriptures. ". . . bears all things, believes all things, hopes all things, endures all things. Love never fails."

Paula looked up at Sister Barnes and was grateful when she took the lead.

"Can anybody in here say their life exhibits every facet of true love?"

Five of the twelve women raised their hands.

"Depends on the day," someone said.

"Love encompasses more than we think," Sister Barnes said, sliding to the edge of her seat.

Whenever she did that, the ladies knew she meant serious business. "And we just throw the word *love* around so loosely without realizing the sacrifice involved with it," Sister Barnes said. "Everybody always says they want to press toward the mark, and be who God has called them to be. God says in 1 Corinthians that the greatest gift is love. And one of the most powerful statements in the Bible is, 'God is love.'"

Sister Barnes looked around the room. All of the women were silent, nodding their heads.

I have so much to learn about love, Paula thought.

"Now, I don't know who that was for, but it was for somebody." Sister Barnes slid back in her chair and opened her Bible. "I'm sorry, Paula. Go ahead."

"No apology necessary," Paula said. She looked at the lesson in her manual. "Our first question is about the order of kingdom marriages. The key verses are in 1 Corinthians 11:3

and the verses in Ephesians 5, starting at verse 15. Let's read those verses silently."

Paula tried to soak in the Scriptures, but her mind combated the truth of every word.

So Darryl is supposed to wash me with the Word and love me like he loves his own body? I might run a close third to his cars—he washes them and loves them on a regular basis. I don't even fare that well if you compare me to his real estate ventures.

Paula read on.

And I'm supposed to respect him? God, You know I've tried. I'm getting up early and praying, reading my Word every day.

But are you respecting him? Those are good deeds, but do they come from the heart?

Paula looked up when Sister Barnes cleared her throat. She slid to the edge of her seat again.

Why do I feel like this one's for me?

"Two Scriptures I want to add that aren't in the manual are in 1 Peter and 1 Corinthians. "1 Peter 3:1–2 says—" she flipped to a page marked in her Bible, "'wives, . . . be submissive to your own husbands, that even if some do not obey the word, they, without a word, may be won by the conduct of their wives, when they observe your chaste conduct accompanied by fear.' It also says in 1 Corinthians 7:14 that an 'unbelieving husband is sanctified by the wife,' and vice versa. That's so powerful, ladies. Your husband can be won over to Christ by the light and love of God he sees in you."

Yolanda raised her hand. "I can vouch for that."

Paula was relieved that a question or the request to expound wasn't thrown back to her.

"My husband was the one who accepted salvation and began to grow in the Lord first," Yolanda said. "I didn't want to hear it." She pounded her hand in the air. "I was too caught up in my perception of church folks and let it keep me from a relationship with God. The last thing I wanted to see or hear about was church.

"For two years my husband kept praying for me. Sometimes I'd wake up and hear him praying on his side of the bed, or I'd tip out of bed and hear him downstairs in the living room. Over time his prayers softened my heart."

A single tear rolled down Yolanda's cheek. "And he didn't stop," she said.

Paula wiped away one of her own. Then a second, and a third.

"And he didn't stop," she said again. "He didn't stop, he didn't stop, he didn't stop . . ."

Paula didn't know whether Yolanda was actually repeating the phrase or if God had sealed it in her head. No matter Darryl's response, she wouldn't stop.

Zora stuffed a tissue in Paula's hand. "Thank you," she said, without looking up.

Paula couldn't stop the tears. She felt the wail rise through the soles of her feet until it nearly choked her throat. Her body slumped over and slid itself onto the floor. She no longer had control.

Someone had knelt beside her, covering her shivering body with her arms. She felt another set of hands on her head and then the voices of women around her. They prayed fervently, sharing her tears and petitions until a peace like Paula had never experienced in life enveloped her. After a few minutes, she was able to push herself up to an upright position. All of the women were on the floor crouched or sitting around her.

"I must look a mess," she said, running an already soaked tissue across her eyes. It was streaked with black mascara and brown eye shadow.

"Who cares what you look like?" Belinda was sitting closest to her. "You just got a breakthrough."

"Amen," the women said.

"Your marriage will never be the same again," Belinda said. She held Paula's face in one of her hands. "Never again, I feel that," she said, poking her stomach, "right here. Deep down your husband is going to come to the Lord and come back to you."

It amazed Paula that she hadn't shared her struggle, yet the women knew.

Paula laid her head on Belinda's bosom and let her sister in Christ rock her like a baby. She drew from Belinda's strength and wisdom. Paula's spirit felt revived.

Sister Barnes's voice had nearly dropped to a whisper. "The Word says that the prayer of a righteous man avails much. It also says in Matthew that whatever you ask in prayer, believing, you will receive."

Two of the other women helped Sister Barnes stand up from where was kneeling at Paula's feet. "Like Belinda said, Paula has had a breakthrough. And she believes now. And if we believe with her, we can pray to have her marriage set back in order and her family to be healed and restored."

"That's right," Yolanda said. She held out a hand to Paula. "I can stand with you on that."

Paula stood to her feet, though she had to hold on tightly to Yolanda and Belinda to steady herself.

"Me too," the rest of the ladies agreed.

"With Paula's permission," Sister Barnes said, "we're going to walk through this beautiful house and pray in each room. Right now," she said to Paula, "God is working on your behalf. It was ordained for us to be here today."

"Please do," Paula said. Yolanda and Belinda kept their arms around Paula's waist as she walked with them to the steps leading upstairs.

Her other group members dispersed themselves around the house with Bibles in hand and the transforming Word of God on their lips. Paula began to cry again. Her prayer for a group of friends had been answered.

36

Zora and Monét rode in silence until they reached the subdivision entrance. Zora came to a slow stop and looked at Monét while she waited for the traffic to subside.

Monét reclined the passenger seat slightly and leaned her head back on the headrest.

"What are you thinking?" Zora asked. She pulled out into the center turning lane and eased into the flow of traffic.

"Marriage is serious business. You have to be so careful about who you connect yourself to. I had no idea Paula was going through that. After the time we've spent with her, she's never let on."

"Didn't I tell you I could always see something in her eyes? I've been telling you that the whole time."

Monét closed her eyes. "I'm so thankful to God that things are about to change for her. No. They *have* changed. I couldn't stop crying. My head is still pounding."

"When it comes to the men God brings and has brought into our lives, we can't afford *not* to pray," Zora said.

"This entire P.O.W.E.R. experience is teaching me to step up my prayer life," Monét said. "God has given us the privilege to petition Him and commune with Him, and we don't use it to our advantage. We've got to be armed for the battle. What's the highest rank in the army? I don't know—let's just say commanding officer. God is our commanding officer."

"How does that Scripture start about the armor of God?" Zora searched her memory, tapping the steering wheel.

Monét snapped her fingers until it came to her. "Be strong in the Lord and in the power of His might." She looked over at Zora.

"In God's might," Zora said. "Now that's some power."

"That's for a Purpose-Oriented Woman Equipped and Restored," Monét said, cranking up Zora's air conditioner another notch.

"That's for a woman going to battle for her family with the sword of the Spirit. Slicing up everything in our lives that's not according to God's Word."

Monét stomped her foot. "Walking through our situations with the gospel of peace on the soles of our feet."

They continued, adding their own flavor to the sixth chapter of Ephesians.

"Holding our shields of faith high, blocking every evil tactic," Monét said.

"Because we're more than conquerors, and we can overcome any situation set before us," Zora said, holding her hand up for Monét to slap. When Monét tried to pull away, Zora wouldn't let go.

"I'm so glad you let Bryce go. Promise me you're finished dealing with him."

"I'm finished," Monét said. She massaged the side of her temples. She wished she could go back in time and erase her life from the moment she agreed to go with Bryce's family. No, back to the kiss that had drawn her in during this last stint.

Then there was Jeremiah.

"Jeremiah really likes you, you know," Zora said, as if she'd read Monét's mind. "Whatever you've said or did to him over the last few times you've seen and talked to him has made him think about something more than work and music."

"You're exaggerating."

"No, I'm not. Preston told me, and you know he's not going to exaggerate something like that. After Jeremiah saw you at the wax museum, he had to have asked me and Preston at least five times that week what you saw in Bryce. Come on, Monét, even Ray Charles could see that Bryce was a counterfeit. I promise. If you'd give Jeremiah the chance, he'd take it."

"Do you still think so?" Monét rubbed the area above her nose. Her headache had moved to the center of her forehead. "He didn't call me at all that weekend, and I haven't heard from him since. I'd told him ahead of time that I was going to be tied up that Saturday, so he was supposed to give me a call on Sunday after church."

"That was before he knew who you were tied up with. And then the fact that he saw you guys kiss had to be another deterrent, I'm sure."

"You're not making this any better."

"I'm not trying to make it better. My job is to put reality in your face."

"There's one reality you missed. Jeremiah lives in Houston. I mean, he's traveling a lot now, but it's not going to last forever."

"I know, I know. And you don't do long-distance relationships."

"But I do long-distance friendships, and I can see how he could be a good friend."

And Monét knew she owed the possible good friend a call.

37

Leave it to God to be as strategic as this. The subject of today's P.O.W.E.R. meeting was children. Belinda had pressed herself to attend the session even though she was physically and mentally worn out. Everyone in the group had grown so close lately. But today, Belinda felt like an outsider. She didn't feel like herself. It was as if she were watching her life unfold on a movie screen instead of living it.

Scene one. Belinda had been back to Baltimore for two days now and had hesitantly left Hannah behind. As much as she wanted her daughter with her, Belinda couldn't handle both Hannah and the extended hospital visits with her mother.

Bernice had been weaned off of the ventilator, but now she was getting prepared for a tracheotomy. The tubes in her throat wouldn't allow her to speak, so she responded to questions with grunts and facial expressions. Her eyes, especially, spoke volumes. They gleamed anytime Belinda or her sister entered her room.

Scene two. Things with T. J. were decent. Not perfect, but decent.

Thomas had performed an all-out strip search and room upheaval when he arrived home that night after Belinda told him about the strange odor coming from T. J.'s room. It turned out that T. J. was guilty of the contraband Belinda had suspected, and the disciplinarian erupted out of Thomas. He couldn't believe T. J. had the nerve to smoke a joint in his house.

That time it was the two men of the house behind T. J.'s closed doors. The next morning and every morning since then, T. J. went to work with Thomas to serve his sentence.

"Yes, they're straight-A students," their hostess, Rhonda, was telling one of the ladies. "One day each of my sons is going to be somebody's husband, and they both need to have some discipline and focus in their lives."

Rhonda walked over and handed Belinda a photo album. Since arriving at her home, she had given every lady a customized presentation through the scrapbooks and photo albums chronicling the lives of her two teenage sons. Belinda was next. She flipped through the books until Sister Barnes called the session to start.

Sister Barnes encouraged them to sit beside a sister they hadn't had a chance to get to know. That meant, of course, that Zora, Monét, Belinda, and Paula would be split up. It was too bad. She felt so much comfort being around them.

A day hadn't passed that one of them didn't call to check on her and the family. At night, usually around ten, they all connected via phone to pray. It had helped her plenty of times when she couldn't find the words to pray for herself.

"How many of you have children?" Sister Barnes asked, raising her hand. Six of the other women raised their hands as well. Rhonda sat forward, proud as a peacock.

"How many want children?" Four more hands raised.

Belinda noticed one of the younger ladies in the group, Aimee, was the only one who didn't respond. She sat with her arms crossed tightly over her chest, locking out the world. Her face dared someone to question her.

"For our mothers and mothers-to-be, we're seeking God's Word about raising our children," Sister Barnes said. "When it's all said and done, the parents will be held accountable, not the day care center or the schools." She paused and looked around the room. "Not the television or the radio."

Moans of agreement came from two of the older women in the group.

"Belinda, could you open us in prayer, please?"

God was doing it again.

Yes, I am.

"Every head bowed," Belinda said. "God, we thank You for bringing us all together safely. As we delve into our study, Lord, show us how to parent according to Your Word. You're the ultimate parenting expert, and we seek Your guidance first. Teach us how to train up our children. Your Word says that if we bring them up in Your ways, they will not depart from them. And most of all, God, show us how to love our children. Love like You love. Amen."

"Amen, Belinda," Sister Barnes said. "You might as well take us to our foundation Scripture for today."

Belinda opened her Bible and found the corresponding Scripture listed in their P.O.W.E.R. study manual, Psalm 127:3–5.

She read, "Behold, children are a heritage from the Lord, the fruit of the womb is a reward. Like arrows in the hand of a warrior, so are the children of one's youth. Happy is the man who has his quiver full of them."

Sister Barnes opened the discussion. "When I reviewed this lesson, God reminded me of how awesome a responsibility it is to raise children. They're like sponges. Whatever they soak up they're bound to squeeze out."

Sister Barnes went on to teach on the value God places on

children as an inheritance, and with the responsibility of directing and releasing them into destiny. Belinda highlighted the Scriptures they reviewed in Deuteronomy 6:6–7; Proverbs 13:24; Psalm 34:11; and others. She had a feeling she was going to refer to them often. Better yet, she'd read them and try her best to live them so they'd become a part of who she was. Until now, they'd only lived on the page.

"For some reason, I never pictured Jesus as a child, other than the biblical story they always tell about His birth," Jewel interjected. "But He was a baby learning to walk, a toddler learning His first words. Mary had to raise Jesus. I mean really. How many of us think we could've done that? She had to teach Him, and she must've done her job, because He was preaching in the temple at Jerusalem when He was twelve."

Glenda laughed. "My son's twelve, and I can barely get him to memorize a Scripture." She shook her head. "Sad, but true. I've got some work to do. I need to study more myself if I want something to pass on."

Sister Barnes studied the faces of the ladies in the room.

"Have you decided how many arrows you will have, or did you at least consult God about the call for your family?" she asked. "You know, God will send children for you to raise, and they won't always be birthed from your womb."

Listen. This isn't just about Hannah.

The ladies raising children—biological and not—had so much wisdom to add. Belinda gleaned all she could, even though she was counted in that number. Thomas Jr. challenged what she thought she knew about being a parent.

Before Belinda knew it, she'd shared her story. Her infertility and insecurities about it. Hannah's adoption. T. J.'s recent reappearance. The fact that his mother, Juanita, had said she was never coming back to get him, that she'd had enough.

"I didn't have time to adjust. Teenagers are so unpredictable. Especially T. J. He's got to sort through all of his feel-

328

ings. I can't imagine what he's going through, so how can I minister to him?"

That was the real problem. Belinda couldn't touch him. She'd always been the one who was called to the rescue. She'd been the one with all of the answers and the unshakable faith.

"We're supposed to launch them as arrows, and I don't know which direction to shoot him, because frankly, we don't know who he is."

Belinda looked around. The faces she looked back into were nonjudgmental. Especially Janice's.

"In time you will," Janice said, reaching for her hand. "As you pray for him and your relationship as a family, God will begin to reveal things to you."

As Janice continued, Belinda learned that she spoke from experience. When she married her husband four years earlier, he already had twin fifteen-year-old daughters and a twelve-year-old son. He'd been widowed when the children were in elementary school, so they hadn't had a woman in their lives during some critical stages of their lives. His daughters' feelings, especially, were locked up because her husband hadn't been a big communicator.

"Communication is so key," Zora said from across the room. She'd been quiet during most of the session. "My mother and I were as close as two best friends, but she still had the line drawn that she was the mother. As she should have. I'd assumed we talked about everything, but I found out not too long ago that we didn't."

Belinda knew Zora was about to share her heart with the group. She'd told Preston's family and had begun to share the news with her church family. From what Zora said, it had meant the difference between her being stuck or moving forward with her life.

"Unfortunately, my parents were killed in a car accident earlier this year." Her eyes traveled to Monét, Paula, and Belinda before she continued. "They took a piece of my life that I may never find," Zora said.

Belinda watched the expressions on the women's faces as Zora told her story. Raised eyebrows, a few dropped jaws, but most with no reactions at all. She could tell they didn't know what to do.

"Thanks to all three of you for sharing," Sister Barnes said. "Whether or not you realize it, your testimonies will help more people than you know."

"That's right," someone said.

Sister Barnes clasped her hands together and shook them with passion. "There are so many children who, for whatever reason, don't have positive influences in their lives. That's why the first ladies of our churches have organized opportunities for us to give back to the community. Glenda, could you read the information I gave you earlier?"

Belinda listened as their project was described. They'd been assigned to spend the day at a girls' group home. They'd spend quality time with them and participate in some much-needed repair and decorating at their facility.

"This is love in action," Glenda said after she finished reading.

Belinda noticed all of a sudden that Zora seemed restless. She'd already packed up her Bible and P.O.W.E.R. manual. Everything about her body language said she was ready to leave.

You're going to have to take her to My Word. She's got one last step.

Belinda closed her eyes. *Yes, Lord.*

38

I'm not going," Zora said matter-of-factly. She stepped forward into a deep lunge to stretch her right hamstring. She'd thought about it all week. She wasn't ready.

Monét leaned over to one side, her left arm stretched across her hip. She stood up straight and posted her hands on her hips. "What do you mean you're not going?"

"I can't take going to the group home. Maybe I can participate in a community service project with another group."

"Why? What are you running from?"

"I'm not running from anything." Zora sat back in a deep squat to stretch her hamstring.

"Then where did this sudden change come from?"

"Have I not experienced two major shocks to my life in the last nine months? I haven't gotten over it yet. I thought I'd accepted it, but I haven't. If anybody's entitled to be on an emotional roller coaster, it's me."

"You're more than entitled to go through your process. But it's not fair for you to withhold yourself from a group of children who may very well need the exact words or touch that you have to offer."

Zora held her hands over her head. She felt the pull down the center of her back and reached higher. She must've slept balled up in an awkward position last night.

"It could've been me. If I wasn't adopted, you never know what kind of life I would've led. I could've found myself abused or neglected. Don't you see that?"

"Yes. I see that you were blessed that it *wasn't* you. God saw fit to take your life down a different path, and you should be grateful."

"I'm grateful. But I'm still not ready."

"What am I supposed to tell the group today when you don't show up?" Monét asked.

"Tell them the truth. And if you don't want to, then I'll let them know at the next meeting."

"Maybe you should talk to Belinda."

"Why? Because she has an adopted daughter? That doesn't necessarily qualify her to speak to my situation."

Zora started the timer on her sports watch and started in a slow jog. Monét, who outpaced her with no effort whenever they ran together, jogged beside her. She matched her pace with Zora's. Their rubber soles thudded against the sidewalk as they started from their parking space, winding their way down the running trail.

Zora picked up speed. So did Monét. Maybe Monét was right. She was running away from the problem. If only it were that easy. She'd run until this mess was behind her. She'd run until the emotional weight and burden fell from her shoulders and her heart. She had lain her burden down for the Lord to carry, but somewhere along the way she'd picked it up again.

When Zora kicked it up another notch, Monét still kept pace with her gait. She'd run until everyone around her who didn't understand was left behind.

Zora broke into a sprint, and after a moment she noticed that no footsteps trailed behind her. The early morning August breeze cooled the tears on her face. Her eyes burned and clouded her vision when she finally stopped.

She moved off of the asphalt trail and squatted down in the grass. The untrimmed sprigs scratched her ankles and made her palms itch, but she was too overcome to stand. Feeling the comforting arms of her best friend around her only made the tears flow harder. When her well for the moment had dried up, she wiped her face with the underside of her T-shirt and stood up.

"I'll go," she said, her face buried in Monét's shoulder. "I'll go." She walked back to the car with her best friend arm in arm.

⁂

"I'm ready," Zora said, walking into the living room from her bedroom. She'd done a one-hundred-eighty-degree turn since the park this morning.

After she and Monét had left the park, they returned to Zora's house to get ready to go to the group home. Her promises posted around the house had made her feel better. God wouldn't forsake her; that she was sure of. He'd strengthened her to come this far.

Monét stood by the front window and pushed the sheer curtain aside. "Let's roll," she said. "I'm proud of you and so glad I wasn't going to have to resort to beating you down."

"Trust me, the mental beat-down I was giving myself was a whole lot worse."

Zora followed Monét outside. She was surprised to see Paula's and Belinda's cars pulled into her driveway. She looked at Monét, who shrugged as if she were clueless, but didn't do a good job hiding she was the guilty party.

"What are you guys doing here?"

"We're in this together," Belinda said, walking up and hugging Zora.

Paula added her arms around the ladies, followed by Monét, until their bodies were so close that they couldn't tell where one arm began and the other ended. They were one.

"And you know, we've been thinking," Belinda said, pulling out of the group. "There were so many powerful people that God anointed to lead His people, and He didn't have them all grow up in their biological family."

"Like Moses," Monét said.

Zora slipped her arm through Paula's and pulled her toward the car. "I guess I need to sit down for this one. This sounds like a planned presentation."

Paula opened the front door of her SUV, and Zora sat sideways in the front seat. She crossed her legs and propped her hands on her knees. "I'm ready."

"Like I was saying," Monét said, "Moses' mother had to put him in the Nile River to save his life. But it's not like she didn't want to keep him. She kept him for three months before she did that."

Belinda opened Paula's back door and tossed her purse on the seat. "Then God made it so that he was taken to the house of the Pharaoh, but they had to find someone to nurse him. And who do you think did that?"

"His mother," Paula said. "And she got paid for it." She climbed into the front seat and slipped on her shades. "And Moses didn't know until he was adult that he wasn't Pharaoh's son."

The women were all in Paula's car. She locked the doors and looked at her watch. "Buckle up. We don't have much time, and I can get us there in twenty minutes flat."

"Dear Jesus," Belinda said. "I'm going to close my eyes for the ride." She reached up and patted Zora's shoulder. "I have kids at home."

"Let's, go ladies," Paula said, backing out of the driveway. "We've got some young women's lives to touch."

Zora buckled her seat belt and turned so she could see all of the women. "You've already touched at least one."

God had put a family around her. It was what she'd prayed for, even though it hadn't come the way she thought.

Thank You, God. If I had taken the time to open my eyes, I would've seen You at work in my life instead of focusing on what I didn't have. Now I see.

Your ways are not My ways. And by the way, you're welcome.

39

Paula

I'm thinking about preparing a lunch and surprising Darryl at his office," Paula told the ladies. She pulled into Zora's driveway and cut off the car. It was a random thought at first, but now she wanted to act on it. She was putting action to her faith. Darryl was the father of her children, and her husband. *'Til death do us part.*

Before, she'd avoided going to his office because she thought the unexpected visit would unfold like a movie scene.

Paula would walk in wearing Darryl's favorite outfit and carrying food that she'd slaved over all morning. When she entered his office, his assistant would try to divert her attention or warn Darryl—without causing too much suspicion—that his wife was in the building.

Then, unbeknownst to Darryl, he'd round the corner with his mistress on his arm, her head thrown back in laughter. An argument would erupt, and the two women would end up playing tug-of-war with each other's hair while Darryl watched.

Enough with the drama.

"That's a wonderful idea," Belinda said. "You should definitely do it."

"When do you plan on going?" Zora asked.

"Tuesday. Before I change my mind."

Monét unbuckled her seat belt and scooted up closer to the front seat. "You're not going to change your mind," she told Paula. "You've come too far and been through too much."

"That's true." Paula was encouraged to hear those words from Monét. After the session at her house, she was worried that Monét would act uncomfortable around her since she'd known Darryl on a personal level. That night, Monét had called her personally to assure her that everything that had happened would be kept in the strictest confidence.

She'd also been able to talk to Monét about Victor. Even before their conversation, she knew that she'd have to cut Victor off. Although there wasn't a physical relationship, she'd become attached to him emotionally. That could be just as dangerous.

"I'm going to call Darryl's assistant on Monday to make sure his calendar is clear and that he'll be in the office," Paula said. "I've never met her before, so I hope she can keep a surprise."

"You've never met his assistant?"

"The first one, yes, but she retired. This lady has only been with him since around June."

"She must've been the one that was going to come to the auction, but had a family emergency," Monét remembered.

"Right. That's her."

"I owe you one for doing those invitations, so let me know if you need help," Zora said.

When it had been time to address the envelopes for Zora's wedding invitations, Paula had decided to lend her calligraphy skill to the cause.

"That's not a bad idea," Paula said, opening her door. "And can you believe I've finally accepted his real estate ventures? I can handle getting rid of some of our extra luxuries. At least for a while." She smiled. "If I'm called to be his help-meet, I might as well lend my skills to his vision. If he decides to leave medicine, we'll be back to living large in no time with my help."

"That's what I like to hear," Belinda said.

"I'm going to do it up. Give him something to remember and remind him what he has to come home to." She stepped out of the car and wiggled her hips. "Pregnant or not, I've still got it."

"Yes, you do," Zora said.

"Well, save it for Darryl," Monét said.

☙

It was a blessing to see Paula with a renewed outlook on life. She knew God would honor their prayers to revive her marriage. If there was another woman, she'd no longer be a threat or a desire to Darryl. And if there wasn't, that wall between them would be torn down.

God, You're so awesome. And thank You for taking the scales off of my eyes.

Bryce was still out of the picture, even though he was trying hard not to be. She'd grilled him until he'd broken and confessed why he was really at the hospital the evening he saw Zora. Guilt had made him try to turn the tables on her friend.

"Why is she trying to be in your business? She has a man, but she doesn't want you to be happy."

That was about the most ridiculous statement she'd ever heard, and Bryce soon realized she wasn't going for it. Monét didn't let up. She was going to make him tell the truth.

Bryce's visit to the hospital had been to see his former love interest and Monét's temporary stalker. This time Bryce had gone too far with playing with someone's heart. When he wouldn't commit to a relationship, she had started to stalk him and anyone else she saw him with.

The woman was emotionally distraught to the point that she'd started to inflict harm on herself. She'd overdosed on sleeping pills, and her roommate had rushed her to the hospital.

If that wasn't an eye-opener for Bryce, then what would be?

Monét prayed that the woman's eyes would be opened to her self worth. Unfortunately for Bryce, Monét didn't plan on hanging around to find out. No amount of begging, no phone calls, gifts, or office visits would change her mind. Ever.

When Bryce had walked out of her loft that day, she'd immediately called Jeremiah.

"I'm surprised to hear from you," he'd said.

"You must hate me," Monét had said. She didn't know what else to say.

"I don't hate you. You're a free woman. You can date who you want."

"Look, Jeremiah. What you saw that day is over. It's a long story about how it started and how it ended, so I don't want to go there. My door is closed to Bryce—literally and figuratively."

She had waited for him to say something.

People had always told her that turning thirty changed your outlook and made you more daring. She'd found out it was true.

"That's closed, but I'm open to you," she had said. "Never in my life have I connected with someone so quickly. I don't want you to think I'm going to pursue you or try to make us into a couple, because that's not the kind of woman I am. I just couldn't—"

"Monét." Jeremiah's voice had been steady. "Our slate is

clean. Do you think I didn't know this was going to happen? I'm a praying man. I knew you'd come to your senses sooner or later. I'm just thankful it was sooner. A brother's never felt a stab in the heart like that before."

"Jeremiah."

"I'm serious. That's why I know you're someone special."

"Thank you."

"And I can't wait to see you again."

"I hope it's soon." *There's that thirty-year-old boldness again.*

"Next Saturday would be nice. Work is sending me up again, and you still need to make good on your promise to show me some of the sites."

"I can do that," Monét had said.

The sun rose before they had found the end of their conversation. Monét couldn't sleep and had been happy to join Zora for a run this morning when she'd called. Her friend still didn't know.

Wait until I tell her this.

※

Zora's experience at the group home had been indescribable. She'd talked to the home's coordinator to see if she could make regular visits. She didn't care how many courses or clearances she'd have to get approved for. There was more that she had to offer. In time, God would reveal His plan.

"Do the mommies have to get home anytime soon?" Zora said, opening her pantry to find her blender.

The women had stretched out on the living room furniture.

"I'm free," Paula said. "Micah is with his grandmother."

"Me too. Hannah is with my sister, and she told me not to rush back."

"Good." The can opener hummed as Zora opened the

frozen can of pineapple orange juice. "I'm going to whip up some smoothies. You ladies rest. Today's my day to serve you."

Paula went from lying on the couch to reclining on the floor. "I'm going to take your advice," she said. "If you can't wake me up later, throw a sheet on me and let me sleep until morning."

"I would get down there with you," Belinda said, propping a pillow behind her head. "But I might not be able to get back up."

"Found a puzzle piece," Paula said, reaching under Zora's couch.

"Good. That's the last piece I was looking for after somebody's child knocked my table over. Snap it in for me," Zora said.

"Leave my baby alone," Paula said. She slipped the last puzzle piece in the empty space. "We offered to put it back together for you."

"I know." Zora dropped two large bananas into the blender along with the juice. "You'd already done more than enough." She laughed at the look on her face. "I'm just kidding."

"Speaking of kids, Belinda," Monét said, "how is your crew?"

"We're still adjusting, but we're doing good."

⁂

T. J. was still having his rebellious moments, but he knew he couldn't push Thomas too far. God had softened Belinda's heart for him.

The night before she had left to come back to Baltimore, she'd been preparing a day's worth of bottles for Hannah and packing a cooler of organic baby food.

T. J. had walked into the kitchen and slumped down in a chair at the kitchen table. He was wearing a pair of jean

342

shorts—that were nearly the length of a pair of pants—and a baggy LA Laker's jersey. T. J. had never put himself in the same room alone with Belinda on purpose.

"I know you don't want me here," he'd said. "Don't worry. As soon as I turn eighteen I'll be out of here."

Why do teenagers think eighteen will be the end of all of their problems?

Belinda had zipped the cooler closed and put it in the refrigerator.

"I never said that." She had pulled out a roll of chocolate-chip cookie dough. "Set the oven for three fifty, please."

He had dragged his feet across the floor. Belinda saw the black scuff mark on the floor. She wanted to tell him to pick up his feet, but now didn't seem like the ideal time.

"You don't have to say it. You act like it."

I'm guilty. "I apologize. Everything was so sudden, and I was in shock."

"You weren't the only one."

His words might've been harsh, depending on the tone, but there had been no anger in his voice.

Belinda knew he wanted her to understand.

T. J. had opened the drawer under the oven and pulled out a cookie sheet. They worked shoulder to shoulder, Belinda slicing the dough and T. J. spacing them out on the pan.

"You and Dad used to want me. I remember."

That had been the first time she'd heard him call Thomas "Dad" since he'd arrived. He usually just walked in the room with him and started a conversation.

"Thomas Junior," Belinda had said. She turned toward him and made him face her eye to eye. She saw the face that she remembered. The seven-year-old who needed to be loved. She saw the person he was now. He still needed it.

"We still do want you. We're going to make this family work."

343

T. J. hadn't looked away like she expect him too until they heard Hannah wake up from her nap in the next room.

"I'll get her," T. J. had said, wiping off his hands. "Thank you for saying that, Ma 'Linda." T. J. walked away.

Ma 'Linda. He did remember. Belinda wanted to hold on to that moment. Even later that day when T. J. and Thomas had argued about the school he'd have to attend, and then again about how T. J. kept his room, Belinda held on to her hope. After all, he'd called her Ma 'Linda.

40

I *can't believe I was scared to surprise my own husband,*
Paula thought. She was putting feet to her faith. Whatever it
took, she'd do.

"When you said you were going to lay it out, you really
meant it," Zora said. She picked up the silver candleholders
and wrapped them in a dish towel. She put them in the bag
along with the tablecloth, china, charger plates, and silver-
ware Paula had already packed.

Paula slipped her foot into a high-heeled mule. It was the
last day for a while that she'd wear a shoe over an inch high.
At four months, her pregnant body was causing her to become
more unbalanced. But this would be a special day—and a special night—to remember. She wanted to look her best.

"Put this in there too," she said. Paula handed Zora a
family photograph in a pewter frame. "Just a reminder."

"When he sees you, he'll have all the reminder he needs."
Zora lifted the bag to her shoulder. "I hope you made plans
for Micah tonight."

"You know I did. He's staying at his best friend's house. I told the little boy's mom we had some family business to take care of tonight."

"You weren't lying."

Paula led Zora out to the garage, and they secured the bag and the hot plates of food in her trunk. She hadn't let Zora see what the entrée for the day would be.

"As soon as I help you set everything up, I'll disappear," Zora said.

"I forgot my CD player and CDs," Paula said. She let up the garage door for Zora to get out, then ran back into the house. By the time Paula came back outside, Zora had backed her car down the driveway, waiting in the cul-de-sac. A few minutes later they were on their way to Darryl's office. *This is going to be good,* Paula thought.

⁂

Paula knew that the hospital wasn't one of Zora's favorite places to be, so she was appreciative that she'd volunteered. Paula needed the emotional support; otherwise, she may have turned around and walked back out of the door once she heard the first tap of her heel on the tiled floor. When they reached the administrative wing of the hospital, the floor turned into a carpeted hallway, and the antiseptic smell was left behind.

Paula walked to the desk that she assumed was Darryl's assistant's. Zora lagged a few steps behind, carrying most of the gear to set up his office. Zora had insisted that she carry everything except the CD player, because she didn't want Paula to strain her body or get sweaty by the time they trekked from the parking lot.

"It's such a pleasure to meet you, Maxine," Paula said to the petite woman sitting behind the desk. Her hair was cut low to her head, and her eyes squeezed into tiny slits when she smiled. She looked just like her squeaky voice sounded. "Dr. Manns doesn't have any idea, does he?"

"No idea," Maxine said. "I made sure he had a reason to come back to the office after his clinic rotation."

"Thank you so much, Maxine," Paula said. "Let me give you a hug." Paula was starting to feel better.

"Of course, sweetheart. I'm so glad to finally meet you. I kept asking Dr. Manns when you were going to come in."

"I'm sorry," Paula said, turning around to Zora. "This is my friend Zora. She's going to help me set up."

"Hi," Zora said, hoisting one of the bags off her shoulder.

Paula knew she'd overpacked it. It must've felt like it weighed a ton.

"You ladies go ahead and go back. You've got at least twenty minutes before Dr. Manns is scheduled back in the office. Don't waste any time either," she cautioned. "You know Dr. Manns is always on time."

"That's true," Paula said, and walked back to Darryl's office. She opened the door, surprised and relieved that the room looked the exact way she'd remembered. For some reason she'd expected their family pictures to be replaced with him and someone else. In fact, on the bookshelf behind his desk was the same picture she'd brought with her.

"Nice office," Zora said, picking up the only stack of papers on a nearby round table. She placed them on the burgundy leather chair near the window and helped Paula set the table.

"You don't know how much I appreciate you, Zora," Paula said, unwrapping the utensils.

"Stop thanking me. I told you it's no problem. Didn't we say we were here to stand by you?" Zora set the white china dishes on the tablecloth. It was a sentimental touch that Paula had decided to add at the last minute. It was their wedding pattern. She wondered if Darryl would notice.

"But you didn't just say it," Paula said. "You're doing it."

"For the last time, you're welcome." Zora looked at the digital clock hanging above Dr. Manns's flat-screen computer monitor. "Let's keep this moving so we can finish before—"

The door latch clicked, and Darryl walked into the room. Maxine was two steps behind him.

"He moved too fast for me to warn you," she said, peeking around his shoulder. "You two have a lovely time." She patted Dr. Manns on his arm. "You have a beautiful wife. Just beautiful."

"Thank you," Darryl mumbled. He pulled off his white coat and hung it on the back of the door.

"I wanted to do something special for you," Paula said. She scolded herself. It made no sense to feel this nervous. *Stop it, Paula. He's your husband.* She handed him a menu that she'd designed on the computer that morning. He read over it before he plopped down at one of the place settings. He didn't seem to be the least bit thrilled.

It didn't matter. She was doing this because God had told her to. Paula looked around the room and realized that Zora had disappeared. She hadn't even noticed her slip out. Her support was gone.

I'm still here.

Paula pulled the prepared plates out of the portable warmer and set one in front of Darryl. He'd since found something more interesting to keep him busy on his Palm Pilot.

Who cares? Her obedience to God would bring a blessing to her house, even if Darryl never looked at her one time.

God, at least let him see that I'm making an effort.

Darryl shoved his Palm Pilot into his shirt pocket and looked up. "Thanks for lunch," he said.

"You're welcome," she said, and set two bottles of sparkling water on the table. *Thank You, God. That's the only sign I need.*

41

The September morning couldn't have been more ideal. Monét awakened not long after the sun took its place in the sky. She felt refreshed. New.

She thanked God that Jeremiah was able to overlook her stupidity and deal with her in a loving way. He was more concerned about her as a sister in Christ than as a potential companion. They'd prayed together for God's perfect will for their lives.

Monét slipped on a light jacket to ward off the chill of the crisp air until the temperature reached the forecast seventy-five degrees. By nine o'clock, she had picked up Jeremiah for breakfast before they headed to Washington DC for a sightseeing tour via the latest Segway transporters. They watched an operation and safety video, then relocated outside to test their two-wheeled machines on the sidewalk of Pennsylvania Avenue.

Monét stifled a laugh as she watched Jeremiah's Segway shoot backward. When he looked up at her, she turned her head to watch the more adept teenage boy and girl in their group turning circles with finesse.

"Don't you say a word," he said, after he finally stood straight to stop the vehicle's inwanted moves.

"I didn't say anything." Monét moved toward him, but kept her distance in case he zipped forward or backward again. The fact that this athlete couldn't handle such a simple piece of equipment was amusing.

Monét liked the preppy look he was sporting today—khaki pants, a red and blue striped polo shirt, and a pair of classic white sneakers. It was the first time she'd seen him in a baseball cap, and he wore it pulled low over his forehead.

What had she been thinking? As fine as Bryce was, he still paled in comparison. She still prayed that one day Bryce would be introduced to the God who was the lover of her soul. Every person, no matter their shortcomings, deserved to know Him.

"You can help a brother out any day now," Jeremiah said. He was standing by the side of his Segway with a look of half amusement and half defeat.

"I thought I wasn't supposed to say anything," she said, stepping down beside him. "We wouldn't have to have this lesson if you'd paid attention during the video."

Jeremiah mounted the Segway again, and Monét instructed him to lean forward to move ahead and tilt back to go in reverse. The turns were performed by a mere twist of the handle. Within a minute, he'd caught on and was zipping around the sidewalk.

The guide led them and eight other eager tourists on a six-mile tour of the nation's capital. In four hours they were educated with facts and entertained with anecdotes about the Federal Triangle, National Archives, Washington Monument, the IRS Building, U.S. Navy Memorial, and others. They dismounted and parked their high-tech scooters when it was time to tour the sites located on the National Mall.

Riding along with Jeremiah against the landscapes, Washington DC never looked so good. As much as they usually talked, they were comfortable in their silence. After the tour, they found a quaint ice cream shop to refuel their energy.

Monét couldn't have imagined a better way to spend the day, and she couldn't have imagined how it could've been better. She twirled her red plastic spoon through the small cup of rocky road ice cream.

"You're the only person I know who goes out for dessert before they eat dinner," Monét said.

"I wanted us to celebrate." Jeremiah pulled off his cap and put it on the bench beside him.

"The sightseeing was nice, but I don't think it calls for a celebration."

Jeremiah put down his double scoop of strawberry shortcake ice cream. He licked his spoon, then stuck it in the pink mound.

"I want to celebrate my move." He reached across the table and put his hand on Monét's. "To Baltimore."

"What? When did this happen? Why didn't you tell me?"

"They came to me about it earlier this week, but I had to make sure it was what God wanted me to do. I was set on staying in Houston all of my life. If I had talked to everybody about it first, I'd have everyone's opinions in my head."

"So you're sure? Absolutely sure?" Monét couldn't believe it. Even her ice cream wasn't as sweet as the words she'd just heard. *God, I can't believe this.*

Believe it.

"Absolutely." Jeremiah picked up his ice cream again and smiled. "Tell me why you're looking like that. What are you thinking?"

"I just can't believe it."

Jeremiah held out his cup for Monét to take a taste of his ice cream. "There's nothing like a surprise when God is in the middle of it. But then again, He's not surprised about anything."

Monét reflected back on the past months. Her life, like the women's lives around her, had turned like the pages of a book. They could've written their own stories—the way they thought best—but God had His own plan. She thought of the verse in Proverbs 16:9, *A man's heart plans his way, but the Lord directs his steps.*

Monét wondered where God's next step would lead her. She enjoyed how He'd been leading her so far.

"Before we go to dinner, I need to pick up the bridesmaids' jewelry for Zora. Would you mind coming with me?"

"That'll work. And as long as I'm being held hostage, you can help me find something for Preston. I want to give him something special for the wedding to show him how much I love and appreciate him." Jeremiah put his baseball cap back on to shield the sun that had moved from its hiding place in the clouds. "You know, man to man."

"I need to get something meaningful for Zora too."

Monét swirled her spoon around in her ice cream. She didn't want to get ahead of herself or of God, but she sensed something more than a friendship with Jeremiah. And it wouldn't be long. This time next year, she may be sending out her own wedding invitations.

42

Zora pushed open the double doors to the sanctuary. In her humble opinion, it was breathtaking. The white multi-sized columns on the altar were draped with white chiffon and entwined with ivy. The columns' formation created an overhang where she and Preston would stand, symbolizing the start of their new home and lives together.

Following last night's rehearsal, Monét and Bailee, the florist, decorated alternating pew ends with shoulder-high candleholders that were also twined with ivy, white roses, and purple organza ribbon.

"This is it," Zora whispered, and walked down the center aisle. She took slow, deliberate steps. She wanted to soak it in before she was swept into the surrealism of the moment. In two hours the path would take her to the next stage of her life. She felt the presence of someone walk up behind her.

"Zora," Monét said, "isn't it amazing? No, it's past amazing." Monét put her arm around Zora's waist.

Zora rested her head on Monét's shoulder. She stood in

awe of God because He'd cared enough about her to heal her heart and to bring a family of sisters into her life. She was on His mind.

I trust You. Before she'd said it with her lips, this time with her heart.

"Are you ready?" Monét asked. Her voice was tender, as if she didn't want to disrupt Zora's reflections. "The photographer will be here in an hour, and we need to get you ready."

They left the sanctuary and walked down the hall to the women's lounge that Preston's mother had reserved as the bridal suite. Everyone turned around when the door opened.

Zora's spunk returned. "What are you guys looking at me for?"

Victoria tilted her chin in the air while Paula applied eyeliner to her left lid. She peeked at Zora through one open eye. "Get used to it. You're about to be the center of attention."

"I can handle that," Zora said. She walked over to Paula's makeup station and admired her work from over her shoulder. "Thank you for doing this. Victoria looks so beautiful."

"Oh, I'm always beautiful," Victoria said as Paula swept a blending brush over her eye. "When my husband sees me today, he'll probably want to skip the reception."

"I bet you won't beat me and Preston out the door," Zora said, throwing her hands in the air.

"Don't be so sure about that. We—"

"Hold up." Monét walked up and hoisted herself onto one of the stools reserved for the bridesmaids to get their makeup done. "Please don't get my sister started. I'm not interested in hearing about my sister and brother-in-law's . . ." She waved her hand in the air trying to find the perfect word. "Relations."

"Why? I'm legal."

"That's just too much information."

The women laughed, and Victoria ignored her sister's

request. Paula jumped in a time or two with a remark of her own. Zora was overjoyed to see and hear the change in her. Even though Darryl still had his days, Paula continued to hold steadfastly to God's promises.

"Zora, let's start getting you dressed," Victoria said, when her makeup was complete and Paula had moved on to Monét. "My mother's going to be here any minute, and that will add another level of drama. She takes her role as honorary mother of the bride very serious. Believe me, I know."

Zora let Victoria steer her to the space in the back of the room reserved for the bride. She undressed out of her street clothes and into her bridal undergarments. With the help of Victoria and her other bridesmaid, Stacy, she fastened the clasps on her low-back bra, stepped carefully into her stockings, then stepped into the hoop slip.

Victoria and Stacy carefully unclipped Zora's gown from the hanger and lifted it high enough for Zora to dip under and then pulled over her head.

"The big day is finally here," Stacy said. She worked to adjust the front of the gown while Victoria straightened the train in the back.

"This is absolutely gorgeous," Victoria said. "Hanging on the hanger doesn't do it justice."

Stacy agreed. "Preston's mouth is going to drop."

"I'm not going to look until I'm completely done getting ready," Zora said.

"Well, you're one step closer," Paula said. She walked over with her makeup case in one hand, dragging the stool in the other. "Okay, ladies," she instructed. "Lift Zora's dress up enough to get on the stool, and then let the gown drop around it."

The bridesmaids followed Paula's instructions until Zora and her dress were securely hoisted on the stool. They helped Paula fasten two large sheets around Zora to protect her dress before they got busy with their own preparations.

"How do you feel?" Paula asked once they were alone. "Nervous?" She used a small clip to pin back the soft curls around Zora's face that cascaded from her up-do.

"Not at all," Zora said. "Ready. I feel ready. Everything about this day is how it's supposed to be."

Paula retied the smock around her neck that was protecting her cream skirt. Without her suit jacket on, it was easier to see her growing belly.

Zora put her hand on Paula's stomach. "How do you feel?"

"Nothing like I felt four months ago the first time I saw you. You remember our run-in at the Harbor?"

"How could I forget?" Zora said.

Paula snapped open a compact and dug around in her case for a clean sponge. "I know Darryl and I have a ways to go, but the difference now is that I see the promise. Before I didn't, because I kept focusing on the circumstances. My new sisters in P.O.W.E.R. helped me see."

"Most importantly, God helped you see."

"Absolutely." Paula tipped Zora's face to the side and blended the makeup on Zora's jawline.

"So Dr. Manns is still coming to the wedding, right?"

"He said he'd be here. He doesn't have Micah to slow him down, at least. I dropped him off at my mother's so we could spend the weekend alone. Darryl may be there tonight, or he may not. It's only my job to set the atmosphere and let God do the rest."

A knock on the door sent Monét to check out their visitor. "Belinda!" Monét called out. "Look who's here, Zora," she said over her shoulder.

"I can't move," she said while Paula blended eye shadow across her closed lids. She was so close Zora could inhale her minty breath. "Belinda, I'm so glad you could come early. I

356

wanted all of my prayer warriors here."

Belinda's heels clicked across the floor. "You knew I'd try my best. I had to get Hannah ready, and then I left her with the men. They were taking too long, so they're coming later."

"Make sure you introduce me to Thomas and T. J. today. I've got to meet the men in your life."

"If T. J. comes," Belinda said. "He was cutting the fool with Thomas when I left Mama's house. I'm starting to see that boy has a problem with authority, especially when it comes to listening to a man. Then, T. J. tries to smooth things over when he comes and calls me Ma 'Linda. I'm way over that one." Belinda let out an exasperated sigh. "But this is not the day to hear about my problems. God will work it out in due time," she said, pulling on the sheet fastened around Zora's neck. "That's an interesting dress if I've ever seen one."

"From the finest Italian designer," Paula said, an Italian accent rolling the words off her tongue. "He dresses all of the stars."

"Very funny," Zora said, waving her hands under the sheets. "There's an exquisite gown under here, I'll have you know," she told Belinda.

"Don't get the bride upset," Stacy said, walking up and joining the conversation.

"No, please don't." Zora heard Victoria's voice in the circle around her, and a second later Monét from over her shoulder.

"Can I open one eye? I feel like everybody is staring at me," Zora said.

"We are," Victoria said. "I told you that you would be the center of attention today."

"No, keep your eyes closed," Paula said. "We're going to unveil you in front of the mirror as soon as I apply your blush and lipstick."

Zora waited as patiently as she could while the women

357

went on around her. After Paula applied her finishing touches and dusted a large brush with setting powder over her face, she unclipped the sheets and helped Zora off the stool.

Zora kept her eyes closed and let her women of honor guide her toward the mirror. She could tell that her back was turned to it.

At that moment, Zora heard Mama Jo enter the room. "I saw the photographer waiting outside in the vestibule." Her voice was rushed until, Zora assumed, she saw her.

"Oh my goodness."

When Zora didn't hear her voice again she knew Mama Jo was probably covering her mouth and stifling tears.

"If your mother was here . . ." she said. Her voice trailed off.

Paula put her hands on Zora's shoulders. "So, are you ready?"

"Yes," she said, but kept her eyes closed while the ladies help sweep her train behind her.

"Open them," Monét urged.

Zora did. She soaked in her transformation, turning to admire the fullness of the dress and how it draped her body. She walked closer to the mirror, admiring the colors Paula had used to enhance her features. Zora pulled down one of the curls framing her face.

"I look good," she said, giving a broad smile to the women waiting for her response.

"You ladies don't look so bad either," Zora said, seeing her bridesmaids in their full regalia for the first time. And Mama Jo, you're one foxy lady."

Mama Jo propped one hand on her hip and shifted her weight to one side. "Well, I do my best." She twirled and twisted around in front of her embarrassed daughters until they grabbed her and stopped her show.

"You ladies need to get moving to take pictures," Mama

Jo said, looking around the room. "Does everyone have everything that they need? Where are your bouquets?"

"We've got it under control, Mother," Monét said. "Our bouquets are in the box by the door."

"Just making sure."

The ladies gathered their flowers and helped Zora maneuver out of the room and down the hall to the vestibule. The photographer led her to areas he'd pinpointed outside as picturesque backgrounds, before bringing her back inside for pictures around the altar.

Zora wasn't worried that Preston would run into her. Monét's and Preston's fathers had strict instructions not to let him or the groomsmen roam outside of the corridor on the opposite side of the church.

"I don't think I've ever smiled so much," Zora said while Paula used a tissue to pat her forehead.

The photographer attached a flash to the top of his digital camera. "Just a few more, and then we'll get a few pictures of the bridesmaids by themselves and let you rest for a minute." He reviewed the digital shots he'd just taken. "After the wedding I bet you won't be able to stop smiling."

"You're right about that," Zora said. She looked around the room while the photographer changed his flash for the next set of shots. Belinda and Paula had retreated to the first pew. Monét sat a few seats behind them, reviewing the ceremony program with the church secretary who'd been appointed by Preston's mother as the day's overseer. Mother Diane had cornered Stacy into a conversation about who knows what.

Zora focused on the photographer's directions and smiled for a countless number of photos.

"All right," the photographer said when he was finished. He slung his camera strap over his shoulder. "Let's get your bridesmaids together so you can rest." He looked at Zora's dress. "Though I don't think you'll be able to sit down."

Belinda and Paula stood to help Zora down the steps, then gathered together the bridesmaids. Once their shots were complete, they helped hurry them out of the sanctuary so Preston and his groomsmen could take photos.

Zora eased down the corridor for the second time in thirty minutes, with the ladies trailing behind and around her. She looked at the clock on the wall when she walked into the bridal suite. In less than an hour, she'd begin the covenant ceremony to join her with her husband.

Mrs. Zora Fields, she thought.

Zora asked the ladies for some time alone and walked to the back of the room. She turned her gaze heavenward. "Mama and Daddy, I know you're up there watching me," she whispered. "I hope your little girl has made you proud." A small puddle formed around the rim of her eyes, and she laughed. "Mama, make sure you keep Daddy preoccupied tonight. I don't want him thinking about what's going to go on down here later on tonight."

Zora felt the familiar touch of Mama Jo's hand sliding into hers. "There's got to be a way we can sit you down for a while," she said. She and Zora walked to the couch in the back of the room. "You need to sit in the presence of God by yourself before you walk down that aisle. From this point forward, your life will never be the same."

Mama Jo dabbed a handkerchief under Zora's tearing eyes. "God has joined you with a powerful man of God, and your anointing is shifting from that of a single woman to a married woman, called to serve the Lord and glorify God in your marriage. Accept that and let the Lord minister to you."

Zora closed her eyes, and the sounds and happenings around her faded into the background. She humbled herself in the presence of God. There was no way she could thank Him for the things He'd done in her life, how He'd covered and healed her. There was no way she could thank Him enough for being God alone.

God, You're so good. I bless Your name. There's no one like You. Absolutely nobody.

Zora was unsure how much time had passed before she felt a gentle touch on her shoulder.

"Your ladies are lining up for the processional," Mama Jo said.

Papa James stood beside his wife. Grey hair had just begun to salt his temples, and he'd let his beard and mustache grow in for the wedding. Their presence together reminded Zora of her parents.

"It's your day, sweetheart," Papa James said. He helped Zora stand and patted her hand as he placed it in the crook of his arm.

Zora leaned her head on his wide forearm and broad shoulder. They walked behind the ladies as they filed out of the room, Mama Jo leading the pack.

When the other ladies rounded the corner in the hall, the coordinator signaled for Zora and Papa James to wait. The processional music drifted out from the sanctuary into the halls.

This is it. This is really it.

Zora peeked around the corner to see her flower girl, Stacy's daughter, taking cautious steps toward the open sanctuary doors. At first it seemed like the five-year-old would make a mad bolt for the exit, but the coordinator coaxed her to move forward. When she disappeared out of Zora's sight, the sanctuary doors closed again.

"Are you ready?" Papa James' clasp tightened on her hand.

"More than I've ever been," Zora said. She walked to the entryway and heard the beginnings of "Seasons," the song by Donald Lawrence that she'd chosen for her bridal processional.

It is your season.

The doors swung open, and Zora beheld the scene before

her. A sea of familiar faces smiled back at her from the left side, and some unfamiliar faces from Preston's family doted on her from the left. They all seemed to marvel at her as if they were seeing her for the first time.

Papa James patted her hand again, and Zora took her first step down the aisle.

Her eyes automatically found Monét standing at the altar, then Paula and Belinda sitting in the congregation with their families.

Zora took a deep breath as her bottom lip began to quiver, especially when she saw Preston. She knew her first sight of him would draw tears, which was why she had avoided looking at him first. Zora didn't want to lose control before she walked down the aisle, but the chance of that happening was gone.

Preston stood waiting for her—her husband, friend, and lover. At that exact moment, she felt God's love.

And Zora cried.

Zora's Cry

Reading Group Guide

There's nothing like a group of avid readers for a lively book club discussion. I hope these questions will help start an entertaining, but thoughtful exchange about the issues in *Zora's Cry*. If you'd like me to sit in with your book club during the discussion (in person or via phone), please drop me a line at Tia@TiaMcCollors.com. And while you're at it, swing by my Web site. Visit www.TiaMcCollors.com.

GENERAL QUESTIONS

What was an issue, character reaction, and/or event in the book that caught you by surprise?

What was the most memorable scene?

Did you see any recurring themes in the book?

Did you imagine a different ending?

What lessons did you learn?

How did you feel after the last page of the book was turned?

The issues of Monét, Paula, and Belinda were intentionally left unresolved. Where do you think their lives will lead?

What were the characters' flaws? What were their redeeming qualities?

Did any of the characters remind you of someone you know? of yourself? Read *Philippians 2:12–13, James 1:5, Romans 3:23,* and *Matthew 7:1–2.*

Zora—

The book opens with Zora's shocking discovery that she was adopted. How would you have reacted and why?

Zora prayed that God would reunite her with her family and felt that God had given her that promise. Though near the end, she was content with the "family" God brought in her life through Monét, Paula, and Belinda, God answered her prayers for a biological family in a way she least expected. Has that ever happened to you? Read *Isaiah 55:8–9.*

Zora understandably became discouraged several times when her search didn't uncover what she'd hoped. Discuss *Hebrews 11:1–6* and *James 1:6–8.* In what area of your life should you apply these Scriptures?

Zora opened the door for her prayer partners to be honest. Are you harboring a secret that's preventing you from moving forward in your life? Who do you have in your life to hold you accountable? *Ephesians 6:1–5, Philippians 2:3–4, Proverbs 12:15, Proverbs 13:20.*

Monét—

Monét knew she and Bryce were unequally yoked. What was her attraction to him? Why couldn't she say no? Read *2 Corinthians 6:14.*

Monét's eyes were opened after learning of Paula's marital problems and thinking about the strange calls she'd been receiving. What does that say about learning lessons?

Compare Bryce's and Jeremiah's attributes. Do you think Monét and Jeremiah's friendship has a true chance to grow?

Paula—

Do you think Darryl was really having an affair or did Paula let her imagination take over? *Read Philippians 4:8.*

What do you think made Darryl withdraw from his wife? How can a wife complement her husband's life? Read *Proverbs 12:4, Proverbs 14:1,* and *Ephesians 5:33.*

Paula's pastor preached a sermon about being the person to set the temperature (like a thermostat) in her household and life instead of reacting to situations (like a thermometer). Are you a thermostat or a thermometer?

It's evident that Darryl Manns has issues of his own. Do you think it's possible for their marriage to be restored? Have you given up on someone? Read *I John 1:9, Ephesians 5:26, Psalms 19:12,* and *Matthew 19:26.*

Even though the act was innocent, do you think Paula should have gone to the coffee shop with Victor?

Paula and Victor found common ground with their marital problems. Why was this dangerous?

Belinda—

At one point, everything seemed to be falling apart in Belinda's life (mother's illness, T. J., marital tension). How do you handle life's challenges? Read *Matthew 6:8, 34, I Thessalonians 5:16–18, Romans 8:28,* and *Philippians 4:19.*

Belinda's insecurities about her infertility resurfaced after Paula announced her pregnancy. Do you think she'd ever completely dealt with it?

How did you feel about Belinda's initial reaction to T. J. coming back into their lives? Was she justified? Read *Psalms 127:3, Proverbs 22:6,* and *Proverbs 31.*

Girls' movie nights . . . shared "dating commandments" . . . career ups and downs . . . the same pew at church . . . and a passion to live as His daughter, even through hard times. This is the real life that twentysomethings Anisha Blake and Sherri Dawson share in Atlanta—until Tyson Randall comes along and Anisha wonders, *Is he the one?*

A Heart of Devotion
by Tia McCollors
ISBN: 0-8024-5913-7
ISBN-13: 978-0-8024-5913-8

If ever there was such a thing as a perfect marriage, Bryan and Nicole Walker had it. Even without the child they desire after five years of marriage, their love for one another is solid. But then, without warning, the very thing they wanted threatens to tear them apart. A marriage that was once unshakeable is put to the ultimate test.

A Love So Strong
by Kendra Norman-Bellamy
ISBN: 0-8024-6834-9
ISBN-13: 978-0-8024-6834-5

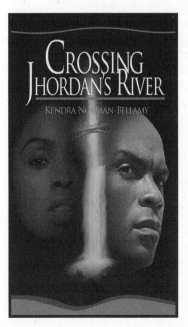

Handsome firefighter Jhordan Adams seemed to have everything a man could desire . . .

- a beautiful, loving wife
- a sweet little daughter
- a steady job
- a strong faith

So why was he pushing away the best thing that had ever happened to him?

A positive story of romance, real life, and the power of love and faith!

Crossing Jhordan's River
by Kendra Norman-Bellamy
ISBN: 0-8024-1255-6
ISBN-13: 978-0-8024-1255-6

The Negro National Anthem

Lift every voice and sing
Till earth and heaven ring,
Ring with the harmonies of Liberty;
Let our rejoicing rise
High as the listening skies,
Let it resound loud as the rolling sea.
Sing a song, full of the faith that the dark past has taught us,
Sing a song, full of the hope that the present has brought us,
Facing the rising sun, of our new day begun
Let us march on till victory is won.

So begins the Black National Anthem, by James Weldon Johnson in 1900. Lift Every Voice is the name of the joint imprint of The Institute for Black Family Development and Moody Publishers. Our vision is to advance the cause of Christ through publishing African-American Christians who educate, edify, and disciple Christians in the church community through quality books written for African-Americans.

Since 1988, the Institute for Black Family Development, a 501 (c) (3) nonprofit Christian organization, has been providing training and technical assistance for churches and Christian organizations. The Institute for Black Family Development's goal is to become a premier trainer in leadership development, management, and strategic planning for pastors, ministers, volunteers, executives, and key staff members of churches and Christian organizations. To learn more about The Institute for Black Family Development, write us at:

The Institute for Black Family Development
15151 Faust
Detroit, MI 48223

We hope you enjoy this book from Moody Publishers. Our goal is to provide high-quality, thought-provoking books and products that connect truth to your real needs and challenges. For more information on other books and products written and produced from a biblical perspective, go to www.moodypublishers.com or write to:

Moody Publishers/LEV
820 N. LaSalle Boulevard
Chicago, IL 60610